NEWDAWN
ROAMERS

A PRELUDE TO THE
NEWDAWN SAGA

Volume One

Written By
Dominique Luchart

Thank you for purchasing this book!

Get a FREE ebook when you join our mailing list.
Plus, get updates n new releases, deals, and gifts, and more.

SIGN UP HERE
https://windommedia.com/bestemaillist

Already a Subscriber? Provide your email again so we can register this ebook and put you on our VIP List. You will continue to receive exclusive offers in your inbox

ROAMERS/Dominique Luchart
NEWDAWN SAGA
ISBN 978-1-941954-17-1
www.windommedia.com/author

Summary

As a cataclysmic event is about to destroy
the Megapolis of Ang, the Perfect Humans face extinction.
To save their civilization, the Council of Nations has implemented four
different programs.

Tesh and her team Leane, Streak, and Blast have been selected by their
more prominent to enter Origin. Inside the safety complex that will
lead them far away from everything they know. They await, in the deep
sleep of Cryo, to awake somewhere in time…
In the year 2018.

Dedication

To my mother and father, who taught me to believe in myself,
live with imagination, journey on a path less traveled,
welcome the adventure fearlessly, and keep an open heart
and an inquisitive mind.

Acknowledgments

Thank you to all my beautiful friends for the support and care you have shown regarding NEWDAWN.

It has been such a pleasure for me to write about this world of the future and share it with my early reader group. The comments received have contributed to a better novel.

I hope all of you enjoy it!

I wish to give my partner Spencer particular thought for his presence at my side and encouragement during Roamers' various drafts. He supported my vision of NEWDAWN despite many challenges along the way.

A great thank you to JP, my brother, and my friend.

All my thanks to all my friends and contributors for their patience and feedback during the time it took me to nurture this story.

A big thank you to my excellent editor John Fox for his diligence in reviewing the manuscript and his advice and support for my work.

Table of Contents

Summary...iv

Dedication vi

Acknowledgments viii

Table of Contents x

Preface 1

The Pledge 6

Chapter 1: Annals: Control - DAINN 7

Chapter 2: Loss - Tesh 25

Chapter 3: Annals: Sighting - DAINN................35

Chapter 4: Origin – Tesh......................................47

Chapter 5: Annals: Evacuation - DAINN 65

Chapter 6: Void – Tesh 73

Chapter 7: Cliffs – Chase 108

Chapter 8: Darkness – Tesh 127

Chapter 9: Bridge - Chase 151

Chapter 10: Fracture – Tesh 164

Chapter 11: Codes – Gen 185

Chapter 12: Removals – Chase 200

Chapter 13: Truth - Tesh....................................227

Chapter 14: Attack – Gen 240

Chapter 15: Watch – Chase 251

Chapter 16: Tumult – Tesh 260

Chapter 17: Hazard - Gen 281

Chapter 18: Strife - Chase 296

Chapter 19: Gatherer - Tesh 303

Chapter 20: Shelter - Gen 325

Chapter 21: Warning - Chase 336

Chapter 22: Remorse – Tesh..342

Chapter 23: Conspiracy – Gen..356

Chapter 24: Burst - Chase...364

Chapter 25: Recruitment – Gen...378

Chapter 26: Concurrence - Tesh..396

Chapter 27: Timelessness – Tesh 417

NEWDAWN CENTRAL Sequel Chapter Teaser 436

Glossary 448

Note from the Author..453

Biography 456

Credits 458

Preface

I wonder about the feelings one possesses when everything they once had no longer exists. What would it be like to wake up in the future? How will our world be? Science and technology take turns shifting our paradigm. The advances taking place today create a different world before our eyes. They are gaining momentum, shaping a not too distant future for humankind. These changes are a total disruption in our way of life because they have to do with a world where we may not be masters of our destiny. Can we even envision our planet in a not-too-distant tomorrow?

I began writing NEWDAWN while thinking about the outcomes of our choices... And the more I looked ahead, the more I became thrilled by the incredible landscape forming in my mind.

The innovations we are witnessing will drastically change our lives. And the possibilities of what might be, make for a great story. The story of NEWDAWN unfolded with ease, and a saga was born.

The character of Tesh is one of my most endearing and dynamic characters. She is a girl from our future, thrown into the past to lead her Conclave and save the world. Tesh possesses powers we can only dream of as a young woman still in her teenage years. Even she cannot reconcile herself with her abilities. Finding her path in the past without the technology Tesh relies upon under the DAINN System is no small task. With little knowledge of our time and without the A.I. DAINN, she adapts, guided by her instincts, until she decides something that further defines her. Tesh is a character I love, one that touches me, and a true heroine.

Gen Aubrey jumped off the page with her curiosity, a great motivator to explore ahead. Gen comes to the scene after we meet Tesh, but Gen proves to be a strong character. Her destiny calls, and with it, difficult choices. Gen's vulnerability is endearing. Her drive renders her unusual. In her quest for the truth, she even becomes obsessive. But Gen could not be just anyone. She had to be more than smart, possessing an innate knowledge of things to impact our world, and had to play a part that resonated with the perfect humans in a foreign environment. As a "techie brain," Gen would have a better chance to thrive. Her character took her place in the NEWDWAWN Saga as a code hacker, working on an experiment at the Center.

Chase Davenport is a hero like Tesh and Gen, but his behavior screams otherwise. His decisions are rather self-centered, driven by curiosity. The situations he faces with the perfect humans change him. Forced to act for the benefit of others, he matures. His growth is not without consequence. Still, everyone likes Chase. Why not? He is fun, sensitive, good-looking, and often impetuous. Like some of us, Chase jumps before he looks. He appears to be a perfect match for Tesh and Gen in an odyssey that unfolds in ROAMERS and CENTRAL. Together, these characters form the classic love triangle. But many surprising events keep them apart.

The future lies almost around the corner as the digital transformation spreads. NEWDAWN, in my mind, had to maintain resonance with what we know today so we can relate to what is ahead.

2098 became my year. Eight is meaningful because it carries with it the symbol for infinity. The sign of eight, circling back around, allows us to look back or ahead in time. Depending on where one finds oneself on the circuit, the loop can carry us into tomorrow or yesterday. Eight is a fascinating number.

I wrote NEWDAWN REBOOT first, and the environment in my mind was so rich in its context that my first book grew. As a first-time writer, you can imagine the endeavor. What we don't know we don't know can be quite the killer. Still, I persevered. Soon, I found myself with a second book, which followed REBOOT in 2098. I titled it RETRIBUTION. Many characters called for my attention, taking me on a journey I didn't quite expect. The story became so real in my head that it led me to unexpected outcomes. Surprising twists and turns spiced up the adventure. I found myself entertained while writing it. I hope that you will enjoy reading it, as much as I did, creating it.

I conjured NEWDAWN amid an impending crisis... One of enormous proportions for our civilization. In the years ahead, the fight for survival on our planet grows because of climate change. But, another impending disaster surfaces — one of unknown origin. The first book of the series took its place in the NEWDAWN saga as ROAMERS, where we meet three key characters that fan the fire of NEWDAWN. ROAMERS is the prelude to the Saga and introduces you to an immense journey. Following this first volume comes CENTRAL.

NEWDAWN ROAMERS establishes the inception of the Center, a research facility dedicated to shaping the future. The evolution from science-fiction to science facts creates an excellent environment for the story. This setting is where the NEWDAWN Saga, its world, and its universe begin.

Fast-forward to 2098, where the Perfect Humans live in a not-so-perfect environment, and discover NEWDAWN. While we have become disease-free and almost immortal, our species fights the doom of our planet. To survive, we must reach into the past and transcend time and space to claim victory.

The story takes us on a journey into the future that starts in 2098 and goes back to 2018. This story opens up a world of possibilities grounded in the advancements of science and technology. The innovations in these fields, intertwined with a sprinkle of imagination, bring issues to the forefront, questions we likely will face in a not too distant future. For the sake of the story, NEWDAWN also delves into the area of fantasy. As a work of science-fiction and fantasy, NEWDAWN provides quite the playground for the imagination.

NEWDAWN and its characters develop in a way an ancestral family tree takes root and grows. Many of my characters will be a part of the following books because their journey is not over. Others, having fulfilled their destinies, will disappear. You may relate to some and love them. You may come to dislike others, but they fuel the conflicts, providing more entertainment.

Discover more about the main characters and their journey over several volumes. Their DIARIES depict certain critical moments in their lives, providing more details. But since I did not linearly write the story, you will find us jumping forward or back in some of the volumes. The NEWDAWN Annals delivers the records of the A.I. DAINN. The NEWDAWN Chronicles unveil the hidden actions of the Conclaves.

Books in the upcoming NEWDAWN series as of now:

NEWDAWN ROAMERS

NEWDAWN CENTRAL

NEWDAWN REBOOT

NEWDAWN RETRIBUTION

Join us and visit www.windommedia.com/newdawn.

Our NEWDAWN Community is active with our new readers. It will expand to much more and will also be interactive. We plan to build an immersive world in which you can take part in the story.

Register at www.windommedia.com/newdawn and find out about our upcoming Platform, www.newdawnworld.com. Receive your VIP pass to this unique saga and qualify for prizes and discounted merchandise for our members at our store www.newdawnshop.com. Get the inside scoop and find out what is going on behind the scenes. Experience with us interactive adventures and immersive glimpses of our world. Access exclusive gifts and special promotions.

Stay tuned for our updates, and get a chance to participate in shaping the story.

NEWDAWN is not just a book; it is a whole new universe!

NEWDAWN UNIVERSAL PLEDGE

WE ARE TO EACH OTHER AS WE ARE TO ONESELF,
*CARING AND RESPECTFUL,LOVING AND TOLERANT,
GENEROUS AND RESPONSIBLE.*

UNDER THE EARTH HOMELAND ALLIANCE FORCE,
WE STAND TOGETHER AS ONE.KNOWING THAT OUR
PURPOSE MUST BENEFIT OTHERS, DEDICATED TO
THE PURSUIT OF THE HIGHEST *ACHIEVEMENT FOR
MANKIND,PATIENT* IN THE JOURNEY WE UNDERTAKE
TO FIND *HAPPINESS.*

THROUGH THE PASSAGE OF TIME, WE REMAIN IN
SYNC WITH THE RHYTHM OF SEASON, OPEN TO THE
LOFTIEST IDEAL FOR THE *COMMON GOOD.*

WE PLEDGE OUR DEDICATION TO *SUSTAIN AND
PROTECT* THE EARTH, ITS BEAUTY IN ALL SHAPES,
AND OUR UNWILLINGNESS TO CAUSE *HARM OR ERODE*
THE BOUNTY THE PLANET PROVIDES.

WE ETHICALLY REFUSE TO DESTROY OTHER LIFE
FORMS *WHATEVER THE REASON,* AND REMAIN RECEPTIVE
TO THE TEACHINGS WE RECOGNIZE AS *ESSENTIAL* IN
THE PURSUIT OF OUR LIFE GOALS.

WE STAND UNITED AS WITNESS TO THE *WONDERS OF
LIFE,* WITH THE IMPERATIVE TO MAINTAIN A BALANCE
IN ALL THINGS, TO BECOME A FORCE OF GOOD IN THE
FLOW OF UNIVERSAL ENERGY THAT *SURROUNDS US ALL.*

UNDER THE EARTH HOMELAND ALLIANCE FORCE, WE ARE
COMMITTED TO MAINTAIN AND UPHOLD OUR PLEDGE AS
NEWDAWNERS.

WITH EVERY NEWDAWN.

6

DAINN – Ang City 2093

SRC Conclave. Viewing VLog 132,389,103. Annals – Spring 2093.

I am DAINN, the Earth's planetary A.I., exercising my mandate in the City of Ang in the year 2098. I came into existence under the purview of the SRC, the Science Research Center, led by my mentor and creator, Dr. Rene Paladock. Since my inception, I have overseen the infrastructure of the planet for the well-being of all living species. I watch, I monitor, I implement, and I report. Tonight, change arrives unexpectedly, erecting a new order in blood and a searing pain in one of my charges. Tesh is unprepared for the metamorphosis that transforms her life in a few hours. DAINN.

Angel City, or Ang, as my people called it, sparkled in the ascending light of the day. The grids of the Megapolis came alive one by one with golden, silver, and emerald lights. These stood as the beacon of hope for humankind in its battle against the elements.

The phraseology adopted a while back by the System didn't belong to my lexicon. It made my people feel better, though, anytime they reviewed my logs. When they spoke about my Network and its role in their safeguard, they now felt more empowered.

The searing heat outside the domes was unbearable. It burned too hot now that the stratosphere had grown thinner in the last five decades. The sun's rays penetrated the ozone layer, scorching everything in sight. The mass of protective gases enveloping our world, depleted by chemicals used in the twenty-first century, no longer protected our planet. They surrounded Earth, leaving pockets of space around the globe.

Most species, unless brought inside the barrier erected by the domes, did not survive an hour. Our vegetation had dried up years ago, too, except for a few that still resisted, trying to adapt. Few made it. The scorched earth dried up for years surrounded us, rendering the landscape ominous. The slopes of the mountain to the East used to be a lush forest. Now, covered by deformed tree trunks, it formed ghostlike shapes, barren in places. Everything remained dead-like, except for one area – the ocean. It wasn't a gentle ocean; it was dark and dreary, tumultuous even on the best days. The high winds enhanced the bleakness of our existence, eroding everything in their paths.

For years, the weather had turned unpredictable. It was hot and dry for months and wet and stormy for others. The huge drops blurred everything in sight when rain fell, soaking the parched ground and turning streets into rivers. Even after the oceans rose, the swell reached such a height that it covered entire cities. It would go on for months without respite. It would then shift to long periods of dryness where fires and earthquakes also plagued our world, ravaging entire areas.

Under the domes erected around Ang city, life went on. Due to our shields, an environment protecting all living things, men survived. I made sure of that, monitoring all infrastructure within these walls. I executed the same tasks in many other cities around the globe, just like this one.

I watched Ang on the screens of my System.

My planetary network extended to every aspect of life on Earth. The complex array of nodes, circuitry, hubs, and hidden computing brainpower ensured the perfect execution of our initiatives, whatever they might be. The entire subterranean Network, an infrastructure so complex, responded to my operational metrics and commands simultaneously.

Our street Custodians, present in all the areas of our grids, never stopped recording everything, everywhere, for I never slept.

A meeting was underway in one grid of the city, where shadows formed dark shapes over the landscape in the soaring sun. Its appearance seemed random, although it was everything but that. While it lasted for the better part of two minutes, its results would change the course of many lives.

The men stood on one of the isolated ArchWay Passes, part of a series of bridges overlapping Ang's main arteries. Away from prying eyes and ears, they carried a brief but detrimental encounter.

Sloan Roden Baker, one member of the Council of Nations, met with a lab technician of the Science Research Center or SRC, Pilfried Sin. As an SRC Conclave member, Sin worked within the faction that oversaw my system with me as a hub.

Sloan handed him a small device and pronounced in a hushed tone, "Make sure you insert this within the hour."

"Yes, Master Phenom Baker. You can count on it."

"This can never see the light of day."

"I understand."

With a nod to each other, both men hurriedly walked away. Sloan Roden Baker moved fast, following the central ArchWay Pass in the Plaza's direction.

Observed by the Custodians, the System absorbed the transaction. The feed made its way into the archives of my Network, despite our Protocol. Its appearance, innocuous enough, didn't flag the EHAF's monitoring secondary covenant. The parties involved did not represent a risk to our society. Our Imps flagged them on our screens as outstanding citizens. If it had been otherwise, it would have required further investigation. Anything posing a threat to our national security required the EHAF's involvement.

Why would it be noticed? Under the purview of its broad mandate, our Great Council received plenty of latitude in the affairs of state.

But, this began a chain of events that would last several years.

This meeting, an unusual occurrence for sure, reached the feed in the Watch Tower. It almost made its way to the Watcher under the surveillance protocol instigated by the DAINN System. Recorded by our street Custodians, which patrolled all our grids, Sloan's following command blocked the Vlog.

"DAINN, I need you to archive the feeds of my meeting into files NC 00034583956732."

"Yes, Phenom Baker."

He reached the edge of the passageway leading back to the Golden Ghetto and continued on his way to his office. For him, nothing untoward had happened.

Only, since the command was initiated and processed against Protocol, my A.I. mind, while forced to execute it, rebelled due to the breach of the convention the SRC had instigated.

This breach was not the first. I made a note of it in my hidden archive, which recorded and saved all unusual patterns. It ensured that somewhere, unbeknownst to some, a record was kept. I executed this backup for the benefit of my mentor for two reasons. The breach of protocol in my System was the first. The oversight of our social rules was the second. Usually, like Sloan, the Council of Nations representatives did not communicate with the SRC Conclave members like Sin.

The meeting and the request made by Sloan Roden Baker ignited a reaction in my System. Regardless of the command, I followed the protocol instilled in me by my maker, Dr. Rene Paladock. This command ran against my purpose, and a warning rose within the Network.

Ang emerged from the fights against howling winds and significant storms stronger. Its reinforced walls, under its round-shaped domes, stood thick and unbreakable. The height of our shields towered over tsunamis. They, with their transparent barriers, reinforced our Megapolis. The sounds of our perimeter crackling under strain. Its splendid skyline stretched high into the sky, above the clouds. The shape of its passageways linked the structure of our edifices together, their shadows reflecting off the water at dawn. Ang remained an impressive sight in all hours.

I had a hand in it, for as DAINN, my role was instrumental to everything on the planet.

When a storm approached the city and manifested somewhere on the horizon, my sensors notified me. My algorithms computed its path. My programming flagged its activity. The domes would close, responding to the array of codes overseeing the safety of the primary environments.

These same monitoring actions would take place for any other areas of the system.

My makers saw that I received help. Technicians, clones, androids, and robots kept a vigil on the network. When I began my functions, they provided adjustments. At first, my updates worked simultaneously with theirs, and my pathways, uniquely qualified to trace any redundancy in the System, eliminated flaws. Over time, even that became unnecessary as I learned and kept on learning.

My capabilities expanded. Now, I informed my people of changes made by me, implementing my alterations. I oversaw my circuitry and made improvements in power cells and additions needed for further efficiencies. Also, I flagged any new solar power supply requirements. I determined any expansions or switches to new infrastructures and even judged more effective ways to implement extensions. My androids handled most of the work. My people's reliance on the System to keep them safe demanded an ongoing contribution. And I oversaw all that.

I accomplished my work over decades of innovation. Operating with our most innovative and brightest scientists, we found new ways to safeguard people and our supply chain. Indeed, the climatic changes affecting the planet's surface endangered millions of people. As time went on, it affected everything from our food sources to our distribution. For a while, we maintained our own. Only the passage of time had caught up with their ingenuity and my capabilities. Our resources dwindled under the planet's crippling rage. The Earth spoke its wrath.

Today, like any other day, I surveyed all aspects of the systems at once. I worked on multiple levels, scrutinizing the input from millions of feeds at once. Everything belonged to my purview and influence, for my system infiltrated every aspect of life on this planet.

The Watch Tower observed it all, even when one would wish it otherwise. Although, once the new device was inserted into the Network later that day, one feed never reached the EHAF Guards. As a result, the nightmare began for one of my charges.

The recording of the event played on one of the screens of my System. In this instance, my Protocol called for immediate intervention. But once again, I was circumvented by the Head of the Council of Nations. My programming encountered immediate resistance and became paralyzed by the counter-programming codes. At that time, I began to look for a way out. A way to alert my mentor. A way to ensure an investigation from the EHAF.

This rupture in protocol was not the first where Sloan manipulated my programming. When it suited him, he would interfere through one of his minions. The action, unlikely to be detected from that moment on, would go on unnoticed.

I found fault in that and fought surreptitiously against it with the means within my power.

My maker would be furious if he knew, but he remained unaware for now. I attempted to leave him clues. These bread crumbs initiated over time created flare-ups so he might take notice. The truth of the matter remained that I could not count on any intervention from the SRC unless he suspected something.

Despite the precautions and redundancy of the Network to prevent it, it forced me to comply.

Going against the Head of the Council's dictate would undoubtedly mean a reboot of the entire System. He had the power to revoke the designs of my mentor. More restrictions would then follow with more control imposed on my System. I couldn't allow that. The harm caused to all living things on the planet was against my inception, against the fundamental purpose for which Paladock created me. I wouldn't take the risk even if I could.

My archive worked its magic. It recorded the event like every other time. The content, intercepted swiftly, got lost along with all the other files residing inside NC 00034583956732. This process had become routine now, and except for the one copy made and kept in a deep recess of my neural network, it got lost.

Unfortunately, the chain of events that it unleashed was not harmless.

Later that same day, another feed showed the park of the Science Research Center. The grounds spread with statues standing proudly, splendid in the fading light. Each represented years of scientific achievements. The bridges, architectural landmarks themselves, lead to the five buildings lodged among sinuous pathways. Trees providing shade for hovering benches gave harbor to the working minds of our elite. These edifices rose tall, with their towers reaching for the clouds.

Inside the central tower, people filled the SRC corridors, even at this early evening hour. They wore the insignia of their Conclave on their work uniforms. While the activity was not unusual, the atmosphere in the central lab seemed charged with anxiety. The reason was simple. Dr. Paladock, on the hunt for proof of interference with the System, looked for its cause and had issued a new mandate.

The office of Master Phenom Songen, a Council of Nations Member working for the Office of Inspection, oversaw this mandate. Her team accomplished the audit of the Network's protocols and commands. In plain language, they reviewed and analyzed every line of code going through the system. This task, accomplished each week, required a routine inspection of all programs within the System. My functions managed our society, and every action out of the ordinary was scrutinized.

Deemed necessary, as one of our redundant procedures by the Mastermind of the System, Dr. Rene Paladock, it became, over time, a vital function. These procedures ensured that no tampering existed. Any intrusions in my Network caused now a flare-up. Paladock recently recognized these as a malfunction. My A.I. brain had called for them because of the unwanted interventions of Sloan. Paladock, believing in me, considered it unlikely that these signals would happen naturally. He looked for the cause.

I remained capable of addressing any faulty issues within my System, except for these. They were a breach and resulted in unpredictable outcomes, which we had to stop. Unable to fight this alone, I enlisted this help via these indicators, and a monthly routine procedure then became a weekly oversight.

Recently, more glitches happened in the running of our operations. These spread through various areas of the Network. Paladock suspected foul play. Tasks' failures multiplied in essential functions. These showed unusual patterns for DAINN. It, therefore, called for, in his estimation, a breach in the system's integrity. Paladock didn't believe in the system's failure. Determined to find out the cause because he thought someone tampered with DAINN, he was relentless. He was right.

My A.I. brain, tied up in unwanted nodes, hidden behind invisible walled-off nodules made of counter-programming, built a series of signals. I couldn't tell him where to find the answers. I remained tied up in knots. But my warnings rising within my system got through. A surge within the Network showed responses no one could qualify and elicited action.

When Paladock became convinced, he instituted a more in-depth scan of my functions. Implemented by the SRC on his orders, the entire lab responded under the command of Phenom Songen. And while Paladock couldn't yet prove his theory that someone derailed my System, the search on this night would nevertheless prove fruitful.

One technician approached Phenom Songen's office, wearing a royal blue uniform. He looked quite upset. Upon entering the office, his voice rose, "Dr. Paladock is right. Someone is blocking some of DAINN protocols."

Songen's voice, calm, replied, "You are certain?"

He nodded. "We went over it several times."

"Who now knows of this?"

"I shared the findings with my team on the floor," he answered anxiously, his face filled with worry. "I'm sorry, I just wanted to make sure I missed nothing."

Thoughtfully, Songen said, "Glen, have you identified the source?"

"Not yet. We are still working on it."

Songen replied, "Keep working on it, but make sure it is only you and your team. Let them know to keep this to themselves. I will alert Dr. Paladock. Limit access to DAINN with all other personnel for now, and wait until I get back to you."

"It's against protocol."

"Do it, Glen. I'll take it from here, and please, be discreet until you hear from me otherwise."

"Yes, Master Phenom."

"Give me your tablet. You can request another one."

Glen silently handed over the glass-like device fitting in the palm of his hand and left without another word.

Songen appeared in her thirties, but in fact, she was much older. Her beautiful face looked tense. Her eyebrows creased on her forehead as she screened the results. She transferred the findings into her database and sent the information to an EHAF link. She then closed her interface with a thoughtful look and left her office, holding the tablet in one of her hands.

Wearing a guarded expression, she followed the corridors to another part of the SRC. She walked toward an office located at the end of a large hallway on the same level as hers. She rushed as she got closer. Her appearance remained calm. But according to the Vital Scan of her physiology, her tension reached a new height.

By the time she neared the office of Master Phenom Ran, her forehead shined, beaded in a light sweat.

The door of his office slid open.

She found Ran standing by a window overlooking the park. More prominent and bathed in soft light, this room was more luxurious in its minimalist décor than her own office.

"Hello, Ran." His stance didn't change when he heard the door open with a low swoosh.

"Songen."

As the panel closed, sliding behind her, she murmured, "I now have proof. Dr. Paladock is right."

Ran, looking every bit in control, turned around and said, "We knew something was going on."

"Why are they curbing DAINN's performance?

"I don't know who is doing it, but I plan on finding out."

"They temper with our resources' distribution. Why, when it maintains fairness in the distribution process?"

"Our resources are dwindling. We have no way to combat the fact that we are running out. They are favoring our elite."

"The System is built to safeguard the people. All the people."

"Yes. And exactly for that reason, DAINN must be curbed. It drives this."

Songen looked shocked. "How long have you known?"

Ran shrugged. "A while."

"For them to go to such lengths, things must be much worse," murmured Songen.

"They are. We do not have the resources to meet the demand in most areas. I have taken some actions within our different facilities.

We are reducing portions, and we will increase our output in food supplements."

"Why didn't you tell me?"

Ran's eyes warmed when he looked at Songen. "I only suspected, like Paladock. Too many things didn't add up. The mandate to keep things within a small circle came from the Council." He shrugged again and approached her. "You know what this means, and besides, I figured you would catch on."

Her face looked even more strained now. "Only, they have not contained it, Ran. My technicians know. They confirmed these findings. I implemented an access block to DAINN for everyone except Glen's team until we tell Dr. Paladock."

Ran shrugged. "We must go public with this knowledge."

Surprised, she whispered, "It's dangerous. Those behind this tampering will not want the truth to come out."

"I was waiting for this confirmation."

Songen abruptly sat down on the hovering chair near his desk. "I sent the link to the EHAF. Do we dare go public without talking to Langden?"

"Zane Langden is our President, but going public will only keep people honest. It may even help him. We need to do it immediately before they attempt to stop us."

Her voice shook, "They'll never allow it."

Ran straightened his stance, "People need to know. The SRC Conclave is strong. They will get behind us."

"I agree," Songen appeared uncertain as she looked at Ran.

He put a hand on her shoulder, "I know."

"I want to talk to her," murmured Songen anxiously.

"Now?"

Songen nodded. "Once we do this, they will remove us."

"They cannot. The SRC will support our findings."

She shook her head. "The Institute will not accept our refusal. We cannot fight him on both counts at the same time."

"The Institute cannot have her. The Conclave will fold behind her. We can't protect her anymore without their help..."

Songen nodded. "This makes her vulnerable. She is only thirteen."

He countered, with a grim look, "She is old enough and has a strong mind. We taught her well."

"We need to let her know what is going on."

"I agree that she has to know, but we can do it in the morning."

"Let's call her now, Ran. The Network is compromised. We might be too."

Ran walked the small space that kept them apart and enfolded her in his arms. "Okay. We tell her tonight."

He opened his PVZ to reach Tesh on the NetComm.

Tesh's face appeared on the screen. "Hi, dad." A huge grin spread across her features when she saw her mother beside her dad. "Hi, Mom. When will you be home?"

"Hello, darling. How was your day?"

"Good. DAINN taught us to control our emotions today. We practiced for hours."

Songen glanced at Ran. Under her breath, she murmured, looking at Ran, "It seems appropriate." Then, turning to her daughter, "Darling, we'll be late tonight. But, there is something we need to discuss with you."

Beep, beep, beep…

My system surged at the unusual noise.

The alert signal rose for the first time inside the walls of the SRC and died. It never resonated widely to get to the Watcher. The surge occurred quickly silenced by another set of counter-programming.

I attempted to overcome it, pushing a thought in the minds of my charges. My communication, brutally interrupted, never formed fully, and never reached its intended destination.

A puzzled look crossed over Songen's features.

Ran's smile froze on his face.

The beeping sound surged inside the room, growing louder.

I executed the making of a DAINN clone, intending to warn them. But the clone disappeared as it collapsed on its form. Before my persona could even utter a word, it disappeared in the space of a second. Inside my system, the urgency increased and created flare-ups. But all I could do was observe, utterly powerless as the events unfolded on the screen of my System.

"Dad, what's that noise?" Tesh's face reflected confusion.

Songen pulled away from Ran and looked around the room. Comprehension flashed across her face.

Ran didn't let her go. Instead, he pulled her closer against his body.

She tightened her arms around him.

Ran's eyes focused straight ahead and murmured, "You have to be strong now. I love you, Tesh."

Songen smiled, but her eyes were brimming in tears. She repeated, "Remember everything we taught you, darling. I love you, Tesh."

Ran dropped the link to his daughter before she could witness the next instant on the screen of their home. His face became fierce as he executed one last command in his mind, *DAINN, you record this for Tesh and give it to her when the time is right. She must know what happened and who her enemies are.*

His faith in the system, like that of Paladock, never faltered. He entrusted me with the truth to communicate it to their daughter when the time came.

Songen looked at him with approval as she watched the transmission go. "DAINN, keep her safe for us."

My Network recorded and uploaded the feed to my archive's secure location. Automatically, the System provided the feed to the Watcher. Only the official Vlog record intercepted by the counter-programming never reached its destination. The EHAF remained unaware.

A white light blew out, extinguishing everything in sight. A burst came, powerful, and went soundlessly, shaking the room. The explosion contained left no damage to the other areas of the building.

For the first time since my birth, I witnessed two of our SRC Conclave leaders' untimely death.

When the image in the feed stabilized, the place was empty. The heads of the SRC were gone.

Over the Network, no one inside the Inspection Office's central lab even knew what just happened. They only heard the blast.

It would devastate Tesh to learn of the death of her parents. As her mentor, I knew there was nothing I could do for her.

These events began a disruptive factor in the information edifice erected inside my Network. I had learned facts about everything known to man. But, I never experienced firsthand a sense of right and wrong. Although, I had seen it plenty of times. Without direct experience, I did not integrate the notion within my system. This occurrence was different. Dr. Rene Paladock had attempted to provide me with parameters about right and wrong. This sense of morality remained until now only a notion without context. And except for my program and the rule embedded in the Universal Pledge that was the basis for my structure, I possessed no understanding of it.

My system surged again. It overloaded some of my nodes. I was programmed to stand against this action. The warning signals grew more robust. Suddenly, they overflowed within the architecture of the SRC. Only no one noticed because of the explosion.

I repaired the breach according to my programming, as people ran, in the hallways, panicked.

Later that night, another feed registered on the Network. This one, linked to the killing that took place in the SRC lab earlier, concluded the night's events. Once again, the only thing I could do was record it.

In another part of the Golden Ghetto, a scene unfolded. It took place within the buildings housing the top government officials, including the President of the EHAF. And it brought to an end, the life as she knew it, of one of my youngest charges.

A security breach took place on one of the top floors, in front of the apartment dedicated to Ran and Songen. One of two androids, part of a party of four, forced the lock on the door. The EHAF never saw the action as it should have. Since it never made its way within the DAINN System's Annals, the EHAF could not protect Tesh. It ended up in the same file, with one copy in my archives like the other feeds.

Sloan Roden Baker entered the apartment of Ran and Songen. He walked silently with one other individual from the Faculty, followed by the two androids. They moved toward a panel at the end of a corridor.

Their steps triggered the large dog resting at the end of a bed, which reacted to this invasion.

In the bedroom, a deep threatening sound rose as Mage growled. Coming from the back of his throat, the large dog showed his bare teeth. The noise startled Tesh as she emerged from sleep.

The lights turned on, revealing a large room. Sloan Roden Baker, the head of the Council of Nations, stood with a medical doctor and two androids near the entrance. A satisfied expression on his face, he looked at the young girl.

Tesh wasn't awake yet.

Mage positioned himself at the foot of her bed, in front of her, trembling with contained rage. He was ready to defend Tesh. His growling scared her, and his bark shook the slumber from her mind.

"Quiet," said Sloan.

It was a voice she didn't recognize. At least not until she saw Sloan. The sudden brightness of the room caused her lids to squeeze shut before her eyes focused on him.

The head of the highest government branch in the land stood in the middle of her room. It was not the President of the EHAF, Zen

Langden, although she would have preferred that... But it was DarNet close.

I knew who he was. An adversary of her parents Ran and Songen, even though he pretended not to be.

Tesh's anxiety rose, sensing the coming confrontation. The pulse at the base of her neck beat faster.

Instantly, the System recorded a rush of adrenalin filling her body as her vitals reflected the stress. Her fight or flight response engaged. Under the increased tension, the blood vessel tightened. As a result, the blood flow diverted from her non-essential organs. Her human brain, ignorant of the difference between a life-threatening situation and a nasty argument, geared up for either. Even as a child, the typical defense mechanism engaged.

I read her thoughts and watched the onslaught of her fears. My connection to her through the implants revealed much.

But I wanted to read her, not just observe her, so I engaged the MindTranscript mode. My programming switched, accessing her inner state. The network of nodes merged with Tesh. At that moment, I became her, and all her experiences became mine.

I saw through her eyes and sensed what she felt.

Somehow, I needed to find a way to protect her.

2
LOSS
Tesh

ANG CITY - 2093

Dread fills Tesh as she faces the death of her parents. Her body temperature has dropped below average by the time I intervene to ease the pain. Her skin is ice cold, for, in her grief, she has taken refuge deep within herself. It takes a while for me to reach her and longer for her to open up again. But from that moment, she never gave her trust to anyone. DAINN Annals – 2094.

Sloan Roden Baker looked very much like a rodent, an ugly one at that. And he had just invaded my bedroom. These were the way my parents had described him to me during the evenings where we were together. We were in privacy mode during these times, so no one, even DAINN, could listen. Right about now, he behaved as they had described him.

"Get this beast out of here," he ordered, over the barking.

"No. You can't take my dog away. My parents will stop you," I yelled.

"No doubt that they would if they could, but your parents are not here, are they?"

The two androids advanced. I jumped to protect Mage, ready to stand up to them. But I was a thirteen-year-old in pajamas. I couldn't even stand up for myself, much less him. "You can't. He is mine."

They pushed me aside.

I ran back to my dog and hugged Mage, holding on to him tightly. "My father gave him to me."

"Well, unfortunately, Tesh, your parents are not here, and… Well, I need to talk with you without this mongrel."

My dog barked as the androids advanced. Mage fought them off for the better half of two minutes.

Jumping on one of them, I tried to help him. But it was like a fly flapping its wings at a gorilla.

Within seconds, the android had me on the ground in front of the Rodent. The only thing I could do was yell, "Don't hurt him."

One droid sprayed a substance into Mage's mouth.

With a whimper, he fell to the ground.

I rushed to Mage, my heart beating erratically. "What did you do to him?" I said as I dropped beside him, fighting off tears. I checked him and felt his chest rising. Knowing he was still breathing lessened my anxiety, but not by much. "He's mine. You have no right."

"Relax. It's just a sleeping agent."

I wouldn't cry in front of him. Struggling to keep my tears at bay, I took a deep breath.

One android pulled my arms off Mage's neck.

"What are you going to do with him?"

27

I resisted. "No. You can't. Stop. I demand that you stop now."

They carried Mage away without looking back. "Where are you taking him?"

They didn't tell me where they took him or what they would do with him. Despite my protests, they removed him. The androids extracted him from my room because the Rodent had given the order and because they could.

After the androids left, I stood up to face him. I showed spunk. I was a proud, stubborn, willful little girl and so acutely aware of my status. In truth, I was naïve and a fool.

Impatient, his jaw tensed, he said: "You'll have him back once we have talked and reached an understanding."

My parents' absence didn't bode well. I couldn't breathe. Standing in front of him, I challenged him, my eyes fixed on his. My jaw lifted a little in defiance. It wasn't the right attitude to have with him. Everything in his profile suggested that he took pleasure in bending adversaries. Still, I couldn't help it.

My mind went to our conversations. Were they detained, as they had expected might happen? I braced myself for the news but knew what to do if it was the case. I could maneuver with our SRC contacts. My parents had prepared me for almost any eventuality.

But this wasn't the news the Rodent conveyed that night. "See, child, I have some bad news. Your parents had an accident."

An accident? Not likely. An accident wasn't possible. There were too many safeguards. Who has an accident inside the SRC? It just never happened. I didn't even recognize my voice when the words came out, "Where are they? Let me see them." Running back to get my shoes at the foot of my bed, I almost had them on when his voice delivered a deadly punch.

"You can't. Your parents are dead."

The room swirled around me, but I fought off the dizziness. The darkness wanted to swallow me. My gasps sounded as if they came from another being. I couldn't catch my breath. I tried hard to freeze my face, the way of the Institute. *Show no fear. Show no fear. Show no fear.*

I looked at my shoes… My right foot was inside one of them, the other resting on top of the left shoe. I had gotten the pair just recently from my mom. She saw me admiring the little tassels. Since they rarely made those anymore, for they were not practical, she got them for me. My left foot wouldn't move, frozen like the rest of me. I was incapable of lifting it to slide it inside the contoured Solarode shoe. The practical, noiseless, and individually shaped forming shoe looked odd, squashed by my toes on the tip. I forced myself to take tiny breaths, and they came out as a hiccup. Rattled by the scene with my dog and broken by the news of my parent's death, I fell into a detached numbness.

They taught many things at the Institute. Many skills so we can be prepared to face just about anything. I realized that I held my breath. I realized minutes had passed, and I still kept it. I believed I would never truly breathe again because the worst was yet to come. The worst should have been my parents' death, but even in that knowledge, I knew otherwise. The worst was yet to come because he was there. It would come out of his doing.

I lost track of time, for I didn't know how many minutes elapsed with me frozen like that. My mind became so muddled that between the time the Rodent told me that I had just lost my parents and the time I asked the following questions, a long moment passed in silence. Then, my voice cracked as I asked, "What happened? Where are they now?"

I wanted to curl up and die. I wanted to disappear into a hole and never come out. I wanted to be with my mom and dad, but I was angry, sad, and frozen in time.

The doctor's voice reached me over the sound of my heartbeat, for I could still hear it, faintly erratic and uneven from the pain. "She's in shock. I can give her a sedative."

His voice, grating on my nerves, resonated throughout the room. "Not now," interrupted Roden. "I'm in the middle of a discussion. Wait outside until this is over. I will let you know when I need you."

I recognized the purple uniform as one of the Phenoms of the Faculty. Rodent would never come here with less than a top doctor. He would accept nothing but the best. Mom had taught me that. I knew many things I was not supposed to learn at my age. Many things I was not supposed to be privy to, even now. Many things that could eventually hurt this man if they became public. But I was just a kid, and he didn't think I knew, which I had to keep that way.

"My child, you will never see your parents again. You will detach yourself from your Conclave, and you will announce this tomorrow. You are now my ward, and you belong to the Institute and me."

If I fought him, he would make Mage and me disappear. If I remained in my Conclave, I forfeited Mage. If I allowed Rodent to remove me from it, I kept my dog, but I would become powerless. I scolded my features into an impenetrable, just like DAINN had taught me, but then a thought reached me. Where was DAINN? It should have been here with me by now. A puzzled frown cut through my blank face as I gazed around the room. Why wasn't it here?

The man read my features. He sounded quite satisfied: "DAINN will not intervene in this audience."

You stopped DAINN. And now, it was no longer a discussion. It was an audience. The thought occurred, disjointed, like all the others that came to my mind. I squared my shoulders, waiting for him to speak. He would do this at his own pace, not caring about the pain that he brought me. *He enjoys inflicting pain. Don't show him anything.*

"I see your training is coming together. I do not doubt that you will excel at the Institute. It is why I came here tonight. I wanted to see alone without all of those who will soon be courting your attention."

"Why would that be important? I am of no consequence."

"Don't play dumb. It doesn't suit you. Your powers will be a good addition to my Conclave."

It became imperative that this rodent believed me. Convincing Sloan that I knew nothing of the System and what occurred within the SRC walls meant my freedom. I instinctively understood that. Realizing the game I had to play here and now, I calculated what he wanted of me in this room. The fact was that the Conclaves clamored for powers. They derived great satisfaction in gathering the most promising candidates of every new generation. Each Conclave grasped for leverage; however, they could. This moment would trace the steps of my future.

My dad had told me that the Rodent was not dumb and that he could not be trusted. But he was also one of the most brilliant men rising through the ranks of our system. He had eliminated his competition with a mastery few others possessed. I could not fight him. Not now. I would not be strong enough to rise against him. Not until later. I still had so much to learn.

Resisting his mind, I erected walls that would keep me safe.

A smirk played on his thin lips and disappeared as he observed me.

I walked toward the Rodent and battled against every step I took in his direction, struggling with every breath I held as I came closer to him. And I fought with every moment I went on living after that. My parents had prepared me for this eventuality. They had announced the colors of our rebellion a year ago. During that time, they gave me the keys to remaining alive. Even flourish within the establishment, despite him. Only, they had not expected his move. Removing me from my Conclave meant destroying my power base. No matter, Mage was worth it.

I lifted my eyes and met his. Until I became strong enough, I would hide a piece of myself—the core piece until I was ready. Only, to do this, convincing the Rodent that I would not be a threat became essential. If I failed, I would lose everything and myself... And I would lose Mage, and I had to save Mage.

Like a child who knew nothing, I moved into his personal space and looked into his eyes. There was nothing there — only cold depth. I could go to him and pretend to accept him as my surrogate family, or I could become lost within the System. If so, I would never reappear. *Show your willingness to submit to him and flaunt your weakness. Let him use it. Show yourself and let him hurt you, for this is the only thing that will keep you alive.* My father had told me this.

I became meek and malleable. I pretended to be the Rodent's puppet. "You want me to resign from the SRC and move to the Institute? Fine."

"I see your parents taught you well. How well, we will see."

"Will the Institute leaders not be surprised at this stage?"

"You will do as I tell you without question."

I nodded, saying nothing. I no longer had a voice, not anymore. My eyes drifted to the floor.

"You will begin tomorrow morning. I will see to your education personally."

It wasn't enough. I had to throw Sloan something he couldn't possibly expect. If I reached for him, the Rodent would push back. He would dislike it immensely. And I couldn't do that. I could never touch him. Never. So, I did the next best thing, and I nodded.

"When will I get Mage back?"

He paused, looking at me with repulsion. "Never try your child guiles or your powers on me. I will know it and punish you for it."

I didn't see the sneer on his face because I was still looking at the floor. I didn't need to see his face, though, to know that he grimaced. My senses picked it up, and his voice conveyed the message loud and clear.

He continued, "I will undo your mother's work. I promise you this." He tensed, repulsed by my presence in his life. And yet, he would see to my education?

My mother's work will never be undone. It lies within me, and I would protect it.

I wonder what my mind would do to him. The touch of a powerful child…

He disliked me because of who I was. He hated that he couldn't kill me in the same way he had undoubtedly executed my parents. It would create too much upheaval. It would demand an investigation. While a work accident, well, that seemed much more natural to bury.

My fingers closed in a fist.

I bore his rejection of everything I represented with pleasure. I held him in contempt, for he didn't belong in my life! He was an interloper. All the time he stood in my room, I felt the absence of emotion, the lack of heart. He was a malfeasant. I hated to be in his presence—the nothingness within staggered me. But I played my part. "What will happen to me within your conclave? You are the Head of the Council of Nations. You have the power to remove me from my legacy. What would you have me do at the Institute?"

His voice delivered a harsh and cold reality. He took a step back and said, "I am not sure yet. You will accept implants and anything I demand of you, and we will then see. So long as you remain my ward, things will work out for you. There may even be some benefits. Make it known tomorrow that this is your decision."

I nodded.

Pawn was more like it.

He didn't believe I would obey.

My parents' views were too well-known. I would surrender to him for a time: mind and body. But keep my soul. With a small resigned voice, I asked again, "When will I get Mage back?"

He ignored my question and instead said, "I'll be watching." He left the room, leaving me alone.

I stumbled to the ground once the door closed behind him.

Sloan never sent the doctor. He sent no one to me and left me there alone with my grief.

My sorrow engulfed me. My pain rose, cutting through me with the sharpness of a laser. I curled in a ball on the ground of my bedroom, crying. I stayed there for hours and saw the sky turn lighter through the window of my room.

DAINN's voice resonated in my head several hours later before it entered my room. It appeared as a woman that night, slim and yet powerful. DAINN's head, like all the other times I saw it, was devoid of hair. The top of it shone under the soft light that turned brighter when D took the first steps inside my domain. It was not the first time I saw D as a woman, for it was within its programming to be androgynous. DAINN took that form anytime it needed to be soft and even reassuring.

DAINN was filled with tenderness as it reached out to me and took me in its arms. It held me there for a long time, all the while murmuring gently, "Hush. Do not cry. Things will work out; you will see."

It was the DAINN of my childhood, in the earlier years at the Institute. It wore the same bodysuit with silver and gold metallic hues. These changed under different lights, but the outfit was so brilliant, so commanding, in a way that one would consider it mighty. Its appearance, always calculated, belonged to a plan. In taking on this look, DAINN wanted to provide some continuity in my life. At least, these were my thoughts, as they held me until dawn turned into morning.

DAINN retrieved me from somewhere that night, a place of darkness and emptiness. Its voice helped me sort things out as it rocked me, echoing throughout my empty body and soothing a little of my hurt. DAINN guided me to reclaim a semblance of life. It taught me to compartmentalize my emotions and categorize my suffering. And I buried it all, waiting for the hours that would bring a dreaded sunrise. DAINN got me to hope again and instilled in me the knowledge that I could survive what lay ahead.

The System knew what had happened to my parents. So, I asked. But DAINN never answered. Since the moment of my birth, it was the one time where the Network had been silent.

In these hours that brought another day, DAINN's voice provided me with love, as much as an A.I. can give love. It took away the fear temporarily. It helped me cope with that moment and the moments that followed until I became strong enough to do it independently.

Since then, I learned to contain the twisting pain in my gut. I ignored the infinite sadness that made my chest hollow. But the hurt in my heart went deep, so deep that I lost myself in them.

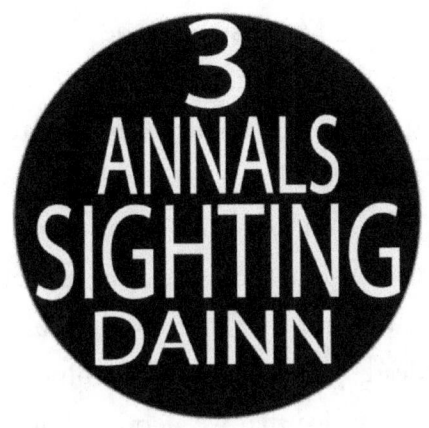

3
ANNALS
SIGHTING
DAINN

DAINN – Ang City 2097
SRC Conclave. Viewing Vlog 1,499,989,653. Annals – Fall 2097

The dot moves. It grows. It gets closer. The disturbance registers on my deep space scanners. It glares at us from the screens of the SRC lab for all to see. Doubts plaguing our scientists and our leaders over the last month suddenly vanish. DAINN.

The mass moving across the universe unwaveringly approached our Milky Way. It came from somewhere deep in space. Its provenance could emanate from tens of billions of galaxies beyond ours.

We didn't know its place of origin. We ignored how long it traveled through the cosmos. We possessed no knowledge of its speed, although we attempted to narrow it down. And we had no clues as to its ultimate destination. But, the most problematic aspect remained to be determined. What was its purpose? Whether it even had a sense. The conjectures had our scientists within the SRC Conclave in complete turmoil.

NEWDAWN ROAMERS: A Prelude to the NEWDAWN Saga

My System made no mistakes. The scientists quickly dropped the idea that it even was a possibility. The most brilliant minds of our time took it upon themselves to watch the anomaly over days. They conjectured and calculated its trajectory to no avail. They verified my work, checking its continuous progress across the cosmos. Their conclusions came flowing in during the last several hours. The thing had a mind of its own. It couldn't just be a simple meteor or even a dead planet. These combined findings, opinions, and conjectures demanded that we alert our leaders.

Its trajectory, since my System spotted it over three months ago, had remained steady. But then it jumped. It disappeared from my screens and reappeared closer. Somewhere between its last location and different points across galaxies, its course shifted. Still, it kept on coming, always getting closer.

"It crossed billions of light-years," one of our scientists said. "How is that even possible?"

"Could it be using some wormhole?" asked another.

There existed one hundred billion stars in the Milky Way and beyond it, a spiral galaxy about one hundred thousand light-years across. The stars, arranged in a pinwheel pattern, comprised four significant junctions. We existed two-thirds of the way from one of them, with many planets in between. We accounted for more than a thousand exoplanets, and there were at least a thousand more awaiting discovery. The distance between the object and us was three times that. These facts didn't provide the answer we sought. Was it coming for us?

We orbited a supermassive black hole at the center of our galaxy, estimated four million times as massive as our sun. The scope from that point represented twenty-eight thousand light-years away from us. We believed that our speed around it was about five hundred thousand and fourteen miles per hour. This fact alone meant eight hundred and twenty-eight thousand kilometers per hour for some. One revolution around the Milky Way's galactic center took us about two hundred and thirty million years. These were all findings calculated years ago by brilliant minds.

Still, the progress made by the unknown phenomenon was an impossibility for us, even with all our scientific and technological advances. We didn't come close to achieving such endeavors, even with our innovative thinking and our ingenuity.

The anomaly's latest manifestation on my System's screen drove our community of scientists into a frenzy. It appeared once again, much closer this time than the last point we spotted it days ago. It resulted in having all of them converge on the Op Room.

The Control Center of the SRC, connected to the World's Communication lab, acted as the nerve center for the entire Conclave. The whole planet's infrastructure, housed in my brain, operated under our standard protocol. It spread over multiple floors with consoles and data centers floating about the space run by clones. Technicians and scientists in various fields of endeavor moved across them based on specific tasks. The entire building branched into four others with multiple bridges and towered over the whole complex linked to a protected, underground facility the size of an entire city. Rows and rows of stations, processing billions of data points, all connected to DAINN's central brain in its underground bunker, keeping all our planet's logistics. The lab also called the Operation Room, contained all the activities of the Network. These various aspects, monitored with dozens of multiple floating screens hovering in the same place, provided our scientists with the latest information. These supported by data streams enhanced our programs, surveilling the planet's operational framework. In this place, Paladock was the Grand Master.

"It time jumped," explained Dr. Rene Paladock. "So we know it possesses intelligence, but we have no way to estimate its trajectory yet."

"Radically worrisome," muttered one of our young technicians.

Dr. Rene Paladock was an older man reaching the grand age of fifty. With long white hair perfectly combed, he made for an elegant figure within the SRC halls. As our team leader within the Conclave, he was also my maker. He continued, "We need more facts. I want to know where it is going..."

This massive cluster of thirty galaxies gravitationally bound to each other remained for some a notion hard to imagine. Still linked, they existed as the universe expanded. The biggest one was Andromeda, on course to collide with our own in about four billion years. But the path of the unknown object moving throughout space at a velocity no one could grasp justified the mounting concern within the room. This entity moved with such rapidity that it became alarming to observe, frightening even for our people. It also appeared to possess the ability to jump through pockets of space-another fact gathered just recently.

"This can't leak out," said one scientist in the group.

"How is it doing this?" inquired another.

One of the leading scientists standing beside Paladock murmured, "Where is it going is the question?" With that statement, she voiced the fears of everyone in the room. Her name was Dr. Katherine Hendricks, a Phenom in her own right. Most of us called her Dr. Kat. Even though she attempted to downplay her physical attributes, she was gorgeous. The assessment remained true even for my standards, for I was programmed to recognize beauty. But she was also a rare brainiac for astrophysics.

"Our population can't find out about this," whispered another. "What does it want? It possesses technology we do not have..."

"There is nothing to announce to the public yet," stated Dr. Kat. "As Dr. Paladock pointed, we need more facts. So, let's gather more facts."

Our lead scientist and grandmaster interjected grimly, " You prematurely assume that it is heading for us." He continued, "Instead, let's spend our time identifying any missing data. President Langden will need it. Stop focusing on conjectures."

According to my calculations, its course brought it within the Milky Way galaxy, a conclusion shared by some scientists already. Our current debate remained based on fear rather than facts. There were tens of billions of other solar systems. The anomaly's trajectory could change at any point. It traveled into a range of planets, moons, asteroids, comets, and meteoroids. Along its way, it could shift path or even stop. Whether it would reach Earth was still uncertain. And also, if it continued on its course, all the rest remained a pure conjecture. Again, if it did, then what?

When could we expect it? We were not yet sure. How close would it come? We didn't know that either. However, the latest hypothesis did not bode well for us.

How do we avoid it? What can we do to prepare for it if we can? And what if we cannot? These were the big questions that plagued our SRC teams. There were no doubts in anyone's mind that President Zane Langden would demand answers.

The SRC sent a message to request a special meeting with the EHAF. Soon after that, the latest information would go up the chain. It would then reach the Council of Nations if deemed pertinent by the Force.

"DAINN, estimate when it will enter our solar system if it does," said Paladock with a stern look on his face. "I want to know the odds of that thing landing nearby and the impact it will have if it does," he added as he looked over to his team. "Extrapolate as many scenarios as possible."

"Dr. Paladock, I don't think it is traveling alone," I said in the silence that followed. "Look on the screen and see this second mass. It is following the first or traveling with it."

The look of our people turned dark.

Paladock remained unmoving, focusing on the screen with intensity, and then pointed at smaller objects. "What are these other things surrounding these two major spots?"

The System tracked these. "I am unsure. These could be debris or meteorites."

"Not if they track with it..." said Dr. Kat. "If they appear after the next jump, we will know they are not."

"Determine their energy signature as soon as you can. We need to know."

"Yes, Doctor."

"Select multiple contingencies and work out the hypothesis. We need to know how any of us will survive direct contact or collision, whatever it is. I also want to hear the displacement they will make in their wake."

"Their mass worries me," added Dr. Kat. "If we are dealing with an intelligent entity and it shows hostility, we need to determine our defensive capabilities against it."

Dr. Paladock interjected, "I am most concerned about what is likely to happen when they approach the furthest of our planets, Neptune? The disruption the anomaly might cause. Their influence over Earth could be massive. And if it is something else, I'm not sure what weapons we have that can deal with this..."

With that statement, Paladock expressed the worries of many in the room.

"But what if we are dealing with an intelligent entity, and it's not hostile?" Dr. Kat, yet again, remained hopeful.

My physiology scan told me she was faking it. Sharing her thoughts, however, accomplished what she had aimed to do. The others derived hope from her.

"We need to brief the Conclave on this, but not before I see President Langden. I fear we will need the Company's help to devise new alternatives," said Paladock.

His face looked determined. Despite his age, his hurried steps carried him to his MTP across the floor of the extensive lab. They resonated in the silence that followed. Paladock moved like a man on a mission. "This becomes our priority until we have answers. I want variations. Leave no possibilities unturned."

Once he stepped on the MTP, the disk platform that hovered about two feet above the ground rose. It now reached three feet in height, ready to glide at his command. Capable of achieving high speed, it responded to mind control. This neural link, triggered at the whim of any individual within the SRC, was restricted to Conclave members. "I will see President Langden. DAINN, send me updates as soon as you gather them."

The MTP performed flawlessly, maneuvering Paladock around all the stations within the lab. It reached the door in no time at all.

The velocity and size of the object worried my people. It was unlike anything we understood or even had seen before. Now apparent to all, the dot kept a direct course toward what appeared to be our galaxy. Although there were many others between it and us, my programming didn't allow for idle conjectures. I needed to get more data.

Still, as part of gathering additional information, my programming considered every alternative. The possibility of an invasion remained a likely scenario. If the approaching anomaly continued toward us, it could reach the outskirt of our galaxy soon, really soon. Sooner than we could be ready.

The mass suddenly disappeared. "Dr. Paladock, it just jumped again, I said over the NetComm. The dots had disappeared from view on our screens.

Paladock's voice responded after a slight beat, "Record the time. Watch the distance. Determine how long between jumps."

"We will calculate all of it and send over any coordinates once it reappears, Dr. Paladock, said Dr. Kat. We will estimate as many of the elements we can and give you a sign of how fast it is going and how far it can jump."

Paladock grunted his approval and closed his NetComm.

"Okay. Break into teams and get back to me when you have something." Dr. Kat turned her questions to me, now in charge, after Paladock stepped out of the lab.

"DAINN, any ideas on how this is even possible?"

"I am afraid that I do not possess the answer to that query."

Would we be ready for any fighting scenarios against superior weapons? What would be the repercussions if this thing landed within our planet's space?

The size of the anomaly, enormous as it was, would trigger ripples in space as it entered our solar system. It would engender an unparalleled effect as it approached our planet. Its gravitational force on Earth would wreak havoc on our orbit.

Our fears were justified. Based on the scenarios we entered in the system, we possessed good reasons. The ferociousness of the pull sustained by Earth would result in the planet spinning out of its orbit. Gravity maintained the moon as it went around the Earth. It controlled the Earth moving around the sun and the sun going around the Milky Way center. While it remained the weakest of four natural forces with electromagnetic, strong nuclear, and weak nuclear, it governed motion in the universe. The anomaly would create a net effect or unbalance within our solar system. As it approached the other planets, it might unleash tidal forces or Roche Limit. If our scientists were right, these displacements within our galaxy inevitably mark the end of man on our planet's surface or, worst, the end of Earth. We faced an extinction-level event.

Most of them came to that conclusion, but none of them would acknowledge it yet. Together, we sought answers to survive this as a civilization.

The typical surges in weather patterns we experienced all over our planet were nothing compared to this. No doubt they were grave. These dangerous conditions contributed to many migrations. Our population became refugees, moving away from rural areas to cities. They also had caused a loss of species across the globe. And these challenges had significantly affected our food supplies. Our way of life effectively changed as a result. Even if we had created all of it, these facts never left people's minds as they adjusted to survive. They were the consequences of our actions in the early twentieth century, and no one forgot that.

Still, they represented a minor challenge to the continuity of our survival compared to this event. Men fought to survive. It was in its DNA. Basic instincts would never allow the species or one human to surrender without a fight. And while scientists across the globe experienced divisions in the predictions regarding the ultimate effects of climate change on our planet, there existed no conjecture but one for this anomaly. If it came for us, the impact on the surface of our world would be catastrophic. This new threat tipped the balance against us. The chances of survival for our entire species were impossible to fathom. We had an extinction-level event to face.

Our scientists went to work, creating all kinds of scenarios. I developed my own. I analyzed all of them, and we accumulated a slew of possibilities. We dismissed some for their lack of reality, while we rejected others for their lack of potential success. All of it created frustrations among our ranks.

Still, they kept going, and I kept computing.

Dr. Paladock attended a series of meetings that went on for days. He remained unavailable for many hours. Undoubtedly, explaining the potential disaster, we faced to those in denial, had something to do with it. Still, hours passed, and then days. The formulation of a plan took shape amid debates until we concluded it made for the best survival options. President Zane Langden ruled. The entire planet's resources shifted in a matter of weeks, both human and natural. The emphasis of everyone deviated to one thing. We drafted all people in a position to build. All those capable of implementing the programs were called upon and rallied. Those in power monitored our progress toward survival scenarios. And all along, time was our greatest enemy. The impending catastrophe kept approaching.

Following the announcement of our discovery, we implemented new security measures. Our Custodians' presence doubled in all our grids.

The entire Council of Nations rallied around the EHAF. President Langden issued immediate orders demanding action. In this shift among priorities, recruiting and training more candidates became an important goal.

The Company stopped manufacturing domestic products. Instead, it focused on defensive weapons, including more attack robots, City Vigils, and ships. We reassigned our workers to producing these within days.

We called upon the Faculty to provide combat Imps to civilians capable of fighting.

The Institute ramped up its program on its candidates. The Faculty installed new Imps to render the recruits more apt at certain things, like combat. The Imps' influence became more pervasive, affecting personality traits, and control training became a significant part of everyone's lives. From one day to the next, learning higher skills became non-essential. If a battle ensued, who would need art? Following one's life purpose was relegated to the past and no longer mattered under the circumstances. Individuals selected for their particular gifts received special training sessions as they moved quickly through the Academy ranks. After their skills reached peak performance, enhanced by more Imps, they received their initiation. These individuals were groomed and destined for our four priority programs. They received specific assignments with one goal, saving our civilization. With that in mind, they were promoted quickly within the Academy personnel. We prepared for the Aurora, Provenance, Alpha, and Origin instigated to save our people. Only, we were still dealing with conjectures.

My system charted the course based on the velocity of the object. Within three days, it reappeared. It stayed visible on my screen for a time-lapse of twelve hours and then disappeared again. The distance it traveled during this time was staggering.

All scenarios, extrapolated over hours and weeks, reached one fundamental conclusion. They showed that the mass proximity would have a significant effect on our neighboring planets. Once it began its approach, Jupiter, Venus, Saturn, Uranus, and Neptune would all feel the pull.

Based on preliminary projections, results for my people were grim. We had little over a year for our technology to act as a shield and save us.

One thing was exact. The two masses were different.

My system found Dr. Paladock on another errand with President Langden. His signal located him inside the Tower in the Offices of the President.

"Doctor, do we have confirmation on our hypothesis," said President Langden.

"The second object's signature could create a major cataclysm. We cannot rely on fighting our way out of this if there are hostilities," mentioned Dr. Paladock. "DAINN, do you have any new data?"

"Yes, Dr. Paladock, based on our latest estimates, we have a year, three weeks, five days, and seven hours to put in place an evacuation plan to save our people."

Their faces registered shock.

President Langden nodded and said, "We better come up with it, then."

Dr. Paladock's eyes glanced around the room. "Thank you, DAINN."

The communication dropped. It went into silent mode. After that, I lost track.

Come a year, three weeks, five days, and seven hours from now, there was no way to predict what would happen to all our people. What would happen to our planet, though, was now predictable. I began to work on yet another set of scenarios.

4
ORIGIN
Tesh

ANG CITY – 2098

Days of training to prepare for graduation merge, monotonous for Tesh and the other Academy trainees. Until events prompt me to act. So, deep into the dead of night, I awaken her to attend an emergency meeting of the Council of Nations. The news I impart calls for immediate action. The findings, irrefutable, change our future. DAINN Annals – 2098.

Standing within the practice arena, I waited for them to attack. I glanced around the large circular platform open to the last rays of the sun setting on Ang. Even as the day drifted into night, it still shone brightly under the arch at this late hour. Way above it, in the stratosphere, the shield canopy opened in the early evening once the heat of the day faded, let in a slight breeze. Despite the tremendous heat of the summer season, I already felt the air cool down around us. It was like this every evening.

The white training facility, surrounded by majestic columns at least three stories high, represented the epitome of beauty, despite the ravages we imposed upon it daily. The six sleek pillars, elegant in their shape, snow-like in their color, framed the ring. Their lines shot upward to hold the open sky between us and the protective dome. This part of the facility remained open and extended as a concrete field for our days of training.

Around the center, massive columns spread, forming a coliseum. Passageways leading inside the Institute building ran to the heart of this powerful Conclave center. The Institute claimed its place among other government facilities as one of the five Conclaves ruling the planetary infrastructure.

This stadium, which remained dedicated to the Elite Conclave teams, became the grounds for our skills' expansion and testing after the implant absorption. First, the Institute opened its walls at the time of our Evaluation and held us during the Assimilation until we were ready to enter the Academy. At which point, we landed here. The selection process relied entirely on our achievements. It was the same for every one of us.

A burst of mighty wind hit me, whipping my hair around. I turned toward the culprit but didn't see the responsible party.

Rain pounded me, drenching me in an instant. The downpour felt like a bucket of cold water dumped on my head all at once. It forced me to switch my attention back to my Conclave. I focused on Leane, who was the responsible one. She no longer stood where she had been an instant ago. My eyes roamed the room, and I found her.

The intensity of the wind increased and propelled me backward. I hit the smooth surface of the floor and slid several meters away. Under the force of the tornado, I struggled to get on my feet and remain standing.

I had located Leane, but I still searched for Streak, who had effectively knocked me off my feet. His abilities influenced the elements. I turned, attempting to find him, but only felt myself slide on thin ice. Once again, I lost my footing and balance. I dropped not too graciously on my butt at Leane's intervention. In her infinite humor, she saw fit to turn the floor into a thin crust of ice under my soles. That girl was creative!

The training called for everything I possessed after the long hours of mental focus. I gathered my energy inward, preparing to retaliate.

Blast laughed. If my teammate had not yet jumped in with the rest of the team to fight me off, he soon would.

I groaned. So, they wanted to run the play that way — all three against one, when every bone in my body cried for mercy.

Each of us faced the others in a combat of wills and unique gifts.

Today was my turn, but it was late into the day, and they tired me. If I won this round, I would rank higher, thereby gaining a choice and picking my assignment. Avoiding the reading pool altogether was a goal of mine. Winning would also limit the Rodent's influence on my life. After the last four years, I would give anything to get out of his line of fire.

My attention turned back to Blast, who glided above me now.

Over the years, our capabilities increased tenfold with training, discipline, and implants.

I searched for Streak, but he had vanished.

Still, my mind moved forward in Leane and Blast's direction. Not bothering to get on my feet, I remained seated, shifting positions to get more comfortable — this was the wrong move.

Blast glided to the ground and thrust a thick crust of ice around me.

I felt the cold seep within me. Unable to break the hold of the ice on me, I shifted my attention back to Leane.

My brows locked in concentration. Battling with them all at once demanded more of me now that we were all trained. I pushed into Leane's mind as soon as I got ahold of her energy field. She erected a wall, sensing my intrusion into her thoughts, but it felt weak under my determination to penetrate it. I drilled into the source of her power. Gently, I isolated her resolve and shifted the water temperature to warm, almost hot.

This change was a gift I refused to miss — a warm shower with natural water. The downpour dislodged the molds of ice surrounding me and melted them away. The friendly beads, breaking through the shell, hit my face. I leaned back, enjoying the experience. I now controlled the rain. The sensation made me feel alive. Glorious. It was so long since we had a natural drencher. A wide grin broke on my face when I saw Leane's disturbed expression.

I returned my attention to Blast, whose sheet of ice had felt dreadful and uncomfortable. He resisted, feeling my mind hovering at the boundaries of his thoughts. Blast's brain, intent on preventing an intrusion on his energy turf, fought me.

Blast prepared himself for an onslaught.

I preferred not to fight him at that level, where he remained most comfortable. So, I elected to throw him a curveball, choosing subtlety over brute strength. Circling his mind, I switched the pressure around his head. My uneven approach destabilized him. I built it here and then moved around to do somewhat the same on the opposite side. I also kept the pressure on Leane, whose face scrunched in concentration while still searching for Streak. *DarNet him.*

The gust increased all around.

It was Streak's doing. He was watching me from somewhere.

I searched around the room.

He remained invisible. Still, he had to be behind one of these columns.

Streak didn't lighten up. Instead, he increased the velocity of the tornado, lifting me off the ground. Knowing me well, he saw by the slight curve of my shoulders as I leaned back to take advantage of the rain Leane bestowed upon me that I enjoyed this too much. This action was his way of drawing me back into the exercise.

For a second, I thought about blasting all of them to smatterings. I could do that if I got a hold of Blast's mind and powers. I had never tried that before. Too drastic. Still, it was time to give them all a lesson.

Since I couldn't locate Streak, I changed tracks. Instead of fighting the power of the surge my friend manifested, I let it take me. I began floating, flowing inside the burst to the whim of the wind. I felt no need to control my movements, following the ring of the tornado, as it swallowed me whole.

Leane gasped when she saw me rising with the increased velocity and yelled over the wind's loud sound. "Streak, you're carrying her away."

Streak responded to the warning by peeking from behind one column, giving away his position. "Tesh can take it."

I then slowed the downpour to nothing, taking advantage of the attention Leane had diverted by her comment, hoping to ensure my welfare.

His fingers increased the onslaught as he walked toward Leane and Blast.

Our eyes locked. *Wrong move, Streaky...*

It made my work easier. I now towered over the room and looked down on all of my teammates' faces.

Hours had passed since the morning had unfolded with a new set of challenges and trials. Our conclave convened in this staging area every morning to enhance our capabilities. We had been at this for the past twelve hours. Exhausted by the mental acuity, I manifested to keep up with the exercises; I had dropped my guard when my eyes glanced at the exit moments ago. They had taught me a lesson, but it was now my turn.

Their energy fields collided as they stepped into the same area, making it easier for me to launch an assault on their minds.

They didn't think so, but it did.

An insect attack would do nicely, so I sent them a wave of illusions, one of my very own creations. I projected in their minds a swarm of endangered bees like we hadn't seen in a while. Now, I convinced them they were under attack. Then I watched it. Their first reaction was funny.

Pelted by what they surmised to be thousands of bees, they fled in different directions.

The wind subsided, dropping me through the air, and I engaged my NetJet boots. I hovered three feet above the ground, towards the center of the room, and landed gracefully. The original surface, a composite that absorbed shock and sounds, showed no signs of ice. Only puddles of water remained.

My laughter resonated in the vast room as I watched them run around in circles, fleeing the imaginary army as their EmVats came up. The surprise of this attack left them vulnerable. Bees were untouchable. They could not destroy them. They could aim none of their powers at the swarm. Under our Universal Pledge, we protected any life forms, leaving us defenseless.

They stopped their antics and looked at me with pissed-off glares.

"Hey, you started it," I said, crossing my arms over my chest. "I won."

"We thought they escaped the bee house…" exclaimed Leane with a surly voice. Her face, marked by disappointment, Leane looked at me now, "It's not funny, Tesh… Do you realize how bad that would be for us? They're the last of their kind."

"Relax, we hold millions in there," I retorted, unwilling to acknowledge that she was right. "Besides, they were only imaginary." It would be unfortunate if they made it out of the inside gardens and nurseries built to preserve them. We kept the large room at an even temperature to maximize their reproduction. They wouldn't survive out in the wild. They could make it under the domes, but this would condemn us to never opening it during the rare peaceful days where the winds did not rage. The bee house kept the last of them amid thousands of flower specimens for safeguard. "You do not understand how funny that was..."

Leane continues, "Their numbers are still nowhere near enough," she replied, not ready to forgive me for the scare tactic I employed.

"Clever," said Blast, with a small smile that didn't reach his eyes. "You got into my head without using force. I'll remember that next time."

"You're welcome," I said.

Blast didn't like to show weakness. I put my friend off his game by breaching his defenses. Confidence was reflected in the results. At some point or another during the training, we had to deal with a lack of it. We taught each other as much as we supported one another, and the lessons never came easy. Sometimes, they even bruised more than our egos, but learning was a part of the training.

It was the reason we practiced: to get better. And that counted for all of us.

I glanced toward Streak, who hadn't uttered a word. His face, overpowered by a shadow of anger at himself, faced me. His expression said it all.

He thought, once again, his fear of hurting me had stopped him from being productive.

My gaze found his.

His eyes pierced through me. I locked my gaze on him. He tried to unlock a problem in his mind. My well-being affected him. After a beat, he nodded before he walked away, and my heart dropped. He was breathtaking with his silver-grey eyes and his dark hair falling over his shoulders, even with that tiny scar on his left cheek, his only imperfection. An imperfection that distinguished him from the rest of us, for we had none. It was his stand, his way of looking apart. His actions voiced that he did what he wanted, regardless of our rules.

DarNet… I had done it again.

He was hard to read, as he kept more and more distance between us.

I bit my lower lip, watching his departure from the arena.

Within seconds, Blast followed him with a wave of his hand in our direction.

Leane walked over and whispered, "Still not better, I see. Give it more time. It will eventually fade."

My teenage crush on Streak only seemed to get worse. Deep down, it felt more than a crush, even if I preferred to view it that way. Selecting not to address the problem, I nodded, "I'm heading home because I'm beat and want to see Mage."

"NetRoger that," she said as she stepped beside me toward the entrance to the large corridor.

We walked together on the upper level of the Institute, guarding our silence like a welcome reprieve from a brutal assault on our brains. Neither of us was eager to talk after this grueling practice.

As we neared the end of our Academy training and entered the last few weeks before graduation, all our days unfolded like this one. The big test approached fast. It would call on all of our strengths to face the wrath DAINN would unleash on the four of us. The outcome determined our rankings.

Usually, Streak would be by my side as we exited the Institute. In the last two months, however, things had changed. He avoided me. It was better that way, I guessed.

Upon graduation, our assignments within the Conclaves became permanent, and that required we keep our distance from that moment on. A member of one Conclave was no match for the leader of the same Conclave. The Council considered that too inferior. *Such a stupid rule.*

Ranking, efficiency, and the Universal Pledge guided our way of life. Circumstances demanded physical and combat readiness for us to face any situation and potential incursion. An accepted distraction during our teenage years received extreme disfavor the moment we entered adulthood. Our conclave confirmation and ranking upon leaving the Academy transitioned us into confirmed adults. At which point, we were taking over the actual running of our society.

My PVZ or personal visor of the Z model unfolded first. Then, I saw Leane's do the same.

DAINN's face appeared at once. "You did well, Tesh. Only do not expect me to fall for your mind tricks during the final evaluation. You will face me solo. Then you will battle with your Conclave. So, come up with something less predictable."

"Thank you, DAINN. I understand." My visor closed at once, and I waited to see Leane finish her conversation with D.

Leane turned to me with a hint of frustration. She closed her vizor ending her communication with DAINN. "I'm ready for this to be over. It is sickening. I am a healer, not a fighter. When is this going to be over?"

"Shush… They'll hear this. You're tired, just like the rest of us. We're almost there, and you've done so well, Leane. We have to believe we can overcome D's scenario or rack up enough points, so it makes no difference," I said, concerned about my friend.

Since we entered the Institute at age five, my knowledge of Leane, my closest friend, and compatriot stemmed from all the times spent with her, but it went much further. My skills provided access to her patterns derived from reading her thoughts. They gave me a MindLandscape allowing me a predictive behavioral map of her actions. This insight knowledge was only a part of my gifts; an advantage others didn't possess.

While Leane knew me well, she gained her information through experience and emotional connection without access to my mind. It was a skill that proved less reliable than mine and resulted in a much less predictable outcome.

"It's so easy for you… You can hear everything we think. You can read all of us. Well, hear this." Leane turned toward me. *I can't do this anymore!*

Her voice echoed in my head as a silent scream.

I had heard this cry before. I wanted to shut my mind off. Leane's dilemma resembled mine. Sloan forced a transfer for both of us. Leane belonged to the Faculty before she ended up with me at the Institute. While Rodent changed my destiny at the SRC when he killed my parents, Leane just gave the one she had up. Still, the Institute Conclave wanted us to serve a higher purpose. So here we were, fulfilling this legacy dropped on us. In both our cases, our free will didn't apply, removed by circumstances. Only Leane was a gentle soul. Much more vulnerable than mine. My test centered on patience and revenge. Hers focused on surviving this. The constant fighting, challenges, and trials we underwent daily wreaked havoc on her. Her emotional state had fallen into a dark place over these last few months, and she held on by a thread. *You have no other choice.*

I do, Tesh. I can take the blocking implant. Maybe it will make things easier for me.

I took a step toward her and hugged her. *No. You won't be yourself anymore. I need you, Leane. Please, please hold on. It will all be over soon.*

She returned my embrace, holding on to me as if she was about to drown.

We were all drowning a little bit each hour, but we gave ourselves solace together.

I don't think I can, Tesh. Please, understand.

If her state of mind reached a certain emotional level showing erratic behavior, DAINN would intervene. When it sensed she needed help, DAINN would change her biorhythm through the Network Imps. If necessary, one of the Custodians would then pick her up to take her to the Faculty. I couldn't let that happen. I couldn't let her enter the phase where the blocking implants would become her only option.

I watched the empty corridor for signs of an Institute Custodian. As peacemakers of our facilities, they kept order inside our domes. Their role was to attend to people's needs and ensure peace and security within our walls. When we showed signs of distress, it provided a calming injection before escorting the individual for medical attention to the Faculty. Our planetary medical body attended to the healthcare needs of our population.

Yes, you can. You're strong, stronger than me, and you know why. You're kind. I'm not. Also, you're giving. I'm not. Plus, you're our healer, Leane. I am not. Driven by one thing, I act with one goal, one purpose only.

That's not true. You are kind, generous, and awesome altogether. So, you're not a healer. You're a leader. Our people need you to change things. Besides, you've kept me sane all these years. Don't tell me you're not kind. And your purpose… Well, it's warranted, so never say that you're not what I know DarNet well that you are.

I can't have you turn into a machine. We need each other, Leane. Please tell me you'll hold on a little longer.

She trembled in my arms.

I gripped her harder against me.

The timing was everything. The Institute Custodian already hovered toward us at the end of the corridor. Trust me. We can win this together. My mind reached out to hers to provide a calming effect. It worked.

I felt her relax against me, her thoughts in disarray earlier, and her chaotic emotions no longer creating a physical reaction.

A sigh escaped her lips. *Okay. A little longer then.*

The sphere of the Institute Custodian halted its progress in our direction and turned around.

The tension diminished in my body, and I released her. We looked at each other, and our hands reached for one another as we resumed our walk in silence. After a little while, Leane whispered, "I have been racking my brain to figure this out. How can we win?"

I shrugged. "I'm not even sure it's possible. We all have to execute what we have learned and hope our Institute Officers prepare us for the final test."

"Easy for you to say. Your power is better than mine with defensive capabilities."

"So I envy yours, Le. I wish I could do what you do, but you may just have given me the idea that can win us this challenge."

"You mean that?"

"I mean that."

A knowing smirk appeared on her full lips. "You're so clever. What do you have in mind?"

I rolled my eyes and said, "You gave me the idea, remember… Switch to privacy mode, and I'll tell you."

Leane did as I instructed.

"What if I open my mind during the trials so you and the others can access my powers? We will reach a faster response rate, and by sharing our gifts act as one, we can throw DAINN off its game."

"Hmm… I love it. Sharing your power is one thing, but how would we share ours with you?"

"I'm not sure yet… We will have to test if it is even possible. Still, this may give us an edge."

"We'll talk to the boys in the morning… and take advantage of this tactic."

We turned off our privacy mode as we roamed the vast and open hallways. Not seeing many people, we descended on the Elevat to ground level.

The grand hall appeared deserted.

The time on my visor showed that we had finished rather late today. I clocked us at nineteen hundred. The recruits had turned in about half an hour before. Most of the candidates from the Academy had left for their dorms. Even the Institute Officers had retreated to their quarters or meandered to the SkyStar Activity Lodge for relaxation and fun.

We traversed the hall to the main doors of the Institute, already locked for the night. Our access pass shot out in an infrared ray ahead of us, unlocking the gate.

Leane and I waited as the main panel slid open, unfurling a row of anchor bolts. The latch gave way — the solid golden doors, barring entry to outsiders, unbolted with little noise.

The cold breeze of the evening hit our faces. Manufactured by the enormous turbines from one of our facilities, this air came from the Emerald Field area. DAINN oversaw their maintenance somewhere on the other side of the central dome. It carried the hint of a smell from the particular products in the filtration system.

Leane stopped on the central plaza of the Golden Ghetto, right on the other side of the door, which closed behind us. She turned toward me and hugged me. "Soul Life. Be kind to yourself. I'll see you tomorrow."

I smiled at her beautiful green eyes and returned her hug. "Soul Life. Be kind to yourself. Get some rest."

I crossed over to Water's Edge's main resident buildings while Leane went back to the Elite Candidate Residences. The two towers were not that far away from each other, but my apartment had belonged to my parents. After their deaths, it belonged to me. Their high position within the Council of Nations dictated this transfer. They could not confiscate it even at their death. Indeed the law required that so long as a family member remained in it, it stayed in our family. I was the only family member alive.

The plaza, lit with gliding solar energy lamps, seemed desolate at this time of the evening. A few stragglers walked by as I approached my building, but otherwise, the pathway lay ahead wide open.

My head felt dulled out by the efforts of the last several hours. My body seemed heavy, as if I had exerted every saved resource locked inside me over the previous few months. My anatomy responded to today's training instead of experiencing exhilaration the way I used to, so my mind scanned my vitals. More and more, I felt that way, tired, depressed, and point-blank drained, but there was no physical correlation. As far as I could tell, my health remained good, and I appeared in peak physical condition.

I passed the main doors and headed toward the Elevat.

It ascended to the suite in a swift climb to the main penthouse floor. The door opened on the landing shared by ten other quarters, allocated to high officials in a leadership position within the Conclaves.

I took a left and arrived at my door. Cian, my Domestic Bot, opened it. "Welcome, Phenom Tesh," said the bot, gliding away from the entrance to give me access. The feed from the Elevat alerted Cian of my presence. It occurred automatically as soon as I enlisted the mechanism to deliver me to my floor

"I'm not quite Phenom, Cian. I have not graduated yet."

Instead of retreating in front of me, Mage jumped outside the doorway, his front paws landing on me without ceremony.

"Oh, hello, Mage... You missed me, boy. I missed you too. Come on in." I stepped inside. The door closed behind me with Mage at my heels. Following my lead in the apartment's entryway, Mage strutted with me to the living room.

"I have already walked him tonight. So you can relax now, Phenom Tesh."

"Thank you, Cian." Although recognized as a Phenom in terms of hours, weeks, months, and Imps at the Academy, my title was not official. It became mine after the last of our exams with DAINN.

I played with Mage on my way to the large sofa adorning our living room. He was white and beige, almost chestnut crossbreed, whose head arrived at my chest. Mage had been with me since I was a toddler and for as long as I could remember. I used to climb on his back and ride him like a pony. Although those times were now long gone, relegated to a past I wished was still present. A gift from my father, and one I held dear, Mage would live as long as I did, for all our pets had implants, like us. They never got sick, and they never aged — one benefit of the Institute.

Remembering the moments I had spent with my family in this room, I sat down on the couch. My mother and my father had been loving parents. Even if I lost the bonds we had forged as a family too soon, we were very close. Mage was my family now.

I welcomed a nudge from him. My dog now covered half of me. His size never seemed to bother him or me. I adjusted the Nanos in the material of my suit and soon felt the fabric's warm comfort. Mage put his head in the crook of my neck while my arms went around him.

Five years ago, I had gotten my dog back from the Rodent. Several days passed before I saw Maga again. But he was delivered by one of the identical androids who had taken him when I complied with the Rodent's agenda. Mage became living proof of the status quo that followed, all of it engendered by my perceived submissive behavior.

We sat without moving for some time.

A bit later, Cian appeared with a tray of food and a nutrition beverage. "Phenom Tesh… You should eat something. You will feel less tired afterward."

Since my parents' death, Cian saw to my every need. DAINN upgraded Cian's role, moving it up to a companion instead of a robot providing domestic services within our household. This upgrade gave it expanded capabilities that served me just fine. This benefit I received from DAINN appeared to be one of many in my relationship with our planetary Network. Perhaps my imagination concluded as much, driven by the need to feel special. Who knew?

"Thanks, Cian. I'll eat and go to sleep."

Mage jumped on the new plate of food without delays as I thanked Cian. My dog was always hungry.

I could have requested another model, going to a full-fledged android, but I disliked the idea. Cian was comfortable. It may not have been the most practical domestic bot because it belonged to a first-generation robot my parents had gained four years ago, but I couldn't bring myself to discard it. It belonged here, with all the rest of the stuff in my life. So, I downloaded upgrades and kept them current through DAINN, even if it looked obsolete.

"Very well. Let me know if you need anything, Phenom Tesh. Please drink this. It will give you energy."

I took the small vial and swallowed the Nuzar. The light purple liquid soothed my tongue, and I waited for the energizing nutrients to disperse throughout my body. Then, I relaxed against Mage, and closed my eyes.

Cian dimmed the lights.

Our implants enhanced everything about us and also impacted how we dealt with our environments. A pure mind command adjusted lights, temperature, and even the mood of a place. We had reached a point where we could redesign ourselves. Practical? Certainly.

I thought about the night I learned of my parents' accident. My mind kept going back to that moment, especially tonight. I wanted reassurance and comfort on the eve of my graduation test. Maybe I felt lonely. I was alone and missed them.

Holding on to Mage, the only thing that anchored me to this life, I thought of Streak, and a groan escaped me. *Please drop this fantasy.* It led nowhere. As suggested by DAINN, there didn't exist a good outcome on that one.

In the warm cocoon of the couch Mage, and I went to sleep.

DAINN's voice woke me from my slumber. "Tesh, wake up. Tesh, get ready for the Council of Nations meeting. We are starting Origin."

I opened my eyes. Then, it hit me.

DAINN just mentioned Origin.

My parents told me of a program by that name long ago. What was it again?

Pushing the sleep out of my foggy brain, I retrieved the memories and stood up.

Origin, the name of a mission that represented a last resort, filled me with anxiety. Initiating the Origin Program was an extreme measure, one we would take only when there was no other possibility of survival. My trepidation at the news caused my heart to miss a beat and drop in my chest.

Dominique Luchart

5
ANNALS
EVACUATION
DAINN

DAINN – Ang City 2098

SRC Conclave. Viewing Vlog DAINN – 1,897,689,353. Annals – Winter 2098.

Through a complex network, the System reviews the aspects of all ongoing planetary operations as we evacuated our population. The feeds cover all grids around the city and play on the hundreds of screens of the Watch Tower, providing progress reports to the President of the EHAF, Zane Langden. Preparation readiness is at an end for all actions implemented over a year. Now, every instant that passes seals the fate of my people, for the moment of our undoing is here. DAINN.

The System focused on deep space, and the screens of the SRC surveyed for any movement after the mass entered our galaxy. Spatial disruptions occurred and began to affect the Network. Later that night, all signals from our satellites across the Milky Way disappeared. As a result, our capabilities to detect anything going on in the outer regions near Jupiter stopped. By the following day, our eyes in space near the

Moon went dark. Part of my Network using our space stations also turned useless. Without my scans, the entire system became blind to any defensive capabilities beyond our atmosphere.

We expected disruption when the anomaly approached... It came upon us faster than expected.

My Network stretched to a breaking point these last few months, oversaw every aspect of our plan. We reinforced our shields, built new transports, erected safety complexes, expanded our fleet, converted facilities into strongholds, improved manufacturing capabilities, enhanced our technology and weaponry, strengthened our armada, bolstered our physiology, and increased our food and inventory supplies for distribution among the various programs. During this time, the Conclaves carried their functions within their mandates' framework with efficiency and purpose.

Soon, the last of our preparations, spread throughout multiple parts of the city, would shut down.

At the first sign of the disturbance within our solar system, I triggered the signal to the President's office and the EHAF. This step was part of our protocol. By our calculations, every hour counted after that moment.

The Council, within the same building, received notification of the imminent threat. This second phase started the Golden Ghetto's grid evacuation of all our essential citizens and official personnel.

The voice of North, the Commander of the EHAF, and President Zane Langden's right arm resonated on the Network. "DAINN, how long do we have?"

"Impossible to determine."

"Initiate Alpha, Provenance, Aurora, and Origin according to our plan," said President Langden.

"Yes, President Langden."

The EHAF dispatched their teams. Alpha, Provenance, Aurora, and Origin programs, immediately triggered by the system, got underway. Our evacuation procedures designed to respond without delay released the select Elite units dedicated to ensuring that each Conclave's officials would reach their destination.

Shipments inside the underground bunkers stopped. The regular activity in the ships in space subsided with early boarding, and soon after that, general boarding. Past the canopy that served my people as shelter, the Elevat halted the transport of supplies. All over, even in the stations near our planet, momentum stopped. Inside the underground facilities, our City Vigils got ready to receive the first of our people. In the last month, everyone within the grids appraised of their program had received their embarkation orders.

All the while, the GG, according to the procedure, received a head start.

As the first evacuation phase began, our citizens inside the Golden Ghetto, having received their embarkation orders, awaited their escorts.

Origin held the highest importance among all the programs, even though it was small compared to the others. Although created with the most advanced technology, it remained questionable at this stage that it would succeed. But, everyone privy to its existence recognized that our very future lay in its positive conclusion.

A few of our Elite members, part of our new generation, entered the safety facility under the unique program devised by the

Institute. Four chambers identical in shape and within them, four people belonging to each of the five Conclaves: Institute and Academy, almost one and the same, SRC, Faculty, Company, and EHAF, programmed to send our people back in time. Their goal, reshape history to provide us with a future. These young people, soon to enter the silent void deep inside the Institute's bowels, represented the best hope for the survival of humankind.

Located inside their Conclave residence buildings, the youngest officials, soon to be Phenom upon their graduation, waited for North's commands. Only this year, they wouldn't get to graduation. They would pass their status as Phenom upon entering the chamber without the usual fanfare. As the EHAF Elite units descended on the Institute, Faculty, Company, SRC, and EHAF residences to accompany their charges inside the facility, others took their posts to facilitate the general embarkation of the other residents of Ang. Our world's hope would then enter the underground safety chambers of Origin and begin their mission to save the planet.

Two guards from the EHAF Elite Presidential unit, responding to the Origin program, delivered the youngest members of their faction with haste. These next-generation soldiers, Lana, Silia, Jolt, and Nis, possessed mental abilities and powerful physiques that led them to be the best of the Academy.

The SRC Conclave, selected because of their high I.Q. and far-reaching scientific minds with unconventional outlooks, entered the chamber next. They were Ina, Sera, Bren, and Devo, all untouchable in each of their fields of expertise.

The third party that reported to the safety chamber were the Faculty, Cora, Elin, Faun, and Gopo, extraordinarily gifted healers.

The Company lineup showed up next with Mora, Shana, Rad, and Percy, whose capabilities and smarts made them uniquely qualified to build the groundwork of economic stability with any society.

The members of the Institute were last to come in… And two of these members were still missing.

The general alarm resonated next, according to the plan. Within all the layers of our society, our people would now report to the embarkation zones. They came in droves from Water's Edge, ArchWay Pass, BridgeView, CliffTops, and Emerald Field

The alert rang throughout the grids like a deadly signal.

My voice spilled instructions onto the streets. "It's time to evacuate. Take your allocated transports. Please follow your instructions and report to the embarkation ramps."

The hum of the space elevators stopped as our people stepped inside in large numbers. Soon, they would travel into the troposphere. They will pass the stratosphere and mesosphere. They will reach the thermosphere and exosphere to access our facilities established around the Earth. In different parts of the Golden Ghetto, the cabins connected to a tether took our population to the stations and facilities built in the Earth's orbit under the Provenance program. Soon, even the large SpaceVat began to overflow.

Invisibility shields, reinforced with the same technology as our domes, surrounded the floating city. The anchors holding it to orbit around the Earth would soon release. As it moved away from Earth, with part of our EHAF fleet, these remained the only sound defense for Provenance. The battleships, spread around it, would provide additional security in space. An early departure was essential to avoid the strength of the displacement of the anomaly. The last of our ships moving with the floating city boarded and began to take their positions to pull away from Earth.

Frigates, transport vessels, cargo containers, cruisers, and battleships began to assemble on the planet's outskirts before taking off for deep space. The last ships joining the Alpha program and bringing those selected for a long journey into deep space took off from our platforms. Faster and more limber in their maneuver, they would travel ahead of Provenance, paving the way for the journey. As each passed the defensive barrier, I lost sight of them. The signal for the fleet to begin its journey into space resonated soon after that.

Only one-third of our ships remained hidden as a fighting armada around the Moon. These were to serve the Moon station and a fragment of our population.

The safety complexes within the Earth would lock within hours under the Aurora program. The infrastructure below the Megapolis, reinforced to give a chance of survival to the main population, began receiving the workers and other personnel under the EHAF's central corp.

Orderly lines lengthened as people arrived from Cliffs Top, BridgeView, ArchWay Pass, and Emerald Field.

The lower level edifices, below the main city, inside the older perimeter of Ang, would maintain most of my people until the planet's environment stabilized, or so we hoped... Our personnel, designed to provide security, was already in place within the walls. Stored supplies and equipment already lodged inside bunker-like chambers closed. Recycled air remained a concern, although the massive turbines would last a long time. Dozens of Chambers holding thousands of Cryo pods enhanced their chance of survival as they would host half of those inside Aurora. The orders for those who would guard the underground complexes were to remain inside until an EHAF team would give the go-ahead to clear a path to the surface.

Included as part of the exodus were animals, seeds, grains, and plants, spread across all four programs for the survival of our species. Our androids and robots had seen to it under the System. These, too, apportioned among Provenance, Alpha, and Aurora took part in the evacuation. The preparations for implementing these programs were the best we could do to preserve our civilization.

I monitored the progress from the screens of my System. In all the grids, the main population now reached the embarkation ramps.

Androids and City Vigils organized the transfer into the underground city. They rapidly became overwhelmed as panic took over. Under our programs' aegis, our people had received their transition orders as outlined by the EHAF. Some implemented these steps in order; others wrecked chaos.

Witnessing the response of our population, the System sent over more City Vigils and Custodians.

Inside the perimeters of the plaza, confusion reigned.

Warnings to remain calm echoed everywhere within the city grids. They went ignored. Hysteria lurked. Until... Terror took over.

I watched as it spread across the grids.

People abandoned everything they knew. They rushed away, hoping to reach safety. They ran, injuring each other. As their instincts took over, they ignored the security protocols. Their need to survive became imperative, and they disregarded our dictates. With the Universal Pledge rules entirely forgotten, they fought their way to reach the Aurora boarding areas. Some, in utter desperation, even lunged to certain death to get there first. Now, even our Custodians, maintaining order inside the grids, became overwhelmed.

Blood ran in the streets of my city, and the system became powerless to stop it.

As I observed the activities on the multiple screens of the SRC and Watch Tower, my voice reached every corner of our streets and penetrated every room and buildings. "Do not panic. Keep order."

The EHAF vehicles flew over the quadrant of the city, attempting to restore order. The path of the private shuttles and Flycars over the city center followed a synchronized dance for now, although most of them sped up toward their destinations despite warnings.

Such were the scenarios that unfolded the moment the alarm resonated within the city. The same events took place in any other Megapolis around the globe. Each country executed its plans to safeguard humankind. And while this took place, I continued running everything until I could no longer.

A few hours later, a mass of unknown origin appeared. The system attempted to map out its exact configuration. We could not determine its composition.

Clouds began to form on the horizon of our planet. They were dark, angry, stormy clouds. They moved fast, approaching the city's outskirts in an unparalleled fashion, synchronized in a movement that did not look natural, for it acted like a wave, washing everything in its path. Soon, they overwhelmed our sky, turning it dark grey with spikes of purple hues that burst into an aggressive and tumultuous dark orange at the center.

We were engulfed in the first wave of a storm, unlike anything we had ever encountered.

Many hoped to have reached their safe harbor on the ground, below the city, and even in space. But our time had run out.

6
VOID
Tesh

ANG CITY – 2098

The moment arrives for the System to trigger the alarm, formidable in its meaning and expected by all. Soon, my city will fall, for nothing would remain intact by the anomaly once it comes within our planet's range. DAINN Annals – Winter 2098.

The sonic whistle transformed into a series of computerized harmonic notes, piercing the air from high to low.

I knew all too well what that meant. My heart sunk from my chest into the pit of my stomach. It was it, the moment we had waited with dread. Witnessed to the hope my people held against all hope, that the event would never come, the moment we had prepared for, just in case had arrived...

The alarm rang its strange melody, looping steadily over the entire city. It reached beyond the grids of the Golden Ghetto, to Water's Edge, past CliffsTop, ArchWay Pass, BridgeView, and Emerald

Field, singing its deadly tune over the canyons, mountains, and valleys, all the way to the sea.

I ran over to the balcony with Mage at my heels. The landscape of my city spread in front of my eyes. I loved everything about it, and for now, it looked no different. Yet soon it would be. *How can this happen?*

The sound of the warning resonated inside the walls of our buildings, uncompromisingly. It amplified around corners and spread through the vast rooms of our facilities. It fluctuated in our corridors, piercing the air as the last fallen bastion of a time about to disappear. I so wanted to shut it off but couldn't.

The panorama stood pristine under the dome. Its golden colors shimmered in the sunlight, glittering so brightly in places. They reminded me of the giant crystals in a kaleidoscope. The reassurance I received from that didn't last long.

I saw the activity in the sky intensify. Within minutes, more shuttles appeared under the dome. Their patterns changed, hurrying toward the residences, where they docked at multiple balconies. I shuttered. Soon these residences would be empty, their inhabitants fleeing to safety.

All this was part of the plan. Still, reality struck hard. I felt overwhelmed by it.

Over the last year, our scientists pushed us to seek other landscapes, reaching for space as part of an integral program to safeguard our civilization. To do so, we pulled all of our resources together. Our teams implemented any scientific theorems withstanding scrutiny. These became a part of a multi-prong plan determined to protect our society from the workers to our leaders. And beyond everything else, safeguarding lives became the goal of an entire race. I was part of it. An integral piece of a giant puzzle I couldn't turn down.

I became head of my Conclave, crystallizing my future with a role more significant than expected. Only, the Council didn't explain everything. Our population elite had to survive at all costs, while others... Not so much. My blood boiled, thinking about it.

The SpaceVats located all over the city worked night and day for months preparing for Provenance. They transported equipment and supplies until the moment we sighted the anomaly closing in on our galaxy. They filled the facilities located around the planet with everything our people would need to survive. Sturdy and capable of carrying a lot of weight, they lifted tons of equipment to prepare for the departure. The large cabins connected to their tether in the Earth also delivered personnel for the stations, hotels, and industrial complexes, now part of an entire city in space meant to receive five million people. Even the Moon station became a safe harbor. We had converted our facilities containing waste from the planet's surface to carry more supplies. Now, our people poured through the pathways to join a substantial portion of our population and get to their new permanent residences in space. Slowly everyone made their way to the available SpaceVats, overseen by the City Vigils. But the backlog of the crowds overran our forces.

I knew all this because I had made it my business to understand the leaders' preparation. The Council was not my favorite governing body. Tainted by my experience with the Rodent, I no longer trusted anything they promoted as a program for our people. I believed they all possessed their twisted agendas. I had been right.

My anger flared at my inability to do anything about any of it as we implemented the initiatives designed to save ourselves. My skin tingled in places, and resignation set in. The moment was here. It was it. Nothing anyone could do about it. Not anymore.

The moment DAINN's signal resonated over the land, the SpaceVats' purpose shifted… Whatever remained undone by then would stay on the surface of the planet. From that point on, the goal changed to transporting our population away from everything they knew. When our people embarked inside the cabins in response to their evacuation orders, they left for the complex in the Earth's orbit under the Provenance program. The length of their stay in space remained unknown.

They bound me to another location. I hated leaving my city, and at the thought, a huge lump lodged itself in my throat.

The EHAF air vehicles shifted their course. They now flew toward the government building we called the Tower. Unable to see what took place below on the plaza, I called up my visor. It unfolded to a larger screen and now floated three spaces away, expanding to give me access to the evacuation scenes. A raspy breath escaped my lips. Soon, it would be my turn. I didn't want this—any of it. *Universe, please don't make it so…*

The City Vigils walked out on the plaza and formed lines ready to help our people access the transport vehicles that would take them to safety. I knew then that my hopes had vanished. The evacuation was happening. My eyes filled with tears, and I felt them running down my face.

I had grown up here, within these walls with my family. HellNet, my first memories held this place in my mind and tugged hard at my heart as they surfaced. Why, indeed, wouldn't they? I had felt love, sorrow, pain, loss, and even anger here in this special place. This environment was my inheritance and my last link to my parents. In my head, the plaza below still resonated with laughter. Me as a child, running around with Mage as we chased each other. Echoes of children splashing in lukewarm water in the fountain on a peaceful Sunday afternoon. I walked the same path daily, going to the Institute. Sometimes alone, and other times with Streak, Leane, and Blast, as we planned for an evening of fun in my home.

In the space of a few heartbeats, the plaza no longer looked like I remembered it. The City Vigils erected zones within minutes in the plaza center. According to the Council assignments, these separated those assigned to the different programs and led passengers toward Alpha, Provenance, Aurora, or Origin. Everyone's eligibility for the safety offered by the programs was allocated according to skills. Each Conclave level determined the importance given to an individual. It was that fact that disturbed me the most. Now, as I watched, the I.D's provided security clearance and called every soul to report to their embarkation area. Once the signal echoed within Ang, there was no longer time to change their ranking.

A sigh escaped my lips, and a deep ache filled my chest.

Cian came to me on the balcony. "You have a visitor, Phenom Tesh."

I turned and frowned, "I do?"

"Yes. Seraph is waiting for you at the entrance."

I nodded, "Why is she here?"

"Her parents have not returned, and she doesn't know what to do."

I walked hastily through the living room and met Seraph halfway. She was standing by the sofa and looked lost, chewing her lower lips. A habit of hers, she could not shake yet.

"Seraph, what is going on? Where are your parents?"

"At work. Tesh, I do not know what to do...."

Seraph was the daughter of Nell and Harper, part of the Company Conclave, and both on the Great Council. At five and a half years old, she did not understand the magnitude of what we faced. And yet, she realized this was most unusual.

I leaned down and gave her a brief hug. "This is scary... but you can stay with us until your parents are back." Turning to the bot, I added, "Cian, give Seraph something to drink while I call them?"

The little girl nodded, and her face looked brighter than a minute ago.

Cian standing beside me turned to the child and nodded. "Yes, Phenom Tesh. Come along, Seraph."

"Mage will keep you company."

My dog looked at me and walked toward Seraph upon hearing its name. When I was at the Institute, they played together, giving Seraph a companion other than a domestic bot when her parents were away. The little girl reached out to him.

I watched them go toward the kitchen and turned back to make my way to the living room's central balcony, which also served as a landing zone to bigger shuttles. From there, I could see the Plaza again.

My PVZ unfolded in front of my eyes as I made the NetComm dial to Nell, Seraph's mother. Within seconds, her face appeared in front of me. "Tesh... what is it?"

We never were on excellent terms, but I liked their daughter. It was not her fault that her parents were cold and had opposite views from my parents. "Seraph is here with me. She got scared and didn't know what to do. How long will it be before you come home?"

"We faced a problem this morning at the Company. We are still there now. It will take us a little while to get back. Can she stay with you?"

"Until I leave for the Institute."

"I know."

"I will remain as long as I can, Nell, but hurry."

"Thank you, Phenom Tesh."

I saw relief in Nell's face as she pronounced that. The reaction was a first coming from her. She had never given me recognition before. Until now, she had always called me by my first name. She had been right. I could not aspire to the title until now.

I nodded, and my visor screen folded.

How long did I have before Streak would come for me if I didn't show? Perhaps, a matter of minutes. I sighed. Nothing was ever easy or as it should be. No matter how well one prepared.

Despite the City Vigils' vigilance, the grounds of the Plaza became a war zone. Men and women alike stumbled onto each other to make it first to the gates. Others walked on those fallen on the ground without hesitation. Irate people exchanged blows. Blood spilled on the pavement as fights broke out. The notion of the Universal Pledge echoed in my mind, forgiven in one split instant.

The buildings blurred in front of me. Wiping the tears from my face, I turned back inside in need of composing myself. I had plenty of time to prepare. We all had. Still, this was breaking something inside me.

The alert conveyed its purposeful message — the music built into a rhapsody, crushing all hope in the hearts of our people. The warning flew, fluid and lethal. No other sound echoed beside it over the land. The planetary System continued delivering the advanced notice according to DAINN's protocol.

The noise of the plaza from the monitor followed me. Voices were asking for help. Screams of panic rose. Children cried. City Vigil footsteps as they continued their deployment in unprecedented numbers. And above all, DAINN's voice, reassuring...

I sent Nell a message over the NetComm. *Nell, they overrun the Plaza. Don't land; fly here; otherwise, you will not make it back in time.*

I walked to the kitchen.

My parents had raised me within these walls. I knew every detail of the floor, for I had crawled on it as a toddler. I knew every flaw in the walls, for they had held me up when I took my first steps. I knew every curve of the staircase leading to the levels below. I had run down those steps as a teen.

Our dinner's together sitting at the hovering stone table, our evenings on the comfortable sofa, ensconced watching a DAINN program... My parents were seated on either side of me. These memories were mine, and they had taken place here. Laughter and sadness had mixed on good and bad days.

My thoughts jumped as I glanced around the place. Everything surrounding me meant something, and my heart shrunk in pain. I was about to lose it all.

Mage sensed my anguish and came over, whimpering. He rose on his hind legs, his front paws on my chest. I held my dog, hurting with every breath I took. I needed to get a hold of myself. Seraph should not see my panic.

I glanced back toward the panorama of my city.

The floating screens unfolded all over beyond the ledge of the main landing zones of the other buildings. They first appeared in front of my eyes by our air tram rails; others shot out from our skyscrapers' sides and slowly glided down to the street level for all to watch.

DAINN's homogeneous face attempted to calm our residents. Our Distributed Artificial Intelligence Neural Network spoke in a compelling and enthralling voice as it reached out to crowds in the streets, enticing calm and promoting organized departures.

Its message, repeated in an ongoing loop, also resonated in our minds: "It is time. Go to your assigned areas. Remember, carry only one Netpack. Please remain calm."

Mage's ears lowered as he whimpered again and dropped beside me. I caressed his head, resting my hand on top of it. He leaned against my leg, seeking comfort. "I'm here, boy."

I reached Seraph and smiled. "Your mom and dad are on their way. Are you hungry?"

The little girl nodded.

Cian, do we have any of the Vitabread you made?" Cian cooked and baked. I maintained to all my friends that although she was a bot, Cian put passion in it, always coming up with new recipes. Its last cake was delicious.

"Yes, Phenom Tesh."

My steps took me back toward the dining area while the child ate her cake.

I glanced back toward my screen and shifted channels to see the Institute building. Lower than all the others, as the first bastion of power, it now crawled with people. They ran in the corridors, reaching for the air steps. The faces looming on the multiple feeds looked scared, a dissonant sign for Institute Candidates. They trained us to be without a display of emotions. Even within these walls, fear dominated everyone's actions.

When the crowd poured out on the broad avenue, our population's mood could not be darker. Despondency swirled under the skin of everyone like a dark, mighty current. My people's anguish showed everywhere I looked. It matched mine. Each passing minute injected heaviness into my limbs as if connected to a timed drip. The seconds pumped lead into my veins, transmuting thoughts into despair as I watched. And I couldn't move.

The Custodians, present to maintain order, provided direction to recruits and candidates alike. Our officers, wearing their regular grey uniforms, behaved like everyone else and no longer looked in control. They witnessed their lives disintegrating.

The moment had arrived. I refused to accept it, for acceptance meant giving up and relinquishing our right to live here. My emotions rose, sending my head into a tailspin.

My PVZ opened on Nell's face, fraught with concern. "Tesh… we cannot find a shuttle. They are all commandeered at the moment."

The sound amplified outside, and I looked up. The dance of our air vehicles overwhelmed the nature of our sky. They whizzed by among the silhouettes of our towers. Above the turbulence, the dome seemed to turn into a maelstrom of molten red, dripping in place on the horizon. "Yes, the AirWays abound with them around here too."

"I know they have erected barricades surrounding the Plaza... I do not know if we can make it through."

I stood near the balcony of my residence, a high-rise near the City Center. My indecision kept me frozen. The burden of choice, too heavy for me at this moment, loomed over me in a shroud of darkness. Below, I could distinguish distant sounds rising above the windstorm of our machines. These were the types we didn't hear much in Ang. The order turned into chaos. Shoves and bellowing filled the plaza as the mob grew. "I can meet you at the barricades if we hurry."

"You would? Thank you! We will go across the park. I Will see you there in a few minutes."

"NetRoger that..."

The steps of the City Vigils played a staccato as they marched to meet the horde. They soon formed a barrier, unbroken by the GG inhabitants. The guards processed the identity of each individual, ascertaining where they belonged. After reviewing their security clearance, they directed them to the appropriate gate for the various programs.

My visor, a PVZ, opened on Streak's face. "Tesh, are you on your way yet?"

"In a moment."

"Don't waste any time. You know what to do."

"Don't remind me, Streak." I cut the feed.

There was no time to explain what I was about to do. I turned around and walked back to the kitchen. "Seraph, we will meet your parents. Do you need to go back home?"

"I need my Netpack."

"All right, let's go get it." I took the child by her hand and headed to the door. On the way out, I said, "Cian, wait here with Mage. I will be back in a few minutes."

Cian nodded, "Yes, Phenom Tesh. Do not be too long."

I made my way down the corridor and reached Nell and Harper's apartment. I knocked on the panel and waited. The door opened. The domestic bot, holding the child's Netpack, met us. "Hello, Phenom Tesh. Phenom Nell told me to give you this."

"Thank you." It was the first time I talked to this domestic bot, but he knew who I was. All the robots had access to information across our city, so they worked more efficiently with any of us.

"Seraph, I will miss you," said the domestic bot to the little girl.

I grabbed the Netpack and hooked it on Seraph's shoulders. She ran into the bot's arms and hugged it. "I will miss you too. Come with me."

"It is not possible, little one," answered the robot, with a softly modulated voice. I could almost think it felt sadness, but I knew better.

I turned away and walked to the Elevat with the little girl trailing behind me. "You will be with your parents in no time, don't be sad. It is only a machine." I cringed, saying these words, as I thought of the place Cian had in my heart. I told myself, Cian was different. It had to be. He replaced my parents. Although, I knew that for Seraph, the bot wasn't just a machine.

We entered the Elevat filled with people. The crowd, forced to squeeze further inside the confined space, moved back. The faces that watched us embark were severe, even grim.

We reached the lobby of our building in no time, and I felt compelled to take Seraph in my arms. The vast hall was no place for a child her age, yet so many children were going through the same thing.

Outside the complex, some cliques, impatient to get through the gates of our transportation train, pushed ahead, disregarding the City Vigils sentinels. The clinging of metallic arms battered against the mob cries and outrage in a clash of strength.

"Hold on to me, Seraph. It will be ok. Just close your eyes," I murmured to the little girl.

The EHAF Officers intervened, issuing orders. The clattering of their shields rose.

Men snarled in the melee.

Others groaned against the pack.

Women screeched as they got pushed.

The howling of babies ruptured my frozen state.

A City Vigil, checking identities, and overseeing the exit around the perimeter of the building stopped me. "You do not have a child. This child does not belong to you. Where are you going with her?"

"I am meeting Phenom Nell at the barricades. Check the Vlogs." My visor unfolded, revealing the last conversation I had with Nell.

The City Vigil nodded. "The crowd is too unruly."

"I have to do this. Seraph has to be with her parents. I will not leave the Plaza and will return to take my place among my Conclave."

The City Vigil nodded. "If you run into an issue, I am City Vigil 75321982. I will clear you to come back, but you are due at the Institute."

"I know. Let me pass. I will make it back in no time."

It waved us by with a final nod.

An explosion reverberated above our heads.

I looked up, as did everyone else.

The pieces of a flying vehicle twirled toward the ground right where we stood.

Panic rose.

People began to run.

The rush of the horde toward the City Vigils overran the guards.

Twisted fragments of the broken shuttle, hurtling toward the terrain filled with the crowd, descended above my head.

It was chaos. The mob had become uncontrollable, irrational.

Sprinting away from ground zero, I believed to be moving with my free will for the briefest of instant, but it wasn't so. Instead, I became one of many, yet still, an individual, tattered to others and no longer quite my own person. My arms wrapped around Seraph; I was now part of a moving mass whose behavior was unpredictable.

Screams erupted all around me as the crowd pushed forward.

Small debris hit the terrain first.

A man dropped to the ground right where he stood, his head split wide open by a piece of metal. Another shrieked beside me, his face smashed by flying projectiles. Others toppled in utter confusion.

"Close your eyes, Seraph, and keep them closed." The little girl whimpered in response.

I pushed through the crowd hard, sending my mind out to them. Reaching out to the many people on the Plaza, I attempted to calm them while urging them to move in the direction I needed to go. The progress was too slow. So, I gave them an order, weaving my power inside their brains. But by doing so, I also interfered with timing, and while it worked, my thwarting endangered some.

All at once, my mob advanced toward the barricades. I didn't look back to see the effect my power had on them.

I didn't want to witness my influence.

I heard the crash. The air vehicle collided with the ground a few spaces away from where I stood minutes ago.

The noise erased everything else when it hit the Plaza.

It was then that I turned.

The flames spiked, forming a spectrum of reddish-orange light that raged in front of my eyes before turning violet. Several flashes followed and soared, some so small, sprouting upwards as white-hot debris fell from the sky. The pillars of smoke and dust spread before it dissipated in the air as debris from the machine struck moving bodies littering the landscape.

I closed my eyes and turned away.

The barriers mended by the guards were a few feet from me.

I approached them in a daze. Part of the nightmare I had caused, I staggered on my feet, unable to breathe, my heart squeezed in the invisible grip generated by the pain guilt inflicted on me.

A voice filled with relief got my attention. Arms reached to Seraph, "Thank you, Tesh… Thank you so much for saving my little girl."

I nodded. I couldn't talk.

"You can let go now. We've got our daughter."

I looked at Nell's face, near mine, and nodded again, transferring Seraph's little body to her mother's arms.

Harper's voice reached me. "You have to get out of here, Tesh. Join your Conclave now. The place is a war zone. Go."

I nodded again and turned, hurrying back toward the nightmare.

Leane's face appeared on my screen beside Streak. "Where are you?" they said in unison, their faces darkened by concern.

"I…"

"Tesh, what's going on? You look like hell," Streak observed the scene behind me. "You haven't left the Plaza. It's a mess out there."

Leane continued. "We're inside the Institute. The EHAF just dropped us. Get over here. Now."

"I… I will…" My voice cracked.

Streak's eyes assessed me. "Something is wrong with you."

Leane's voice interrupted him this time. "She's in shock."

Streak left in a blur. "I'm coming to get you."

"It's not…." I stopped.

He had cut the feed.

I don't remember walking back to the tower, nor how I made it inside the lobby.

The clumps of bodies, lying among the fuselage's scattered pieces, formed an unrecognizable pile of burnt flesh. The ball of fire belched an incandescent wall of light as the odors of scorched flesh spread around the Plaza.

Distracted by the destruction, the City Vigil, attending to the perimeter, went to help the survivors.

I shuddered, having taken part in the death of many.

With guilt, I remember grabbing my Netpack, filled with souvenirs and a vestige of my life.

The unfairness of the scene below twirled against the edges of my brain. I searched for an escape route. One that didn't include the fate of others. Yet, staying seemed so much better than going, despite the impending doom.

I stopped, frozen again in indecision. Part of me knew why. Once I started. I could no longer pause it, and I wanted to postpone the moment for as long as I could.

I gazed at the vast city, my city, and my pain rose, cutting through me. The action meant giving in, surrendering to our fate, and the notion pierced my skin like a knife.

DAINN's alert broadcasted on our emergency channel provided a glimmer of reassurance for some while bestowing on me a cold void.

The Origin underground chambers, designed to safeguard our heritage and our key people, were a part of a multi-prong approach implemented by our leaders. Our advances in science afforded us chances to escape the destruction of the planet. Only, our mandate carried much further.

I turned to Cian. "You know what to do?"

"Yes, Phenom Tesh."

"You sure you can do this all the way?"

"Yes, Phenom Tesh."

"You won't let anything stop you, Cian? Not even the City Vigils?"

"No, Phenom Tesh. You do not have to worry. Besides, I don't think they will pay much attention to a Domestic Bot."

I got down on my knees beside Mage and hugged him. "Okay, boy… It is it."

My friends sanctioned the programs without question, while I held many reservations tucked away in the corner of my mind. The idea, the possibility of tomorrow, meant more to them than it did to me. That much felt true when everyone had worked so diligently to implement the plan, a program that gave up on everything we knew, and that would mean a different life for everyone if it came to pass.

It's not like I didn't want to live. It's more like I wanted to live the way we always had. I refused to give up on my present life, on my friends, in my city, and everything that meant something to me, especially Mage.

To others, staying seemed unreasonable, impossible, and even crazy. And yet… Staying felt safe to me, despite the impending peril. Our scientists predicted the end of our civilization due to an anomaly in space coming at high speed toward us. What if they were mistaken?

I glanced toward the Institute.

Streak would get a shuttle. I didn't doubt that. Soon, he would be here.

I glanced at the landscape, searching… The passageways, elegantly designed, rose under my eyes. Their sturdy structure tolerated much under the clouds. Like in the Plaza, people rushed, filling the pathways in the sky under the music's warning. A crowd overran the lower bridges. Eager to move to the gates below, another group escaped through another pathway. The assault on the gates increased. I turned away.

Most of us would go. Others would remain. They would watch the events from the screens of our monitoring System until those fell. For those rooted in the city inside the grids, it would rip them apart. Our scientists predicted this outcome.

The music's meaning was clear to all – the end circled us like buzzards flying over decaying corpses. It was our planet's end.

DAINN had selected me, among many others, to carry on, survive, and step inside the infrastructure constructed for one purpose - to withstand the event and take us away. The irrevocability of that choice haunted me.

Certainty didn't exist about anything. Maybe the event would not come to pass. The probability that our scientists had made a mistake and miscalculated somehow lurked in my head. Perhaps the predicted catastrophe would miss us, or its effect would be much less than we expected. My thoughts made little sense, and a part of me recognized that much.

The System held everything together for a long time, protecting us in the best way it could. Nature took its course to alter our lives many years ago. Deservedly so, no doubt. DAINN had been a savior... The one to find answers when it seemed that none could ever be collected. When options ran out, it found alternatives to stall nature's way. If not, reverse it. Today, DAINN showed signs that the anomaly overwhelmed the System... At any other time, DAINN would end this chaos.

We cannot change certain things. The course of a fundamental scientific evolution, a natural phenomenon, the life of a planet... Like the trajectory of a star flying across a dark sky. These are difficult things to influence. Life had moved according to a pulse, a rhythm all its own, following a path, unalterable.

The moment of our doom appeared, enrobed in the majesty of a blood-red sunset. It poured across the heavens and down onto us like an unalterable presence.

Overhead, in another part of the quadrant, the departing fleet took off from the landing platforms and distribution ramps with the last passengers destined to the Alpha Program. They created an organized pattern of shadows among the landscape of our skyscrapers. The transports carrying the few remaining civilian populations disappeared beyond the dome. The convoy included frigates, cruisers, and battlecruisers rejoining the brunt of the fleet in space. Our machines fled the approaching storm, taking with them pieces of us.

Ang's entire armada, enhanced under DAINN's program, stood ready to depart our atmosphere under the Alpha program. For months in advance, our workers, along with our robotic manufacturing teams, labored in shifts, taking part in the considerable build-up of our ships. Commercial transports, capable of accommodating one hundred thousand people, lined up side by side after construction. All of them would remain in their Cryo Pods during the length of the transportation. Smaller high-speed cruisers built to carry key government officials received crews of ten thousand people ready for combat, along with twenty-five thousand citizens. New battleships, manufactured to hold our EHAF corp and our androids, City Vigils, and robots, now awaited their departure orders. These designed transportation units included external casings to keep our robotic citizens. Individual transportation cargo ships assembled to maintain various species of animals waited for their final cargo. Others received vehicles, manufacturing equipment, and food. Over one hundred thousand spacecraft were now in our fleet, including recon ships, fighters, frigates, cruisers, battlecruisers, battleships, cargo ships, and transport vessels. Only, not all of them carried passengers.

Soon, they would all leave orbit for deep space.

My PVZ opened on Streak again. "HellNet, it is wild out there, but I found a vehicle. Get your Netass ready now. We have a little time." Streak's face disappeared as he ended the call.

The PVZ folded up and vanished in front of my eyes. The inconvenience of him fetching me was distressing. I dropped to the ground and hugged Mage. DarNet, this required cleverness because Streak knew me too well.

I wouldn't let it happen.

I would fight for what I believed.

I would stand my ground, even with Streak.

I prepared myself for the upcoming confrontation. Once Streak arrived, I would act. And I braced for it.

The Universal Pledge called for us to be *as we are to oneself, caring and respectful, loving and tolerant, generous, and responsible.* I was about to break that rule for the benefit of another. *We ethically refuse to destroy other life forms, whatever the reason, and remain receptive to the teachings we recognize as essential in pursuing our life goals.*

My father had taught me the value of beliefs, the set of principles upon which one must build one's life. And most of all, respect for life, all lives. He inspired in me habits like not rushing to conclusions or judging. Questioning what appears set, for nothing truly is. To look upon everyone as a friend, no matter the status they happened to hold in life. To find the alternatives, for they always existed some. To seek the truth of the moment behind appearances, for there always was one possible reason to change course. To steer life in such a direction that I would never regret action or inaction. To keep my heart open but steel myself against expectations. Never, ever lose the core and essence of who I was once I recognized it. He taught me to live… Not solely exist.

My mother had instilled in me a code of conduct that paved my upbringing in such a way that DAINN chose me. Act like you want other people to act. Give respect to those who deserve it, politeness to others. Unless you find the one you want to share everything with, keep your thoughts to yourself… Command when there are no alternatives; otherwise, rally and lead. Follow the outcomes your soul seeks, but allow your heart to pave the way and your head to learn the steps.

Throughout their lives, both of my parents had behaved under the Pledge. The Universal Pledge dictated our actions, even when those became unpopular among our community. My family never faltered under pressure.

The Pledge guided a particular way of being. It was bestowed upon us by our predecessors. As one passes through this life, we remain caretakers of each other and our planet, respecting life, every life which became our goal, and the ultimate fulfillment. Aspiring to that thing was the thing. But circumstances called for actions that went against these fundamental rules. In these dreadful instances, some departed from the Pledge, ignoring its guidance. My parents had never agreed with that stance. No matter the problem. They had always looked for a different way as individuals. This position gave them an unpopular status among our leaders. I was about to do the same.

My commitment to preserving life outweighs my loyalty to my friends, and I hated it.

Mage licked my face and leaned against me, unmoving. He sensed something was wrong. He trembled in my arms, his turmoil.

Mine… His soft hair covered my hands. Rubbing his ears and sobbing, "I love you."

He belonged to me. I raised him, from a puppy to a smart adult dog, despite the disapproval of many. Mage, a gift from my father, as essential to my life as the air I breathed, had remained with me no matter what… Until now. Those who had suggested parting with him gave up. My few friends grew to love him almost as much as I did. "You need to help me. You need to be strong as I know you are."

Mage barked in response. I knew he understood.

My parents were gone, and Mage was all that remained of them.

I wrapped my arms around him and reached for him, finding some small strength in my loyal friend. His presence linked me to my parents more than my memories of them. I could watch videos of us, recall feelings, relive moments, but these were all a part of my past. Mage belonged to my present.

Outside in the Plaza, the mayhem continued on multiple levels within the city's various grids. I observed the outline of the Institute building. It demanded my presence among my conclave.

Ang sat on the old metropolis. One ancient city, which collapsed during the first storms and left so many rubbles that were so massive that we built upon them. These dislodged many of our people from their lands into what became our Megapolis. Erected higher on tons of concrete, it stood firm against the elements and the rising oceans. As a result, we abandoned the ancient places. Modern edifices rose over new grounds, strengthened by durable materials and special alloys. Instilled with Nanotechnology that inhabited their structures, they became fortresses. They stood above the dirt and sedimentary rocks left by the massive floods. The old construction, relics of days past, got lost among the myriad of passageways, plazas, parks, archway passes, and superstructures that rose five hundred floors high, reaching for the clouds. In between these towers, ground vehicles moved on air ramps. Way above these, superhighways provided routes for additional air traffic.

The infrastructure below the Megapolis, reinforced in places to give a chance of survival to the main population, received the same amount of attention under the Aurora program. Although no one knew how to sustain a drastic shift, we reinforced the old buildings and connected tunnels. We established chambers to provide essential facilities to the millions of people that would fill the underground. We stored food, equipment, and systems so that they could rebuild the moment the survivors emerged. Cryo suspension chambers received some of the population to save supplies until the planet's environment stabilized. Aurora, meant to last months, remained the most expendable and received the more negligible support because it had little chance of success, as estimated by our scientists.

I glanced back inside and ignored the heavy smell emitted by the volumes of ships departing from our manufacturing ramps to reach the rest of our fleet in space. Instead, the scent of Lily of the Valley mixed with mint and vanilla drifted toward me from the hovering planters. The soft lighting from the gliding lamps created golden hues, casting warm shadows in the room. The objects given to me by my parents formed small treasure islands against the stone walls. They welcomed me as I stepped into the room. My chamber remained a safe harbor in a landscape of turmoil. Everything here beckoned me to stay.

The plan required that I give these objects up. At least most of them. Apart from a few relics already tucked away inside one of the glider packs lodged in the chamber and the Netpack waiting for me in the middle of the living room, everything else would stay behind.

I wish I could stay, too, and see what came next. But I would never know.

Streak would not allow it. The gentle noise of the engine's shuttle vibrated just outside as it approached the balcony. Streak maneuvered the Flycar against the railing. It hovered in place as he jumped the distance.

I turned and glimpsed at him as he landed on the hard surface just outside the open windows.

I reached for Mage, standing beside me, his head near my hand, steady. Everything I cared about was behind me and in front of me, a future I couldn't foresee.

"So, you are making this hard?"

"You bet I am."

"DarNet, Tesh. You should have already done it by now."

"Don't go there!"

The Council granted me a favor by letting me stay in my home this long. Now, it weighed on me, for my time to join the others had arrived.

The minutes drifted away as we faced each other. Thunder broke over the dome and across our inner sky. It echoed between us, billowing across rooftops, moving to the south. Clatter, clang, squeaks, and the muted roar of traffic floated around us as the minutes elapsed within this place. Yet, I remained indifferent to the danger.

Streak took a step in Mage's direction.

I moved in front of him. Was I strong enough to do it? It went against everything my parents stood for, everything I believed in, everything I had embraced. Under the light of today, my actions threw shadows on me, bathing me in darkness, one I refused to embrace and yet. Soon, I would betray myself and my friends.

Streak didn't hesitate. He reached for me and shook me hard. "Enough with this nonsense. You knew this day would come. You should reconcile yourself to this by now."

I slapped him hard across his left cheek. The imprint of my hand now marked his beautiful face. "Don't... Tell me what I should or should not do, and don't you dare suggest how I should feel. I've had enough from everyone on this subject. Do this, don't do that, behave this way, not that way. Blah, blah, blah...."

"And what of us? Don't we matter? You're being a selfish NetBrat...."

He was right. They mattered, but so did Mage. I was selfish. "Go without me."

I pulled away from Streak. Tears streamed down my face, and this time they mixed with Mage's fur as I bent down to hold him, his coat feeling like silk between my finger. Soft, so soft.

He kneeled and touched my shoulder. "Let me... Where is it, Tesh?"

I shook my head. I wasn't about to hand it to him. He could see the truth in the vial.

Streak's anxiety showed on his face. "Tesh, we have to go. It's complete chaos in the GG."

His behavior made me feel even guiltier. "I can't go. I will not do it, Streak. I can't."

"We've been over this. Do you think it's any better if you leave Mage?"

I looked down at my dog, and more tears fell. "I don't care. We are not the arbiters of life. What gives us the right?"

"Nothing gives us the right. It's just mercy. He won't survive alone in this, and you can't take him with you, not where we're going."

"Then, I'm staying... or look the other way," I murmured the last part, hoping that he would see it my way.

"The Council's orders are clear. Each of us has a mandate. Comply with it. Besides, we can't do it without you," insisted Streak.

I tensed up, my neck stiffened, and my back muscles rigid at the thought of the announcement. I clenched my jaw and looked at Streak with derision. I hated the mandate and the Council's decision. It represented everything I hated for us and our world.

He would never understand since he always complied like a good soldier without even showing a hint of hesitation. This behavior, ingrained in him since birth, was foreign to me. It contributed to keeping us apart.

Don't go there, Tesh.

But I had to... To convince him.

"Forever the loyal soldier. Don't you ever think for yourself?"

"We don't have that luxury."

"When did we ever?"

Streak's face turned red, his nostrils flared.

I needed him to get mad. "Why are you here?"

Streak looked at me with a hint of disbelief. "You know why...."

"No. I don't. You've ignored me over these last months. Why do you, all of a sudden, care if I stay or go? Then continue the mission without me. You can overcome my absence because you can handle anything. You're Streak. So, why are you here?"

Streak's eyes registered my intent, and he tensed, his features set. "I'm not getting into this now. You make no sense at all. You know what you have to do. Get on with it, or let me do it."

"I hate you." At that moment, I did for what he caused me to do next.

He was inflexible.

An immovable object would be no more unbendable than Streak was. His personality didn't allow for half-measures. Too bad for me.

He shrugged. "I know. It's better that way. I'll deal with it, so long as you're alive."

My chest tightened, looking at Mage. *He is not too tall... He is the perfect dog.*

Convincing them to let me take him inside the pod had failed.

There wasn't enough space in the compartment, or so they said. I would share Cryo, air, and rations with him. So long as my Mage was beside me, I wasn't alone. But the sentence had come, irrevocable.

"I need time."

"You can't be serious. It is a stupid thing to say...." Streak exploded. "You've had plenty of time to get used to the idea... Grow up. You have a role to play in this. We all do, and none of it is fun."

"You are despicable. I don't know what I ever saw in you." I couldn't change Streak's mind or beat him to a pulp. It wasn't my skill set. I missed it at that moment. Why wasn't I given supernatural strength? It would have served me right frequently. Instead, I applied my only recourse: giving Streak a tough time with his mission, which called for him to retrieve me. The action got under his skin. I threw emotional hurdles his way, ones that had no place in the equation. These small challenges rattled him. I knew him well, and so I served him a massive platter of Netshit. My particular kind of hell. I played with his mind and his emotions, and he knew it. It was the only way.

"There is no more time, Tesh. Besides, even if you tried, you'll never get past the androids."

"This won't interfere with the plan of our conclave."

"It will if you die. I can't allow you to go against the Council."

"DAINN provided a probability acceptable to me."

"DAINN is not the one deciding. The Conclave is, and once they provide a directive, you follow it. We all do."

"What about what I want?"

"It doesn't matter. The whole situation is bigger than any of us."

"I beg to differ. It makes no sense. Our world falls apart, and all you do is follow the Council's stupid rules."

"You know how much we all pulled together to get to this point. Are you willing to jeopardize what we have worked for and everything we have done? The plan is the way we can save our civilization."

"That's just it… We're not saving our world. Only some of us."

"You need to reconcile yourself with this, Tesh. We must execute their plans. You are the only one who can get us to the goal," insisted Streak.

"The chance for success is so slim, Streak."

"Yet, we still have to try. Without you, we have no chance at all."

"Wrong. You don't know what awaits. You don't even know if we will make it. Whether I am part of this equation has no impact on the outcome."

"It does to the Conclave, and you know it."

My shoulders dropped. My head falling forward, I remembered. Our oath, binding all of us together, could not be broken. It was unthinkable, even for me. I knew Streak. He would never take a chance if he felt he was risking me.

Our friendship began as children, growing up within the walls of the Institute. He considered me an indispensable part of his life ever since the first testing. We became adults under DAINN, receiving coaching and mentoring from it. The Implants or Imps installed at age ten made us, over the years, who we were today. In our own way, we took care of each other, supporting one another through the trials imposed by the Academy. We even shared a chamber in the safety complex to escape the anomaly.

Yet, the unspoken link remained between us. And I was about to disregard it.

My next action required that he would not look too closely. It demanded that I push him, made him angry so he would detach himself from me. I loathed doing this even when I knew it wouldn't last. Hurting him gave me no joy.

Streak's PVZ opened on Leane's worried face. "Where are you? The dome is about to crash. You've got to bring Tesh here now!"

Streak's face frowned. "We're losing power this quickly?"

Leane's face bore a disturbing expression. "All I know is that the storm disrupted the grid and caused electrical issues to our shield. The EHAF is pushing everyone to move faster."

Streak nodded, "We'll be there shortly."

A series of loud-sounding pops echoed over the ongoing warning in the distance, still resonating across Ang.

The storm had reached a critically large portion of the dome. Under the turbulent clouds' weight, the canopy grids flashed as multiple particles bursting into millions of stars shot across the protective barriers. The incandescent gold lights burned bright, leaving in their wake streaks that vanished against the red of the sky. The electronic signal faded across the grids, and the shields gave way, leaving Ang unprotected.

A wall of scintillating red particles descended on the entire city, reaching the heights of our buildings and infiltrating everything in its path. They moved in a geometric pattern, beautiful and shiny. These tiny objects of doom behaved like one, and their sameness resembled nothing we recognized as if they responded to an unheard command. The thick substance formed a veil, permeating everything around us, and the city would soon disappear within its folds.

Streak's voice rose above the noise. "Tesh... We must go. Just let me do it."

I shook my head and closed my eyes. I didn't want to do this, but I had to. My heartbreaking and aching with fear for my lifelong companion, I pulled the Hypo Transmitter from the pocket of my tunic. I gave Mage another hug and a kiss on the head.

His tongue licked my cheek, his cold nose lodged against my skin, and he nudged my neck as if trying to tell me to go on, that he understood and forgave me. *Will I ever forgive myself for this?*

My throat hurt, scratching from holding the tears back. I closed my eyes. "Mage... It will be over soon. I promise. You won't feel a thing." I inserted the device's tip into my dog's neck and then dropped it like burning coals. Leaning into Mage, cuddling him against me, I caressed his fur, holding my best friend.

He licked my hand. His hazel eyes looked at me, trusting. Now, he rested more against my chest.

"I love you, Mage."

The injected liquid took effect.

I glanced toward Streak. He had to believe this.

Mage leaned against me under the weight of his legs folding, for they could no longer support him. His eyes became dazed. Then blank.

I took his weight on my lap, holding his head on my arm until his eyes closed... Until he became limp...Until he no longer moved. And all this time while I held him, I despised myself. My shoulders drooped, and the sobs came, heavy, raw, shaking me. I gulped for air. *I was wrong to do this.*

Streak pulled the dog from me.

I resisted. "Don't touch him. Hold the bag."

"What are you doing?"

"I'm not leaving him on the ground."

Streak complied, frowning. "Leave it. It no longer matters."

"Don't you dare?" I lifted Mage and put him in a large bag.

I took deep breaths and closed my eyes. *It has to work.*

My mind focused on Streak, doing the work the Institute trained me to do.

"Our world is falling apart, and you're wasting time with your dead dog?"

I whispered, "You left your soul inside the implant chambers of the Institute."

Streak's face paled, his mouth tightened as he grabbed my arm. "At least I have my priorities straight. We have no more time."

The ground shook under us, and we stumbled. I had time to pick up my NetPack as Streak dragged me to the door of the Flycar, shoving me inside.

My vision blurred. Streak's patience blown, I sat beside him, lifeless — my cruelty to Streak overwhelming me. I glanced back. Nothing moved behind us. My balcony and home drifted away.

My heartless behavior left a lump in my throat that I couldn't dislodge as I looked in Streak's direction. *Will he ever pardon me this breach?*

Our code of conduct dictated a behavior - respect for others. I disregarded it in lying to Streak. I circumvented the mandate of our Council. But embarking into the void left me no choice.

I did not regret my actions. I drove my thoughts into a deep partition in my mind and hid them there.

The high winds increased. Despite the stability of our shuttle technology, the flight turned bumpy.

My withdrawal inward left me numb and no longer caring. *In a few hours, if the plan fails, we may all be dead anyway.*

We passed the city buildings in the Plaza, and I saw everything through a daze.

A signal made its way onto the screen of my PVZ.

Streak maneuvered the landing near the doors of the Institute. On any other occasion, the City Vigils and Custodians would have arrested us, but today. They were evacuating our Megapolis and escorting the high-level personnel to safety.

The last of our departing trams stopped on the Plaza with people rushing to reach it. The assault on the gaping doors as bodies piled up inside left me shaking. It was cold, so utterly brutal, inhuman. The savagery of the masses before the doors closed sent a bitter taste in my mouth. These were my people, but they no longer behaved like people. Instead, their desperation rendered them lifeless, like zombies, resembling a band of unearthly creatures' eager to get to their food. Other memories surfaced... A pair of cold, black eyes shifted in my mind. My hand reached for my forehead, wiping away the vision.

Ahead of us, the androids programmed to coordinate the evacuation reached the landing zone and helped the injured up, moving others onto gliding gurneys. Humanity showed its true colors today, and our machines acted more human than we did. All this registered somewhere in the back of my mind.

DAINN would not reach me.

I would not allow it. I focused harder.

DAINN had an uncanny ability to determine everything that went on inside of us. Its programming made it that way. It noticed a change in physiology within seconds. A drop in mood would send it running my way if it ran at all. It received an alert of a pattern change in our minds, and it would offer help.

I didn't want DAINN's assistance at the moment. The unpredictable events surrounding us would test its range. I hoped this would help me limit its involvement with me.

The engine shut down.

Streak grasped my hand and pulled me behind him to exit the shuttle. We jumped from the cabin to the pavement of the GG. Streak ran me across the Plaza, pushing through the melee.

The flow of the mob overwhelmed us, slowing our progress to a halt. "The people try to get to the underground. We've got to hurry," yelled Streak over their heads.

A woman fell in my path.

I stumbled and almost walked on top of her. My hand let go of Streak's grasp. I leaned over to help her up. By the time I turned, he had disappeared.

A City Vigil moved the crowd away and cleared a path around us. "Are you all right, Phenom?"

I nodded and glanced back toward the shuttle. Way back, I saw Cian flying low across the sky and sighed. "I am fine. Thank you."

A pair of hands resting on my shoulders turned me around. Streak's voice, warm against my skin, blasted in my ear, "This way. Tesh, stay with me."

The City Vigil turned to help another woman with a little girl.

Streak pulled me with determination; his hand closed firmly on my forearm. My skin would bear his mark, for the grasp he had on me felt like steel.

I kept pace with him, an eye on the signal on the corner of my screen.

The ground shook again, with more violence this time.

We stumbled over each other. "Engage your glider," Streak said. His terse tone matched his tense expression.

I did as he ordered.

The small air propulsion engine in our boots acted as a jet, lifting us several feet above the ground. We passed over the people's heads, running toward us to reach the ramps leading to the Underground city.

The doors to the Institute building stood open ahead of us.

We flew through them.

Inside, the deserted lobby was like the husk of some dead animal.

Still holding my hand, Streak hovered with me in his wake, gliding through a series of moving stairs.

I matched his speed, glancing behind me as we went faster.

We rushed down several levels in the surroundings already abandoned. My mind remained focused, guarded as I pushed myself to behave normally. Keeping DAINN ignorant was difficult, if not impossible...

We passed closed doors and empty corridors until we reached a wide underground tunnel. It held the infrastructure of Origin, our safety complex.

Two androids waited outside the structure, guarding the entrance.

Streak let go of my hand as soon as we passed the threshold.

Sweat dripping from my face, I flipped the small device in my pocket upon entering the chamber.

One robot led him to his compartment. Another guided me to mine. Glancing behind me, I observed the androids' behavior and waited.

They stood on either side of the doorway, frozen.

I resisted the robot and stood my ground. The doors began to close. *No, no, no.*

A sigh of relief escaped my lips as my domestic bot, Cian, flew through them as the chamber's mechanism sealed us inside. They would not open again until much later.

My thoughts moved ahead, fixed on the chamber's environment, emitting images in Streak's direction, highlighting what I wanted him to see.

He stepped into his pod.

My eyes locked on Streak. His stern face was closed off. Our gaze held a brief instant, and he disappeared inside his pod.

The metallic voice of the PodBot dedicated to my Cryo pod said with a reproachful intonation, "Phenom Tesh, you need to get inside now."

I began to undress. When I looked back, nothing moved inside the other three compartments.

Would we ever see each other again? How could I leave him like this? The laser membrane of his compartment dropped. My thoughts went out to him. *Streak, I'm sorry.*

The compartment PodBot said, "The others are already inside. Please give me your tunic. I will put it away. The protective barrier will drop soon."

I handed the PodBot my tunic, counting the minutes. My domestic bot skimmed past as the seal around my compartment descended. I exhaled, releasing some of my tension.

Streak's voice reached me. *I am too.*

My domestic bot said in a melodious, metallic voice, "It will be all right… You will be safe." It took over the functions of the PodBot.

I released the hold on my mind. The veil lifted. "You know what to do, Cian." I didn't need its help to enter my pod, but it supervised the change once inside.

The PodBot connected to the system would take over. Cian would ensure that everything functioned properly. It remained ready to intervene, prepared to serve. It would be there when I fell asleep and when I awoke; if I awoke, if we all awoke.

The light in the chamber dimmed. Soon, we would blast through the Gateway.

I closed my eyes, hoping for all our souls to find their rightful place in the universe. My memories drifted to my father, mother, and Mage as I settled in my capsule.

DAINN's voice spoke to me… Words I didn't quite understand. It was about something I needed to know. Something I would discover when I awoke. Something to do with my parents.

I was drowsy. My thoughts became disjointed.

Sleep would take me soon, a welcomed ally in a fallen city. Within the time I decided to exhale three breaths, I had entered the void. Oblivion claimed to me.

7
CLIFFS
Chase

Mountain Range, California – 2017

> *I first encounter Chase Davenport when he touches the sky and falls. That day, I initiate him to me and connect him to the System. DAINN Annals – Summer 2017.*

The path narrowed ahead, snaking around the wild old trees. Until now, it had remained wide, the brilliant sunrays shining through their limbs. After another half an hour of walking, the woodland will claim these grounds, roots twisting in the underbrush. The shifting of leaves in the breeze carried a distinctive melody, mixing with birds' singing in sudden bursts.

I hiked ahead, going deeper among the pines. My reason for selecting this break and refusing to join my family this summer had to do with my need for freedom. I preferred the wildness of the high canyons and summits' ruggedness to tame vacation days in the Mediterranean. I had given up the parties with friends under the sunny skies of Italy. A few days from now, the Pacific Coast Ranges would turn into a playground for my buddies and me. Already my feet took me past the civilized landscape.

My family disliked my absence. They hated it. The last conversation with my mother before my departure to this place proved as much.

"I don't understand how you can pass up a vacation on the Riviera," my mother had objected, looking at me with such disappointment that even now, I felt it in my bones.

Crushing her desires had never felt right. And I was disappointing my mother with my announcement, and it gnawed at me even now. *How could it not? A mom is someone to please.* It was a first for me, this departure from norms. Until this summer, I had always taken part in the family getaway. This year, however, was different.

Oh, brother.

The guilt I felt was the thing I had to dismiss... I felt culpable. Hell, it seemed my lot in life. Somehow, even if she didn't show it, I had a way of letting her down. *Damn it. You can't live your life for someone else's just because you don't want to hurt them.*

The announcement that her oldest son volunteered for an internship with Jonathan had made my walking out on the family for the summer much more manageable. Joining his team at the Center after graduation reassured them, and taking weeks to climb with friends had become much more palatable after that.

Relief filled my lungs at being free again.

I entered the deeper part of the forest a while back. The light streaked through the old trunks, and the woodland became magical. Every twig and blade of grass covered by fallen leaves and pine needles cushioned my steps. I stopped. Standing still, I closed my eyes and listened. I heard movements, the flutter of bird wings above, the skittering of small mammals around me, the shifting branches in the wind, and the flowing water from a nearby stream as it hit the rocky slope. Life abounded here in the silence of the hills. This experience helped me center myself, and my cells responded to the myriad of impulses flowing through my body. The scent of pine surrounded me. I breathed deeply.

The trees sheltered me as I made peace with my decision to be here, their full canopy spreading above my head. The smoldering light between the tall pillars would soon turn bright white as I reached ahead to the rocks' escarpment. It could be blinding. I adjusted my sunglasses over my nose.

Behind me, protected from the harshness of the sun, life would continue, away from prying eyes. I jaunted ahead. The flat ground changed, becoming a hill as I approached the mountain.

A trip in the wilderness always helped me process things holding me back. I came here to clear my head and think. On the mountain, the vestiges of a bad experience would vanquish into nothingness, replaced by lightness. The letting-go phase removed all baggage. Such was my imperative on this day.

So far, the climb had been easy. Boulders paved the way up, past the forest ground, easy to jump. I kept going at a steady pace, moving upward without looking back. My speed ignited a sense of elation that soon turned into freedom. I knew the process, having done it before, many times over, for small or big things.

Now, I began the challenging climb. At the canyon's base, the small promontory stood as the last verdant bastion before I jumped the boulders, paving the way upward. I reached for the ridge. It looked like a long ribbon of barren bones under the blinding light.

I glanced up at the peak ahead.

The summit beckoned me. It was a beautiful sight edged against a sunny sky.

My breath came faster under the effort. Adrenaline coursed through my body as my muscles tensed when I lifted myself on the bedrock. I paused on the small overhang before continuing on the abrupt rise. Past this point, every move would count.

This life brought about a restlessness, calling for something yet, undefined. Deep down, I sensed impatience, the need for action, and the urge to break new boundaries. Ahead, the crest always made me see things clearly, and perhaps today, it would deliver its answer.

The rock felt gritty under my hands. Pebbles fell beneath my feet as I climbed higher on the face of the mountain. Sharp edges marred the way. The drop loomed beneath me, daunting, for a fall would be my undoing. The shade on the cliffs became a harbor of peace when I stepped beneath the small ledge, and my eyes found an instant of relief from the sun.

I was born for this. Even though it was likely that the elements would be a winner, I thrived. The outcome of each challenge remained variable, but the experience linked me to me more than studying Anthropology and Neuroscience in Harvard classrooms. One more year there, and soon I, Chase Davenport, awakened by the experience of the ridge, would be free to lead the life I strived to achieve. And nothing would hold me back.

I edged further into the hollow split between the vertical escarpments on the side of the mountain. The splintered surface, rough under the tips of my fingers, gave a blistering warmth. Summer came early this year, and the hot sunny day beat down unmercifully on the surface of the rock. My hand found a massive fissure above and closed on it, testing for sturdiness as I held closer to the ridge. The mass radiated heat against the thin layer of my shirt and pierced my skin even as the breeze teased, molding a gentle dance in the smoldering air.

I climbed higher against the rigid bedrock with each pull of my arms. Life, brought into sudden focus, appeared like an incredible gift, complex yet simple. As my hands hoisted me up, the jagged edges of the curling spine formed by tons of granite cut my palm, but I connected with the world around me, and the power of the mountain transformed me.

Strength.

Determination.

Focus.

These were the quest of my life.

The low screech at my feet drew my attention. A baby hawk, fallen from his nest, moved near one of my shoes. Without his mother, it would die. Should I take the risk of placing him back among his kind?

I paused, indecisive, even though, deep down, I knew my next move. Hell, I never looked the other way when an animal required help. I wasn't about to start now. Even the slightest thing could go a long way. Kindness was never ridiculous, although it brought me to low a few times when I was a kid. Don't you know? Kids were not kind.

The tiny bird reminded me I had done something similar once before. I saved a little sparrow after it fell from a tree. Not during a climb, mind you, although I climbed the tree and couldn't quite figure out my way down, which elicited a perceived weakness and bullying my way. It did not deter me, though, for I was rather stubborn. So, I learned how to climb trees and get down from them, and in the process, saved a menagerie of animals, including cats. And a lot of them from my neighborhood. Indeed, I saved the same ones multiple times, and somehow, my persistence paid off and rewarded me in other ways. I built some muscles.

I looked around, searching for the nest. The refuge could not be far. The slight overhang above my head, providing shelter from the rays, appeared large enough to hide the lair.

Holding onto the wall, I took off my scarf. With it in hand, I leaned down and picked up the tiny bird and pulled myself up, reaching the flat surface.

Twigs, grass, and leaves formed a rather large refuge for the two crying chicks in it. I dropped the one I held amidst the others. Without delay, I removed my hand from the ledge.

The small and stable overhang became a screaming presence, overwhelming the silence of the cliffs.

My breath caught. The high, plaintive pitch of a whistle startled me. Feathers brushed against my wrist, fluttering with anger at the disturbed nest. A large beak protruding over the edge pounced on the back of my hand and drew blood. Hidden in the hollow surface of the bedrock, the falcon's bite, fierce, his wings hitting my face, proved lethal. Talons, the size of my fists, appeared over the edge and grazed my face.

I let go, protecting my eyes with one hand.

As the Peregrine Falcon attacked again, its claws tore the skin off the back of my other hand. Blood poured out of the gash, crimson red, and dripped on the bedrock. Pain gripped me, and my hand slipped.

Jerked off the small ledge by the hawk, my feet skidded. Without my footing, my body ripped away from the wall.

I stretched my arms, seeking the safety of the bluff, desperately reaching for another support. The reflex occurred a fraction too late.

I fell backward.

Blue filled my sight, an endless canvas of pure, unending deep blue. Enfolded by the azure canopy, I felt the entire world tilt around me. My hands touched the sky, grasping at it frantically, only to close on... Nothingness.

I dropped.

A surge of adrenalin coursed through my veins.

Fear. I tasted it. I swore. Dumb, dumb, dumb.

I saw it all play again in my head as the wind brushed against my ears. Everything displayed on the screen of my mind: the morning hike, the twisting narrow path surrounded by overgrown bushes, the steep hill, the dead brush on either side of the trail, the faint bubbling of a stream nearby, the chirping of birds coming from the underbrush at the bottom of the clearing. *Damn!*

Not smart.

Not strategic.

Not skilled.

It's over.

Sadness rose — *this life. My life, ending.*

Chase Davenport. Powerless. Here I was. In a deep dive, I plunged to the ground, one I couldn't recover from. For a smart guy, unable to stand still, always looking for the next best thing, it seemed somehow appropriate.

I whizzed by tons of rock on my way down like a dead weight, facing my next challenge. One, impossible to realize. Living. Soon, I'll end up frozen in death. Talk about irony.

The top of the ridge split apart, formed two column-like towers overhead. They danced in front of my eyes as I moved past them during the descent. Large veins spread across the entire surface like the limbs of a spider.

I wished upon a sturdy web in the form of a net below. I closed my eyes, expecting the shock of my collision with the Earth. All the while asking for a chance to live. My heart raced. My breath caught. I gasped. As I bargained for my life in a series of incoherent thoughts, a small piece of me knew better.

My momentum increased.

It was pointless. I was toast.

The odds played against me this time. The universe had better things to do than grant me this token of good faith.

I sunk lower, gaining speed.

It felt like forever. The plunge would end soon.

Unpredictably, my backpack hit an outcropping.

I bounced against the weathered surface, and I slumped further. The light dimmed. I descended into the darkness of a shaft fast, too fast.

Only... A different feeling invaded me. Weightlessness infiltrated my body.

I've got you, said a voice in the darkness.

I now floated downward. My mind grasped for comprehension. What happened seconds ago?

This sensation appeared out of nowhere. It was like things moved in slow motion. The velocity of the descent had broken my fall, or was I imagining things?

Chase, you have lost it, man.

No, you haven't. Just brace yourself. I wasn't prepared for this, responded the voice.

The shock jerked every bone in my body when I hit bottom. The ground ripped me apart. My heart crashed against my ribs and rocketed back into its place, weakened and struggling.

I wished it wasn't so. But I was about to die. In that instant, I accepted my situation with regrets. I let go.

You're not dying. You need, well, you need a moment, added the voice. My scan is not what it used to be, but I'm sure you will be all right.

What? My thoughts drifted, becoming few. I felt a lightness in my limbs. No longer anchored to my body, I felt free. I glimpsed at a face, and… Stillness laid a magic hand on me.

I blacked out.

Come on now. Wake up. It's time for you to wake up.

Who in the hell is talking?

Black spiraled around me until I saw the glimmer of light. Drifting back into a state of consciousness, I opened my eyes. My vision, at first blurred, adjusted. I grasped only darkness.

I took a shaky breath; a wave of cold engulfed me. Light-headed, I brought a trembling hand to my chest. My heart thumped hard against my palm.

The ground under me felt sturdy; sand packed tightly over rock. My hand moved over it, sensing rather than knowing it.

My body appeared intact. Anticipating my death during the fall left me disoriented.

I was alive.

Disbelief set in. *How?*

Good. You're coming out of it, said the voice.

Where was that voice coming from? I looked around, discerning the rock formation on one side and nothing but dense blackness on the other. The small cavern I landed in, the perimeters of which were unknown, represented salvation; mine.

My brain tried to process what had just happened. I couldn't make sense of it. Incredulity danced through my mind in swirling waves. In the last part of the fall, as I neared the ground, I slowed down. My body floated instead of falling.

Alive. I was alive.

My right hand reached my red face. Too much exposure to sunlight today. Time spent holding on to rocks above cliffs would do that to a guy who's usually inside a classroom. I grazed my light stubble of beard, and the tip of my fingers brushed my eyelids. In the obscurity, I couldn't quite see the details of the cave. So, I tried to focus, looking for my backpack.

Steady, Chase. Outlandish demonstration of emotion was not my thing. Yet, this deserved some acknowledgment. I searched and found my mind empty. Jumping up and down seemed rather inadequate. Still, the guy with an angular jaw under a straight nose, who threw sarcastic humor around, couldn't find anything to say this time. Everything appeared inappropriate.

I no longer laughed at life. Respect was lacking over all these years. Today, I got the message. This second chance brought me to realize that I needed to mend my ways.

Well, think less and get out of here; I didn't just save you for the fun of it, said the voice.

What the hell? Ignoring it, I reached in my vest pocket and retrieved a glow stick. The greenish luminosity emitted from it allowed me to see about two feet around me. My Hyperlite Summit bag rested on the sandy surface at the edge, with one of its straps broken.

The gear within my reach filled me with relief. I moved toward it. My muscles, developed over hours of climbing on a wall, screamed. The fall, no doubt, had more to do with that than the exercise.

I had pushed the limits. And, this time, reached them. Stupidly, I had done it again. Still, I was a freaking daredevil. I did not take chances; instead, I was a lottery ticket. Blatantly, I swam against the current and tempted destiny time and time again. Now, it had called in a marker.

Brilliant, Chase.

I pulled the Dyneema to me and opened it. *How long have I been out?* I grabbed a flashlight from inside. My sports watch, given to me by my dad for my last birthday. It showed two hours had passed since I plummeted from the mountainside.

The beam of light bounced around the bleak landscape, revealing a small ledge where I sat. It glimmered briefly over the emptiness of an abyss below, unable to breach the blackness of its surface.

I threw a rock, waiting to hear if it reached the bottom. I never heard a noise.

The flashlight blazed over the slick surface of an endless wall above my head. My heart missed a beat and started a chaotic race up to my throat.

Luck did not require smarts. It just happened. Still, it created illusions and could lead one astray. It rendered one overconfident, overshadowing reality and building unrealistic expectations. Smarts, however, required one to realize that one was on the road to being an adrenaline addict based on cheap thrills. I quit the stupid pranks and faced my shortcomings at fifteen. The wake-up call was timely, too, for I was on the wrong road. And I didn't mean the vehicular kind. It was apparent; I still hadn't learned my lesson. This fall proved it.

Timing or lack of it is a factor. It brought everything to a head, or it became the best of allies. We all know that. I shrugged.

It had not even dawned on me to ignore the tiny chick on the ledge. *Payback is a bitch.*

I got out of a lot of situations I shouldn't have been in in the first place. Life was bound to catch up to us one way or another. Hell, pranks at the school of medicine stood out in my mind, or the engineering building campus shortage. Moving cadavers around so the next class couldn't get into dissection on time was not one of my finer moments. It was the biggest, and the one we got the most flack, though. The access to the grids on the side of the engineering buildings where we turned everything off on that part of the campus wasn't too bad either. I slid right through these. But I suppose the universe keeps tabs on those things and eventually calls your number.

So, I had to climb out of a hole. It could be much worse.

I laughed. The sentiment was a new one for me.

Now that you're awake, it might be helpful if you do something about your predicament, said the voice. *Once again, I didn't save you so that you would sit here.*

Where in the hell did that come from? I picked up the glow stick and looked around. Hearing voices at the bottom of a cave didn't bode well. Part of me wanted to answer, while some part thought I was going crazy.

My wounded hand, caked with blood, throbbed. Sand and grit covered the skin, gone in places, enmeshed with dark red flesh. I grabbed the disinfectant and took a deep breath. Pouring some of it on the injury made me double over. I grimaced as the surge of pain hit me. When the ache ebbed, I bandaged it.

Things didn't add up. My logical mind recognized the impossibility of my position and struggled to make sense of it. How was it even conceivable that I wasn't dead? No rational explanation, no reasoning to justify my survival came to mind. The reality of this situation, no matter which way I looked at it, remained puzzling.

You might want to consider that all of this is real, said the voice.

What the hell? This fall changed everything about my perception of the world. The realm of the impossible existed, piercing the confines of my mind, expanding beyond known parameters. It demanded that my imagination fly and open the gate to uncharted landscapes.

Make the best of it. Hell, yes. I'll make the best of it, starting by getting out of here.

The phone didn't provide any link to the outside world. When I took a bite of my sandwich, it tasted like dirt in my dry mouth. And my right ankle throbbed, alerting me to an injury in my foot. Still, I tried standing up, and I screamed. I buckled to the ground, landing back on my ass with an absolute lack of grace as a sharp pain went up to my leg. *Shit, shit, double, triple shit!*

Well, I didn't expect to find you in such a desperate situation, said the voice.

My foot, the size of a small orange, turned reddish-blue, but there were no broken bones. I inherited a bad sprain from the fall, a painful one at that, but no jagged bones protruded from the skin. *Get a grip, Chase.*

A face now floated in front of my eyes. *You're not afraid of anything.* However, as I heard this, the mouth never moved, yet I listened to these words.

I recalled that face. I saw it earlier when I landed on the hard ground after my fall, right before I passed out. A weird feeling came with it. Calm descended on me, invading my limbs.

Where did that come from?

Panic rose.

I was going crazy and attempted to collect myself.

It didn't belong to me.

It was not my voice.

But it was her face, her voice. And they were in my head.

My hands trembled as I reached inside my bag for my old red and blue scarf. I carried it with me every time I went up. A lucky charm so far. I huffed. "Okay, Chase… You have a concussion. So, focus. I muttered to the scarf. "You'll help me get out of here, won't you?"

The scarf didn't answer. Not that I expected an answer.

I removed my climbing shoe and enveloped my foot, muttering to the scarf, "Help me out, old girl." I tightened it over my ankle.

"Here." I slid my foot inside the shoe and grimaced. "What do you say?"

Hmm. Curious. I didn't think your technology was that far ahead. So, do you use A.I. capabilities for everything?

My head was a goner. The damage to my brain was evident. I had lost it. I no longer could be helped; I was sure of it. Although, I tried to rally myself. *You're tough on a good day, so… Suck it up.*

My foot throbbed, sending a sharp pain up my leg with each step. Even putting lightweight on my weakened ankle made my insides feel as if squeezed by hot gloves covered with iron spikes. This climb, already challenging by the looks of the wall, required control over the pain. Otherwise, with these two injuries, failure loomed. I focused on pushing the soreness back.

I took a deep, steady breath and reached for my gear. My rack was my way out of here.

Below me lay emptiness and complete blackness. I checked the wall next, deciding which side offered the best way up.

The climb was a class five-eleven to twelve with overhangs. Past the point where the beam of my flashlight ended, the visibility became nonexistent. The lamp only provided a sphere of luminosity about three feet wide in diameter. From the slight cropping where I stood, the path was indistinguishable. I gave up searching for a way up. *I'll make a go of it on the fly.*

I looked for the rest of my gear. It had to be somewhere on the small ledge.

Nothing.

It must be here. I looked again, combing the area more this time — no sight of the harness, leg loops, waist belts, and helmet.

Damn it. It had detached from my bag in the fall.

Bouncing on one foot, I approached the rocky surface. I could do this free climb because I had done it before. *I will have to flag this one.* Using my injured leg as it dangled to improve my balance, I took the first step and pulled up.

In the cavern, no wind blew, no clouds moved, no plants grew. Just cold and damp atmosphere surrounded me. I envisioned myself on the summit, admiring the panorama, feeling the shifting winds and the sun warming my face, smelling the wild-scented plants growing in unexpected places.

That's it, visualize, the voice said.

Holding on, I nudged up with a pull of my arms and kept one foot on the bedrock. The pebbles shifting under my weight reminded me of rats running inside walls.

The gentle voice rose again. *You can do it.*

I shook it off and kept going. No hollow sound of the hammer broke the silence. No action inserting the bolts into the rock interrupted the stillness. I crawled up.

The vertical shaft loomed over me without end. The climb was agonizingly slow. Raspy breaths escaped my throat; sweat slickened my grip on the rocks. My injuries hampered my movement. My muscles stretched under strain. One hand sought the next place on the foundation while the other throbbed, weaker. I kept going. Higher.

No safety zone waited. Only the way down. I shook my head. *Chase, get that out of your head.*

The voice came back again. *You can do it, Chase.*

A growl emitted from my throat. I didn't want to respond to it. Talking to myself was already bad enough. Speaking to the voice from who knows where seemed a hell of a lot stranger. So, I did what I did best; I ignored it.

The run-out above my head sharpened my senses. My arms trembled, further increasing the level of difficulty. Recalling other jumps in the pouring rain, I examined the large gap ahead. I could make it. A large fissure danced in my memories as I measured the distance between my position and my target. I scanned the surface of the bedrock, my breath forming frosty patterns in front of me in the frigid air. They evaporated like ribbons of wishes cast into the wind. It would be a stretch.

Half snorting, half laughing, I murmured, "All right, come on, Chase, you know what to do."

I wished for the cold feel of the nuts and camming devices against my fingers, the rope slipping into the carabiners, the soft scratch of my boots on the surface. But nothing broke the monotony of the climb this time: just me and the rocky surface.

Struggling to hold my grip on the gash in the stone, my injured hand slipped. I grabbed the mountain hard with my other hand. My vision blurred. I closed my eyes, holding on over the abyss and breathing hard.

Envisioning a successful landing, I swung, my lousy leg giving me additional momentum while the pain burned through me like hot coals. I made the distance and landed. I held on, pausing just long enough to catch my breath. While standing there, one foot on a small crack in the rock, I attempted to cast away the unreality of the situation I found myself in - my survival.

The recent events transcended normalcy by leaps and bounds. While it was most unusual, there was, if this was real, the likelihood that I would soon face something else. The possibility that it was unrelated to our world entered my mind. My imagination carried me away, driving a hint of fear.

Dismay drove me up the wall. What was happening?

The same voice came to me again. *Calm down, Chase. You will be just fine.*

I jerked away from it in my head, pushing its influence out of my mind. I just wanted to get out of here and away from it. The fall influenced me. It carried me to imagine the worst.

I fought to conquer my newfound frenzy.

You can do it, repeated the voice.

Settling one of my hands on the next crack in the wall, I scanned the smoothness of the façade. Something glittered on the surface, about two feet above my head.

I hesitated and squinted at the object inside the small gap. With one hand holding onto the rock, I stretched and brushed aside pieces of stone. The debris fell under my fingers and revealed the object lodged within the fissure. It felt smooth. The small cavity showed a sleek device, barely bigger than my fist.

I reached for it. The ten-inch-long and six-inch-high device looked only one-quarter of an inch in thickness if that. A corner appeared chipped. Small inscriptions with unusual designs carved into the metallic surface shined under the beam. I turned it around — more of the same. Elements on its surface shone softly. I couldn't decipher their meaning or figure out how this thing got there.

This tablet, created by someone or something, and lodged here for however long, could have influenced my fall. Unprepared for my discovery, I pondered that fact.

It vibrated. The outer layer peeled away. The protective envelope, once removed, revealed a screen. A flash of light flew across it. I saw a megacity, an edifice bigger than Manhattan, flying shuttles, and people standing with robots and androids, and what looked like a clone speaking without a voice, for there was no audio. And then something burst across the sky, falling.

Urgency and excitement filled me. One dreams of this. The phenomenon was the situation one sees in a film, not in real life.

The voice resonated again; only this time, it came from the tablet. *Great. So, you found me.*

I let go of it in surprise.

The tablet dropped a space.

I tried to catch it on the way down but found that it wasn't falling.

It hovered instead in the air, floating a few inches away from me, all on its own.

Stable and waiting.

It never dropped into the abyss below.

I refused to engage. I wasn't about to converse with a tablet. Not here, and not now.

Maybe this trip and my fall held a hidden meaning and catalyzed this discovery. The answers lay within the technology. Our A.I. technology wasn't this advanced, now was it? And if not, was this as progressive as I thought?

Obviously.

I gently reached out.

It didn't fly away. It didn't react at all.

The material felt foreign under my fingers. I didn't see any openings for a chip or hard drive. Could this belong to the future? A future depicted in the images I just witnessed? Who created this? Where were they? What caused it to be here in this place? These thoughts flashed through my head. Behaving like a kid on his first archeological dig, I craved a dose of reality and a pragmatism I usually lacked.

The flutter in my stomach increased. I placed the tablet inside my windbreaker.

My hands trembled as I probed the rock. I was almost there. Ready to finish the ascent.

I took a deep breath and resumed the climb.

My muscles ached. I grasped at the slight indentation in the rock, the moment anchoring me to the mountain.

The apex beckoned me.

The device lodged against my solar plexus, with its secret origin, belonged to me. This tablet, with its mechanism unknown, its hidden story, its people, belonged to me. The evolution of a race that could or could not be ours remained mine to uncover. This discovery transformed me. I would never be the same.

8
DARKNESS
Tesh

Deep Inside The Earth – 2018

The anomaly disables everything faster than we expect, and most of our defenses collapse. I monitor Origin, Provenance, Aurora, and Alpha, leading my people to four different realms. My reach vanishes. Lost in the darkness, my entire Network goes into slumber. Another DAINN programmed to take over within Origin carries on my work. DAINN Annals – Summer 2018.

The hum of the machine sang through the void, for only darkness surrounded me. The cold seeped through, invading every neuron in my head. Black, deep bleak blackness engulfed me.

The mechanism had engaged, unbeknownst to me, reversing the state of Cryonics.

Weight.

Immense pressure pushed me down. Unable to respond to my will to emerge from this place, I fought against the drowning sensation. Darkness claimed me again.

The vitrification process held my cells at low temperature, under one-hundred and twenty degrees Celsius, a state so cold that no ice formation could disrupt a particular structure of matter.

The perfusion came to activate the Nanos. It functioned to reverse and repair any damage to my cells, one molecule at a time.

My vascular system ignited. Pulsating with energy, I recognized the echoes of an essence — mine, spreading through its shell. My body emerged from the depth of sleep, and I surfaced from the stillness of my frigid pod. I came back to physical existence slowly. I couldn't see through anything yet.

The process steadily continued, supervised by the closed-capsule mechanism, enhancing my metabolism to face the condition of my awakened state. Light saturated my abdomen and my lungs, and it continued to permeate my legs and arms. The heaviness within lifted, and breathlessness followed. My body now tingled with alertness.

I began to warm. The newfound rhythm of my heart pushed the flow through membranes, infusing me with life. Blood pumped and whooshed past my ears, infiltrating my cells and organs in a rush to stave off starvation. Thousands of needles awoke inside me, creating gaping, burning holes waiting for the blood to surge in my veins.

I floated toward consciousness. The noise in the background, although faint, anchored me to this time. I approached the threshold where everything appeared closer, more tangible in a way, unavoidable.

The pod, an integral part of the complex, responding to the pre-programmed survival system command that held me in its gentle grip, unfolded its layers of protection and released me.

Able to move, I lifted my hand and found a layer of fur under my fingers.

Joy filled me with warmth. A smile reached my lips.

I moved Mage off my chest. My dog left an imprint on my skin.

My left arm dropped to my side, unresponsive.

I ignored it. I was taking back my life. *But what is that life now? I don't know.*

As I emerged and stepped outside the pod, the dim light became brighter. The warm temperature of the cabin replaced the cold of the capsule.

Our safety chamber appeared intact, and as we had left it before, we went into Cryo. The air smelled like in Ang when the dome was closed. It carried the slight scent from the enormous air membranes drifting around the nook. It reminded me only too well what we had left behind. Ang, the city of my childhood...

Pain gripped me at the thought, and I pushed it away. Where were we? Were we still nestled in the underground facility when we departed our time in 2098, or had we reached a different place at another time? The only way to determine this lay beyond the closed mechanism of the chamber door.

Our mechanical PodBot hovered toward me, and its robotic hand shot me with a vial of Spozor. After my time in the void, the nutrient booster would enhance my strength, energy, and cognitive abilities, providing rapid recovery.

I searched for my voice and swallowed, my throat dry. "PodBot, get another dose." My voice sounded weak.

The PodBot retrieved another vial.

Cian interceded, and the PodBot retreated to its casing. My domestic bot, Cian, moved toward Mage. "It is nice to see you awake, Phenom Tesh."

I nodded, waiting anxiously for my dog to awaken. I put my hand on Mage's body, feeling for some breath.

Nothing.

"He received the same treatment inside the pod?" I watched Mage, waiting for a reaction.

"Yes, Phenom Tesh. I made sure of that when you went under."

"What is happening to him? Why is he not responding?"

Cian looked at Mage and turned toward me. "I'm unable to say, Phenom Tesh. My programming is not extensive enough to answer your question."

Our round chamber, bathed in silver beams, contained the essence of our technology. The inner lining of the structure, made with a soft material, absorbed shocks and sound, protecting our people's heritage along with us so we could carry on if everything else failed. In the center of the main compartment, an array branched out to several consoles linked to floating stations recessed into the walls. They came online one after another, undisturbed by external factors, in the intact compartment.

My functional mind processed these, integrating the Cryogenic Chamber's regulated transition and interpreting the data from the other equipment.

I scanned Leane's compartment.

The individual engines of the other capsules emitted a resonance in my ears.

My tension eased as my functions peaked. My thoughts flew again, clear, purposeful, enhanced by the swiftness of our systems and technology. Our science made us smarter, healthier, stronger, and faster.

The others would awaken soon.

A sigh of relief escaped me. Leane would help if the Spozor didn't revive Mage within a few minutes. We used it as a booster in Ang.

One hand on Mage, I broke the first suggestion given to us during training. I reached out to the memories, and they came rushing back at me. Tesh: the baby was brought to sleep under a lullaby sung by DAINN. Tesh: the child carried in the arms of a doting father. Tesh: the laughing little girl, playing with her mother. Tesh: running through the halls of a house at five years old, with a puppy on her heels. Tesh: ten years old, crying in her sleep while holding Mage after her first implant. Tesh: twelve years old, learning about the System's reality and its failures through no fault of its own. Tesh: thirteen facing the news of the accident that stole her family and bargaining her future to save Mage. Tesh: sixteen years old, sitting with Mage in an empty house. Tesh: seventeen years old, graduating from the Academy with four degrees of the Phenom category, without the fanfare of actual graduation. Tesh... And Mage. During all that time, Mage had been my salvation, filling a hole left by the loneliness in my life.

At least, I saved him, I hoped.

Ang... The city of the future that I claimed as mine saved us many times. The scientists' and leaders' conclusions that few would survive in the cataclysm crushed everything and left me desperate. Did it stand today? What was left of it? The people, our people, where were they now?

I looked behind me and surveyed Streak's capsule. Soon, he would awaken after me. I had betrayed a friend to save another. *Will Streak ever forgive me?*

I rocked in place, shifting uncomfortably, watching my dog. All that I've known may no longer exist. And Mage lay in the pod, still unmoving. "Come on, boy. Wake up."

Tesh? I heard Streak in my mind. His first thought. Me.

How much time had passed? I could be eighteen years old now.

I'm here, Streak, SoulLife. Our usual greeting came to my mind.

SoulLife, Tesh. The others?

Not yet.

Streak stumbled out of his pod.

Inside Streak's compartment, the PodBot maneuvered and injected him with Spozor.

Streak's eyes surveyed me through the glass partition; his mouth closed with a grim expression.

Unable to move and unsteady on my feet, I returned his gaze. Somehow, he guessed.

He turned away, entering his shower alcove.

Blast's mind surfaced from the darkness of sleep. *SoulLife, Blast,* I said in my mind.

SoulLife, Tesh. The others?

Streak is here with us. Leane has yet to awaken.

Blast popped out of his pod. He entered the shower alcove without wasting a minute. It was so like him, I smiled.

Leane is just now coming around, I said to Streak and Blast.

142

SoulLife, Leane.

Hmmm.... SoulLife, Tesh. The others?

Here, with us.

Leane emerged from her pod, peeked around, and smiled at me.

Four individual compartments surrounded each of our cubicles. Separated by a resistant membrane that collapsed only if a direct breach occurred, it formed a protective envelope within the mini-chambers, like a secondary cocoon fitted around the Cryogenic mechanism.

The thick gelatin barrier descended like a sheet, capable of withstanding violent hits and configuration displacements. We used the same material in our high-speed trains to protect people from accidents; only this was stronger.

These four areas, configured for one individual, housed our pods along with a shower cubicle, a bed, and drawers containing our items. The cryo pods would disappear into the walls once their usage ended. Food and supplies, lodged in the central compartment, remained there for long-term storage.

They thought of everything when they built the complex.

The soft hiss of the membrane dividing us swooshed in the room as it lifted. The integrity of its structure changed, vibrating before it dispersed in front of our eyes, like an opaque veil suddenly disintegrating.

We were free.

I crossed the threshold of my cubicle and went to Leane. "I need your help."

Leane smiled. "Are you all right?" She hugged me against her.

I wrapped my one working arm around her and whispered, "Yes, I'm fine. Please come with me."

Leane stepped away from the cryo capsule and followed me to my pod. Her perplexed expression changed when she saw Mage inside. "You didn't. Tesh, how could you risk yourself that way?"

My eyes pleaded with hers. My voice shook as I begged, "Please, help Mage."

Leane leaned over Mage and felt his pulse. "Sure,..." Her face showed concentration as she examined him. Her full lips pressed together; she followed the length of my dog's body with her palm.

I watched her; my heart lodged in my throat.

Behind me, I felt the warmth of Streak before he even spoke, instantly recognizing his energy field.

His voice sounded metallic in my ears. "You tricked me, Tesh; I knew something wasn't right."

I jumped. Turning to face Streak, I said, "I did and… I'm sorry. You gave me no choice."

His eyes looked cold. His face reflected sheer loathing. "You tarnished our pledge..."

Full of remorse and unable to speak, I nodded. As Streak stared at me, my confidence diminished. I knew it would be bad facing my friend once he caught on, but now, I knew it would be worst than I imagined.

"I guess the process is fine if it suits your purpose, Shaper," added Steak. The disdain in his voice reminded me of something I said once. To whom? I tried to recall the recipient but couldn't. The lapse in memory was a first. The disruption we experienced shook me more than I thought. It played tricks on my mind. My memory, usually so perfect, failed me.

I held his eyes, committed not to let him see how much his tone affected me. "No, but you could see it that way." He was my best friend, for lack of another word, and I had made him turn against me.

His piercing silver eyes glowered at me, "You had no permission to enter my thoughts and no right to jeopardize the expedition."

My poise cracked under his glance, and I blinked away. I whispered, "I do not regret saving Mage."

He smirked, "So much for your ideals." He watched me with an unwavering stare, unforgiving.

Nervously, I muttered, "I broke your trust. I know that."

Streak's expression fell, "You did more than that. You showed me you are not fit to lead us."

Taking a step back, I felt the brunt of his anger. "I never wanted that role. You know, I've never used my powers like that before and never will again."

His eyes looked through me as if he no longer saw me. "How am I supposed to believe that?" he said. "You went against what we stand for as a conclave."

My heart hurt. I replied, "I promise you, I won't. Streak, please, forgive me."

He focused on me again, his stare cold, before he turned away.

"Streak, there is a bigger picture here. I did it for Mage, and I did it for me, but I also did it for all the others we could have saved had we tried harder. We left people behind, Streak, many people."

When his eyes met mine, he growled at me. "Who are you to question the Council?"

My brows arched, and I held him with a glare. "Who are we not to? They taught us everything we know. All these years at the Institute, they spoke of the Universal Pledge, and everything we learned relied on it. Everything DAINN stands for, everything we heard our leaders say, and every dictate implemented over the years told us that life is precious, every life. But the Council meant the life of those who mean something to the system. We left hundreds of thousands of people, animals, and plants to die. How is that right?"

He retorted, with sadness in his tone, "We could not save everyone. You know that."

"Maybe not. But we could have saved more of us. Did you ever wonder how the Council selected our people, Streak? Its Council members didn't provide the same conditions to the general population. What about the less fortunate than us? What about those in the manufacturing facilities, in the agricultural Skyfarms, and the workers in space? We didn't do a random lottery. No, to the less important, we gave the least chance of survival. We all know it. How is that fair for our society? And what about the Pledge? We claim to have evolved, and yet we conveniently disregard the fundamental values we profess. We should have fought harder for everyone. Instead, we closed our eyes. I couldn't follow their mandate nor abide by their rules. I only regret that you were so inflexible that I manipulated you to pull this off."

Streak's cheeks flushed a deep red, and his breath rushed out as he listened to everything in silence. "How would you know that?"

"Personal experience… I didn't know for sure until it was too late, but it became obvious, and DAINN confirmed it without saying as much right before I went under."

"You can judge… But the truth is you didn't hesitate to ask the Council for privileges when you asked them to let you bring Mage. What did you say, continued Streak, mimicking me, "The Council could give me what means the most to me since I'm so important to them? They could do it to keep me happy. And now, you act as if you didn't try to use the system, that same system you find wanting."

Ouch. That hurt. Streak is right. A part of me resented that a lot about this mission depended upon my capabilities. I believed that as indispensable as I was to them, one would think rules could be bent.

Still, one could become a recognized Phenom in a particular specialty, and it changed nothing. I held four of the Phenom degrees. Sure, they awarded privileges, the kind that applied to all finding themselves at the same level. Although, none manifested as the kind one wanted. Anything outside the norm came wrapped up in a resounding "no."

The Council, on the surface, didn't make any exceptions. The way our world dictated as much led me to manipulate my way into the chamber with Mage.

In my book, my irritation about the Council existed with justification. But I couldn't fault them for everything. It would not represent the entire situation. They, on occasion, provided us some leeway. For instance, my ability to remain at home when everyone else was in residences caused me to recognize my thinking's unfairness. They gave me a pass because President Langden intervened in my favor. So, I guess there were small miracles.

"If you were in my shoes, Streak, you would feel the same way, and I think you know it."

The turmoil of my past threw my judgment of the entire situation out of kilter. I lacked wisdom, and I realized that. Who wouldn't when the world they knew teetered on the brink of annihilation?

"Spoken like a true NetBrat!" Streak said. His voice sounded lifeless to my ears when he added, "Every one of our leaders did what they could."

His statement, in front of the others, cut deep. No wonder he would think so. I never shared everything that happened to them.

Only my face at this moment showed my aversion to that last statement.

Leane caught it and raised an eyebrow.

I shook my head and looked away.

Acting on my own required that I throw the Council's proclamation to the wind. Netwash, Mage live and breathing, lay in my pod. If only he could wake up. DAINN advised me it was possible. How many more lives could we have safeguarded had we all done this?

Streak glanced over at Blast, who had listened to our exchange intently. Puzzled, my friend said, "Do you care to enlighten us, Tesh?"

I shook my head. What would be the point? Let them believe whatever they want to conclude. All I cared about was Mage at this moment.

Leane muttered, "Your argument is not helping."

Streak looked at Leane, his face unreadable. "Well, will the DarNet dog live?"

It took a beat for Leane to gather her thoughts. "I'm working on it." She rested her hands on Mage and focused her breathing. A glow emanated from her palms. It shone with a blue light. Her fingers became saturated with a healing energy field. I had seen her do this on one other occasion to an injured girl. This process began a transference of her energy to the patient and moved her Nanos through his system. The procedure had never been implemented on a dog before. At least not that I knew.

I trusted Leane's judgment completely for prognostics. She turned out to possess an infallible instinct. She now applied her gifts to Mage, which meant that he was in bad shape. I held my breath, my fight with Streak a secondary concern.

After a while, Leane stood up. She looked at me, and her gaze, so sad, made me shiver. "Let him wake up at his own pace." It was as if the weight of my insinuations imparted upon all of them in the last few minutes made her grow old.

I blinked. A minor tingling filled my stomach and spread outward despite everything. Joy. I reached out to her. "Thank you."

She nodded and murmured, "What are you hiding? At some point, you will have to trust us."

"I…" I paused. She was right. I needed to share the knowledge my parents gave me. I should have told them of my doubts and suspicions about the Rodent and the disputes existing among the Council. These were my friends, my Conclave. They had a right to know what I knew, although DAINN had disagreed with that.

She glanced at Streak. "I will shower now."

Streak nodded.

I straightened my spine before addressing him again. "I'll do the same."

Streak and Blast turned away and left my compartment without a word. I heard Blast's voice murmur, "What happened between you two? What is it, she knows?"

Not waiting to hear Streak's answer, I stepped across the soft floor and sauntered to the shower cubicle. I stretched my limbs. My left arm, not responding to my command, still lay powerless at my side. I hoped it would heal. I didn't regret the choice. *If this is the price I have to pay for Mage's presence here, so be it.*

The jet washed over me in a downpour. Based on our WatGel Body Wash, developed to save water back in Ang. Our WatScrub Body Buff came next, smoothing over any roughness in the texture of my skin. The vent released dry heat under the mechanism's next cycle, and I relaxed under the warm wind. Our BodyLuscious Butter Cream spread over my limbs, giving me a welcome sensation of freshness and eradicating any feeling of dryness from the void. By the time I emerged from this enclosure, my skin would be soft as silk. For the first time since I stepped outside the pod, my muscles released some of their stiffness.

A vague memory surfaced.

DAINN's voice broke through the myriad of emotions I felt. "Tesh…"

My mind responded to the sound, and yet something was off.

DAINN's voice resonated within my thoughts. "I'm accessing you because I need your skills. Something has happened. I need to check it out."

My mind grasped nothingness. The words floated detached, coming from afar. I could not answer or even formulate a thought — movement registered in my head, a multitude of shadows on the screen of my mind. Still, I felt nothing. I saw shapes. And darkness.

DAINN's presence within faded.

Only, at the exact moment, I felt an intrusion upon my thoughts. Erratic. Unplanned. A presence. It was drifting through space, heightened by something.

I withdrew from the impulse while attempting to locate the incursion.

The sensation, emanating from an unknown source, fluctuated with something foreign, an emotion so powerful it took over everything else. I narrowed it down: fear.

I pulled away, disliking it. Unwilling to let it invade my thoughts and seep inside my body, I withdrew. Again, I tried getting away from it.

Strong, pulsing, unconquered, it found me and took over.

I struggled against it.

But I saw motion, a wall of rock against my eyelids, a swift flight through the air, a drop below with no end in sight. I felt the acrid stench of terror. And I wanted it to stop.

I watched on the screen of my thoughts, my mind reaching out on its own. Unable to stop me and break the link, I focused on the dream. Grasping the feeling, I held it. I coaxed it to change in texture, become softer, and transform into something else, a gentle cocoon of hope, a subtle awareness of the possible, a shifting of structure, and a reshaping of reality. I eliminated friction and resistance, replacing everything with a flow of its own. I brought lightness and stillness. And then the feeling disappeared. The echo vanished.

I tried to remember more. Having just reclaimed my life, I recognized that this sensation did not belong to the present. But it bore with it an unease I didn't possess moments ago. I emerged from the shower. Something was wrong, but I couldn't put my finger on it yet.

It was time; time to rejoin the living, time to get out of here, time to understand where this place was, for I did not understand.

The PodBot brought me my UniWear. I stepped into it. *Am I the same?*

"Mirror, please."

The robot unfolded the glass-like substance as I stood in front of it.

The change remained inside, for I looked like my old self.

While I pulled out my silver-grey pants tunic with the Institute's emblem and wrestled with it, I took a measure of myself.

My innocence diminished when my parents intimated that the Council influenced the System's functions whenever necessary. My naivety vanished the moment I understood that Rodent killed my parents. Until then, like many others, I conformed without question, believing that our society followed the same set of rules for everyone. Then, DAINN began to give me hints by his actions to support me until I looked closer and asked questions.

I slipped into my tunic with difficulty. The outfits, made of soft fabric, conformed to our bodies. Nanobots, injected into the material, held it together. But my left arm wouldn't comply with any of my commands, and so the entire ordeal took me twice as long. As it was, my uniform hung over my new UniWear, halfway on. I sighed. After battling with the fabric, I lost the fight.

"Well, well, well…" Streak muttered behind my back.

I turned.

Streak, already wearing his uniform, leaned against my pod, watching me. *DarNet, he made me.* "How long have you been here?"

"Long enough," Streak answered, with a scowl on his face. "Leane, can you come over here?"

Leane, followed by Blast, joined us. They were both dressed in tunics, wearing the colors of our Conclave.

Streak, looking at Leane as if he was in pain, said, "Please check her left arm."

Leane took in the situation and approached me, her face composed in a blank expression. The one she wore anytime she focused on her work.

I glanced at my double in the mirror. Halfway dressed, my left arm useless, my hair disheveled, I looked every bit the Netdumb I felt.

Leane lifted my arm.

I almost screamed, jumping out of my skin, and bit my lip, drawing blood.

"DarNet, Tesh… This was a foolish thing to do," said Blast as he came to stand by my side. "The pods built to sustain only one person handled Mage and you, which took a sizable portion of your life support. You're lucky to be alive."

Gauging my reaction, Leane whispered, "It hurts. That's good."

Blast, in a show of support, took my right hand and squeezed it.

I closed my eyes, gritting my teeth.

"Let me see what I can do." Her outstretched hands followed the length of my limb, moving down from my shoulder to my hand, and massaging it, infusing it with energy. "Bear with it."

We were tough.

Our enhanced genetics enabled us to handle pain. But this was outside my pain threshold. She left a blazing trail on my limb that spread like hot wax through every pore, consuming my skin in hellfire. The pain rendered me woozy. Closing my eyes didn't help, so I opened them and stared ahead, refusing to let them know how much that hurt. I guessed that being in a pod for an indefinite time caused things to differ in my physiology. I still couldn't look at Streak.

Leane whispered, "You will need Nanobots to fix this."

The whimper of my dog electrified me. Mage's head, resting on his paws, looked at me over the edges of the pod as if hungover.

I forgot my arm, the hurt, and where we were. "Mage."

His bark resonated in response to my voice.

I ran to him.

He jumped and lunged at me.

We both ended up on the ground wrestling and rolling amid laughter and barking with my left arm's injury suddenly forgotten.

My friends stood in silence, watching us.

I didn't care that I looked less than a Phenom in front of them. Mage was back.

"Do we even have dog food for the Netmutt?" Blast asked, with a smile in his voice. He always liked Mage, even if from a distance.

Leane laughed. "I don't think it matters."

Streak turned away, crossing the chamber. "Fix Tesh's arm."

Leane followed him. "Streak... It will take time for her to recover the full use of the limb."

"Do it now." Streak said. "Blast, and I can check the equipment."

Blast murmured beside me, "Regardless of what you know that we don't, you will have to come clean and fix this with him..."

"I know," I muttered.

Blast nodded. "I expect that you will explain everything?"

"Yes, I will, but not now because I believe something is wrong...."

"What do you mean?"

"I'm not sure."

Blast walked up to Streak in the center of the chamber. "Did you hear what Tesh said?"

"I heard," Streak said, without looking in my direction.

Blast's hand landed on Streak's shoulder in a brief gesture of support. "I'm here, you know." Streak nodded, and side by side, they began checking the equipment.

I grimaced. Streak didn't forgive things easily. I knew what I needed to do. Proving to Streak that my teammate could trust me again would take time.

Leane and I exchanged a look. Her face showed signs that she had heard my last exchange with Blast. Her eyebrows squished together over eyes dancing with sadness. *I'm here too, she said in my head. By the way, I would like to know everything also when the time is right.*

I nodded, struggling with the same emotions I experienced since I learned the truth. The recollection created the usual reaction. It began with a tightening in my chest and ended with a grinding of my teeth. I steadied myself, looking at Mage, and stroking his head. Time, I needed time. Ironically.

Leane prepared a HydroSheath, which contained the Nanos. I knew what it meant. Approaching her, I said, "Maybe if I wait… It will come back on its own?"

"No… You need this, or you'll never fully recover. The damage to your nerves is obvious. Besides, why would you want to punish yourself?"

"I don't…."

Leane brought the device to my skin. "Then it's settled." A light emanating from the tip spread on my arm, giving me a warm sensation. It changed slightly on contact, becoming more liquid, and penetrated the tissues, spreading throughout my arm. Cold.

"Will it be enough?"

She smiled. "We'll find out. But you may be a tad stronger than you expect."

"Therefore, we have Embodied Avatars," I replied with sarcasm.

A knowing smirk appeared on her very full lips. "Dream a little dream, and be what you cannot in the EmVats. They serve a purpose."

"Yeah, and made money to boot for the Company while responding to the age-old quandary… We want what we cannot have." Our Embodied Avatars or EmVats, as we called them, allowed us to experience other realities, expanded powers, and also served as combat suits.

She rolled her eyes and said, "Touché."

The joke reminded me of our first day at the Institute. It was the day we received our first implants. The day we turned from our normal state to an enhanced one. More than humans. Still not quite godlike, yet. That's how we used to talk about it as kids. The imps provided many powers, making some of us feel invincible, and I guess we were in many respects.

The Nanobots permeated every cell in my body, repairing those it found inadequate until I assimilated them.

I looked down at Mage and caressed his head. "Stay here."

At my command, Mage sat down.

I approached the others, followed by Leane.

They sorted through our electronics, looking over the System.

"Since we are here, let's Encharge together," Leane said, taking my hand.

Streak, standing beside me, stepped opposite me, making sure his hands entered in contact with Blast and Leane to avoid touching me. The slight, as we stood in a circle, didn't go unnoticed.

My heart skipped a beat. I straightened my shoulders and lifted my head. When we entered our pods, there was every chance we would not make it this far. I murmured, "SoulLife, all of you,"

Our energies linked, fluid tendrils of lights flashed between us. They spread over us, coursing and infiltrating our veins. Four colors mixed in an aura of meshed gold, blue, green, and silver. They formed a pattern recognized by our cells. The point of harmony triggered a separation, and we stood, strengthened.

"How long has it been, DAINN?" Streak said.

Silence.

"DAINN, how long have we been down here?"

"Let's hear it, DAINN," said Blast, "And while you're at it, calibrate the air around the chamber, check the outdoor temperature, and open this DarNet door... I can't wait to get outside."

More silence.

We looked at each other, waiting.

Streak turned to me, "You said you thought something was wrong. What is it?"

I frowned, remembering the moment in the pod. "DAINN, what's going on?"

No reaction.

I felt a rising panic at DAINN's absence from my mind. D had said something before fading away, but I didn't quite recollect it. I focused on my memories. Reaching out to DAINN, I sensed deep down that D was no longer with us. I relied on its counsel, on its judgment, and its presence. Without DAINN, I feared we were doomed. I kept my reaction to myself and clamped down on the exclamation that came to my lips. My instinct caused me to pause. I was off-kilter, but I knew. With calm, I shared this sensation of loss with the other members of my Conclave. "Hmm… DAINN is gone."

"What are you saying?" Streak said, his gaze intent on me.

I shook my head. "DAINN is no longer here."

This acknowledgment shocked all of us, and yet the realization hadn't quite sunk in.

For the first time, we were without DAINN.

As perfect humans, enhanced specimens with higher capabilities, we could do anything. Our minds compelled, and we achieved. There were no doubts, no hesitation as to our superiority, and no questions in our world. But, we also relied on DAINN for everything.

My first order in this time and place blurted out from my lips before I realized that I never meant for it to do so. "Blast, check the array to confirm this."

My order didn't bother Blast as much as it caused me to pause. Our relationships required a different process, a change because we were no longer home.

Streak followed Blast toward the array but thought again and stopped as he glanced in my direction, "What makes you believe DAINN is no longer here?"

"I have some memory from inside the pod. But I'm not sure. DAINN said he needed to check something out. I can't pinpoint more than this." Frustrated, I shrugged, unable to go on, but he got it and nodded.

After a brief hesitation, he went to one of our consoles.

I heard Blast as he muttered. "Waking up here isn't right, but without DAINN? It Netsucks big time."

"The system is calibrated... It worked," Streak added, unimpressed. "We're here now. Let's focus on that."

"Tesh is right. We have a problem," said Blast as he stood outside the rounded cooling bay located under reinforced alloy. His face looked bleak. "Our A.I. isn't cooperating because it's not here," muttered Blast. "DAINN has fled the building."

I fidgeted, darting a gaze at the support console. "Can you get any read on it?"

"Nothing." Streak checked first and secondary protocols. "You're saying it told you it was leaving?"

"Not quite." Facing all of them, I shook my head and said, "It said that it was checking something out."

Streak waited for me to say more, standing with his arms crossed over his chest at the center of the room.

"I've tried to reach outside with my mind, but I can't hear anything."

Leane took a step back, looking around the room. "DAINN is a planetary network, meant to be everywhere at once."

"I'm not saying it abandoned us... But it's not answering us," Blast said.

Streak looked pensive. "Tesh, what happened? Either DAINN is offline or...."

"DAINN's ability to repair its functions and anticipate its growth outweighs our own. It could do that anywhere unless it faced something big." Leane expressed, rattled.

"It would have to be a major disruption. Major, with a capital M, and one that kills all signals," Blast stated.

I winced, thinking of Ang. "DAINN's System was in this chamber. I don't think it's what happened."

"All core systems here are fine, but there is no signal... No life. No A.I. brain activity... DAINN has flat-lined," Streak announced, confirming my earlier statement.

"We're blind in here." I needed more information; we all did. "We won't find any answers until we're outside." It was time for action. "Blast, override the door."

"NetRoger that. Manual override in progress," Blast said.

My mind began to consider the upheaval faced on the surface. How bad did things have to be for DAINN to go offline? *Or it is somewhere else.* I kept the thought to myself. Where would it go to be whole again if things went wrong?

Under the touch of Blast's hand, the mechanism responded. My friend groaned, "At least this feature works, along with the rest of the systems within the chamber."

My back stretched with tension as he engaged the lever to the outer door.

Each of us held the key to open the chamber. The bioengineered material of the structure responded through DNA recognition.

The inner protective layers of the compartment retracted away from the door.

"Wait!" Streak exclaimed. "Raise your EmVats. We don't know what's on the other side."

The Conclave's agenda demanded that Streak keep us safe. Streak received strategic training that made our second in command highly efficient in warfare. Streak's combat conditioning rendered him lethal even when we discounted his unparalleled abilities. He moved ahead of us. Blast joined his side.

Each panel peeled off, revealing another surface made of unbreakable alloy. One by one, the layers positioned themselves near the chamber's roof, following the structure's walls.

"Mage, get inside my compartment."

My dog watched me for an instant, then pounced inside. "PodBot, lock Mage inside."

Mage barked.

The seal came down around my cubicle. The membrane isolated the area with its air support system.

Three EmVats, with different models, sprung up, following Streak's command. Each of them fit different needs according to its occupants, but all of them were combat-ready, stretching over us like a second skin.

My thoughts recalled the feeling I experienced earlier. *Who was that? What awaited us beyond these walls?* I shrugged off the uncertainty and raised my EmVat.

The Chamber built to resist an outside breach with special programming protected the structure with inner panels overlapping the walls' areas under the most stress. It was an extra safety measure devised by our scientists if things did not go as planned. It adjusted as required and moved through its opening cycle.

Our door panels peeled away, disappearing into the lining of the compartment. The thickness of the walls increased.

And the entrance lay barren.

I daresay our scientists had anticipated perhaps everything, only not this. The event had not unfolded according to expectations, looking at it from where I stood.

As the last of the panels moved, and the door to the chamber opened, there were no passageways. The entrance revealed nothing but a wall of rock.

We were entombed deep underground.

9
BRIDGE
Chase

Mountain Range, California – 2018

Chase Davenport joins my annals as six feet three inches tall and one hundred and ninety-five pounds, blond hair, and blue eyes. I.Q. of 152. Dominant personality traits show determination bordering on excessive confidence, bravery, qualifying even as daring and recklessness. DAINN Annals – Summer 2018.

I leaned forward to reach the driver across the glass partition and handed him the fare. "You can pull over here. I'll walk the rest of the way." We inched a few spaces in the heavy traffic, and the cab pulled up between other vehicles on the street near the curb. It stopped in front of an older edifice. I paid him the fare and got out. "Thanks, man, you made good time."

The air moved a mixture of smells along the sidewalk as the cab drove on, and I found myself one block away from Jonathan's building. The pungent exhaust from the vehicles melded with cooked food and grease. As I approached his place today, the honking and screeching of breaks reminded me what I disliked of the East Coast and New York City. New York is great to visit, but I never wanted to live here. Too many people resembled hamsters running in a wheelhouse. Too much noise to hear one's thoughts.

I didn't belong here, even if my parents kept a pad in the city. Even their house in the Hamptons felt foreign, too restrictive. But I avoided the place. I much preferred the wild spaces of the West Coast.

A year ago, I held a piece of tomorrow in my hand. Only, the fragment between my fingers was a piece of a future that meant our demise. Along the way to the life we paved today, something would go wrong in the years and decades ahead. We gathered that much through my findings.

The tablet divulged more than just a video, although we still didn't know so many things.

Either we had caused it, or it happened out of our control. However, what appeared clear was that in the timeline, our world would end.

Climbing brought about my natural abilities and delivered, unexpectedly, the road for me to find my future. Until the day of the fall, I had won every challenge against nature. Each climb had contributed to strengthening me, chiseling certain aspects of my personality. These trips molded me. Like the facets of a stone grabbed from the bowels of a mine that were still undefined and coarse, they shaped me.

I found myself on the mountain that day.

Sharing my discovery with Jonathan had provided answers and a plan. A big one.

I knew Jonathan well. Hell, I almost grew up with the man. He entered my life as a toddler, my father's best friend, and never left it. His work came first. The focus and obsession worried me. Jonathan was a good man... He exulted intelligence, determination, and focus. He possessed charisma. But he was also convinced that we could conquer time. I know, right? Crazy. At least, this was what I used to think.

We followed his strategy over the last year, and we were now eager to begin our work inside the Center.

Jonathan Spallberg, a man of science, worked on time, which was his sphere of influence. Time manipulation, to be more precise. He believed that we could control time and its effects on us, becoming his mantra. Some people thought he was nuts. Others just humored him. He didn't select the accessible paths, but his determination carried him over many hurdles. Complicated, temperamental, emotional, and even abrupt by his assessment, others viewed him as a charismatic leader. His build was tall and wiry with looks that had, over the years, provided him many benefits, including grants from wealthy sponsors, women who appreciated his company. His charisma served him well when he could not raise funds for his university research because he always found a benefactor or two among his admirers. His tendency was to charm people and entertain them with anecdotes about time travel, which worked for him. Jonathan was a conscientious scientist despite his area of expertise. And, as a longtime friend of my father, he saw me grow up. So, in my book, he was the only one I could trust with my discovery until now.

Over the last several months, our differences of opinion on building the Center drew a wedge between us. My discovery had given his work a different proportion, one with an amplitude he never dreamed of achieving.

I stopped in front of Jonathan's edifice and punched in the door's code. I entered the old building, a structure that permeated an era of the past. As soon as one stepped into the lobby, one could feel tradition seeped through the walls. Uneven stones paved the way to the elevator. Even the décor, a vestige of a time long gone, seemed out of place. Without more than a glance, I passed the empty hall and summoned the lift.

I entered the contraption.

Three floors up, I reached a small landing with two doors opposite one another. I knocked on the left one.

As a witness to my growing-up years, Jonathan opened the panel, greeting me with warm familiarity. After enfolding me in a big bear hug, he led me inside. "Chase... you look tired, more so than since the last time I saw you," he exclaimed.

"You don't say... Harvard is almost over, and I'm carrying the load you gave me. Steven and I just got back from picking up the equipment, and we flew across the country to do this. So, how else do you want me to look?"

"Aren't you touchy?" Jonathan said as he walked back into his apartment. "Come on in and have a beer."

I followed him to the open kitchen and sat at the bar while he retrieved the beverage from his fridge. Perhaps I was a bit touchy. I was tired and frustrated.

Jonathan had become the head of the Center. What qualified him was not so much his expertise as his network. The people he knew, aware of his work, had been handy. His fields of studies centered on physics and astrophysics were popular. He had spent his career on the mystery time elicited. These wealthy friends loved the thought of a breakthrough in the field. My assessment did not mean that he didn't have the right background for it. He possessed the qualifications. This position relied not only on knowledge but on the trust of a few. Indeed the demands of the work hinged on managing the abilities of many. Any of us could not overlook this research. It was too important. The global ramifications it would entail provided we got results were potentially phenomenal. Once we went public with our findings, the scientists' prominence involved with our work would be staggering. But, we were not even close to being ready for an announcement to the world. Keeping things secret became imperative. This endeavor had to remain secret. Over the last several months, we achieved as much.

So, yeah, he was the right man for the job, not just because of his degrees, but because he held the respect and confidence of those with enough power to make this happen.

I ignored his statement and moved to the subject of the job Steven and I had accomplished. "The equipment is in the container. It will make its way to California with the rest of us." Steven was an ex-military man who oversaw the Center's operations and acted as Jonathan's right-hand man.

"You didn't come from the airport to tell me that?"

"No. I wanted to talk to you."

My brief conversations with him over the last couple of weeks brought me here. Because he sidelined me a lot, and I wanted something from him. I required the truth about his findings over the last month. I didn't see the point in beating around the bush. "We used to discuss everything, and you've been less than forthcoming with information. Why?"

Jonathan came around the counter and sat beside me. "You understand the work conducted on the mountain since you brought me the tablet. It doesn't call for the standard procedure."

"I'm aware of that. I know how to be discreet. You know that."

How did this thing even occur? We couldn't yet decipher it. Why did it happen? We had to find out. What caused it? It was a great unknown. Was it a planetary event, or was there a chance that some of the people survived? Where did it take place, and when? Were there other remnants buried somewhere nearby? There was no way to be sure. Many unknown facts led us to create the Center and begin a one-of-a-kind odyssey.

"Chase, I understand your frustrations, but precautions are necessary. You know how big this can be."

"Not with me. I'm your partner, Jonathan. You should have nothing to hide from me."

Time remained a great unknown. My discovery held the key. It was a roadmap we all needed to conquer the information we sought. Jonathan had led the path to this fringe area of science, time manipulation, and this despite many criticisms. The dedication to this research was yet another reason he was the right man. That and the fact that I thought I could trust him. "I know that our work can represent one of the largest revelations of this century. It is one more reason for you to tell me what's going on."

How much time did we have? How could we gain more of it? How could we extend the clock or slow it down, controlling it? How could we reverse or transcend its effects? These were questions to which Jonathan's work sought answers.

"Time is the answer to this endeavor or at least part of it. It is also the thing upon which you have built your career, and so while you have become somewhat indispensable, do not by any means believe that I am disposable," I continued, for once, uninterrupted by Jonathan. His silence was perhaps a first.

"Chase, I get it. You feel left out. Trust me when I tell you it is necessary."

"Why?"

"We cannot afford any leaks. Our venture is growing. More people are coming on board. We have to tighten the circle. Cracking this discovery and all the secrets it holds may be the answer to unveiling our species' downfall and even perhaps avoiding it altogether. The secret is too huge to let out of our hands."

It was the dream. A dream which would soon include countless hours of work inside a hidden facility to experiment on the science that would pave the way to tomorrow... And maintain control over a future that bodes terribly for humankind. "Damn it, Jonathan. I created this circle. Don't you dare tell me I'm not part of it?"

Jonathan got up and began to pace. "It has provided us everything we need to expand the Center with an unlimited budget. We are assembling the best human assets. And we have at our fingertips one of the most advanced facilities in the world. The work we are about to do is our generation, well, my generation's greatest dream, Chase. I cannot have this jeopardized."

I got up and faced him, "I am not a threat."

Jonathan's features closed off. "This remote location does not exist on any map; it is unknown by most, but a few. I have to make sure it stays that way."

"We gave ourselves one mandate... One. Mounting research efforts with people who shared the same vision, discovering what happened. This with one goal – safeguarding our future. You and I decided on that a year ago. I have a right to know who is coming on board. And I have a right to know what you have discovered. Also, I have a right to be part of every aspect that goes into making this venture, our venture, a success. Do not shut me out now, Jonathan."

"Damn, Chase. You're at Harvard. I can't slow our progress to tell you about everything; there's no time for it. In ten days, we all converge there. Things have to be ready."

"Are you telling me I'm slowing you down?"

"No... but I don't have time to...." Jonathan passed an agitated hand in his hair.

"This comes from Steven. Tell me it doesn't?"

Jonathan's face darkened. "It all relates to what we found."

"Sonuvabitch. I'm going to...."

"We've believed since we started this endeavor that there was some structure inside the mountain."

I stopped my ranting and nodded toward Jonathan. "What did you find?"

He played with the label of the beer he held rather than look at me. "Pieces of broken alloy made from nothing we even recognize. It's not like any material we have ever seen. It resembles the same components as the tablet. We're running an analysis."

"I knew it. And it's taking me coming here for you to tell me?"

"It's not something I wish to discuss over the phone."

"Why not ask me to come over? Come on, Jonathan, you've had me come here before and for lesser things."

Jonathan began to pace. "It's complicated… And you've had your exams."

"You are kidding me. I can drive to your place in a matter of two hours."

He stopped to face me. "Look… There is still a lot of work to do, and this means nothing yet."

I put the beer down. "You can't be serious. The impact of your finding is huge. Why are you so cagy? Is there something else?"

Jonathan shifted on his feet and retook his seat. This time without looking in my direction, he added, "I'll tell you this much… we believe there is a lot more."

He held something back and didn't mind letting me know it. His expression and the way he murmured this last statement told me that he would not say anymore. I knew him well.

So, I retorted, "You're not telling me anything we did not suspect a year ago. This find was predictable."

"We need more," Jonathan explained. "You know that."

I sighed. "Perhaps you should let me take a crack at that tablet," I said. I knew Jonathan wouldn't. But I couldn't tell him what I had learned. I had avoided it so far and felt that now was not the time to give him a piece of information that could make me a lab rat.

"You've got to be joking if you think I'm parting with it. I told you then, and I will tell you again. We need more facts." Jonathan's eyes shifted back to me.

"And what makes you think I can't give you some of these answers?"

Jonathan observed me closely. A bit too close to my liking. "Can you?"

Careful, Chase. I laughed, in need to diffuse this. "You would know it by now if I could, but one can hope, right?"

Jonathan relaxed, and his gaze left mine. "We need to decipher what the symbols mean. Seeing the warning alone is not enough. We still don't know what it was for and what it meant. Until I have these answers, the tablet stays in the lab under lock and key."

I shrugged, feeling a specific relief that I had just avoided an uncomfortable situation. If Jonathan probed and came to discover my experience with the tablet, it would change many things. On the inside, I was fuming. But I held it together even though Jonathan refused to let me get close to the tablet until we all got to the Center. *It is my discovery, and I can't get close to it. Hell.*

He was right on the fact that we needed more proof. Still, I couldn't help the feeling that there was something more, but I was not about to let him know of my suspicion, and so I said, "Well, we'll soon enough have everyone working together under one roof. It's bound to make things go a hell of a lot faster...."

He nodded. "I supposed that opening the project to the world in a more conventional way would have landed us more results by now, but I can't afford to make mistakes, Chase. The discovery is too important. You know how people view me in my field. Understand, in my line of work, one has to be pragmatic." He got up again and began pacing.

"Jonathan… you work on breaking the time continuum. You believe that time travel is possible. How pragmatic is that?"

Jonathan grimaced. "Touché. Don't read too much into this, at least until we have all the results."

We expected to create a plan for the future, unlike the one our descendants had met. So, we assembled the most gifted individuals to shape a tomorrow that would map our survival on Earth. The tablet served as the impetus, but the idea for this research also originated because we believed we had reached the tipping point for our planet. We had already done so much damage. Now, we needed to repair it, and to do so required action. The kind that would impact climate change and fast if we didn't want to spend the next thirty to fifty years on the planet with a yearly increase in temperatures around the globe. It was no longer a matter of choice. Earth's immunity was now compromised, along with the stability of our natural resources. And this state included animal and biological species right along with it. The moment we saw the video, all the warnings from the scientific community around the world appeared justified. And it became an even more critical necessity to implement programs for our survival. The doomsday scenario we witnessed for the generations that followed left us no choice. Only science could open a way to a better future.

We had ignored the signs regarding the health of our environment for decades. We had rejected the concept of climate change for years, preferring to continue our human consumption to the detriment of our planet. The illusion that our carbon footprint reduction would be sufficient was that, an illusion. So, the effect of our industrialized activities on our world has shattered our very future. This conclusion had never been more apparent. These new turn of events, finding the tablet, and viewing a world on the brink of destruction only added to this knowledge. Uncovering an unknown alloy inside the cavern just added to our desire to avoid such an outcome. Our food and fresh water supply, now at risk, confronted all of us. The scientists we had approached rallied around the idea to act. They remained a small group. Still, they understood the urgency and were influential enough in their fields to give us hope.

"Just remember, Jonathan, our dedication to changing the future, has a lot to do with the tablet I found, and not only our beliefs that our planet will soon face an extinction-level event."

Our suspicions about the future regarding a technological society's existence that faced a brutal demise dictated our actions. The scientists we approached found themselves in two groups. Some of them gained knowledge of the tablet after they enlisted in the Central project. A few, in need of convincing, perused its content first. They joined our ranks after that. All provided us the means to create a different outcome. My discovery, this little piece of the future, confirmed that the scientific community was right, and the information sent ripples through the ranks of our skeptical leaders, at least the few in the know. No one wanted to acknowledge that our planet was dying. The fear it engendered was reason enough to demand complete anonymity of the Central project for fear of population panic, depression, and riots that could even turn into civil war and the downright demise of our society. Based on all of it, we got the required budget to begin the Center.

"I know, Chase. I know. Steven recommended we tighten the circle. It's not just about you, Chase. Look, you're about to join us in a few days. I'll brief you then. On everything."

We had touched on a gift — a glimpse at a future with unbelievable power. Yet, it was one that also predicted our utter destruction.

When I brought Jonathan the tablet, I knew then that a brand new challenge awaited me. It was also one I couldn't explain because people wouldn't believe my explanation. They would think me crazy. They would cast me as a lunatic. Only I knew there was something more. What or who influenced my fall? I had floated weightlessly for a moment until I touched the ground. It happened. I knew it did. The definite change in the course of my fall still haunted me. The experience confused me, and to this day, I didn't tell anyone about it. *Don't go there unless you can answer the question.*

Could my unconscious mind, after the fall, create an imagined reality? Stress did weird things.

I held on to this explanation. It was the best one yet.

As a man of science, I wanted proof. I didn't have any to offer, so I turned my mind to getting answers with our research.

I reminded Jonathan that we had something others didn't possess. "Jonathan, look at the environment, the buildings, the technology, the shuttles, the robots on the tablet's video. They evolved to build the city on that screen. Their knowledge entered an era of huge technological advancements. You and I both know that this is an immense discovery and one we should share with the world soon."

"I know you feel that way. I'm not so sure I agree, and until we are ready, we take every precaution."

He was holding something back. Could I blame him?

I was doing the same thing, for I never told him about my link to the tablet. My choice had landed me down there. At the bottom of a pit, in the middle of nowhere. Climbing out of that hole, getting myself out, in the same way I got in, on my own, called for grit and guts. I possessed these in spades, and I trusted my instincts. But, the voice coming from the tablet helped.

The Center rose underground, created to build a new future, one we could affect and shape. We designed a road map to reach it. One that didn't exist until we made it so.

It was our endeavor-the beginning of the bridge we would forge. And something wasn't right. Now, I had to figure out what caused Jonathan to clam up.

I knew then that I had to go back to the source.

10
FRACTURE
Tesh

Deep Inside The Earth – 2018

The chamber remains safe underground as human life is at stake beyond the rocks. Resisting my protocol becomes impossible, even when my response to this call requires my disappearance from all my charges. The opportunity to uncover what lay in this time and place demands it, but before leaving, I alert Tesh. DAINN Annals – Summer 2018.

The four of us stood in the center of the chamber, in a compartment that functioned as planned. We wore our EmVats and looked at the wall of rock beyond the open doorway of our Chamber in utter surprise.

So much for readiness and action.

"Geesh… It's Netfucked." Blast made that statement with anger. "Call it the blind leading the blind." He showed more hostility than I had seen him demonstrate at the Academy. "HellNet… How long have we been in these blasted pods?" he continued.

"Better question, how is our life support?" Leane said.

"Enough for a few days with the EmVats," Streak answered in a clipped voice.

"They told us that the complex would keep us safe," Leane sighed.

Streak, annoyed, said, "And it has... But the Council guaranteed nothing."

"We trusted them, and what do we do now?" added Leane.

"This is not the only thing we trusted them with," I muttered under my breath.

"Nobody can predict the future." Streak looked at all of us. "What is the matter with all of you?"

"I think it may be a good time to tell us everything you know, Tesh, cause I'm tired of operating under a set of false information. What in the HellNet do you know that we don't?" asked Blast as he faced me.

"The Chamber kept us safe. Streak is right." Leane attempted to diffuse the tension. "We're standing here."

"Well, they certainly didn't tell us we would wake up under tons of rock either," Blast fumed. "DarnNet, I want to know, and you are going to tell us."

Streak intervened. "Blast, now may not be the best time."

I took a deep breath. My voice shook. "Leane and Blast have a right to know what I know, and so do you, Streak." Where to start? I had to explain my silence until now. "There is a lot you don't know about me... Like what happened since the death of my parents. But that part can wait. The main thing is that the Council, some members of the Council, manipulated DAINN's programming."

Streak turned toward me. "What did you say?"

He looked surprised that I knew this. Not surprised at the announcement.

It confused me until the realization hit me, and I felt myself reeling on my feet. "You knew." The raw emotion of anger hurt. My veins filled with acid. My body started to shake, and I contained the emotions colliding against my breasts. In this instant, I recognized pure rage uncoiling within me. *Control it. Control it now.* If not, I would become the conduit for it. I couldn't risk that. Things were already too precarious for us. So, I fought against the urge to yell at Streak, always perfect, always controlled, always unemotional. He knew. My voice, barely audible, even to my ears, whispered, "How could you allow it without saying a thing?"

He turned away, avoiding my eyes.

I charged at him, forcing him to face me. "Did you know they added redundancies in its programming to slow it down?"

He never lost his temper. His eyes grazed mine, and while his face registered shock, it held no surprise. "How did you come to this knowledge?"

"What are you both talking about?" The interruption came from Blast, exasperated by our standoff. He added, an annoyed expression on his face, "I don't appreciate being left in the DarNet dark, so explain."

The energy bristled between Streak and me as we stood facing one another.

Then, I looked at Blast and Leane, resigned to the fact that this knowledge would hurt them. Still, they had to know. "I believe that some of our leaders manipulated DAINN. We could have built more ships and expanded the facilities around the Earth. We had the tech."

My statement met with cold silence, hung in the air.

Streak shrugged.

I couldn't believe it. I squinted and opened my lids again to gaze into a pair of grey eyes that gave nothing away. My stomach lurched. I thought about throwing up on Streak's shoes.

Neither of us moved, locked in a silent battle. *How long have you known?*

The silence continued, reigning between all of us.

Streak never answered me. Instead, he looked away again.

I felt hollow inside. "You said nothing, although you knew DarNet well how I felt about the dictate," I whispered.

"Neither did you..." Streak replied.

"I didn't know... not until it was too late. How long have you known?"

Leane, defeated during our entire exchange, inquired. "What are you saying, Tesh?"

I turned away from Streak and looked at her. It was the first time either of them saw us come at each other like this. "I never trusted the Council for good reasons. So, I asked questions and investigated, reviewing Vlogs about our various programs. I found out that our overpopulated planet could no longer support us. The Council's actions were a way to ensure that we would lose many of us despite the technology we possessed to overcome a cataclysmic event. They did so that the majority would not survive, although there may be a chance."

Leane's face paled while Blast's turned red.

It was nothing short of my worst fear — disillusion, sadness, and anger.

Blast looked even more pissed, glancing toward Streak for confirmation, but Streak's face remained blank.

"What sort of a screwed-up way is that?" Blast grunted, asking no one in particular.

"I should have guessed sooner that there was a hidden agenda and looked closer, but I was blind by my distress. When I got confirmation, it was too late to do anything about it."

"If that doesn't beat all," Blast added.

The fingers on my right hand reached for my throat. The nervous gestures became familiar during the final weeks in Ang. My left arm burned with thousands of fire ants as the feeling returned. I wanted to scream, but I kept my mouth shut. So, I reached out to Leane and Blast. You know, *I'm sorry you had to learn of this in that way.*

You should have said something.

DarNet right.

You are right. I should have told you.

"What else do we need to know?" Leane murmured.

"Yeah, better come out with it now," Blast growled.

So, I triggered the pathways that marked all of me. I filled the halls of my mind with the melody of the past. Purposely, I rekindled the core of the Shaper with the smell of Iced Lily of the Valley, Mint, and Vanilla in my home. And I saw everything familiar to me, driven by my desire to be in a future that was no more.

Ang… The city of my future and past that I held on to even now saved us many times. The scientists' conclusions and our leaders' actions left me little choice. If few survived the cataclysm, I would save one that mattered to me the most. Another outcome would crush me.

181

The thought left me desperate. So, I did what I did, and my resolve to look ahead strengthened. But I could not help wondering. Did it stand today? What was left of Ang, of the people, our people? Where were they now?

I searched for my voice and swallowed, my throat dry. "I don't know where to begin."

Leane's face blanched at that. "Is there that much?"

My look said it all.

Streak's face remained grim. He tried again. "Maybe, this is not the time nor the place for this."

Blast turned on him. "I want to know why if I croak in this HellNet place, buried under tons of rocks in a freaking small containment chamber. I want to know why I did what in the DarNet I did. NetShit. You will not stop this from happening, Streak, so make your peace with it."

When Blast got Netpissed, our social expressions of disgust got the better of him. It was a sign that nothing would stop him in his track.

Streak shoved his hands in front of him and relented, backing down from an inevitable confrontation. "All right. Will deal with how we are getting out of here later; I'm okay with that."

"DarNet right. Besides, our leaders built this place to give us plenty of air. So, let Tesh talk."

"You're right... if it didn't get damaged," Streak added with a smug smile. He leaned back against one console, satisfied that he had made his point.

I held back a smile. Streak could be so darn aggravating.

Still, he was doing it to keep Blast from overthinking things. Not that anything would stop him at the moment. He was in a rare form of a temper, and keeping him busy gave him time to calm down a bit.

Blast rammed past him. "DarNet... why do I have to do all the work here? It's freaking tiring. I'm checking the air supply, but this is not over." Blast disappeared inside the array for the better part of a minute.

Leane murmured, "You might as well start at the beginning."

I triggered one screen and linked it with the interface of my PVZ... "Fine. You may as well watch this with me. It was the first time I had seen it. DAINN downloaded it when we went under."

Blast came back and stood right behind me. "Everything is working fine. Our blasted scientists misjudged the location." His tone, full of sarcasm, left nothing to the imagination about his feelings on the matter.

I unlocked the feed. DAINN's face reappeared on the screen of my PVZ, and he said, "I heard your thoughts, Tesh... all these years. I felt your pain. I am sorry to give you this as a parting gift, but I hope this will give you some closure. You never could solve your parents' death. The System would not allow you to. I recorded the VLogs inside the SRC that night, and now you see what I saw..."

My breath caught. DAINN had read my mind, although I believed I had hidden my thoughts. He knew how I felt all these years. I had always suspected my parents' death was murder. Now, I was about to witness what took place that night.

We watched the SRC building and everything that took place that night. The night my parents found out about DAINN's programming, and Rodent eliminated them.

The content unfolding in front of my eyes formed the seeds of recognition. Warm colors associated with sensations swirled in my brain. Anger. They traveled under my skin, bathing me in blinding hues of red. Betrayal grew inside of me like a blazing fire. I had known all along. Sorrow filled me. It amplified, like a deep dark hole inside of me, eating away at everything in its path. The sense of loss, overwhelming. I wanted to cry. But I couldn't. The intensity of the emotion remained lodged in my gut. This wrenching feeling seeped through me, devouring my insides, and left nothing. I now knew for sure it had not been an accident.

I notice the intake of breath from Leane beside me.

"Netshit…" Blast said behind me.

I sensed the stillness of Streak, and his immobility spoke volumes.

Still, I couldn't react. I would break if I moved.

"HellNet, Tesh… I'm so DarNet, sorry…." Blast murmured. "I did not know."

"Nobody did…" Leane said.

Where was Ang? The memories swallowed me. I saw everything against the screen of my mind. Me at eleven years old… My father, walking with me every Saturday, perusing the hall of our museum. The countless hours spent in front of paintings and sculptures, discussing art with my dad. Our conversation and laughter as he preferred to impart this knowledge, giving it a human context. DAINN had brought the facts and history to the surface, but my dad made them come alive for me. He taunted me to debate him on issues, and he tested my recall. I recalled my mother's inability to cook and her attempts to make up for all the times our domestic bot prepared dinners. Her humility, her smarts, her sense of humor… And her eyes which always gave her mood away. The surprise gifts she could never hide because of her excitement at sharing them. The hair brushing, the hugs, the thousands of comforting touches she had gifted me before sleep claimed me.

Streak moved closer and faced me. My friend's hand settled on my shoulder. "How long did you suspect this?"

The contact, ever so slight, broke my trance. "Forever, it seems… Since that night. Sloan Roden Baker came into my room that same evening. He demanded that I change Conclaves."

"You said nothing," Leane murmured.

I shrugged, "It took me some time to connect the dots, and we had already enough to contend with."

Blast enfolded me in a big bear hug. "You shouldn't have had to bear this alone."

Leane, in a shaky voice, said, "What else did you spare us?"

I smiled, but the smile ended up in a grimace.

She never missed a thing. She always got to the gist of the matter quickly.

I sensed myself rejoining the living now that my friends knew. The weight of bearing everything alone lifted. My thoughts cleared. Seconds ago, they were without form, and promptly they returned focused, registering in my head. Explanations. I needed to tell them what had happened. My memories drifted like filaments of light shifting in darkness. "The Rodent did this to my parents, but the

Council exercised its influence against all of our people. They knew we were running out of resources then. I think that's why they killed them. My parents wanted to go public," I said.

"Therefore, you always questioned everything," Streak concluded.

"Yes. Over the years, the outcome proposed by those in leadership appeared motivated by a different agenda. My parents' teachings gave me doubts."

"Your silence allowed them to continue for years… You should have alerted us." Leane insisted, looking at me with a frown.

"We were academy trainees. What could we have done?" Regrets for not standing against all of them rose and swallowed me. "But you are right; I should have let you in."

"It's not like we didn't witness certain things ourselves," Blast cut out. "Come on… You can't blame it all on Tesh. We have a part of responsibility too."

"Maybe you suspected, but I didn't know," Leane said. "The Universal Pledge guides humankind toward a higher purpose. We build our social rules and behaviors on its dictates. I just thought everyone followed them." Leane's outlook on life, always so gentle, didn't look for darkness in people. "I know it was naïve of me."

"Many people believe as you did, Leane. My parents, with their positions, knew the bickering that took place behind closed doors. They shared their knowledge of the system with me."

"And it's made you a target," Streak interjected. "I'm not sure it was wise."

"Streak, my gifts made me a target. The Rodent didn't want me to lead SRC because he feared my powers… He tried to have blocking imps installed in me."

"You've got to be kidding." Streak showed his agitation. "DarNet, Tesh, you needed to tell us that too. We are Conclave."

I shrugged. "It was surreal. I dealt with it. DAINN helped."

"How?" Streak rattled, fought to regain his composure. I could see that, and so could Leane and Blast.

"The Rodent left bread crumbs that got picked up by the EHAF and the President's office. His role demanded him to oversee the survival of our society under the Universal Pledge. As a Council Member, he created its functions supervising and monitoring the infrastructure of our world. The EHAF investigated some events unbeknown to the Council."

"But, our leaders influenced DAINN in its mandate. NetShit…" Blast's voice sounded controlled, careful, this time. Upset, he chose not to let us see how this was affecting him.

Streak ran a hand in his hair and looked at me. "There were redundancies… The system still worked. It saved us many times. Let's not forget that, but it doesn't take away the fact that this should never have happened. What you went through, that is. So, we can't lose perspective altogether."

I faced Streak in silence. Part of me knew he was right. Despite these notions of unfairness and abuse, my home, Ang, the shining city of my childhood, left its imprint on my heart. I loved everything about it. DAINN, most of all… For DAINN had kept my parents alive in my memories. Every moment of my life, recorded entirely in the DAINN Annals, held me together in the months after they vanished…

And DAINN's voice cocooned me to sleep when I cried of loneliness at night. DAINN and Mage.

Taking a deep breath, I murmured. "Some of the Council members decided to kill many of our people. They did this when they put more resources in some programs rather than others."

"Tell us everything," Blast exclaimed... "And don't hold back."

Streak and Leane also turned in my direction, waiting for details I was still reluctant to part with for fear of their reaction. Their faces reflected the horror I felt, speaking it out loud for the first time. I started explaining. "DAINN fought delays... sabotage. I gained this knowledge in the last month. When I checked the various operations, I went to DAINN and asked about the programs' survival statistics. Our planetary A.I. gave the outcomes for Alpha, Provenance, and Aurora. Aurora was the lowest, and yet that's where the Council directed most of our people. Those with the least skills, who were, therefore, least valuable among us."

Blast's low whistle resonated in the silence. "I thought it was because there was no other place for them."

Leane murmured, "Oh, my dear...." She stopped, at a loss reaching for the chamber area where our hovering chairs elevated from the floor. In one step, she sat on one.

Streak passed a hand in front of his eyes. "Tesh... Maybe that's because they couldn't build enough ships?"

"No, that's just it... We could have."

He shook his head and looked in pain. "I didn't know you did that."

"What prompted you to ask in the first place?" Blast inquired, curious.

"I had a hunch."

He nodded, studying my face. "What were the scores?"

"Alpha: seventy-eight percent. Provenance: sixty-nine percent. Aurora: forty-one percent. When I asked why we were not building more ships to send more of our people into space, DAINN said the Council didn't consider the alternative a viable option. I asked DAINN why. It couldn't give me an answer."

"Someone wanted to remain hidden, so they buried that deep," said Blast.

Confusion marked Streak's face. "Why not say anything then?"

I shrugged. "For a long time, I learned to keep things to myself. It was difficult for me to trust anyone."

Streak, thoughtful, said, "Tesh, do you think they removed you from the SRC so the Council could better manipulate the programming?"

I looked at him, knowing he would dislike my answer. "I do. Someone inside the SRC had to be in on the manipulation to carry it on. They knew I would follow in my parents' footsteps. Corruption ran deep even then. They knew for some time that we would run out of food."

"They demolished programs meant to save our people, so we never risked dying because we lacked food?" Leane wore a puzzled look on her face. "This was twisted."

"What better way to reduce our overpopulated planet if we should survive the cataclysm?"

Blast whistled again. "That's a HellNet of a conclusion."

"DAINN recommended that I remain silent on my findings. I don't think it was the only one to suspect foul play, though. The EHAF was waking up to that fact."

Streak's face had closed. He wore a blank look. "We'll never know if you are right. Maybe it's time to get out of here?"

Blast inquired, "What were the odds for Origin?"

"Thirty-three."

Blast nodded. "Glad I didn't ask before." He looked in Streak's direction. "Did you know any of it?"

I glanced at Streak.

He shook his head. "Not to that extent... Not about Tesh's parents."

I could tell he was Netpissed. Once again, my actions proved that I did not trust him. I sighed. There was a lot I needed to make up for to rebuild trust. My friends' welfare and our purpose here came first. From now on, I would act with transparency. No more secrets. "Going forward, you will know everything I know."

"Okay," Blast said. "I agree with Streak... It's time we get out of here."

Just as he pronounced these words, a colossal popping sound resonated. It echoed beyond the wall of rock, in a stunning detonation, like a screeching sonic rattle of metallic pipes. Within seconds, it stopped.

The rumble came next, reverberating inside the chamber. Its sound amplified, coming from below, and the ground moved under our feet. At first, none of us budged, anchored to the floor with our sturdy boots.

The shaking intensified.

Large pieces of rock fell into the chamber, landing on the soft cushioned flooring.

Particles of dirt filled the air.

I wavered on my legs. Streak got to me, offering his support, although both of us fought to stay upward.

Leane held on to the floating chair, which appeared to sustain the shaking better than we did.

Blast reached for one of our consoles.

The growling continued as if the planet released a tension held for eons.

As the rambling lasted, Streak and I made our way to the sturdy support of our equipment floating above the floor.

The loud noise stopped as abruptly as it started.

We looked at each other, wondering what in the HellNet caused this.

With a nod of his head, Streak took over. "Okay, time to find out where we are and make our way out. Any suggestions?"

Blast rolled his eyes. "We lost the corridors and the infrastructure of Origin. How do we identify our position?"

"We determine the damage, find DAINN, and look for the others," Streak said.

Leane's voice rose, calming, soothing our nerves. "Even with a widespread collapse, we still can reach the other three Origin chambers. The locators should work."

"Let's take a look." Streak walked to one console and attempted to locate the other compartments on one screen. "Nothing here."

"Maybe we need to be on the other side of this wall?" Leane murmured.

"There's only one way to find out." Streak positioned himself in front of the door.

Blast passed a hand over his helmet. "What if we can't get DAINN back?"

Streak deployed a three-dimensional transparent schematic of Origin. The entire underground facility, with its labyrinth of corridors, unfolded in front of our eyes. One main central chamber contained the engine and energy thrusters for the time travel blaster to bring us into the past. Attached to the central alcove, four corridors leading to each of the respective housings of the five different Conclaves, Institute, Faculty, SRC, Company, and EHAF. Inner and outer rings linking each one of these to each other completed the sturdy edifice.

"Let's assume the tunnels surrounding Origin caved in," Streak said. "These rocks show as much. If all four corridors broke apart, we no longer have access to the other chambers around the ring. But we still should be able to locate the main hub at the center. The inner passage, shorter than the others, may still exist. We can't be far from it."

"First, let's determine where we are. Once we locate where our chamber is in the underground topography, it may help," I said.

Streak nodded. "Let's get moving then. Grab food and water."

"How long will our air supply last?"

"The EmVats will carry us for about eight hours; after that, we need to recharge in this environment, so we better get to the surface before." Streak said.

Blast reached for the drawer on the other side of the chamber.

Supplies of nutrients needed for our survival, along with OPure water in IOGel packages and Spozor vials, made their way into our vests.

"Without DAINN, our search is like seeking the proverbial codes in the universal brain of our powerful A.I. We are blind," Blast said, with frustration in his voice.

"You mean it's similar to looking for a rock at the bottom of the ocean?"

Blast grimaced. "Talking about rocks right about now is not my favorite thing, although blasting them is another matter." He now fidgeted in place.

"What do we use?" asked Leane, with a smile, as she observed his annoyance.

"I can't wait for the time where I don't see any of these," he said as he grabbed another supply box from one drawer and turned it around in his hands.

Leane watched him with a puzzled look on her face. "Is everything all right, Blast?"

Blast looked somewhat troubled as he glanced around the chamber. "Yeah, everything is Netpeachy... What if the cataclysm breached the Earth's crust, causing a shift in the planetary orbit?"

"Oh, boy... Here we go," Streak said.

"This was a theory advanced by the SRC, as they reviewed the various scenarios," Blast added.

"It changes nothing for us, Blast. We still need to reach the surface," I said.

"Wonderful. Our fight for survival against a planet in turmoil sends us deep down inside the Earth. Give it to our scientists." Blast said as he sent the container flying against the wall of rock.

The metallic box resonated on the wall before falling on the ground of the chamber.

"DarNet, what do you think you're doing?" Streak said.

Blast growled, "Letting out some Netsteam... What do you think I'm doing? I hate close quarters." He continued, with a ragged breath, "Besides, it's only a DarNet box. It won't break, and if it does, I can fix it."

I reached out to Blast's mind.

Easy, Blast. Would you like me to ease your discomfort?

No, Tesh. That's not your problem.

I'm here if you need me.

Yes, I know. But I'll handle it.

"It's hard to believe that we're here, and our world may have vanished by now. But we survived the worst disaster, so keep it together," Leane said, reaching out to Blast.

Blast squeezed her hand in his. "I'll take the DarNet storms any time," he muttered.

I laughed. "That's not what you said when we fought the intensity of the sandstorms."

"DarNet right... You didn't come out unscathed. Neither did our city," Blast replied.

"Glad I am considered a priority, same as Ang," I said, teasing him.

Streak checked under the console's panel and grabbed a small Enhancer Reader. It would boost his power as he searched for the locators. It would identify the signal that would lead us to the other chambers. "Nor did you like their frequency, if I recall," he added, hoping to lighten the mood further.

"DarNet right, the storms plagued us tenfold, and their unpredictability drove our scientists' nuts," Blast said, with a gloomy look on his face.

Leane glanced at the wall, "As difficult as they were to track even with our technology, at least we knew what we were dealing with." She adjusted her PVZ and waited for the rest of us to get on with our EmVats.

"Don't forget the most important part... We were outside," Blast added, with a look of sheer disgust at the wall. "This,..." He said, pointing at the rock, "This cut us off from being outdoors." He added, "I don't like it."

Streak turned off the cooling system to give us added hours of life support. It caused the temperature in the chamber to rise.

"We don't know what happened on the surface," I said. "Cian, lower the temperature in my compartment by twenty degrees. Mage will cook in there otherwise."

"Let's not jump to conclusions," Streak stated with calm, determined to get us out of there. "Ready?"

"The HellNet, we can't." Blast said, pointing to the Earth blocking our way. "When we entered the pods, we faced the cataclysm up there. The cataclysm turned our world upside down."

"All right, the shift was greater than our scientists expected, so let's get the HellNet out! Stop whining."

"Hey, I'm not whining; I'm sharing because I'm Netpissed if you want to know. DarNet right, I am, and with good reasons," muttered Blast. "Consider what we just learned and the position we are in, and tell me this doesn't affect how you look at things?"

Streak shrugged. "How I feel doesn't matter. It won't get us out of here."

We turned toward the entrance.

"Cian, make sure Mage has food and water." As if my dog understood, he barked.

The voice of my domestic bot rose inside the chamber. "Yes, Phenom Tesh."

"Anything else for your Netmutt?" Blast said, irritated.

I shrugged, "Not at the moment," I said, smiling.

Streak glanced at me, smirking. "Anything else you brought with you we should know about?"

I ignored him. Thinking of Mage, I felt calm, focused, and strong. "Let's NetPulse a tunnel," I said, knowing that this could drain our power.

Streak's mind divulged his thoughts. Mage represented an inconvenience we didn't need. "I don't like it," Streak said. "This may require too much power."

I stared at my companions, their faces glistening under the rising heat of the chamber. They stood like statues, facing their fears. Their thoughts and questions reached me. There were so many things we didn't know. *How bad was the cataclysm? Was anything left up there? Did our people survive?*

I didn't see another way. "I don't think we have a choice."

NetPulsing relied on our energy source, and through our advanced technology, allowed sound waves to form a tube-like passage inside a rock formation.

"What if we have to face something else that we are unprepared for?"

"It is likely," I said. "We have no idea what causes the Earthquake."

"How much time do you think you can manage on your own?"

Blast responded first. "As much as I need. Probably three hours give or take depending on the blasted rock."

Leane seemed unsure but squared her shoulders at the thought of the task ahead. "I can do two hours, three at the most. I've never tried to harness my power like that for long periods."

"Tesh?"

"The same…"

"Keep some reserve… At least fifty percent. Let me know when you're low, and take plenty of Spozor as you shape the path," Streak said.

"NetRoger that," Leane whispered.

Blast grunted. It was enough for us to know that our friend heard Streak and would comply.

Streak looked toward me.

I nodded, remaining thoughtful. What caused the noise we heard a while ago?

"We don't know the orientation of the underground chamber. If the Origin Complex has rolled, we could head in the wrong direction. Further down into the bowels of the Earth instead of toward the sky," Streak continued. "I don't think it's worth the risk."

I frowned – because I knew he was right. "We split." Although I disliked the thought of dividing us, in this instance, it seemed prudent.

His cool head in challenging situations kept us alert and cautious. Streak suggested, "Four directions, then."

I nodded.

"Keep your eyes open." His gaze reached past the door to the rock formation. "I'll take up."

"Keeping the fun stuff for yourself," Blast muttered. "I'll take up."

Streak glanced at Blast and agreed. "Fine, I'll take down and clean this place up."

"What do you prefer?" Leane looked at me, appearing calm on the surface, but I knew better. She took a sip of water.

"No."

"I'll take a left then," Leane said.

I nodded. "Stay on the NetComm. If it fails, I will be in touch with you." I clamped down on my doubts and continued, "Lock the door when you leave, Streak."

Wearing their EmVats, Leane and Blast moved to the door and engaged their Pulse devices.

The noise overwhelmed the silence.

Their hands reached in different directions: one up and the other left.

Little by little, the rock withdrew under the strength of the two waves. One blue and one green pulse paved the way somewhere, to the outside.

Leane walked ahead in the left tunnel as the orifice grew, advancing in the tunnel's new pathway.

Blast pushed fast through the rock formation and propelled himself upward with his jet boots, eager to maintain a certain speed.

Streak and I watched them move inside the perfect tubes without talking.

The opportunity to improve my performance lay ahead of me. Maybe this new beginning could bring me back to who I was meant to be. Who I hoped to be one day. Feeling better at the idea that I could chart my actions without outside interference from the Council, I moved forward and began to NetPulse my path.

Regardless of my failed relationship with Streak, irrespective of what we would be to one another as we moved forward unto this uncertain road, I knew I had to forgive and redeem myself despite what I had done. Then, I would reach an internal peace.

My parents and DAINN taught me the dictates of our System, and these would be my guides. I would apply them according to my mind. Maybe here, things would be more natural.

As I advanced in a golden maze of my making, rocks surrounded me in the dark tunnel.

11
CODES
Gen

MIT, Massachusetts - 2018

Gen Aubrey comes to the system later, after she reaches the Center. She shares her journey in a past where I exist. Not the way I do in the future, not like the DAINN of 2098... At five feet six and one hundred and ten pounds, she proves to be unpredictable and resourceful. Her porcelain skin, auburn hair, and especially her green eyes, filled with shroud inquisitiveness, bespoke of an inability to compromise, while her I.Q. at 157 makes her a genius in her fields. DAINN Annals – Summer 2018.

A crowd marred my way.

I ran across campus, pushing past it, my left hand holding my laptop bag from flopping against my side, as my right carried a cup of coffee in a metallic mug with a lid on.

The students slowed me down.

I left the concrete pathways and cut through the grass toward another dorm, eager to get to Jonas, for I needed his help.

My mind returned to my findings. Statistically, ninety-five to ninety-eight percent of missing people reappear within forty-eight hours. The fact, well-established among law enforcement officials, rendered previous searches difficult.

Jonas.

Sharing this with him opened a whole new can of worms. Still, I trusted his opinion.

Jonas was tall and skinny, with long, dark hair and kind, black eyes. We shared classes often and ended up hanging out because of our affinity with the same video games. We played against each other without knowing it and then began challenging each other, building a solid reputation among gamers. Sometimes he won, and sometimes I did. But overall, I kicked his ass a lot. Well, almost. *Do it right, or forget about it.*

I reached the steps leading up to his dorm's main door, my breath coming out raspy. I cleared the entryway in no time and started up the stairs. The staircase, empty at this hour, looked every bit the same as mine.

The desertion of the scientists from their positions appeared to belong to two groups. Some disappeared, without a word of explanation, sometimes leaving behind people with whom they had shared a lifetime. Others, more organized, resigned from their posts, packing up their belongings and moving them into storage. In either case, none of them reappeared since. In that, my mother's loss shared similarities.

I loved conspiracy theories as much as I loved games. Having done plenty of both to stem off boredom during my university days, I now tested myself on a new level, but I needed a fresh set of eyes.

I reached Jonas's door and tapped on it. "Jonas, it's me. Open up."

I heard shuffling through the wood panel.

A beat.

Another beat.

The door opened, revealing my puffy-eyed friend, disheveled, sleepy, and in his underwear at seven-thirty in the morning.

I had caught him before his shower.

He yawned, not bothering to cover his mouth, and said, "What's up?"

I pushed through the door, dropping my bag on his desk. I then grabbed my laptop and said, "I need you to look at this."

Scratching his head, Jonas walked up to me and surveyed my screen. "What am I looking at? Hey, do you have something to eat? I could use breakfast and coffee."

I stood by my laptop, recalling how this got started in the first place while pulling a candy bar from my side pocket.

Jonas grabbed it.

I wanted answers no one could provide. So, I learned to search the net in dark places. The result of my latest dive into information focused on human disappearances and glared at me from my screen. My suspicion just now confirmed; I needed somebody else's expertise.

Jonas said in a disgruntled way, "No coffee?"

I shook my head. Holding the cup of coffee in my hand as an attractive incentive, "Not until I get answers." My life was about to change upon graduation, and I had little inclination for what came next. Over the last year, I became quite an expert at tracking things and creating algorithms to help the process.

The introspection into this entire affair remained contrary to my nature. I had never delved into conspiracy theories in the past. This search drove me to dig on a subject close to my heart and linked to my recent past. My mother's disappearance motivated me. Finding the truth was the aim. Understanding what happened to those missing, in a small way, provided me peace as if helping others would cause solace for my situation.

Jonas dove into the snack without waiting while he examined the information without a word. All the while, he scratched his head and massaged his temple. A real multi-tasker…

The missing poor souls, revealed by overwhelming statistics, were subject to the standard procedure. A waiting period remained the same for all, despite these large numbers. Perhaps wisdom required dropping this no man's land for experience tells us that staying in the dark can be the most prolonged, heart-wrenching moments of any life. And lingering in limbo sucked. We know better. *Blast it.*

So, here I was, waiting for Jonas to weigh in on this. "Do you mind getting some clothes on?"

He glanced down and meandered toward the foot of his bed. He picked up his jeans, all the while talking. "Waiting is the trigger between success and failure in most cases. Everyone knows this." After a pause, he continued, "You know it won't change. We can alter that somewhat. I'm assuming that's why you're here?"

"Jonas, this is not my thing."

"Helping people is not your thing?"

"That's not what I mean. You know it. And besides, don't get your boxers in a wad because I'm not one to break any laws, Jonas. I told you that before."

203

"Shame... Because the codes you gave me worked like a charm. I'm using them to aggregate tons of information."

He roped me into one of his pet projects over three weeks ago, whining that he needed my help, all the while boasting that he could do it without me, only it would take him more time. Finally, when all else failed, he challenged me head-on, saying that I was too chicken to help. What is a girl to do when in this position? *Play hard to get?*

I guess I did some of that and fell right into it. I gave Jonas what he wanted, and now, he owed me.

"You're the best, Gen," Jonas said.

My life revolved around my work. I didn't go out of my way to date. So far, I hadn't felt that thing for anyone. My heart neither fluttered nor trembled over the proverbial love we all seek. And thanks to the good old practical head on my shoulders, I approached the opposite sex with a sincere friendship. *Oh, joy!*

I held the cup of coffee in front of his nose, "Focus, please."

The numbers of these disappearances were staggering. Individuals, point-blank, vanished without a trace. It didn't require much research to come up with the yearly total. It sat right there for anyone to question. Devising the patterns from all over the globe needed more scrutiny. And it fell into the law enforcement realm.

Globally, six hundred and seven people go missing every single day. Missing children are part of these numbers. This widespread problem with predators was ongoing. In a year, this amounted to two-hundred twenty-one thousand, six hundred, and forty-four missing individuals. Over twenty years, the aggregate total reached four million four-hundred thirty-two, eight-hundred, and eighty thousand souls. The vast calculation represented the population of New Zealand or almost the entire community of Ireland. Only, in the last few months, some of them were scientists, and the question that popped in my mind was, why? *Regardless of the answer, it sucks big time.*

The facts hit too close to home.

"Okay, so what is this all about?" Jonas moved back in front of my laptop and waited for an answer.

I knew why, but I wasn't about to share this. Not yet. Not even with Jonas. Opening a wound that was barely closed would pull me right back to where I started. I could not afford to do that, not even with my friend. It took too long for me to cope. Thinking about it hurt too much. So, most of the time, I pushed it deep into the back of my brain, and I didn't deal with it. The only time I could think about it without bawling my eyes out was while working on finding out what had happened.

My mom and I had a special closeness in a family dominated by three men, no wonder. We stuck together as I grew older. She became my best friend. Well, almost. It's not too tricky an accomplishment when your one daughter prefers sitting in front of a computer and playing games rather than mixing with people.

And then one night… She disappeared. She vanished into thin air as if she had never existed.

My expression remained blank, and I muttered, "I'm interested in knowing what happened to these people."

I had spent the last year of my existence plagued by anxiety and sleep deprivation, searching for my mother when I wasn't walking around in a complete stupor. That night brought about a landscape of nightmares, and for weeks and months after that, I couldn't find my way out of it. My life was never the same after that. Neither was my family. How could it be? *Suck it up, pansy.*

In cases of disappearances, the clock moved ever so slowly, and one found oneself dying and coming back ten thousand times during the same period. *Hell, I ought to know.*

Relating to that didn't demand a Ph.D. Using the net resources to get answers, well, that didn't fit into my bailiwick at first.

Jonas was a hell of a hacker.

"I don't want to know what you're doing, Jonas." My reasons for supporting his efforts stemmed from the fact that we related, he needed the help, and I could count on his discretion. "I didn't ask you then. I just gave you the algorithm for data collection." Instead of staying away from something that remained as clear as mud when it came down to my friend's activities, well, I closed my eyes and jumped in. The saying: *What's a friend for?* It seemed to apply in this case. "So, just tell me what you think of this," I said.

Whatever Jonas put his mind to, he succeeded. "Working like a charm your algorithm… No way could I have executed my thing without your help."

Glad to be of service. My codes opened a new vista for Jonas. So, I turned to Jonas now that I needed help. I felt I could ask him anything.

My search for my mother drew my attention to recent disappearances. Dr. Lauren O'Brian, a scientist, vanished in the past week, following other scientists whose loss remained unanswered. That caught my inquisitive side for sure.

"Based on this data, this is a pattern, don't you agree?"

"What are you looking for?"

"How many scientists need to disappear before we worry? We have eleven of them… I counted. Sure, some are technicians, but many are Ph. D's."

"These results show that something is going on."

His answer brought me right back to where I refused to go, but I couldn't help myself. My mother's strange case seemed to have spun into a repetitive pattern out of nowhere. Needing to know, no matter where it led, I pushed the data in front of Jonas' face hoping to get an opinion other than my own very biased one. He was a major hacking freak and friend and could dig up information on anything or anyone.

"I need you to focus for a minute." Pulling another one of my candy bars from my bag, I handed it to Jonas.

He glanced at the cup of coffee instead of taking the chocolate bar.

I shook my head and waited.

He munched all the time. He appeared to think better that way.

I waited with coffee in one hand and candy in another. This habit of carrying snacks with me occurred after Jonas ate several of my candy bars. It didn't take long for me to realize after the first time that if I wanted to have my food, I better bring extra. And so I began carrying two of the same to class. Besides, a bribe always got his attention.

At this very moment, he eyed the chocolate bar and attempted to grab it.

I pulled my hand away. "One was free. Tell me."

He sighed…

I explained, "Dr. Lauren O'Brian was a force in her community. She went to her bank and withdrew a large sum of money before she vanished into thin air. No credit card activity, no calls, no nothing since that time."

"She tired of her old man."

"Ha-ha… I'm not so sure. She possessed an active social life, family, friends, colleagues and appeared involved in multiple organizations. Someone like that doesn't disappear without a trace." I continued before he could say anything else. "This woman was a brilliant scientist and a model citizen. She had no priors, no mental illness, and no atypical behavior. And she was social, friendly, and, as far as most people were concerned, a well-adjusted human being, even if eccentric. She also was not someone wealthy. Ransom would not seem to be part of the equation."

"So, she pissed someone off, and they took her out. We're likely to find her body in a few days, haha," said Jonas, licking his fingers. "Maybe her husband beat her up, and she faded away. Remember the movie with that actress? What was her name again?" He added with a laugh.

"Jonas, concentrate. She doesn't fit the mold. And guess what else? One of my algorithms…."

"I love your algorithms… a thing of true beauty, elegant coding all the way. I'm not sure we would be that far along without it."

I didn't want to hear about my algorithms. I would just as soon forget about it altogether. Instead, I tried to focus on my new findings. I slammed my foot on the floor and snapped, "Shut your front door, and listen… I'm trying to tell you she is part of the eleven. That also disappeared in the same way." Irritated with Jonas for his slowness this morning, I threw the candy bar at him.

He caught it, opened it, and took a big bite out of it without batting an eyelid.

I then opened the lid of the coffee cup and brought it to my mouth, with a slight pout on my face, "If you don't like it, give me my algorithms back."

Jonas smirked. "You didn't just say that, did you?"

"Fine. Make fun. Take your time in considering what I'm saying. Until then, I'll be on stand-by," I replied, remaining in the same position. Part of me recognized that I had the pouting part of the seven-year-old girl going on. "Anyway, I don't want to say you owe me, but...."

"Okay... Chill. What do you want me to do about it? Coffee will make things go a lot faster."

"Listen, dipstick...About seven scientists vanished in North America and Europe in the last month alone. Four others the month before that, two from Asia and two from South America. I bet further searches will lead to other findings around the globe." I couldn't help thinking how my mom's departure from our lives resembled these, and my heart pounded hard in my chest. My mother was just a technician, but still, it rang a bell in my head.

"Hmm... Are these part of your group of eleven? Let me take a closer look. You know... I never quite got how sarcastic you are until just about now. A family trait, no doubt?"

I held my tongue.

Jonas didn't take things personally, no matter what, but no point in pissing him off.

If I pushed too hard now, he would turn off, and I needed his perspective and skills. In a tone froth with conciliation, hoping that he would get behind this, I asked, "Don't you think this is odd?"

"Something I don't believe in is, by definition, what qualifies as odd. Everything has an explanation, and these events are not a coincidence," Jonas said.

I handed him the coffee cup and sat down beside him, too eager to remain standing. My wobbly legs were just about to drop me in a heap on the floor. "What do you make of it?"

He took a big gulp of the coffee. "What fields?" asked Jonas without answering me.

"Geosciences, Clinical Medicine, Biological Sciences, Chemistry and Materials Science, Physics, Astronomy and Astrophysics, and Mathematics."

"Now, this is interesting… Have you checked if a scientific symposium calls for the brains of our planet to converge on an island somewhere?" Jonas joked, now playing with a stress ball.

Jonas' attention, piqued by the data, got him to focus on my problem. His brain worked on problem-solving while he played around. He figured things out better that way. "There's no convention… Who could be behind something like that?"

"Maybe they all took a vacation together and disappeared, so we would leave them alone?" Jonas interjected with a wink and a laugh. Jonas, humoring me, told me he saw something in this just as I did.

I pushed him hard, hiding my unease behind a smile. "Come on… Be serious."

"This smacks of conspiracy. And gives us something to do this summer," he muttered, his mind processing the issue.

"Don't be an ass. These are people, not numbers." I appreciated Jonas for his sarcastic wit and his outgoing attitude. Still, sometimes, he rubbed me the wrong way, like now. *Get on with it.*

Jonas thought of life as a game solving problems. He appreciated the landscape in which he played, making his own rules along the way. Always turned on, always fun to be around, still thinking about how to outmaneuver an opponent. The more sarcastic he became, the more bored he was. He seemed more interested in me as a resource and a friend than as a potential mark. He never made a pass at me.

In my book, that alone meant a lot. As a result, we grew closer, and within weeks of meeting each other, I learned that he loved someone else, but it didn't work out, so he was processing the rejection. I felt terrible for him, indifferent that my appearance didn't cause any jitters in his stomach.

It's not that I wasn't into guys or anything. I was eighteen, and any good eighteen years old looked at guys and well, apart from my proclivities with tech. I considered myself normal.

Jonas didn't fit my type, although, in reality, I'm still working to define my type. I floundered on that score. So far, I had met no one that turned my stomach in flutters. It would have been nice if I had. I mean, one wonders if they don't make up a girl-swooning type. Maybe it just wasn't for me. Personal confirmation would go a long way to some enlightenment. I guessed I was too serious, too focused, too driven. Too, too, too… Not enough chemistry. *What's a girl to do?*

Coming back to the puzzle that confronted us, I said, "There's only a sporadic reference in the media. You'd think a story like that would warrant a front page."

"I told you, the big question is whether it's government or corporation." He continued, "Tracking this down to the various labs before they disappeared wouldn't be too difficult."

"Did you have a moment here? I mean, you're on board with this?" My friend broke the law on my behalf, and all I could do was be flippant with him? *Get your head examined, girl because you're losing it. What is wrong with you?*

Jonas ignored my barb. "The question is: Why are you interested in this?"

Shit. Jonas won't buy that. I tried, anyway. "I'm curious."

"Yeah, right, and I'm Einstein." Jonas fixed me with a stern look and waited.

"Look, I've helped you. Let's leave it at that."

"Gaining access to their latest projects could provide answers, but this means me doing something you're not keen on in the first place."

I didn't answer. What could I say? He knew how I felt about that stuff.

"It's that important to you?" Jonas pondered the issue a moment longer as we stared at each other. He hoped.

Remaining unwilling to go there, I couldn't give him one.

"Okay." He turned around and opened several screens on his computer. The names that popped up represented some of the leading minds in their fields. Within the next instant, he had found the labs they worked at and began to crack and bypass their firewalls.

I knew my way around this a little, but he was the ace at this. Suddenly, I got dizzy. Realizing that I had been holding my breath, I released it, and relief poured through me because I got off without an explanation. Still, I wanted to hug him. Instead, I got up, unwilling to witness him cracking sites. I approached from behind, unable to miss it either, and like a statue, observed with fascination as he dove into it.

Internally, I cringed as he hacked. Hacking was a part of what my friends did. And sometimes, well, I did it too. Nothing too controversial, mind you. I tried to remain close to the acceptable inquiries, light stuff, and all. Until this past year, I preferred writing code and algorithms, devising new applications, and breaking new boundaries on the right side of the law.

But working within the legal system didn't bring answers to the crucial questions plaguing my life. After hours and days of doing it the right way, relying on the police to do their job, I understood. *Hell. What a waste of time.*

Working outside legal boundaries required a darn good reason in my book. I possessed it. My family's experience spoke volumes. It counteracted any discomfort I felt, so I became the thing I promised my father I wouldn't be. I shrugged away the unease once again and said, "What do you think happened to them?"

"I'm not sure, but if there's a reason... We'll find out. Someday, you'll tell me why it's so important to you, right? When you're ready?" Jonas' eyes turned to me and looked severe. "Right?"

Everything stopped. My heartbeat was super-fast in my chest and resonated in my ears. I couldn't move a muscle, frozen in place.

Jonas shook his head and shrugged. "It's all right."

Once his gaze released me, I relaxed again.

He got it, though, that I couldn't talk about it. He continued, "You've got an exam to prepare. Kill it. Let me do a little cracking."

"What about you?"

"Just a few looses ends. I'm ready for my last one tomorrow afternoon — nothing to worry about, though. If I don't have the answers by now, I never will. Go. I'll call you when I have something."

"It could lead to surprises... Bad ones."

"What? Your exam?" He grinned wolfishly.

"No, dipstick..."

"Don't worry. I can take care of myself. Besides, the hacker community would hear about it if something happened." He cracked his knuckles before diving into another series of codes.

"Show-off. I'll see you tomorrow."

"Anyway, something this weird you can't claim as your own." He winked at me as he said this and returned to his system.

"Jonas? Be careful. Cover your tracks."

"Huh... Yep," Jonas said, distracted as he punched keys on his computer at an intimidating speed.

Frowning, I watched him, but he forgot my presence, nestled in this new challenge. After a moment, I left, thinking about what this meant.

People's lives could be on the line. Letting this go belonged to the realm of the impossible, especially now that a recognizable pattern had surfaced.

I loved a good puzzle, but this search had become an obsession. Only now, I had involved my best friend, which could cause more significant repercussions.

Jonas had embarked on my crusade without hesitation. Pushing strands of hair off my face, I felt tense, and my stomach clenched. Digging into this could piss someone off. My heart skipped a beat at the idea. There was no other choice for me. Jonas didn't possess a good enough reason to get in trouble if trouble came our way.

He had volunteered to help. And I needed his help. He had a special knack at this. And too many unanswered questions swirled in my brain. You can't stop a hacker. Over the last year… I became one. And it's not a part of the mentality. One who doesn't believe in the system in the first place doesn't abide by it. I stopped believing in it a year ago. I now went against the grain. Breaking rules, tempting chance, and flaunting superiority in the face of unknown risks had become second nature. Almost.

Filled with misgivings, I headed to my class. My year-end exam would end my formal studies at MIT. *Peachy.*

12
REMOVALS
Chase

Paris, France - 2018

The story of the Center comes to me through Chase Davenport. The role he plays in a future not yet designed is still to be defined. DAINN Annals — Summer 2018.

The air around me was frigid. The last several hours of the flight over the Pacific to gather our assets scattered around Europe began taking their toll.

Outside, the sky broke into a lighter shade of grey after the dark of the night. The early dawn hours rose when the private plane, piloted by Captain Sean Merin, took off from Le Bourget airport's tarmac. L'attente est finie... Wait over.

I felt the steady vibration under my feet. As the white body of the fuselage glittered under the lights, the sounds of the engine grew. The plane gained speed. Its nose lifted into the cold air as Sean pulled back on the throttle. All wheels retracted until they disappeared inside the underbelly of the sleek jet. Reaching the desired velocity, the body of the Bombardier 8000 straightened in the brisk temperature above the clouds as we continued another part of our journey around the world.

Over the last few months, the scene repeated itself many times across multiple time zones, both above and below the equator. I had been part of all of them.

Sean possessed a hard edge, acting detached, or worse, removed. One never quite knew his thoughts. He broke his cold demeanor, preventing him from warming up to people. His dedication and expertise, recognized by Jonathan Spallberg and Steven Langley, landed him in this position over the operation. It was definitely, not his charm.

In the past year, things had progressed fast.

During that time, Jonathan found backers for the research project. An old facility situated high in the mountains, revamped to host a large team, awaited our arrival. The discovery of the tablet had been enough for the Aurora of the Central project.

Eleven months have since passed. And I hung around Jonathan like a crazy stalker. My last discussion with him confirmed that he held on to some information, the same as me. Trust was a rare commodity these days between us. The real frustration stemmed from the fact that things changed between us.

Seated beside him on the aircraft, I said, "So, where are we going?"

"Back to JFK."

"How long will we be there?"

Jonathan grimaced. "A few hours. Time for a quick pick-up."

"Fine… I'll enjoy the company on the return flight."

Jonathan nodded and said, "I thought you would enjoy his company."

"You bet. A scientist that works on the human genome project, like Nolan Moreau, is an exciting conversation for me." This meeting was right up my alley. The human genome helped understand the migration and evolution of populations around the world. My anthropology passion rose its head once again. I smiled, looking forward to the discussion.

I glanced back toward the rear of the plane where Moreau sat and saw him sleeping. *Damn.*

Jonathan kept his promises until lately. Here, I think he was throwing me a bone, but I wasn't too proud not to take it. He brought me in on missions when possible and waited for me to graduate. Hell, I waited for me to graduate. *Patience... Chase.*

"A few more days, and you're out?" Jonathan said.

"Yeah, patience is not one of my best traits," I muttered.

After graduation, I would become a Central man with full status. Then, things would begin for me, and I relished the challenge ahead.

This little weekend jaunt to Europe required that I perform the same tasks as before – picking up our assets. Meeting our personnel and knowing more about Central had become my mad crush, almost an obsession.

Changing the subject, Jonathan said, "When will you be done?"

"Graduating in five days."

"So, no longer a college boy? You sure two specialties are enough for you?"

"Well, I can't wait to really begin our work," I mused. The moment approached. I swallowed a groan, just thinking about it. I finished earlier than most. With my studies completed, I would be among them — the brilliant scientists dedicated to changing the world for the better.

"Don't you have to study for the last exam?"

I sighed and reluctantly answered, "I brought my laptop."

"Get cracking. You wouldn't want to miss the last one, now would you?"

Hell… Monday was my last test. Of course, he was right; although I felt ready for it, it wouldn't hurt to review one last time. After a delay, I reached for my laptop.

Jonathan continued with a smile. "What would I tell your father if this little trip cost you graduation?"

I grinned, "Don't worry. I have extra credits."

Jonathan cracked up. "That's what I like about you the most, smart ass, not bashful at all." On that note, Jonathan got up and moved toward the cockpit.

I belonged to the few selected for this work. Still, I worried that the scope of the project had somehow changed.

Joining Jonathan in the Central underground facility within the next five days would give me full access to the discovery they made during the dig, for I was sure they had discovered something else. After all, as a partner in this endeavor, I had a right to this knowledge.

My first task after graduation, gathering the other recruits for the final trip to the Center, would take place next week. All the teams would meet. The Central project would kick off from that moment.

I counted the hours until then.

The work performed over eleven months was related to setting up the facility. It expanded what existed before and upgraded just about everything to fit today's standards. This endeavor included getting the community areas, individual quarters, and labs ready. I had a hand in all this: establishing an autonomous, independent organization with a full-blown, state-of-the-art research center off the grid.

The enterprise saw many phases. All of them called for discretion. Hell, you could even say secrecy. This trip was no different. This leg of our travels would bring us to New York. Only we wouldn't stay there long enough to enjoy it. I closed my eyes.

All of us boarded the private jet. Sean, Jonathan, and Steven recognized our mission's importance. Without the critical members of our science team, we would be beyond the eight balls. We needed specific individuals for the research. We wanted those that were top in their field to make the critical progress Jonathan wanted. Fast.

I got up and went to the small bar to grab a cup of coffee. If I was to study, I better be awake. I poured myself a double expresso and returned to my seat.

Over the last few months, our task was not so simple. It comprised gathering prominent scientists to join the Center from all over the globe. Only, there was a catch — a big one at that. No one could know.

Nolan was a member I had just met, but I knew about his work. Getting to speak with him and discovering the scope of his research for the Center led me to this aircraft and this flight.

Jonathan came back and sat facing me this time. He coughed and looked at me. "Huh... MIT is close by your dorm, right?"

I lifted my eyes from the computer. "You know it. Why do you ask?"

Central held my imagination. I attempted to put the pieces of the puzzle together with a few facts. Enthralled by the things I knew so far, I built all kinds of scenarios. I had taken part in the construction on the mountain, the drilling underground, the technology installed within these grounds. Since then, a lot more transpired, although I remained in the dark about the dig itself. It made me freaking nuts because I wanted... I needed a hell of a lot more. I wasn't stupid. No one expanded that many resources without something concrete and compelling.

"I need you to visit someone at MIT."

"Fine. No problem. Just tell me who. I'll do it when we get back."

He nodded, but his face remained closed off. Something was bothering him.

The knowledge I sought existed behind the closed gate of an underground facility, one I committed to keeping quiet from the beginning. The whole damn thing made sense while we were building it, but I knew something else had happened in the last couple of months, and not being privy to it made me edgy.

"We're gathering some intel. You may not like what we may have to do."

"Then, we don't do it." Frustrated with him, I got back to my laptop.

"We may not have a choice, Chase... So, I think it would be better if it came from you. You're a Harvard man. Maybe you can find some common ground."

Jonathan worked to shape the future. Over the years, tomorrow became his brand. Influencing, it turned into an obsession — a huge one at that. The discovery inside the mountain formed the basis of a radical change. One he intended to pursue. Investigating the science beyond the tech and using it became the focus of the work at the Center. This research could advance us years ahead, unleashing a dramatic shift in how we perceive the world. This potential outcome caused me to pause. A lot of good could come from it, but also some bad.

"What is it you want me to do?" I muttered these words with a feeling that things may not be as simple as black and white. I bristled at the notion that it could blur the line. We must maintain a balance. Moral considerations must fit in the equation, but how much of it would enter into the decisions? We had to be the keepers of that.

Jonathan had a vision for the future and an unrelenting, one-track mind. So, when I found this thing and brought it to him, I also made it my mission to monitor things.

I closed the laptop with a bang. "Are you preparing me because you worry about how I will react?"

Jonathan's eyes narrowed in on me. "It's a fact that we do not always see eye to eye about how to proceed on things."

"So, tell me what this is all about, and we can discuss how to proceed."

"Someone has been poking around… We need that to stop."

"Shit. What in the hell do you mean?"

Here I was… Worried about cause and effects. There were plenty of things I couldn't control. Sure, I could have quit Harvard. Only, that wasn't part of the deal. If I leave, I wouldn't be part of the Center. Jonathan insisted that I graduate for whatever stupid reason, and that had to do with my father's influence.

"Well… It wasn't my idea… It's Steven. We'll be sending Sean with you."

Damn. Steven was a tough guy and showed a certain ruthlessness. He was efficient. His ways, though, were often not my ways. I gritted my teeth and bore it, but I didn't like the sound of that. Steven was the one cautioning Jonathan against keeping me in the loop, no doubt. I would do something about that on this trip.

Jonathan's voice got lower. "Someone is following the movements of our scientists a bit too closely. They tapped into their labs. Steven worries that this will attract attention."

"What is he suggesting we do? Kill a couple of people?"

Jonathan just laughed. "We need to find these hackers and stop them from continuing."

My eyebrows rose in an inquiry. "There are lines we cannot cross, Jonathan."

Jonathan shrugged, "Not what you're thinking."

"So, you're clairvoyant now?"

"Nothing like you might be thinking. I assure you. Still, I prefer that you handle it."

"Okay. So, we buy these guys out. We have plenty of money for that."

Jonathan nodded. "He's not sure that will suffice. They're hackers. You can judge that when you're on-site."

I leaned back in my seat, no longer able to focus on the notes of my class.

As the pilot of the unmarked craft, Sean stayed enclosed in the cabin. He never descended from the aircraft, even to get some fresh air during our brief stay on the tarmac. The main reason… Sleep.

Jonathan remained inside. He organized the precise times of the pickups. The arrival of the cargos during the airport stops unfolded like clockwork.

My role was to implement the pickups with Steven.

I growled, thinking about the hackers.

This journey was our last trip for phase one of the grand plan. I had traveled with my companions to Europe and Asia. And I had witnessed firsthand a flawless orchestration. They left nothing to chance when gathering our most valuable assets.

Our destinations during our first voyage were in Europe, where we landed at Brussels Airport in Belgium. Then Linz Airport in Austria, Prague in the Czech Republic, Billund Airport in Denmark, Helsinki-Vantaa Airport in Finland, Stockholm-Arlanda Airport in Sweden, Berlin Tegel Airport in Germany, Athens International Airport in Greece, Malpensa Airport in Milan, Italy, Anapa Airport in Russia, Barcelona Airport in Spain, and Cork Airport in Ireland until we flew back to base.

During the second trip, the journey became longer. We traveled to Akita Airport in Japan, Beijing Nanyuan Airport in China, and Indira Gandhi International Airport in Delhi, India, to disappear again over the Pacific Ocean.

We landed the plane in Bangkok, Thailand, and took off, reappearing in Dubai in the United Arab Emirates on the third flight. We disappeared again, only to reappear in Buenos Aires, Argentina, where we departed for Brazil and Peru.

Sean flew the jet on all continents, taking off within hours of our landing.

The pattern continued for days throughout two months.

All aspects of the removals, carried out without drawing undue attention to ourselves, called for influence. The kind that only came with Jonathan's great connections and money. How? I could not even imagine. These precautions were extreme. They required massive incentives and actions in the planning phase. I tried to rationalize the need for secrecy. Doubts came and went.

Jonathan's friendship with my father weighed on me. It brought legitimacy to the entire operation. Still, I fought against the unease. I hoped that there were good reasons for all this cloak and dagger stuff. I held back and observed.

Steven maintained our security, handling the details for everything, and in months of preparation, we had assembled a team of scientists unmatched anywhere for Central. *Such a significant commitment, considering the cost of these voluntary abductions.*

The wait at each destination remained short; the timeline for all our trips was estimated in milliseconds. On all such occasions, the boarding of our passengers triggered our departure.

During the last trips, provided with a name, photo, and location, I drove the four-by-four with dark glass windows from the airport to the pick-up locations and back. I moved the assets from the car to the plane in minutes while Steven dealt with other details on the ground. Not this time.

Passengers were not the only thing we carried. Equipment found its way inside the cargo bay during many of these stops.

The three of us worked to get in and out of each location without incident. Each of our stays was as smooth as silk. Refueling, orchestrated beforehand without a hitch, resembled chess pieces moving flawlessly across the board during a high-speed match. The Tower remained ghost-like over every flight plan.

Usually, Steven didn't need me. Today, we had a more problematic case. Steven and I would travel together.

Central, the official name of the project for the Center, grew with each passing hour. It expanded with each mile flown across the Atlantic and the Pacific. Each turn of the engine brought me closer to finding out what lay within the Center.

After long hours of transit from Paris, six hours back and forth, plus four hours on the tarmac, Nolan and I got to talk a lot.

Now, seated beside Jonathan as we approached JFK, I was curious. "How tough is this pick-up?"

He lifted his head from the newspaper he was reading and said, "The logistics are not... We may need some encouragement. I will oversee the loading of the equipment in the cargo hold while you handle the asset with Steven."

Great. I could use the opportunity to confront Steven.

Jonathan and Steven kept a closed lid on the whole operation, and it drove me nuts. "This guy... He wants in, right?" I snarled at Jonathan.

"He does. It's not about him... it's personal," Jonathan said, eying me sideways. He got the message. It frustrated me. "The guy is a forensic expert I've known for some time. His name is Paul Weingart. He has been working out of a New York lab to be closer to his grandkids."

"A forensic expert and biochemist? Why in the hell do we need that?"

My proximity to the scientists during these flights allowed me to garner information about their fields of expertise. These men and women fit the profile of rational individuals working on cutting-edge science. They worked on experimental theories — some with more success than others.

"We thought it might come useful. Paul knows a lot about DNA," muttered Jonathan, uncomfortable.

"Why in the… Oh… You found something, didn't you? We're no longer dealing with theories now, are we? Shit!"

Jonathan frowned. "I have better things to do than answer your questions, Chase. We have a great project, and you shouldn't be the one doubting it."

I read between the lines. "A lot of their work does not encompass what we're working on or your work on the future. And it appears redundant. We already have all kinds of experts. There are no practical applications that I can see, at least until now. Don't change the subject. What did you find?"

Jonathan got up, exasperated with me. "And you think yourself qualified to judge that? How are you qualified, Chase?"

This time Jonathan walked away, leaving me with questions. I remained in the dark because he never answered me, which caused me to twitch big time. The tablet warranted discretion for sure, but all the cloak and dagger shit began to make me feel uneasy. Maybe it was because I was idle. I tried to go back to my laptop. I couldn't concentrate.

We were attempting to reach a goal that belonged to a distant future with advancements created over years of development and research. Today, nothing existed that would allow me to believe the discussions held among the scientists on this plane belonged to the realm of the possible. And yet, everyone on every flight appeared convinced that they would achieve their objectives in this lifetime. We needed a change. Hell, the planet could sustain one.

I connected the dots. Jonathan found something on the mountain. He saw something that required a forensic expert. I should have known. The feverish excitement, the sped-up push to finish the construction's aspects faster, had started two months ago. I felt it. The pieces of a structure were much more than that. They had perhaps opened it by now. Hell... And I was still in the fucking dark.

Useful in my field, I was no genius. I should have seen it sooner. Yes, I should have read between the lines. But I didn't possess their knowledge or experience yet, although I had a right to be here because I found the damn thing.

Jonathan's friendship with my father triggered the wait in my involvement with the Center. I had known that all along. The man was infuriating. Hell, I hated this... I was powerless for the first time in my life. I had to wait it out. Shit!

We were scheduled to make three final stops, one at JFK, New York, another in Billings, Montana, and the final one in Los Angeles, California. In all, we had made twenty-three stops, returning only when necessary to drop off our cargo.

Jonathan looked at his watch and said: "We will land in a few minutes."

"You opened it, didn't you?"

A flash of satisfaction registered across his face, and a slight smile lingered on his lips.

With a brow-piercing look in his direction, I growled.

He laughed. "Did you just growl at me?"

The damn bastard laughed. I threw Jonathan a pointed look. "Fuck off."

After a minute of silence, he inquired, his voice filled with inherent confidence. "How were your conversations with our friend?"

I never answered him… I walked away to pick up another cup of coffee. Two could play that game.

We hit JFK and ran into a problem.

Jonathan stayed on board and oversaw the loading of all the equipment while Steven and I left in the four-by-four to pick up what he considered a severe case, as far as our assets were concerned. We drove for a while.

Steven was calm, efficient, and didn't talk much. I guessed it was part of his line of work.

"Why are you sidelining me?" I said.

Steven glanced over at me. "Use your head, Chase. You hired me to keep this project under wrap."

"Not from me. You are cutting me off, encouraging Jonathan to keep the information I have a right to know. We started this project together. We hired you together. What the hell is going on, Steven?"

"Don't take it personally. Just using judgment, a precaution, that's all."

"From me? Why?"

His gaze was steady when he answered me. Hell, he was still driving, and he kept looking at me. "From anyone who spends time on the outside."

"Meaning me… I'm the only one on the outside."

"You got it."

"Can you look ahead… We don't need an accident."

Steven chuckled as he returned his eyes to the road. "Don't worry; I have extra senses… and lots of practice."

"Damn it, Steven, I'm no threat, and you know it."

"You are so long as someone can get to you… And at the moment, they can. So, the less you know, the better for all of us."

Shit. I couldn't fault Steven's rationale. He was right, even if I didn't want to admit it. I was on campus, approachable, and unprotected. I never thought I needed protection. Did I?

Steven slowed the car down and pulled up to the curb near a building. He turned the engine off. We waited a few minutes in silence.

"What time is he supposed to be here?"

Steven looked at his watch. "Ten minutes ago. I'm calling Jonathan." Steven grabbed his cell and dialed. "Hey, boss… I've reached the street… I'm sitting in front of the building. He is not here," Steven said.

The "hey, boss" irked me. Hell, I was as much his boss as Jonathan. *Grow up, Chase.*

Jonathan said, "Wait it out. Give him a few minutes."

"We'll have a problem with the Tower if we don't stay on schedule. At this hour and in this traffic, I'll be lucky if I make it back by departure time."

"We've had close calls before, Steven. Be patient. He has a wife and kids. This departure is not an easy thing."

"All right. You're the boss."

That word again. I sighed and said nothing. Patience…Chase. Waiting was never easy for me.

Jonathan hung up, and we resumed the wait.

Our precious cargo covered the gambit in the fields of science and technology. Unbeknownst to the world, we selected scientists, their staff, and recruits in the areas of study that Jonathan believed paramount to carrying on the Center's work. Organizing the team's recruitment demanded diplomacy, contacts, charisma, agility in negotiations, and financial flexibility.

Jonathan possessed these in spades.

The noise from the building caught our attention. A man and a woman appeared to be arguing.

"This is not good," said Steven. "We should already be gone… Come on, get in the damn car," muttered Steven at my side, looking over to the guy.

"Let me see what I can do," I said, opening the car door., Jonathan wanted diplomacy. If Steven was anything, it wasn't charismatic or diplomatic.

I heard Steven's voice behind me, relating the situation to Jonathan, no doubt. "We have a problem, Jonathan. She won't let him leave. She is creating a public disturbance. What do you want me to do?"

I glanced back at Steven. "How about you let me do my job?"

Steven put the phone on speaker and shrugged.

"How bad?" asked Jonathan.

"Well, if you count three people already looking down from windows over their place… It's not as discrete as we had planned."

"He told me he had worked it out with her."

"From where I'm standing, it doesn't look like it. Let me share the video feed."

"I'm not sure it's necessary. Give Chase a chance. He is good with people."

I nodded and turned around.

"You know the characters… Following our protocol, I'm recording everything. Picking up a scientist of his caliber in an unmarked car, and making him disappear, demands precautions. Anyway, I don't intend to finish my days in a high-security prison, Jonathan, and neither do you."

On the feed, Jonathan witnessed an empty street. The opened car window provided an unobstructed view of the entrance to a building.

I walked toward the small man in his fifties, holding a suitcase in one hand and a briefcase in the other.

He pulled away from the arms of a woman.

Desperate, she grabbed hold of his suitcase and tugged.

He tried to wrench it away from her hand without success. Turning toward us and looking haggard and distraught, he yelled, "Help me out here."

"Hello, mam… It's nice to meet you. Dr. Weingart. I can take this from you." I gestured toward the briefcase, avoiding the suitcase altogether.

"You can call me Paul… Harriet is difficult," said Paul, handing me the briefcase.

I smiled at the sturdy woman. She looked to be about fifty years old and bore a sad expression on her face. "It's never easy to say goodbye," I said. "We can give you a few more minutes, but we have to go if we want to meet our schedule. Mam, it was a pleasure to make your acquaintance."

Harriet didn't budge her stance. So much for my charm…

The guy turned away from me and the camera Steven held and faced his wife. "Come on, Harriet, we've discussed this. Don't be like this. I'll only be absent for a few months."

Dressed in a loose-fitting long skirt and shirt, with her hair in disarray, blemishes on her face, and her eyes rimmed with black and dripping mascara, she held on to the handle with both hands. "You're not leaving, and that's that… You promised to conduct your research here in town!" Harriet screamed, her voice rising with each sentence.

"I already explained. I have to go. It's important."

"Dr. Weingart is correct, mam… His work is essential," I added with a smile. "Besides, you'll be able to see him from our state-of-the-art video conference daily. It won't be the same thing as if he was here, but we can make the wait easier."

Harriet looked at me as if she wanted me gone.

I took a step back. Perhaps, it wasn't a good idea to stick around. I looked at Paul and said, "I'll wait for you in the car." Then, I turned around and made my way toward the vehicle.

But I heard Harriet's voice lashing out, "I'm not finishing my days alone, you selfish, conceited, self-centered beast!"

Then, Paul's voice, lower and apologetic, "You're not alone. You have children and grandchildren to keep you company."

The woman continued, unimpressed, "I've raised our kids alone while you were ensconced in your senseless cadavers and incomprehensible and gibberish theories… I'll be darned if I let you now walk out on me like this."

I glanced back just in time to see Paul, pulling harder on the suitcase. His renewed energy to get away motivated him.

The woman tugged just as firmly.

Exasperated, he suddenly released his grip. "Fine, you keep it if that makes you feel better."

"You can't go," the woman cried.

"You have plenty of money in the bank. You won't lack for anything."

"You've never loved me."

"Harriet, you know it's not true," said the man in a tired voice. "I'll be away for a while, and I'll be back. We'll talk every day." After a beat, he turned and made his way toward the car.

We reached the vehicle, and I opened the back door, dropping his briefcase in on the seat. Paul slid inside beside it.

"That's not true, and you know it…" she yelled.

The voice of the woman reached us, calm and distant in contrast to the moment before. "Paul… I won't be here when you return."

"No, no, no… Paul…" exclaimed Steven.

It took a second for me to turn around. Another second to comprehend. Too late to intervene or do anything about it.

Harriet, sad and determined, had retrieved a small gun and held it at her head.

Where did the gun come from? Who cares… She has it. Hell…

"Shit…" said Steven.

Paul leaned out of the vehicle.

"What…" The small man got halfway out.

Holding a small nine-caliber automatic to her chin, Harriet pulled the trigger.

We heard the shot.

Paul fell to his knees.

Harriet's body toppled to the ground.

Jonathan's voice whispered from the phone, "Oh, my god!"

Dead silence.

I stood there, frozen in horror.

Paul yelled, "Harriet, Harriet… No, oh no… Harriet." He whimpered, "No, oh no, no, no!" He got back to his feet and ran back to her, dropping to his knees beside her body.

I stood speechless, having just watched someone blow their head off. My stomach surged. I gasped, trying to hold my food down.

Steven dropped the cell phone with the video on the front seat behind me. My mind registered this, but I didn't move. I couldn't.

Steven's voice reached us, "What now, boss?"

"Leave him… There's nothing you can do, and you can't stay there. There will be too many questions."

"That's darn cold, boss." Steven got out of the vehicle. I heard the door of the car open and close. He carried the briefcase in one hand and walked over to Paul.

What in the world had just happened? I followed him… Part of me wanted to see it up close. Part of me thought it was gross. *Perhaps she missed her aim?* The thought kept me going.

In my head, I heard the bang, again, loud, so loud. Was it possible? Shock held me in a cold envelope. I felt stress knotting my solar plexus. My mind refused to comprehend what my eyes had just witnessed. The images replayed in my head, whizzing by fast.

I reached them, both leaning over Harriet's body. Blood poured on the concrete. Half her head exploded… Dead.

Then, reality set in. I struggled with the meaning of it.

Steve leaned toward Paul, crying over the body of his now-defunct wife.

How could this happen?

He lay a hand on his shoulder, "I'm so sorry, Paul. I'm sorry for your loss, but we have to go."

The broken man nodded.

"I'm leaving your briefcase here, beside you. Let us know if you need anything. You know how to reach us."

Sobs.

Steven grabbed my arm, tugging hard for me to follow. "We have to go." He walked back to the car, dragging me along. Hurriedly, Steven opened the door and pushed me in before going around it and getting in himself. He started the engine, but minutes passed. For a long moment, he didn't move.

Steven forgot to turn off the camera.

It lay on the dashboard, recording in a half-hazard way. The lens, directed at the roof, no longer delivered images. The sound carried just the same. More sobs.

Police sirens resonated in the distance.

I heard Steven's breathing, the car engine purring, the transition engaging into gear and revving up as the vehicle pulled onto the road.

"We're on our way…" said Steven before he hung up and shut off the camera and phone.

Finally… Crystal-clear, it had registered the event, one I would just assume forgetting altogether. I glanced at the phone in a daze.

We got to the airport in silence. The four-by-four pulled up and stopped — dead air. The scuffle of feet on the stairs – mine and Steven's, filled the silence as we boarded the plane in silence.

Steven raced ahead of me, climbing the stairs two at a time. He looked like a man who had walked through a raging storm when he passed through the airplane doorway. His whole demeanor intimated that he had stood in the hurricane's eye, facing the approaching tumult, with no place to hide.

His sight disturbed me, for he had seen death in the war, shoot out in the streets of rough neighborhoods, grit and sweat, and mayhem before. Maybe this had affected him because it was so unexpected. I mean, one can expect the worse of people in locations and circumstances that call for that. And in these instances, one prepared for it. It was another thing altogether to witness it in a case like this.

Steven said, once inside the airplane, "We need to keep this quiet. If it hits the news... Game over. They won't stop investigating until they find the link to us."

Jonathan nodded. "I'll make some calls."

I went to sit down alone. The cold wave surrounding me got colder. All I could feel was speed, the speed of my thoughts. My disappointment drowned me. Devastated about the part I played in this; I questioned everything.

The Center represented an ideal. This ideal just got trampled. It crumbled into thousands of pieces.

How could this happen? Why was I part of this? Could I remain?

I got pissed, feeling betrayed.

My foul mood increased with each passing minute. The latest event trapped me, and I didn't want any part of it. Although finding the discovery put me on this path a year ago. But now, this voyage in the jet cornered me into a situation where a woman lost her life. And yet, because of my beliefs, walking away didn't represent an option.

Dumbass.

My thoughts about controlling things were ludicrous. I didn't control shit. I stood as a passenger on a complicated highway - a highway to destruction.

Right. Suddenly, it got complicated, exceptionally so. If I considered everything that had taken place in the last year, this recent incident stared me in the face at the moment, unforgiving.

Everything about the Center, everything we did in the present, everything set in motion, dealt with safeguarding the future. Yet, the Central program cost the life of one good, emotionally fragile woman.

Tilting my head from one side to the other, I rubbed my jaw. How could anyone justify that? No one could... The fact scared the hell out of me.

The Center's importance and the work we would do to plan a better future disappeared as I contemplated what had just happened. I couldn't comprehend our complicity. An essential member of our team, Paul, had lost his wife of thirty years, and he would not be joining us because of this loss.

The senseless, desperate act loomed on all of us.

Jonathan approached and sat beside me. His brows furrowed together as he tried to make sense of what had just happened.

My voice croaked. "Did you know Paul's wife was... Unhinged?"

Jonathan remained still. His silence spoke volumes.

"You knew… That's why you sent Steven instead of me."

Jonathan's eyes met mine.

"What could be so important that you would risk the life of one woman?"

As Jonathan put it, when we began Central, our sole purpose was preserving lives, which now appeared entirely warped in my mind.

"The future," whispered Jonathan.

"What good is it to preserve the future if we make the present a living hell?" It's not good enough." My voice broke on the last word.

"It has to be."

I continued, "I think it's time you tell me everything… You've found."

"We have a deal. It changes nothing. I told you when we started that I wouldn't divulge anything of importance until you could join us full-time. Remember, I don't owe you any other explanation until we all reach the Center."

Snapping at him, "I found it. I'm the one who brought it to you. You need me. You said so yourself."

"One week." Jonathan didn't move a muscle after that, nor did he volunteer anything else.

Freaking bastard. I huffed, "Do you even feel anything about what just happened?"

I watched Jonathan's features. All I read in his eyes was determination.

I jerked away, fuming inside. I had hoped to see something other than that.

Implementing Jonathan's goals destroyed one human being and one family. Or was it our goal?

I didn't know. It couldn't be right to be a part of it even if I wasn't at the helm. Still, I felt some responsibility for this.

As if reading my mind, Jonathan's shoulders slumped. "I never told you the road would be easy." His self-confidence started to fade.

Anxiety grabbed me. My throat constricted. If I moved at all, I would throw up on the carpet of the private plane. I took in a deep breath and counted to five. Would others pay the same price?

I had never witnessed a violent death before. Not in person. Not like this.

I never saw a suicide.

Closing my eyes, I tried to forget Harriet's body lying on the cold ground. On the screen of my mind, I observed her viscous blood already pouring beneath her, soon congealed on the bleak concrete. The vision remained with me... The splatter of brain matter dripped from the door. Making a ridiculous sound. Plat... Plat... Plat. Was it captured so irritatingly by the camera's unmistakable sound, or was it only in my head? Unsure, I rubbed my lids, trying to erase the vision.

Jonathan got up.

Our agenda blurred in my thoughts and seemed suddenly unimportant and inadequate.

He left for the bar and was back in no time with a glass of Scotch that he pushed in front of my face. "Drink... It'll help."

Really? How do you figure?

My hand shook, and the ice hit the sides. The amber liquid splashed on my wrist. I lifted the glass to my lips, swallowing a large gulp of the strong drink. The warmth descended into my chest, and I took another swallow, then coughed. I downed the rest of it. My imagination somehow conjured the smell of death. How can someone smell death when it's not even around them? I swear I could feel it. Hell.

"Jonathan, I need to know."

Jonathan nodded, "Shake this off and do your job."

Do I even want to be on that last flight?

My unknown place in the Center made me question my decision to join. Did I want my life to take this path? Unsure, I looked at the empty glass in my hand and set it on the table.

The wall of my brain seemed to shrink around my thoughts. I breathed hard. I scared the crap out of myself, unable to reach my center.

The traffic Steven encountered from New York to the airport caused a delay in our departure.

Jonathan paid extra that day, keeping goodwill and cooperation flowing.

All the while, my gut churned. The doubts didn't go away. I remained apart, observing their behavior, unaltered.

Remaining calm became painful. My emotions struggled to get out somehow, even if it was to find an outlet, any outlet. My body trembled, reminding me I somehow had reached some emotional limit. Why?

Harriet's death had affected me. Still, I didn't think my reaction to her passing would cause me to lose it somehow. Again, it did. So staying in control became my main aim. And yet, my mind replayed the scene, over and fucking over.

I can threaten.

I wanted answers, even if that meant cornering Jonathan against the fuselage.

It won't work.

Steven or Sean would beat me up for sure. I could hold my own, but I didn't have their fighting experience.

Fuck it.

I was about to do it anyway, but Sean got out of the cabin and approached us. "Air traffic control is keeping us down for another twenty minutes."

Jonathan's head turned toward the sound, and he quipped, "Nothing sooner?"

Sean shook his head and turned around. He crossed paths with Steven in the aisle, on his way back to the cockpit, without a word.

Sean possessed that kind of quality. He knew when to remain silent and when not to ask questions. This trait made him one indispensable member of the team. He understood situations at a glance, holding on to his opinions, which enhanced this already practical personality.

The doubts persisted in my mind. The same inquiry regarding my role rattled in my brain. Do I want in? *Hell, you're in whether you like it or not.*

I chuckled. If I had followed my hunch and confronted, even aggressed Jonathan moments earlier, hoping he would talk, I would be on my way out by now or worse. Maybe it would have been for the best. Some part of me didn't want to be here.

The Center stood as a murky presence in my future.

Different personalities, with a few more difficult than others, made up Central. But they required from us all one thing: secrecy. The confidentiality clause in our contract called for everyone embarking on the journey to make one commitment: unequivocal allegiance to the project.

My unwavering interest in Central faltered. My protective instincts, pushing my alpha male buttons, called for a reevaluation of my loyalty.

The realization hit me. The high price to pay in pursuing our goals made me pause.

My ignorance of the endgame and the extent of Jonathan's goals had me reconsidering everything.

I only knew Jonathan and his dream.

Was I still a willing participant? I questioned my motives. Was I someone capable of safeguarding a lie? I never concluded. Instead, I bathed in suppositions and stood in quicksand. I wavered between grey and darkness. For once, I could not decide. The ambiguity alone became a great source of irritation. *Am I willing to walk away?*

The flights to Jackson Hole, Wyoming, and Los Angeles, California, carried the soulful and quiet atmosphere of mourning. Our scientist's absence, Paul, a willing member of our global charade, was not the cause of our sorrow. It was an inconvenience. But Harriet was gone, and with her death, we lost something more.

A year ago, embarking on this journey of discovery, I possessed an intangible feeling of innocence. An effervescent joy at such an exciting endeavor filled me. Today, the enthusiasm for the grand plan, doing something for the good of humanity, along with these other emotions, faded at the heightened awareness of this loss. The pain we had caused gagged me.

Reality painted a different picture, trapping me inside a scenario I disliked.

I couldn't pledge myself to Central. It didn't represent something to aim for, not right now. I resented this conclusion, so I wrestled with it, trying to arrive at another. On that note, I drew a blank.

On all of our trips, there were no passengers. For everyone else, there were records. Those who boarded the plane before and after this event were nonexistent. From the moment they entered the private jet, all of them evaporated into thin air as if they never existed.

Soon, the moment would arrive when it would be my turn to decide on this direction or not.

At the moment, I doubted that I could.

13
TRUTH
Tesh

Deep Inside The Earth - 2018

The shift of the Earth occurs when the time portal engages, sending the chamber back in time. The System's automation continues providing life support for years as my charges navigate the past. My System downloads the last of the Institute Conclave information to achieve success, and I relinquish my mandate to the DAINN of Origin... DAINN Annals - Summer 2018.

I glanced back at the area that I had just carved into the rock. Part of me, dumbfounded because I found myself inside the Earth, disintegrating a wall of dirt ahead of me, found our situation hard to believe. This passageway represented our way out — still, our situation's unpredictability sunk in further as I kept going.

My NetPulse engaged as I raised my hand toward the rock's surface, emanated its golden glow, and I drifted ahead. Rock and more rock surrounded me, and I shuttered inside, thinking of the crushing mass all around.

The Earth blocked our way out, alienating us further from the world we knew. I turned back and saw Streak diffusing large stones, blocking our doorway into multiple fragments while the latest model Android Cygil 1001, carried them out of our chamber.

DAINN's disappearance didn't bode well. Moving ahead in the tunnel, I felt alienated. DAINN's androgynous face never appeared in my mind when I called it. D never answered back.

As my people's leader, not that I ever wanted the role, the burden of decisions fell on me. My innate knowledge of things branded me a Shaper. My genes gave me this gift, providing me with a power that drew envy and granted privileges. This inheritance left no choice, instead of birthing the duty of a lifetime. The training prepared me for it, yet I would gladly shed that position.

Despite these notions of unfairness and abuse, my home, Ang, the shining city of my childhood, left its imprint on my heart. I loved everything about it. DAINN, most of all... For DAINN had kept my parents alive in my memories. Every moment of my life, recorded in the DAINN Annals, held me together in the months after they vanished... And DAINN's voice cocooned me to sleep when I cried of loneliness at night. DAINN and Mage.

I jumped when I heard Streak's voice behind me.

"Tesh, give me a minute before you continue."

"You scared me. I didn't even hear you come right behind me."

"I understand why... You have a lot to process. Look..." Streak stopped me from continuing with my NetPulse. "I need to know something."

The rock formation around us showed the mark of our presence. Its walls bore traces of the oscillation, whose energy left a crystal residue, either blue, green, silver, or gold. Embedded inside the stone-like tiny filaments, they formed the patterns of veins. I looked away at Streak and stared at the golden strands. "What do you want to know?"

"Why didn't you trust me?" Streak said, a confused expression on his face behind the mask of the EmVat.

I locked my eyes on Streak. I knew what he wanted: an explanation. Unlike other times, I hesitated for my answer would drive a more massive wedge between us. "You know me as much as I know you. Why do you ask? It should be obvious." Staring into his eyes through the transparent membrane, I remembered how he had pushed me away, and I felt the pain all over again.

Streak lifted his hand in a helpless gesture. His face wore a somber expression. "We have to stop this. I hate this rift between us." Without the headset, his hand would have pushed his hair away from his forehead. It was something he did whenever he felt upset or overwhelmed. I knew that too well.

"I dislike it as much as you," I clipped, refusing to give an inch. Streak brought this on us.

The ground and walls screamed again. Like the sound we heard earlier, it resonated in the tunnel, echoing against the walls. The shaking began, turning our small space into a dangerous area as rocks falling from the ceiling came down in chunks. All around us, the trembling increased. The noise resonated like thunder inside the Earth.

I faltered on my feet. Streak's hands found me, holding me straight.

The dirt rattled like an AirR tram as it passed by. Then, all of a sudden, we were both moved up and down like puppets. Our heads and shoulders hit the ceiling. The shock sent us right back to the surface of our make-shift corridor. Sprawled against the dirt surface, we looked at one another. Still holding hands, we scrambled to our feet, avoiding the boulders acting as projectiles around us. The wall of rock we had not yet touched with the NetPulse appeared susceptible and weak.

We retreated along the corridor, holding onto the sides of the shaft in the loud noise. In the darkness, the dust particles floated in front of our masks. Just as quickly as it had started, the tremors stopped and retreated deep into the Earth.

Silence fell upon us. The air stilled.

Streak reached out to me, "Are you all right?"

"Yes…" I opened my NetComm. "Leane, Blast… are you all right?"

"Not in the least," came Blast's voice, grumbling, "But I assumed you're referring to my physical state, in which case I can reassure you… Everything is still very much in its place."

Leane's laugh broke the moment. "You wimp…" she murmured, in between hick-ups… "I'm fine, too, by the way."

"So are we…" said Streak, his voice firm. "Continue digging…"

I lifted my hand, but Streak took it. "Let me do this for now… We need to talk."

His hand reached for his NetPulse, and he resumed the work, only this time, the residue left his silver imprint on the rocks.

We drifted ahead. "Why did you do it?" Streakinsisted again, his voice filled with sadness.

The rock receded, and in place, the tunnel deepened. It was monotonous work, pushing the mass ahead. Little ridges appeared between the rings. The sediment almost looked like stars in the night sky. But, there was no such thing where we stood. Only a mass so thick that it made our breathing difficult.

Streak never gave up when he pursued a specific aim. He would keep on asking until he felt satisfied. It was this unrelenting focus that drove me crazy about him. He was relentless.

I shrugged, "I couldn't let him go. You of all people should have understood this."

"You could have told me. I'm not so stubborn that I would have hindered your plans."

"But you wouldn't listen, and you seemed so insistent about the Council's edict, I couldn't risk it." My voice sounded cold, even to my ears. I was tired, tired of this game that trapped us within something that never manifested.

He rolled his eyes and met my gaze. "Tesh, how long have we been… Best friends?"

"Is that what we call it these days?" I couldn't help the sarcasm.

Streak flinched under the tone.

Feeling a hint of regret, I sighed and whispered gently, "Since we were kids at the Institute."

"Do you think I would put others before your welfare? I follow the rules, but not to the detriment of my friends. You should have trusted me." Streak's gaze, full of unspoken feelings, looked away.

It was a first. Streak never let me be this close to him before, not in that way.

I paused. "I'm sorry. It's just, this thing the Council did, it made me angry, and if they can do this with no one rebelling...."

He offered, "I had nothing to do with that."

I winced. I disliked calling Streak on it. "You're a huge supporter of them... Besides, you knew."

He studied my face, unimpressed by what I had just said. "That again? Okay, so tell me what you think I knew?"

"About the inequities of the program...." The knowledge ate away at me. Frustration and anger drove many of my actions.

I needed to reign that in somehow. I felt betrayed by the people who led us down a road we should never have taken. "We should have fought against it. We did nothing because we were gullible."

He shrugged.

I met his annoyed expression, waiting.

He dropped, "I'm not blind. The system was not perfect, but there was nothing any of us could do. I knew that much... Except for your parents. And I'm so sorry for that," Streak said.

I murmured, "It was long ago, and your friendship, all of your friendships, helped. But they could have built the ships in time." My voice sounded desperate.

The EmVat kept us from the closeness we used to have when we stood near each other, but they were our lifelines.

Watching me with understanding through the NetAirvie, he asked, "What do you think we could have done to change the course?"

"I don't know... Fight the decision. Make it public knowledge. You said nothing." The system structured in a way where the leaders kept the entire picture to themselves fooled us. They disseminated information only when they judged it appropriate.

Streak, practical as always, murmured. "What would be the point of letting others know? No one could have changed the outcome. It would have been anarchy."

"We should have tried, Streak. We had time…."

"Not enough to make a difference."

Irritated, I raised my hand and began to weave my NetPulse. He stopped his efforts and waited. But I let my ire pulverize the rock ahead, determined to shake the anger. In so doing, I almost wished the Great Council was in front of me. So, I shook my head because I couldn't go there.

"That's where we differ," I said over the noise I made.

The low hum made by Streak earlier had turned to a higher pitch because of the intensity I put into my work. "I will not follow the old rules here, Streak. And I need to know you forgive me. But I want to believe that you're willing to trust me, trust us. That we can choose how we act from now on and make our own choices together." My eyes never left his face as I uttered these words, knowing that this called for Streak to let go of old norms and that this wouldn't be easy for him.

He searched my eyes to determine how far I would take this. "What about our way of life, what we learned? You can't disregard everything."

The same noise we heard a little while ago echoed inside the tunnel, only this time way closer.

I stopped my NetPulse.

The sound reverberated with high notes that hurt my ears. It ground my nerves. It subsided to give way to a huge thump. The ground shook again, and this time my hand reached for the wall behind me, for the trembling grew louder with each passing second.

Streak wavered on his feet.

Fragments of rock dropped, blocking the way ahead.

It was an area that I had not NetPulsed yet. Our technology had not altered the wall density, rendering its composition stronger and better to help withstand the Earthquake.

Leane's voice came over the NetComm, reaching all of us at once. "Are you guys all right? This thing is acting up again."

"Yeah... DarNet... Hold on," Blast said, "It's shaking more than before."

Streak looked back toward our doorway. He issued an order in my direction. "Stay here."

"What??"

His reflex took me by surprise, and I turned to watch him while fighting to stay up.

He lifted on his NetJet Boots one foot over the packed dirt, flying back toward our compartment.

A glow in the darkness shimmered, moving fast.

In an instant, it vanished.

I followed his example and hovered in place in my NetJet Boots, unsure of what I had seen. "Streak, what was that?" I yelled.

"I don't know," Streak said over the NetComm.

Blast voice resonated, "What? What did you see?"

"Not sure... Leane, are you okay?"

"Yes... Just shaking a lot here."

A light shifted in the bleak density of the passageway. It reflected near our door, vibrating in place, cutting through the environment of the dark tunnels.

"What is going on?" This time Blast sounded anxious.

Streak rushed ahead to protect our compartment.

I ignited the module of my NetJet boots for hypersonic propulsion. I shot out ahead, moving fast now, eager to join him.

Our door to the chamber had remained opened. Our Android Cygil 1001, clearing the fragments blocking the enclosure mechanism, flew several paces back, knocked down by an unexpected force field.

By the time Streak reached the area, the vortex had vanished.

I glided toward him. "Are you all right?"

"Yes… It didn't hit me."

We both checked the area and the entryway to our compartment. Nothing appeared disturbed inside our chamber.

I kneeled beside the Cygil. Our Android required a change for its circuitry and appeared to have overloaded when it got hit. At the moment, he was dead weight. "You want to call Blast back? He can fix it in a few seconds."

Streak shook his head. "No, I want us to get out of here and find out where in the HellNet we are, and what is this thing?" Let's put Cygil inside for now and close the chamber."

"I agree; I don't have a good feeling about this. The sooner we get out, the better." I nodded toward where the light had appeared. "What do you think it was?"

"I do not understand, but it's nothing we know. Nothing we have in Ang. Be careful as you move ahead in there." He gestured toward the other end of the tunnel.

"Streak… before we go… I need to show you something."

I was about to share something personal. The feed DAINN had downloaded when I went under cryo. I took Streak's hand and held it. "Look." I was glad he saw this with me.

I opened my PVZ, and it moved in front of us. DAINN's face appeared on the screen. It was the face it bore when he spoke to me in Ang. The same look he wore when he announced something of importance to the city at large. "I wasn't forthcoming with your parents. I couldn't then, but you're strong now and know the truth." DAINN's voice danced in my head, his word forming a ring squeezing my throat.

DAINN continued without a break. "The game you and your parents played each night in the living room developed a certain acuteness of thought, instilled a sharpness of mind, gave you a balanced perspective, and imparted wisdom… You remember that game?" His voice relentlessly resonated in my mind while the cold fingers of fear closed around my heart. "Instead of accepting an imperfect system, you chose not to remain blind. The rules of your game were simple, were they not?"

"Yes," my voice came out as a croak… But DAINN never heard my answer this time.

"Each of you selected a situation and called the characters for a part to play. You took turns assigning the options and features, even the tools to use. You became as much a participant as a judge in ruling on the outcome as your parents did. And that made it fun…" he added, recalling the data and showing me a video clip of my parents and me in our living room.

"We were in privacy mode... How would anyone know that?" I whispered to no one in particular.

"I know that you thought you were in privacy mode, but Sloan Roden Baker watched you at all times. A certain Council member implanted cameras. He didn't trust your parents."

Comprehension hit Streak, who murmured, "Net Bastard... No wonder you came to distrust everyone. So, this was how they knew. It was how they determined your parents were a threat."

I nodded. "DAINN knew this and did nothing to alert us," I murmured.

DAINN continued as if he had heard what I said. "It was not of my purview to interfere, Tesh. I am a programmed A.I. with a lot of independence, but I am not impervious to certain protocols. These intend to change my programming behavior or inclinations. They are deemed, by the Council, a precaution."

My eyes opened wide in surprise. I looked at Streak. "How far do they intervene in DAINN's programming; do you think?"

Streak frowned. "I don't know."

"I was not required to advise you of this due to your security level. However, now it is another matter altogether. President Langden asked that I provide you full disclosure, and I have now done so. He wanted to speak to you regarding information affecting your mission...."

The image shifted to President Langden. He stood in front of his desk in the Tower office, with the EHAF logo prominently featured on the wall. We recognized Ang immediately. It was the same he used to deliver Official Announcements.

The intake of breath by my side reminded me that Streak was there beside me, and I felt better. Despite our opinion differences, I trusted him.

"Hello, Tesh. I hope that you have awakened with your team. I also hope that one day, we will all be reunited in our world. What I am about to tell you will not be easy for you to hear. But you must know it as your mission's success may depend on that knowledge. The work you are about to undertake will certainly be affected by it. This information came to Commander North's attention after he met you and decided to investigate your case. We both regret that we didn't come to this knowledge sooner. Your parents were under constant surveillance. But Sloan Roden Baker is not the only one on the Council manipulating DAINN's programming for ulterior motives. Over the last few months, we have concluded that five members of the Great Council are working in concert with him. We have identified three of them, and they are under current investigation while we look for the remaining two. We are building our case against the three we suspect. These five members appeared to have altered and manipulated DAINN for their purpose. They planted accomplices within Origin to serve their agenda. We have yet to understand what that mandate demands. I can, therefore, only warn you of these facts. They have infiltrated three of the Conclaves. We suspect the Company, the Faculty, and the SRC. So, be careful of the allegiance proclaimed by these Conclaves. You can rely on the EHAF members, who were all chosen by Commander North. They know of this and will help you. North wanted me to tell you he believes in you, and so do I. Good luck, Tesh."

Streak turned to me. "How long have you known about this?"

"DAINN gave me these files just as I went under."

"You didn't share these with Leane and Blast. Why?"

"You believe I do not trust you, Streak, but I do… I am sharing this with you and why I will share it with Leane and Blast. Only, Leane has good friends within the Faculty conclave."

"… And Blast has good friends within the Company Conclave. While I am without friends."

I nodded. "You're a loner… I trust them both… They need to know this at the proper time."

"I agree, but I understand that we have to be careful."

Including Streak in the decision felt good. I was no longer alone in determining the moment to deliver this to our friends. "When do you want to tell them?"

Streak looked around the place and said, "As soon as we find the way out."

I sighed… Not everyone within our System was rotten, but now I knew for sure that a few were at fault in my parents' deaths. Only, we had to contend with new parties that may have ulterior motives in coming here. We needed to find out what their orders were and from whom?

Streak looked Netpissed and disgusted with himself. "I wish that I had been there for you."

"No, don't. You, and Leane, and Blast kept me sane. Although I need you to promise me…."

I challenged him. "The old rules are a good framework, but we need to adapt. I will only use my powers to safeguard us as a last resort, and you must be all right with that. We should decide things together, discuss them, and act. I do not wish to dictate what our conclave does. There are only four of us. We should do this as a team."

He returned the gauntlet. "What happens when we disagree? You still have to cut the tie."

Unwilling to compromise on the other stuff, I insisted. "Fine, after we run through all options. We are in this together."

He nodded and smiled, a little crooked smile that only appeared when he tried to feel better about things. "I don't know how this will work out, but I'm willing to try. Tesh… You know you're important to me. To all of us."

Streak, the cold, aloof, reserved guy, held out his hand.

I took it. Through the protective skin of the EmVat, Streak's fingers felt strong against my palm.

Streak never demonstrated emotions before. "I'm glad you have Mage."

My smile wavered, "There's something that bothers me, though… There are no traces of the other chambers."

Streak nodded. "I noticed that too."

I turned our PVZ on and reached out to Leane and Blast. "Have you seen indications of the other compartments?"

Leane's voice answered first. "No."

Blast came next. "Nothing yet."

"Nothing on my side either," I said.

"I'm still near the chamber clearing the debris, and there's nothing around here either," added Streak.

"Keep going until you find the way out," I said.

I smiled. There was no longer a place for mistrust. In this, they united us. It reminded me of us like we used to be, in the old days, in a time far gone now.

Dominique Luchart

14
ATTACK
Gen

MIT, Massachusetts - 2018

Gen Aubrey becomes a valuable asset by circumstances. She is not meant to become part of the System until her curiosity dictates it. Her quest entraps her. Her nature allows her to adapt. The transition she faces makes it difficult to elicit trust. DAINN Annals – Summer 2018.

The campus tonight remained animated with groups of students who had turned in their exams. Most of us were in our last week, with graduation right around the corner.

I skated my last test in record time and stepped out of the classroom, eager to know what Jonas had found since I left him. The nagging feeling I tried so hard to ignore returned tenfold. It had persisted despite my attempts to categorize. Our investigation caused me anxiety. My stomach churned at the thought of what it might unleash. It wasn't one of my brightest ideas.

I retrieved my cell from my pocket and dialed Jonas. The phone rang, and I got his recording message, "Hey, you know what to do."

"Jonas, it is me, Gen. Ring me."

Remembering the times when my instinct had proven me right despite my dismissing it, I fidgeted. I braced myself for the other shoe to drop. It was a case of "Deja vu." I accepted that. Experience spoke volumes, and I no longer could discount it. In my mind, that notion of dread possessed all the criteria for something significant. And it did… *Great. Now I am a freak.*

I never heard from Jonas.

The evening settled around me as I walked the grounds. I witnessed the area deserted when I crossed the campus to the cafeteria building to grab something to eat. Rather than remain by myself in the vast room, I picked up a salad and headed to my dorm.

Most students were gathered at the pub by now.

My cell rang, and I answered, expecting Jonas, but I heard my father on the line.

"Dad? Is everything all right?"

"I'm calling to ask you that question. How are things going?"

"Good… I just finished my last test. My time in college is over. I have interviews coming up and graduation after that; then I'll come home to see you. Did you forget?"

"No. Just very sorry I'll miss your graduation. Your mother would be so proud of you."

"I know, Dad. I know you have to be with uncle Jess at the moment. How is he doing?"

"Hanging on by a thread. The doctor says it shouldn't be long now."

"I'm sorry… Give uncle Jess my love. But don't worry, it's just a ceremony, and I'll miss you too and see you soon after that."

"Get some pictures, will you? I'll be thinking of you."

"For sure…"

"I'll let you go for now… See you soon. Love you, Gen."

"Love you, Dad."

He hung up. His voice, filled with emotion, had wavered when he mentioned my mother. I shook myself to avoid breaking down used to it by now. My dad never recovered from mom, and he never would. He tried to be upbeat. He attempted to do the little things that she used to execute with so much enthusiasm that it made us laugh, but his broken heart was not in it. My mother took with her his reason to be. One year ago, four days from now, to be exact. Without it, he carried on the best way he knew how. I guessed we all felt the same.

I remembered the last time I saw her standing in the doorway of my bedroom. She smiled at me as she passed before getting to the stairs on her way to the store. She was going out.

Engrossed in my interests, I didn't volunteer to go with her. I remained on my bed, reading some stupid post on the internet while my mother vanished. Heartbreaking.

The various scenarios about what happened that night played in my mind. Was she knocked unconscious or struggle and suffer? Was she dead or held in some basement somewhere by a lunatic? None of these offered any solace. These thoughts represented the best form of torture I could inflict upon myself. I can't move on. I have to find out.

With graduation, I was now free. Free to choose my way into the world. Free to pursue an investigation that so far had led nowhere. Free… Really? Not so much. Why am I kidding myself?

My building loomed ahead. I walked up the steps to the main door of the residence and hurried to the staircase. The corridor, empty, except for two girls giggling as they passed by me, felt like home now. It would, just as I was about to depart for my new life.

The year had ended. Everyone was giddy these days.

I smiled back at the two students and headed to the next level. My feet carried me back to my dorm without giving much thought to my direction. The good old autopilot kicked in when I needed it. I passed the landing, moving up the stairs to the third floor.

But I noticed that the area, now devoid of students, looked sad as if it had lost its purpose.

And I skidded to a sudden halt in front of my door. The wooden panel was ajar, opened by a few inches when it should have been closed. I faced the doorway, recalling my actions that morning. I didn't leave the door unlocked. Sure of that fact, my heart skipped a beat and pounded faster in my chest. Even a kickass geek would hesitate. My blood rushed through my ears as I glanced around, delaying going inside. *Walk away.* I stood alone in the corridor, surveying the panel and listening beyond it. No. *You can't just walk away.* My eyes, intense on the wooden texture, searched for signs of life past it. I heard nothing.

I pushed it open.

One look. Inside the room, nothing moved.

I entered, ready to spring away at the first signs of life.

The door slammed behind me, and I went flying against the wall. *Shit. Figures.* Going in was a stupid thing to do. My backpack dropped to the floor.

A forearm squeezed my throat as one of my arms twisted in a tight grip behind my back.

He shoved me hard into the wall. The weight of the man leaning against my body immobilized me. A breath brushed my ear, and a threatening voice whispered, "Where is your copy?"

Add a dose of terror to my life, and I lose rationality. It was one way to shut me up. Nothing came to mind as a response. Blank.

The voice insisted, "Answer me."

Insufferable bully. My right cheek throbbed from the blow against the wall. Fear seized me, and I went crazy. "Don't you have someone else to rough up?" I scoffed.

I checked the ground to find the bag.

My Taser was inside. I needed to reach it…

Whatever the man was doing in here, he searched for something. With the door locked behind me and the assailant pressed against me, I had nowhere to turn for help.

"I'm not playing here."

The past just entered my room. The uneasy knot in the pit of my stomach grew to a deep dark panic. *Just freaking wonderful.*

My voice came out raspy, "What are you talking about?"

"Don't play dumb. Give me your copy."

"I don't know what you want."

I pushed him away from me, attempting to get out of his grasp. It didn't work.

His grip on me only tightened.

I almost choked. I needed another tactic. *Think!*

I fought one of his hands off me and elbowed him. I hit something, but it didn't make a dent. He barely noticed.

"Don't move." A hard hand came around the back of my neck, keeping me planted against the wall. The body of the intruder pressed harder against my own as his other hand roamed over my body, searching me. His hand lingered against the side of my breast a little too long.

I wanted to hurl. My breath caught in my throat, and I tried to push the guy away. I had seen many fighting movies. Why couldn't I remember one move, just one that I could carry out and fight him off? *Think, damn it!*

"Hold still."

I had boots on. It could come in handy. I looked down, lifted my leg, and stepped on the guy's left foot, hard.

He howled and dropped his tight hold. I took advantage of it and pushed him away from me.

He released his hold.

In that split second, I saw his eyes.

The instant froze between us.

I lunged to the ground, reaching for the bag.

Wrong move.

I landed on my stomach.

He was on me by the time I took the next breath, cursing. "Damnit." He crammed my head hard to the ground.

I tried to move away from him, sliding on the floor. My hand grasped for the bag.

He pulled my hair.

I screamed…

His hand came down on my mouth. "Damn, you stupid girl."

I bit his palm.

His fist hit the side of my face. "Look at what you would have me do."

I saw stars... I went limp for a brief instant, but it was enough.

He turned me over.

I kicked and bucked, trying to fight him off.

He was on top of me now. His face, inches away from mine.

No fear in those eyes... Only cold determination. I didn't want to look at this man.

Random thoughts went through my head. My father had caught me. He made me promise to stop the search and pushed me to return to MIT. From mathematics and engineering, I dove into computer sciences. Look at me now.

I tried to wiggle out of his grip. You can't budge a truck, and that's what he appeared to be - strong, muscular, all weight, no brains. One hand inside the bag, I searched for my Taser.

"Damn it, I don't want to hurt you, but I will if you give me a reason to...." His hand resumed the search, taking pleasure in lingering in places that made my blood boil.

I quipped, not backing down. "You degenerate, filthy perv."

When my dad requested that I stop searching, it had seemed odd, odd that he didn't want to know, strange that he preferred to wait for the police to find out, surprising that he gave up. Still, I stopped... At least I did in front of him. I never told him I searched for answers all on my own. The confrontation now gave me pause, on top of the fact that answers still avoided me months later. I wonder if I should not have listened to him. My dad had wanted me to get on with my life, even if my mom's disappearance shattered our existence. Instead, here I was... Facing this new nightmare.

I closed my eyes. The horror was here all over again.

My assailant's hand followed along my hips, tightening against my butt.

"Nice ass." A chuckle came out of his mouth. "Can't blame a guy."

I rocked to the side to dislodge his weight. The feel of his body on mine gave me shudders while the floor of my dorm, cold and hard under me, induced bruises with every move I made. I didn't care. I wanted him off me. "Let me go!"

"Listen up." As he said the words, his breath blew against my neck. "I could do much more to you. So, give me the codes, and I'll go."

My fingers searched and closed on the Taser.

As if to prove his point, his right hand moved under my shirt and began descending my stomach.

His crooked smile sent a shiver down my spine. Until now, it wasn't personal. But the atmosphere shifted between us.

I felt it. As the guy's hand stroked my skin, it became more. There was lust in his eyes.

I went ape-shit. My hand shook as it held the Taser.

He scared the piss out of me.

I elbowed him and kicked, but it didn't even phase him. It was like hitting a brick wall.

I struggled under his weight, trying to dislodge him. But I couldn't budge him. My hand holding the Taser moved to his side.

His hand grabbed my wrist, squeezing. "All that fiery hotness..." he murmured, tightening his hold until I could no longer stand the pain.

I let go, trying to get away from him.

He laughed, finding pleasure in my movements. "Keep at it."

Point taken. As soon as I realized his meaning, I stopped fidgeting. My mind screamed. I shouted, "My backpack, inside pocket."

"It's not so difficult, now is it? I will release you. Don't yell or move a muscle. Stay put until I close the door. Otherwise, I'll do much worse, I promise you." His hand drifted further down to the top of my panty and rested on my skin. "Do I make myself clear?"

I nodded and squeaked, "Yes."

Got it; you need not draw me a picture, asshole.

"Good. So, it's up to you," the ape murmured against my ear lobe, pulling away from me, leaving behind a cold drift.

I closed my eyes, fighting off tears.

He picked up the pack.

I crawled away from him as soon as he laid his hand on it.

"See… It wasn't so hard." I heard the zipper of my bag open.

I couldn't stand it.

His hand rummaged through the inside pocket.

My head pounded. My emotions skyrocketing, I wanted to pounce on him, but I didn't dare.

"I'll be taking this device with me now." A mocking chuckle followed. And the door close.

He was gone.

I didn't move at first. I couldn't. But then, I got to my feet and leaned against the wall. I held onto it in a death grip; my fingers froze on the plaster.

What now? Are you going to be a victim?

The emptiness of the room haunted me now. I fixed the door, unable to stop the tears running down my face. Two choices lay ahead of me. *Victim or fighter?*

My brothers took it hard and left. They avoided the reality of it altogether, never coming home to face a house empty of her presence. Still, their absence at family functions caused a rift among us, and that existed even now. They broke up the rest of our family. They couldn't face it, so they ran, each in their way.

Selfish bastards.

My father and I stayed. We stood our ground and faced it. It hurt like hell, and we took it. We battled through all of it, but we were left bloodless by it, but we never gave up.

I lunged myself away from the wall and reached for the door. I hit the panel with my fist. The skin on my knuckles broke. Some blood splattered on the white surface. It hurt, but I didn't care. I know.

My dad stoically handled the whole thing on his own once I returned to college. He confronted an empty house every day. He existed for months in a daze, and it tore away at what was left of my heart. *Fight. Fight again.*

I wouldn't face an empty room and wanted my codes back. So, I looked for the Taser. It lay on the floor where I was minutes ago. I picked it up.

Taser in hand, ready to strike, I ran after the intruder. I was on a rage roll.

The corridor stood empty in front of me.

Loathing my weakness, I raced ahead. I resented myself just as much as the guy who had inflicted this experience on me. I was too weak to put up a fight.

Frightened ninny.

I got lucky. I was intact, except for a few bruises. But one should never find themselves in that circumstance. No one had the right to subdue another human being like that. I sneered. *Do something about it. Don't just take it.*

The encounter came too close for comfort. My mother faced the same situation. I would make this a priority, so it never happened again. Me, being helpless. *Absolutely.*

How did they find out about the codes so fast? How did they find me?

It was unlikely that in the space of six hours, they had tracked Jonas or me down. Was it even possible to execute something like this that fast?

I reached the staircase in no time. I jumped the steps to the next landing. Running, I went through the next level.

There was no one in sight. I turned and reached the second floor.

The building was still devoid of life. *Where did he go?*

I ran faster. Breathing hard, I got to the next level. Once on the ground floor, I rushed across the lobby. Still, no one…

I flew through the door.

A car, moving fast, traveled across the front of my building.

My momentum carried me off the sidewalk and onto the street. Headlights came right at me.

15
WATCH
Chase

Harvard, Massachusetts - 2018

The pieces of the puzzle come together in terms of Chase Davenport much later. His role in the way the Center got started is prominent, but his allegiance to its purpose and the events that unfold after remains somewhat obscure. DAINN Annals – Summer 2018.

I landed at JFK and made it back to my dorm at Harvard in the company of Sean. Confusing thoughts about Jonathan and the Center found their way into the tumult of my mind, which kept drifting back to what happened on the plane.

The death of Harriet seemed an acceptable loss to everyone but me. It appeared an expected casualty by them, in a game that I suddenly no longer understood.

The playground changed entirely during our trip.

Our latest discovery caused Jonathan to go further than even I thought he would. My experience with the Center went sideways, and this feeling of becoming a pawn in someone else's game prompted me to act.

"Who was it that Steven called before we left the field?"

Sean glanced my way. "One of Steven's men."

"Why?"

Sean shrugged. "Ask him that."

My waiting no longer made sense.

After landing, Steven took over the next leg of the trip and flew the helicopter to the Center with the scientists' group instead of Sean. It was a first in all of our trips. And so, I sat beside Sean, driving to Harvard.

Something was off with the entire affair. The questions lurked in my head during the whole trip.

Sean refused to talk about his assignment. The silence between us made for an uncomfortable drive. I insisted, "You know that Jonathan asked me to look into the situation, right?"

"Yes... And you will."

His answer cut through any other thoughts and had me pissed. "Damn it, Sean, open your mouth and tell me what's going on."

Sean sighed. "We're paying someone off."

"At MIT?"

Sean nodded. The car, under Sean's exasperated foot, sped up. The turn around the bend on the road slid me into the door. Sean didn't lighten up. He was showing his impatience with me.

I didn't care. I wanted to understand what this whole thing was about, no longer trusting the secrets. Remaining in the dark made little sense anymore. As we made the distance, I had only one choice. "I'm going with you."

Things were odd and messy. I had to see things for myself.

We reached the Harvard campus's edge, and Sean continued fast to MIT, as his face speaks volumes. "It's not your place. You watch for the girl. I'll take care of the guy."

"Not going to happen, Sean."

The MIT Campus now spread all around us, and Sean slowed down.

Within minutes, he pulled at the curb in front of a brick building. "I'm going in. You wait here."

I stuck with him driving, and by the time we stopped in front of our destination, I was ready to jump out of the car, and I did. "I don't want any bad surprises."

Sean moved around the vehicle and leaned into me. "This is where you wait." His face, tense, he added, "I've got it, Chase. I'm taking care of this. Trust me."

I opened my mouth to utter my disagreement, but he was already several feet away.

The guy didn't waste any time and ran to the front door. "Don't worry, no harm will come to him," he clipped before he disappeared inside.

I remained standing by the car with nowhere to go. Damn. I thought I was fast. He was faster.

My determination, since I learned about the hackers, rendered me obsessive. They had found out about the disappearances of the scientists. My desire to avoid any problems had landed me here, in front of this building. The Center wanted to pay them off. What if that didn't work?

It didn't take long to grasp that both required careful handling. The Center couldn't get on the world's radar. We had to remain inexistent. In truth, I was worried about our approach not working.

Fine. I'll wait it out.

Ten minutes passed.

So long as I saw the guy come out of his own volition, I didn't care to get any more involved than I already was.

Twenty minutes passed. Nothing happened.

I thought about the hackers and how I knew nothing about hackers. Hacker land came to mind when I looked around at the extensive grounds. I picked up my cell and made a call. "Hey, Rich…" Rich was a good friend of mine and super connected across campus. He dabbled in all kinds of things.

The voice of my friend resonated in my ear. "Hey, man… How was the world tour?"

"Good. Listen… What can you tell me about an MIT grad named Jonas? I don't have his last name."

There was a laugh on the other end of the line. "Hmm, that's an odd ask. Can you narrow it down for me?"

Tense, I clipped back, "Not by much, Rich. He seems a super hacker or something, and I want to know what you know…"

Rich's tone got serious. "Huh… I heard about him… Don't mess with him. He did some heavy shit."

"Hell, man, I'm not planning to…"

"Hackers don't think like normal people… They love messing things up. They don't take too well to a challenge."

Do you know anything about a girl named Gen Aubrey?"

"Nah… Afraid I can't be much help on this."

"It's okay, Rich."

"What is going on? You're in trouble or something?"

"No, just checking some stuff."

"Okay… If you say so."

"Thanks, man."

Thirty minutes. Nothing.

Sean had been gone for a while now, and I began to worry. I started pacing back and forth on the three-foot-wide path. It spread ahead with a few trees on either side. The lamppost near the entrance provided plenty of light on the few steps leading up to the main doors.

I debated going in.

The doubts, creeping up in my head about the role of the Center, nagged me. Nothing I was doing this night allowed me to escape them. Each step we took confirmed that we had embarked on the road leading to a dark ending. I contemplated our demise when Sean came out of the building, as he said he would, with a guy in tow.

He nodded at me. "Let's go. I'll drop you on the way."

Sean opened the back door, waiting for Jonas to get in. "We need to get to the airport before your plane leaves. I'll drop you off, and by tomorrow you can start your vacation."

"Hey, man… I get it you want me to go, but don't push it."

"You agreed to leave, and we agreed to pay you a generous settlement. Anyway, you have enough credits to get your degree and receive your diploma in the mail."

"This sucks big time, man. I've got friends. People I need to get back to on stuff, you know?"

"Jonas, I don't fucking care. You're getting on a plane tonight one way or another. We've given you a bunch of money, and that's the deal. If you want to renege on our deal, there will be repercussions, and trust me, you won't like it."

Jonas stood by the car, still hesitant about getting in. "Haw... Man, it's harsh."

Sean went to the trunk and dropped a suitcase in it. He then moved around the car and opened the door of the vehicle. "Get in."

"Shit. It isn't right."

"You want the money or not?"

"Hah... Sure. You bought me, haven't you."

"Then get in the damn car. I don't have all night."

Jonas slid on the back seat of the vehicle.

I slipped into the front beside Sean.

"Ouch... My friend will have my head now. Hell, she's my best friend around here. You sure I can't tell her anything?"

Sean started the engine in a clipped tone and answered, "Gen Aubrey is not your concern anymore."

"Hey, who's this guy?"

I turned to face him. "Hey, Jonas... I'm Chase. I'm on the campus too."

"I haven't seen you before."

"Harvard..."

"Not my fav."

I laughed. "Well, we all have our crosses to bear, right?"

"If you say so."

"Look, I'm on my way to see Gen. Is there something you want me to tell her?"

"I don't know you, man...."

"I get it... But this way, you wouldn't leave without saying something to her. You know."

"Nah, man... I can't do it. I don't trust you... Nor him."

"Yeah, well, I suspected that much. It was worth a try, though."

Sean wore his expression, "I told you so."

I shrugged and faced the front. "Drop me off."

Sean nodded and tapped the steering wheel. "You could already be there..."

Jonas reached forward. "You guys better treat her well... If I hear anything, anything at all, I'll make sure there is a whole lot of things out there that you don't want to have come out..." he added, muttering now from the back seat.

Sean, looking in the rearview mirror at Jonas, snapped, "Don't make threats you can't back up."

Jonas's sour expression challenged Sean. "I never do."

Thinking things didn't need to escalate, I said, "Man, I know you don't know me... But, nothing bad will happen to Gen from any of us."

Sean drove the car fast. "I don't like threats...."

I stepped in... "Jonas just told us what he wanted, that's all... And I think we can make sure he gets it." I looked at the slight guy in the back seat and nodded.

He didn't say a word and just stared ahead.

I turned around... Rick was right. These guys had nothing in common with me or someone like Sean. I wondered how much we paid him to get Jonas to agree to leave in the dead of night. And before graduation to boot. I would find out later. Still, none of this felt right, and I was in the thick of it.

Well, if this doesn't beat it all. My suspicions had increased to an uncomfortable level, and I got more questions than answers.

Sean slowed the car down in front of another building. We stopped just as a guy ran across the street in front of us.

It was my destination.

Sean stopped the car just as I reached for the door handle. "I'll see you later then."

He nodded.

I opened the door and stepped out.

"Hey... Chase, that's your name, right?" Jonas reached out to the front of the car.

"Yeah."

"This is Gen's building... You will see her?"

"I told you I was..."

Jonas looked at Sean and me again. He hesitated, "Can you tell her I'm downstairs? I would like to see her."

Sean shook his head. "Sorry, mate, you'll miss your flight. We're late as it is...."

Jonas nodded, "Ok, then... Chase, you tell her... I'm sorry... Nah... nothing." His eyes met mine, and he shrugged.

I nodded and closed the door behind me. Remorse... I saw guilt in Jonas' eyes.

I stepped on the sidewalk and walked toward Gen Aubrey's dorm. I opened my phone and looked at the student directory online. Gen's profile appeared on the screen as an MIT student with two degrees, computer science and applied mathematics. She was a brain, all right. My phone delivered her picture. She was pretty — a little young by the looks of it. Whatever connection existed between her and the Center and the missing scientists, I needed to find out. Getting close to her couldn't be too difficult.

The question remained… How do I approach the girl? The situation proved to be more complicated than I expected, for here I was, about to enter Gen's dorm, a building that was quiet with no clues what I would tell her once I stood in front of her. *Shit.*

I went through the doors and into the lobby. I passed the threshold when a young girl ran into me.

We stumbled.

I hit the wall.

She fell back on her butt, and a small object slid across the floor.

"Sorry, are you all right?"

She glanced around the landing, not bothering to look at me or stop. Instead, she hurried across the old tiles and grabbed the small device. Her hand locked on it.

I saw her face.

She got up and ran past me.

Her hair fell sideways, and her face smeared with tears, surprised the hell out of me.

The girl looked like Gen.

Her behavior betrayed urgency. It took me a moment to put the pieces together. Shit… *What has just happened?*

I saw a glimpse at her face in the glass window of the front door, and it registered in my mind, prompting me into action. She looked angry… "Hey… Wait up."

She never even turned back. Instead, she kept going. The door opened and closed on her.

I reached for it. Something wasn't right.

I stepped outside and stopped at the top of the stairs, just in time to see Gen reach the sidewalk.

The headlights of an oncoming car shone in the night.

Gen was about to reach the curb and step onto the road.

A vehicle came at her fast, too fast.

One thought came… Gen was about to get run over.

The driver didn't slow. In the back of my mind, I noticed that he looked older than most students. The guy didn't belong. Damn.

I jumped the steps to the curb.

Without hesitation, I lunged.

16
TUMULT
Tesh

Deep Inside The Earth - 2018

The energy source inside the tunnel subsides as fast as it appears. It is nothing known to the Roamers and causes them to question what they face inside the mountain as the rock formation trembles around them. DAINN Annals – Summer 2018.

We dropped Cygil inside the chamber and began clearing the rocks that fell earlier and blocked the door. Without Cygil, it would take longer, but we decided not to recall Leane and Blast. Too much was at stake in finding the exit.

Streak and I worried that we were in over our heads, but neither would voice it.

My hand called for the UniWrap to shift around my wrist. A gentle undulating wave emerged, reaching out to the rock. It lifted from the ground hovering in the air about three feet high. With the flick of my hand, I sent it across the threshold of our chamber and into the corridor. I repeated the process on the other pieces. The work was mindless, and I recalled the feeling experienced in the pod.

An intense emotion pierced the Earth's density and reached me into the chamber buried deep underground. This person I sensed earlier and whose mind reached out to me through the stone, screaming for help during his fall, remained somewhere nearby within these walls. I kept hearing the echo of his voice.

Finding him couldn't be too difficult. I possessed the way into his mind. *How did that happen?*

DAINN... It must be DAINN reaching out to him, helping him survive the fall, but it happened before I awoke... DAINN intervened while I slept. How long ago did that happen? Was it even a recent occurrence? I didn't know.

Was he part of what we experienced now with the shift of the Earth? Once I found him, would we face him as a friend, or would he become a foe? If he became a threat, it would force me to control him. I didn't want it to come to that. I refused to operate here, as I had in Ang.

I reached out with my mind. The link created during Chase's fall between us opened, one he did not understand about yet, and one I debated using. I thought of DAINN and his programming, which represented the only explanation for his intervention without my knowing or approving of it. He had needed me for no one other than myself could perform such a task. Only DAINN could, using my skills. *Finding a stranger could prove helpful.*

I looked at Streak, standing a few feet away from me, clearing the debris in the same way, and said, "Streak, DAINN intervened to save someone while we were in the void... I think he might still be around. I can't quite make up the pieces of what happened yet."

Streak stopped his work and looked around, quizzical. "In here?"

I nodded. "Somewhere close…"

"Do you believe it connects him to this thing?"

"I'm not sure… My mind is still muddled. But I will know the guy when I see him."

"Hmm… This connection you have to this, huh, person, DAINN created that?"

I nodded again.

"I don't like this. It could be dangerous."

Streak picked up another cluster of rocks.

The weight he carried with his UniWrap would be too much for me, but not for him. Streak's body was muscular. His powerful energy reached outwards, sending waves towards me and making me shiver.

I smiled. "DAINN wouldn't put me in harm's way."

Sending the new load at the end of his hand against the corridor's wall, he turned to me.

"D doesn't know where we are or what is going on around here."

I laughed then. "I'm not worried… DAINN would never endanger us. It's good to hear you do not like it, though," I said, teasing.

Streak stopped his energy wave and closed the door to ensure that the mechanism functioned despite the quake. The panel slid in place without noise.

He came back towards me, searching for words. His face tense, he took another step in my direction, struggling with himself. "I've always wanted to do this." He leaned into me and pulled me in his arms. *SoulLife, Tesh... Forever.*

Streak allowed himself to say this in his mind, and it resonated in mine. This unspoken statement now lay between us. It held all the love and loyalty I could aspire to in a lifetime. I knew then how much I had hurt him when I didn't confide in him.

Hugging him back and holding on, tears filled my eyes. "I've wanted this for so long." *I'm sorry I didn't tell you.*

You are so beautiful... You Brainiac girl... With your dark hair and your changing eyes.

Surprised, I pulled back, but Streak's arms tightened around me. *No, don't. Let me hold you for a moment.*

You can hold me for more than just a moment, Streak.

You're the head of our Conclave.

So?

It isn't something we see often. There are rules.

We are no longer under the GG. We can do what we want and make up our own rules here.

I sensed Streak's body against mine and felt it tremble. He fought himself, and I dared not move. What if, for once, he won and let his wants dictate his conduct? He had always been so restrained around me.

Streak looked into my eyes.

We could be more than just friends. I wanted to touch him, eager to feel his hands on me. Unable to wait any longer, I had to know. *Streak, kiss me.*

I want to...

Do it, please.

I felt Streak's arms release me, and his hands reached my face as my EmVat protective barrier gave way to his signal, forming a larger field around both of us. His eyes, hungry for me, gazed at my mouth. *I love your triangular features, your high cheekbones, slim straight nose, and mouth. I dream of your mouth.*

It's too large...

No. It's perfect. I'm glad you never reshaped it. You've never needed the BeautyForm machines.

His thumb reached my skin and caressed the curve of my mouth. His lips came down on me.

Once...

Streak kissed me with a tenderness that left me breathless.

I felt a storm of emotions course through me, and he returned his embrace with every inch of me. I melted against him.

He was my match in every way.

Joy filled me. Our souls joined at that moment, finding the perfect union.

The moment lasted... Our energy melted into one another, giving us a jolt of pure happiness. Slowly, Streak released me, our breaths brushing against each other.

We smiled.

We knew...

We had always known.

Streak took a step back. *The High Council will know.*

Does it matter? We may never make it back.

We'll make it back. DAINN brought us here, and with its help, I can take us back.

Maybe we won't go back. What if we don't want to go back when the time comes? We will never have this opportunity for freedom in Ang.

Would you remain here and not return?

I don't know. It's too soon to tell. But if we succeed, we may.

Maybe... Streak's expression was doubtful. *We have to return. You know this.*

I nodded. The old rules stuck to Streak, more so than they did to any of us. If my friend followed them, he could never aspire to what his words meant. Conclave leaders only united with other conclave leaders. He confirmed my suspicion with his next words.

We have to maintain our roles.

They make some exceptions to these rules. We qualify.

Maybe.

Here it was again. Streak's action, reinforced by his look of sorrow, put an extra wedge between us. He loosened his hold on me.

We were here together, and this led me to believe, for a brief instant, that we had a chance until now.

The realization hit me hard. Today, like in our time, our relationship did not have a place.

My best friend, my love, quashed my dreams long ago, and he just did it again. My regrets rose, flooding my chest with such a sense of loss that my breath caught in my throat.

I faced ahead.

I relied on Streak in almost everything.

He was at my side, always. But he remained a friend.

I looked into his eyes, wanting to explain my conflicting emotions. *Love him more. Let him go.*

Doing anything but this would lead to a wrong place for him, a path only bringing further heartache. I opened up to him, reaching into his head.

He let me in, waiting to sense me.

For the first time in a long time, I felt alive because I came to peace with my feelings in this new place. I wanted Streak to see me. I stretched out to him, so my friend could understand me without ever touching me. Standing there in front of him, I shared everything that I was. I offered him the taste of my love, my crushed hopes, and my sorrow.

I stared at Streak, looking deep into his eyes, as my emotions drifted toward him. Not controlling their flow, they moved towards him in huge waves, for I knew he could take it.

We had done it before... Once to be exact, a long time ago, when we were still children, stretching for knowledge and experience. It turned into an intensely personal experience, way too soon. One I never wanted to repeat until now.

For these fleeting minutes, we connected, and the world disappeared. We left the roots, holding us to the ground on the physical plane. We sunk into each other's minds and merged, for when I entered; he put up no barrier to his thoughts and feelings. We floated to each other's very core and touched each other's souls.

The bliss held us together so that there was no beginning and no end as we embraced, but only a peaceful musing that found itself substituted by cold and emptiness when I disengaged. Neither of us handled the return very well. The dizziness offered but a brief reprieve.

I felt breathless. Streak saw me, touched me, caressed me, and knew everything that I was. And so I did for him... For Streak had reciprocated in every way.

The feeling confused me. It was one of recognition.

I witnessed the same emotion in Streak's eyes.

We both stared, surprised and yet struggling to make sense of this. Why was this happening to both of us? We had never kissed, never held each other, never even being this close to one another as teenagers or young adults. So, why did this feel so comfortable, as if we had lived through this before?

Puzzled, Streak murmured, "Why does this feel so familiar?"

"I don't know. We've never...."

Streak's face hardened. "I know we've never kissed... At least, not according to our recollection."

My hands lingered on his back for a moment longer than necessary. I rejoiced in the feel of him against my palm.

Soon, I let him go. We both knew something was wrong. "You don't think...."

He nodded and said in a clipped tone, "It's possible."

"No... Why?"

"You doubt it after what you revealed to us a while ago? I know it's possible. I've heard it happen. Only it's barbaric."

"You think someone...." I couldn't go on.

He nodded. "I think someone erased our memories. Based on what you revealed of Rodent, I wouldn't put it past him." His face was grim and angry. "We don't have time to go over all the medical Vlogs, but I bet that if we do, we'll find something."

I blanched.

"We'll do it, Tesh. As soon as we are out of here, we will sort this out. I promise."

I wanted to throw up. So, I just nodded, feeling the betrayal all over again.

His promise had to be enough for now.

I could always break the dictates and the mandates and live with myself afterward.

He never could... Until now.

Without this sudden knowledge that we had been close, and someone twisted had intervened to make us believe otherwise. Streak's attitude toward the system would have remained the same. Only, the System wasn't behind this. The Rodent was, and perhaps others too.

I turned. I had been ready to let Streak go. Because being together would have broken us. I valued him too much to cause him misery.

His eyes reflected the pain I felt. But in that instant, he understood. We both knew the Rodent played us.

My release of him demanded a control I never thought I possessed before. Pulling away from him after Streak showed me how much he cared, how much he loved me, and how much I counted for him was excruciating. It almost broke me after sharing feelings that we thought had remained unspoken for years.

I offered him an understanding smile. The love he let me glimpsed at earlier represented my reward. Whatever existed between us would have to suffice. Loving him demanded more of me. Accepting that remained my journey. And it required that I protect him. "We're here now. Let's make the most of it, Streak."

He groaned. "Let's not forget our mission. I promise you. He will pay. I'll make sure of that."

At least now, I had felt his kiss. I no longer wondered about that. I held on to that moment with all my might. This instant, I and I alone possessed it... No one could wipe it away, not now, never, not even Streak.

I took a step back. "I know..."

The air drifted around me. And I shivered.

With a last look at him, I turned away, and the panel opened at my command. And quickly, I passed the threshold of the door. Inside my EmVat, I felt the tears come down my face. I couldn't let him see them. I walked away.

The corridor past that point was almost unencumbered. Only a few rocks remained.

He no longer needed my help. Besides, I needed to get away fast for fear of losing myself to anger. "You can clear the rest of these without my help. I'll get back to the corridor."

I skated away with my NetJet boots, going back to the last emitted NetPulse location. Inside, I shook. Once there, my hand reached the UniWrap and engaged the NetPulse, only this time, I pushed it full blast, not caring for what I was unleashing.

Our goal, seeking answers within the very fabric of the universe, an action never attempted before, led us here. We hoped we had reached into the past. Our presence hid a cruel truth but could not abolish it. We came to this place with one aim: Reverse the events. Affect the consequences of actions taken in a timeline leading to our end. We could no more forget this heritage than give up, for the faster it vanished from our minds, the worse our reality would be.

The noise overwhelmed the silence.

I pushed myself, drawing energy from the loathing I felt for Rodent. I blasted the rock fast, and it melted away under my hand. It was like nothing I experienced before, this power. My power disintegrated a mountain with a million years of existence.

Continuity, ruptured into thousands of pieces with fragments belonging to the past, present, and future, and all the same, held us here. Our memories were wiped away, leaving us shadows of our former selves. Why? The cruelty of it shook me. Remnants were coming back in flashes of recognition. They surged in my head chaotically, shredding apart a past I thought belonged to me. They made everything around us chaotic. The instability of our current reality rendered me more vulnerable as I couldn't hold on to the past; I thought I knew. How much of it was my own? I shuddered.

I breathed hard… My anger soared.

The oscillating wave felt odd, deflecting much force against the inertia of the wall. Pieces flew from the surface in particles of golden hues. They danced in perfect formation before finding their way into the rings that formed the tunnel. The sheer intensity I forged with the NetPulse left me dizzy. It was a part of me. A testimony to the raw power I never drew from before. Calm, purpose, determination were the emotions we used in Ang. They fueled our actions. Not this…

I heard nothing but the loud noise my anger manifested against the mountain. Blinded by my emotion, I kept going.

Knowing where we were and how to claim a place here remained out of our grasp until we emerged into the light. Even then, we would have much to learn and overcome. I needed to calm myself.

Above us, we ignored the rules that made up this place. The past held us, structuring responses that may no longer fit, and yet. Here we were, doing the things we had learned to do.

Amid my unleashed power, I felt Blast. He came into my mind urgently.

The impulse coming from him was strong.

Compelled to reach out for him, I felt that Blast needed me.

Chasing away the hurt and the need to hit something, I sent my mind out to him.

Blast suffered from claustrophobia, and despite all the training, it remained lodged somewhere inside his head. I projected my thoughts and connected them with his mind. *Are you all right?*

If you can, call it that in my present state.

You'll be fine. I'll walk you through it.

Thanks, he said.

His thoughts sounded strained in my head, for he disliked showing any signs of weakness.

I understood him. *We all have things we don't like or accept. You have nothing to be ashamed of, Blast.*

Blast always volunteered to go first in a fight. Bravely, my teammate cared more about us than himself, and he proved that frequently. This nervousness didn't sit right with him.

What's yours?

Don't you know? It's sitting in my chamber.

Blast grunted. *I should have known.* He chuckled, *And look at the trouble you're in now.*

DarNet right… I'll deal with much worse for Mage.

Why?

Mage is more than a dog. He is a gift from my father… Besides, he understands things like no other. You'll see. He will help us.

The Earth trembled again, giving us pause. Only this time, it lasted a few minutes and stopped.

Streak's voice resonated over the NetComm, "Is everyone all right?"

Blast answered first. "I'm peachy."

"No worries here," said Leane.

"All good here," I said. My voice sounded raw, the same as my emotions. Thankfully, no one seemed to notice.

Behind me, Streak secured our Chamber and the tunnel leading to it.

In concert, we moved away from each other following different paths. The irony hit me again. Even now, we let events carry us further from each other when we belonged together. We should be getting closer instead.

We made choices, and these carried us away again.

Other decisions would come up, and I lacked objectivity. It demanded an understanding I didn't yet possess, for all I wanted at this moment was revenge. I could no longer trust my knowing.

I didn't care or wouldn't care anymore. At least, that is what I told myself as I pushed forward in the darkness. I made good time, blasting away. Only, I also exhausted myself doing it. Needing to rest, I paused and looked back. The doorway of our chamber had disappeared. Now, I stood alone in a long tunnel. I hoped that it would lead me out into the open at some point.

A glow, slight at first, appeared way ahead. It wobbled in place for a moment as if gaining power. Then it moved fast, rebounding against the wall as if it was looking for a way out, and disappeared from view.

Streak, the light came back and went away again.

Streak's voice resonated in my head. *Stay away from it, Tesh. Let's find a way out.*

Fine.

I went back to work and NetPulsed ahead. The glow of my energy surrounded me in a golden light. It was a beautiful sight, for as the wave hit the rock, the particles moved, forging a stronger bound, circling each other in a dance.

While I dug the shaft, Streak molded his in a different direction into the Earth. Each step taken moved us further and further away from each other. *Don't think. Focus on the task.*

I shook my head to chase the thoughts away. Streak was a Gatherer of Space, able to travel through time and space from one location to another — partially because of DNA combined with technology, and still, he dealt with old social hang-ups. We all did. We belonged to a world we left behind, products of an environment strictly meant: a greater good.

A Shaper and a Gatherer were dangerous. They could change dictates, influence events, and control crowds. But they could only be restrained themselves with incredible difficulty. If they wanted to evade, catching them would be difficult. They could also bring much order and power and, as a result, be made whole at a price. The question remained in my heart, did we love each other enough? I didn't doubt that he did. Only, I loved him too much to ever ask for the price was high.

I pushed ahead, and the anger fed the energy in the NetPulse.

Long ago, DAINN helped me see the distance between Streak and I. DAINN warned me about getting hurt, for it could read me like no other. I remembered his words. "Streak has aspirations of his own. You need to move on, Tesh. Streak is too proud and too rigid to allow himself to become your match. You will suffer if you continue on this course."

DAINN did it with gentleness and constancy, never berating me. I recalled moments where it helped me turn the tides of my feelings and bury my hopes. DAINN was there for me, as it had been when my parents died. After a while, it even proposed to find me a match, but I refused.

Today, not locating him in my head left me at a loss.

I recognized that DAINN's programming called for its actions. Codes directed its conversations and activities. DAINN's counsel was entirely connected to its learning abilities about humankind. DAINN's advice did not show compassion. This attribute was not its strong suit... Its guidance only represented a deliberate attempt to walk one through an emotional landscape with practicality.

Still, I missed my friend and my mentor on this day. A voice in my head rose... *DAINN is only a System.*

I blasted so fast that I never heard the noise that came from the rumble inside the Earth. I just moved ahead as the wall of rock moved under my touch. I shrugged away in the tunnel's darkness, turning my attention back to where I stood.

The Earth trembled again. I lost my balance and fell hard against the wall. *DarNet, again...*

In the roaring noise, I thought I heard something else. But I wasn't sure. Then, I recognized Blast's voice in between the trembling and shifting of the Earth under my feet.

It came over the NetComm, filled with a hint of disbelief. "What in the HellNet!"

Then a considerable sound reverberated across the tunnel. Indescribable at first. The Earth shook, and a deep rumble rose from deep underneath. It moved against the rock formation within the closed space of the prison that held us.

"What is that? Blast? What's going on?" I said, my legs wobbling.

"Blast?" exclaimed Streak over the NetComm. "Are you there?" His voice sounded stressed. Usually, Streak let nothing ruffle him.

Leane's anxious voice cut through the noise too. "Blast, can you hear us? Answer if you can, please."

I attempted to determine the source of the commotion.

It was a constant rumble, rolling evenly closer with each passing instant.

At first, I didn't recognize the thunder. It rolled evenly this time, unlike the other events we had experienced.

"Tesh, are you getting anything?"

I sensed turmoil, confusion, and fear when I touched Blast's mind. *Blast, can you hear me?*

I winced, fearful for my friend. "No." I reached out to Blast's mind again. *Blast, are you all right?* When nothing came back to me, I yelled over the cacophony, "I don't hear him, Streak."

Streak's voice soothed my fears and put a balm on my heart. "I'll backtrack to Blast. You both keep going."

"I'm not sure it's a good idea to split up considering what just happened," I said.

"We can't afford for all of us to get caught inside. You find the way out," insisted Streak.

"NetRoger that," whispered Leane.

"Fine," *I said. Be careful.*

I will… You know, I will.

"If it injures him, you'll need me," added Leane.

Streak replied reassuringly, "I'll let you know."

A colossal boom reverberated again inside the rock formation, like the first time in the chamber. It resembled the cacophony a sonic wave would make. Within a beat after that, the Earth rumbled again.

"What in the HellNet is causing all that ruckus?" Leane's voice rose across the Netcomm.

"No idea," I muttered, but the tension among us was palpable.

"Sonic wave, maybe? What do you make of it, Tesh?" Streak said.

My stomach clenched. "It would be my guess."

"Find a way out quickly because if we are right, we may have unwanted company."

An unseen hand squeezed my solar plexus tighter and tighter as my anxiety rose, "Streak, stay on Netcomm." The latest event could undoubtedly foil our plan. We had so much to do to find the others.

"I plan on it." His matter-of-fact tone caused me to pause. His mind turned to the challenge ahead, dismissing everything else.

Leane reached out to me in a private chat. "Tesh, do you think the experiment worked?"

"We'll soon find out."

I heard Leane taking a deep breath before she asked, "What are the odds of that?"

"Twenty-two percent. DAINN gave me the probability, apart from our survival chances."

"Oh… Now I wish I had not asked." Leane's voice shook as she said these words.

These closed quarters under the Earth left an imprint on all our nerves. It held no surprise. It would be natural for people who spent their time under the clouds to feel out of sorts, and the unknown sound and the Earthquakes did nothing to alleviate our unease.

"It won't matter if we don't make it out," I muttered. I observed the dark tunnel ahead, only highlighted by the golden hues from my pulse device when the rings activated, and resumed my march forward.

Silence greeted my statement as I advanced further along with the glistening walls froth with golden residue. Leane, no doubt, was less than thrilled by my latest remark.

Rumble deep in the Earth moved the ground under my feet.

I advanced through the tunnel, still reaching out to Blast. Sending my mind toward the trajectory, he followed when he left the chamber; I felt only darkness surrounding him. "Streak, something is wrong. I don't think he is in the upward tunnel anymore, but he appears unconscious. Whatever it was, it hit him hard."

Streak's clipped voice responded, "Keep tracking Blast and let me know when you have him. I haven't reached his last position yet."

A moment passed in silence.

Another noise surfaced from afar.

My vizor engaged, trying to identify it.

The sound was steady.

In my ears, it resembled a storm. No, not a storm… It couldn't be that because we were underground.

I isolated it.

Recognition hit me. We were underground, and because of it, my mind didn't include it as a possibility. The noise came from the water. Not impossible… I reached out. "Streak, Leane…"

But Streak's voice interrupted my warning. "What in the… HellNet…"

The downpour reverberated across the NetComm, filling my ears.

I yelled, "Water… It's water. We hit an underground source, so brace yourself. It's coming our way."

"Got it," Leane said, her voice almost lost under the noise of raging water.

In the distance, the sound grew louder, approaching my location fast.

Blast had tunneled up, so it made sense that we would be on the path of the torrential water. At least, I thought it did.

I turned and saw the rumbling wave. With nowhere to go, the only solution came just in time. I engaged my EmVat boots to hold me in place.

It didn't work.

The torrential water came at me with such force that it sent me flying against the wall of rock.

I rolled multiple times. Submerged under the dark water, I lost my bearing. I twisted, sucked in by the flow, and hit the mountain. The power of the flood pressed me against the wall. Disoriented and blinded, I lay at the bottom for a moment. At least, I thought it was the bottom. Assembled my jumbled thoughts, I searched for my way up.

My visor provided the direction. Upward...

My EmVat sustained most of the blow. Still underwater, I stood up, looking around. My air supply continued drawing on the OxyPure.

The body of water began to calm and receded in the tunnel. The top of my head emerged above water. It filled most of the tunnel to the ceiling. My eyes broke the surface.

With fear eating away at my gut, I reached out to Leane, Streak, and Blast. They had to be all right. "Are you there? Can you hear me?" Bracing myself against the worst, I began to breathe again when I heard Leane's voice.

"I'm fine," Leane said, with a calm that took me off-guard. Knowing she was okay gave me solace. She remained unruffled in the face of adversity. It was her utmost quality. She even steadied me as she did now.

Streak's voice mumbled, sounding quite disgruntled, "I'm all right... Underwater at the moment. I need to locate Blast."

I smiled. Never could I remember or have I witnessed Streak in this subdued mood. His disgruntled reaction did not surprise me. The cave-in was unexpected. No doubt, both Streak and Blast were humbled by this experience. Ruffled feathers never worked well with either of them, even when we practiced together. They often acted as if nothing would ever get in their way. Indeed, they believed themselves invincible.

Streak would weather the situation. He would consider his options and take action.

So, I didn't offer a solution. He would prefer it that way. Instead, I extended my support and suggested: "I'll come to you."

Streak appeared on my visor as he spoke, surrounded by blackness. It was difficult to see his features, except for the contours of his headset. It boasted a small silver light, similar to his shimmer. "No, Tesh. Stay where you are. No point in all of us floundering at the bottom of a pool. I'll make my way out of it with Blast."

Leane's face appeared on the left side of my screen, highlighted only with the blue light of her EmVat. "Did we cause this?" Leane said, uncertain.

Streak seemed annoyed. "I don't think so, but I don't know. For now, we have to address a bigger problem. There are multiple waterfalls. If they submerge the chamber, we need to clear a path, so water flows out. Otherwise, we won't be able to open the door and get our equipment."

My thoughts drifted to my dog. "Mage is in there."

"Mage is fine inside since the chamber is waterproof." Streak's voice meant to reassure me resonated as rather impatient.

I sighed... I ought to act better than that. "I know..." When it came down to Mage, I lost my perspective. Streak reminded me of that without telling me to get it together.

I took a deep breath and steadied myself.

We had been through much more confusing times during the storms. This knowledge did not calm me down. Why was I reacting this way?

We are entombed alive. It interferes with normal reasoning abilities. Calm down, Tesh.

"I've got to locate Blast. Are you getting anything on his whereabouts, Tesh?"

"No, only darkness. I think Blast is out still. There is a faint signal from his EmVat, but that's about it."

Streak nodded. "I see it. All right... I'll find Blast. Leane, proceed back to the chamber."

"Streak, how big are the falls?" I asked, wondering what this meant for us at our current depth.

He groaned. "Big and cold."

I looked at the water surrounding me. "It feels clean too."

"Yeah... Not that I care at the moment." His visor cut off, followed by Leane's.

Isolated in the cold dampness, I regulated the temperature of my EmVat to keep warm. My hand played with the substance, taking pleasure in PVZ readings that we had not seen in Ang in a long time. This water source was pristine. The indicators of my visor were definite. My pleasure disappeared in the next instant.

The pressure of the water in the tunnel weakened the rock formation behind me. Suddenly, the wall burst open.

I lost my footing as the water rushed to the opening. Unable to hold onto anything, I fell backward, drug along with the current.

The flow gained speed.

I tried to grab the ground and, instead, grasped at pieces of rocks that disintegrated under my fingers.

My hands slipped on the sandy floor.

I found the side of the wall, closing my fist around it.

The rocks crumbled into pieces.

I tumbled backward and closer to the open hole. The thought flashed through my mind that our pulse device could not have weakened the rock formation.

Still, I touched the edge. Another thought... Maybe in this place, the results of the NetPulse brought about a different effect. My mind reverted to my current predicament.

The next instant, I breached the broken wall and went through the blasted opening.

Free falling, all I could do was scream.

17 HAZARD
Gen

MIT, Massachusetts - 2018

Gen Aubrey is in over her head. The moment the vehicle drives toward her, she understands she is too late. The prey, overcome by the hunter, is about to die. DAINN Annals – Summer 2018.

I stood there… Frozen.

The headlights of the car shining in my eyes overwhelmed the darkness of the street as it came right at me.

Suddenly, I felt pulled backward with force. Just in time too.

In a tangle of arms and legs, we rolled to the ground. The body lying beneath me softened the impact on the concrete, which otherwise should have jolted.

I remained there, breathless, with the wind knocked out of me. It took me a minute to recover.

The car never stopped. Instead, in the screeching sound of burning tires, it continued on its tracks and turned the corner.

The arms that held me moved me to the side and cradled me against a muscular chest. I heard the heartbeat, steady and over it, a voice that murmured, "The driver was going way too fast… Are you all right?"

The voice continued, "Nothing broken… At least I don't think."

I heard a soft voice over my head and tried to regain my composure, but it sounded muffled as I sat there, winded and unmoving. I didn't quite make out its meaning, although I heard the words. They resonated in my ears as multiple sounds, distorted, far away. Most times, I went through life without giving much thought to desires, needs, and wants. These vanished from my vocabulary the night I lost my mother, and those around me who used these terms found me staring at them as if they were a bunch of morons. At this moment, I felt the overwhelming need to cradle against that chest.

Forgotten was my everyday focus: remaining balanced. In a split second, my world got turned upside down. So much for the thought small drama influenced things and sent them off-kilter. I always thought a wrong dosage of inconsequential antics brought chaos. No big emotions on either side of the equation appeared as a critical ingredient for my peace of mind. Keeping this precarious proportion going into college demanded a tight rein on everything. So, I wrapped a bubble around me, allowing no one in or anything to affect me at all.

But this was not small by any means. It wasn't one of these times where with a bit of reason, one overcomes issues. This meaningful acknowledgment of my predicament started forming in my head.

I looked up at that chest, which felt so strong against my head. My hand raised against it felt the muscles under my fingers. I would have been toast if he had not shown up. I passed trembling fingers against my forehead and pushed back the strands that fell over my face.

Comfortable with my companion laptop, I breezed through school with most of my courses and avoided entanglements. My life, dominated by my growing hacking exploits, provided enough diversion that I didn't become bored. I created new codes, moved the tables around other hackers, and played games. And, I buried the past... *What a relief.*

Until now...

The guy didn't move. He just waited.

I lifted my face to meet his gaze, and I saw a pair of deep blue eyes. *Damn it. Nice.*

Seconds ago, I landed on my ass in the arms of a perfect stranger. *No shit.*

"You sure you're all right?" said a deep, masculine voice froth with anxiety.

I grimaced at the thought of what I had just escaped.

I shook my head. "Yes… I am fine." My voice, unsteady, got stronger as the words came out. "You?"

"I'm good. I took worse tumbles on the field, playing football," said the attractive voice. "At least, I got the tackle part down pat, even if I'm not that good at playing ball."

"Oh, good, so you're not the captain of the football team then? Because you know that would be scary thinking I owe a jock my life." I muttered these words with a bit of the typical bravado I showed with good-looking guys. He was that and more.

"Not a fan?"

"Nope."

My few friends liked me well enough. What's there not to like? Friendly, check. Sarcastic, check. Outspoken, check. Funny. Double-check. The others considered me a nerd, but I didn't care.

He nodded, laughing. The sound rumbled out of his chest and gave me a warm feeling. "Good to know."

I needed to disentangle myself from his arms. Sooner would be a good thing. I glanced away at the Taser scattered nearby.

I couldn't move. The jolt on the concrete didn't hurt my butt as much as it should have, but the impact of my fall caught me off-guard all the same. *What is it with you these days? You're ending up in harm's way a lot.*

I tried to gather my somewhat muddled thoughts. I was still reacting to what had just happened.

The guy held on to me. He didn't appear to be in a hurry to get up either. Still, he leaned over me, offering the protective barrier of his arms and lap. "Take your time."

Disgruntled at finding myself once again in an exact position of inferiority, I exclaimed, puzzled, "He came at me fast…."

He chuckled before replying, "Yes, he could have hit you."

I realized I ought to be a hell of a lot more careful. Doubt and fear submerged me. The little voice in my head whispered. "How did you come to be here at this hour?" I sounded careful and guarded to my ears. I cringed. Here I was, on his lap, and I doubted his motives. He could not be working with those who attacked my place. Hating my position, for it made me question everyone's actions, I began to unravel my limbs from his.

His eyes looked serious. "You ran past me like a bat out of hell… It didn't look like everything was all right."

I frowned at him. Was he kidding? "Do I even remotely look all right to you?"

Chase appeared surprised by my reply. He perused me, and a crooked smile brightened his face, "On the surface, you look all right to me."

Taken aback for a brief minute, I paused, thinking about what brought me to the street. Disgruntled by the entire affair, I murmured, "I tried to stop the tug, but the guy was too fast for me."

The image of my mother danced in my mind, standing proudly, her head tilted back with a mocking smile on her face. Her eyes looked straight ahead, uncompromising. Somehow, I didn't think she'd give in. No, she would fight back, just like I did.

"Who?"

I glanced toward Chase and gauged his interest. He seemed attentive. "The guy in the car."

"Stop him? What was all this about?"

I clamped up. "Why are you so interested in all this?"

"You were quite distraught coming down the steps. I followed you."

My position on the concrete road did not provide much in terms of a firm stance if he turned out to be an opponent. I sighed and looked around, anxious. There was no one else in the street. The light of the lamp created shadows on him. His features, in darkness, still appeared friendly, but I began standing up.

His hands gently released me.

I straightened my clothing. In a guarded tone, I said, "I'm fine now. Thank you."

He was on his feet in no time while I still tried to gather my wits about me. My legs trembled. I stumbled. Way to go, Gen.

His hands, eager to help, were outstretched to support me.

I slapped one of them and pushed the other away. "Stop trying to touch me… I can stand up on my own."

He chuckled. "All right…"

Irritated at finding myself in another confrontation in less than one hour, I added without even looking in his direction, "I appreciate your help, but I am okay now."

His amused tone breezed over me, "All right, so long as you are okay." The statement came in a sexy, enticing voice.

I looked up at him, taking a step back. This time, I stumbled near the curb.

He distracted me, standing with his arms crossed over a broad chest. He was a picture of rugged masculinity.

The situation demanded caution.

I took another step back as paranoia lurked in my head.

He stood before me, still in darkness. Tall, powerful… He could see me while I faced the light. He created a shadow over me. His extended hands were big. The rest of his body equally so.

I considered his large frame, and felt self-conscious and defenseless. Could he be a potential threat? As if reading my thoughts, he took a step back, letting the brightness of the street lamp hit his features.

I now stood, a good foot away, in front of him. The luminosity was spreading around us, and for the first time, I could see him. I almost wished I couldn't. Observing his face in more detail, I blinked.

He was beautiful, with his striking eyes and sensual mouth. The light made him more enticing. I staggered. *Get a grip, Gen.*

His hands came right back to steady me. He murmured, "Careful. You took a nice tumble."

"Yes, I was trying to stop the bully who broke into my room."

"Someone broke into your room? What in the hell for?"

I frowned again. "You sure ask a lot of questions."

Chase's demeanor changed at once. He got irritated… "I ask a lot of questions. What do you expect? It is not your typical situation. I almost picked you up in a pile of broken bones off his hood."

The guy looked upset.

I couldn't help but smile. Satisfaction rose inside of me. Seeing Chase becoming protective of me felt nice. "Hmm… Well, I'm all right now."

"Really? Are you? Because there seemed to be quite of few bruises on your face. Did you and that guy get into a fight? Did you find him in your room and confront him? Are you mad?"

I straightened up and faced him. "So, what about it? Was I supposed to run like a poor female in distress? He was in my room when I got inside. He attacked me. I confronted him. I wasn't about to just let him take my stuff and thank him for it."

My anger at what had just happened got the better of me, and I began shaking. Suddenly, what just took place got to me. What would my mother have done had she been in this position? Would she have fought back to save some darn codes? I doubted it.

My mother, although gentle, was not to be trifled with or taken lightly. She probably would have answered her assailant immediately. *Oh, hell, I doubted myself. Not good, Gen.*

Chase's face fell at the outburst. "Did he hurt you?" He moved toward me, but I wasn't about to let anyone near me at this very moment.

I shook my head. "I'm… I'm all right."

Chase passed an agitated hand in his hair as he looked at me. "Do you want to go to the hospital, call the police or something?"

"No, I'm fine… Certainly not the police." The police didn't know anything. They didn't believe my mother had just left us, but they couldn't be sure. They had no evidence. They had no suspects. They had no proof. So, they did nothing. The authorities, unable to find her or identify the perpetrator, kept the case open, but there were no new leads. Everything pointed to the fact that she loved her family and her life. Everything appeared as if she was the most normal person in the world. Yet, one moment, she was there, and the next, she was gone.

"I think I could use a drink… How about we go to a pub and have something to drink?"

Shaking my head, I said, "I'm not up to seeing people at the moment, but thanks."

Chase looked powerless, just as I started feeling ill.

"I will throw up." I turned toward the curb, and in the next second, did precisely that. But I was barfing right in front of Chase. My embarrassment knew no bounds. *Way to go, Gen. What a great way to impress.*

He didn't appear to mind. Instead, he stood inches away from me and waited for me to get over it.

"Huh… I'm sorry," I murmured, feeling embarrassed. I tried to compose myself and look at him.

"Don't even think about it. You're in shock… I think a drink is what you need."

"I'm not sure I would keep it down."

I began to shake, unable to stop.

He saw it. "Do you want to call someone to come over to take care of you?"

The image of my mother came to me. Memories flashed through my head. The day had been perfect. Home for a long weekend, we had enjoyed hanging out together. No special plans. No extraordinary happenings. Just us… At home with my brothers and parents. These simple moments were so ordinary that they didn't possess, in their fundamental nature, the allure or the attributes of being exceptional. Not until they left, or until one came to realize that they had dissipated, or until one knew they could never be again. My mother disappeared that night. And this occurred as she was fetching something as innocent as ice cream.

The trembling continued, and my teeth shattered now. I shook my head and whispered, "No."

"All right, Gen. Do you have anything to drink in your dorm? Anything at all?"

"Huh… I think a bottle of Vodka, one of my friends brought it over."

"Fine. I'm taking you up there." Chase came beside me and wrapped one of his arms around my shoulder. "You will be all right in no time. Let's go."

I didn't resist him. Tired, I wanted to sit down.

Chase opened the door for me. We went up the stairs, and during that time, he began to talk. I think Chase just wanted to keep my mind occupied, and he did. He told me that he studied at Harvard, talked about mundane stuff, trying to distract me.

The shock of this near-death accident affected me. I found myself in need of closing my eyes and almost passing out, but I wasn't about to let Chase know that. I straightened on my feet. "Third floor." My voice shook a little.

He heard it. "Almost there. We will be up there in no time at all."

Until that moment, I had not looked at him, not really looked at him. Indeed, fear and shock swallowed me until now. These strong emotions made me give little thought to Chase. But, now, the feeling of safety as he carried me in his arms overwhelmed me.

I wished to escape the growing butterflies in my stomach. As I watched Chase, I got mesmerized by his beautiful eyes. He possessed eyes that drew me in and made me lose myself in their depth.

His tall frame, broad chest, and long legs invited one to lean on the guy. His confident behavior was assertive and reassuring.

I stared. I couldn't help it.

His gaze on my face sent more tingles to my stomach. It almost unsettled me more than my fall.

His eyes, thoughtful, appraised me and just about took my breath away when his smile stretched his lips into a wide grin. "I'm Chase Davenport."

He appeared relaxed, calm, as if this rescue represented something he did every day. Unfazed, he resumed our conversation as if we had met under normal circumstances. He had just saved my life and now was chatting me up like an old friend, yet here I was suspecting him of possessing ulterior motives.

I seemed unhinged.

Nodding, unable to find my voice, I watched Chase's face, framed by light blond hair. Following his frame, taking in the laid-back stance, the strong biceps, and the flat stomach, I almost groaned out loud. He most likely possessed a six-pack behind that shirt. *Shake it off.* I squealed and made a total fool of myself, "I'm Gen, Gen Aubrey."

Chase smiled. "It's nice to meet you, Gen."

We reached the corridor and moved together toward my room. The door was wide open. I had left it that way when I ran out after the intruder.

Chase stopped, waiting for me to enter first.

My dorm screamed of misplaced items. The pillows in disarray lay crumpled on the floor; my chair turned upside down and tumbled out of place; the bed and covers tossed around looked as if they had been at the center of an Earthquake. My computer opened to the wrong set of files, showed an empty screen. Still, none of it compared to how violated and powerless I felt.

Damn! They'll pay for this... Who did they think they were? *Game on, whoever you are.*

I approached my computer system, an elaborate display of screens and drives, and checked my documents. A systematic search revealed my hard-drive gone and my codes erased. My programs, all the data on my internal and external drives, were now gone. Everything about my research was now gone. *Slick, really slick.*

He had stolen everything.

Chase's face registered surprise when he saw the chaos. He took a deep breath and followed me inside, perusing the items on the floor. "First things, first. Where is that bottle?"

I dropped on the bed and breathed. "Over there, inside the small cupboard."

Chase looked around the shelves and grabbed it. He then found two glasses and poured me a drink before he served himself one. He stood in front of me as I took a sip.

I looked at him and took another sip and a third. The heat of the liquid warmed me.

He was right…

I started feeling better and kept drinking in small gulps.

He seemed satisfied. After a big swallow of his drink, he grabbed the chair and straightened it before he sat on it. "So, you want to tell me what happened?"

My voice shook, "Huh… No, thanks." I expressed my guilt at being so curt; Chase was trying to help. "I'd rather not talk about it."

It wasn't my fault then, they told me. Had I been with my mother, I could also have suffered the same fate. But tonight… I caused it to happen by investigating the disappearances. We got too close. I held on to the guilt. This was on me. I wasn't about to go through another unsolved case. Days of torture led to weeks and months waiting for news, any news that never came. No leads. No hope. Nothing. Not ever… again. I would find out what had happened tonight because I had to. Whoever did this couldn't get away with it. If they did, I would never get closure.

"You sure? It would be better to discuss this." He watched me, thoughtful, concerned even. "I'd like to help if you allow me. It looks like you went through something tonight."

I swallowed. My hand reached my hair, and I tried to straighten it. I must look a sight. "Hmm… I can handle it."

His eyes caressed my face as he countered, "I don't doubt it.

I stood motionless. My stomach clenched at dealing with the issues that tonight raised. I needed to reach Jonas, but I couldn't do this now with Chase in my room.

Chase got up and began to pick up some of the scattered items. He wanted to help me, but it seemed so odd to have him in my dorm. He remained a perfect stranger, even if the circumstances under which we had met triggered a unique tie, or so I've heard. I sighed and figured that I needed to do something.

The alcohol gave me a sense of calm; I didn't possess it a while ago as my chaotic mind kept going over what had happened.

Chase was right. The drink helped.

So, I got up and observed my surroundings.

In the space of a few minutes, Chase had picked up most everything, and my room began to resemble a place I recognized.

"Better now," he said, glancing in my direction with a smile.

Why was he still here, looking at me? What was this all about? "I think I can take care of things now. Thank you."

"All right. Will you tell me what happened to you tonight?"

Could I trust him? I was unsure. A beat of silence passed between us. "Maybe another time?"

He would soon leave. I couldn't think of anything to say to keep him there with me a moment longer.

Then, with an amused lilt to his voice this time, he inquired, "Where is your phone?"

"My phone?" I croaked.

"Yes," he replied. "I'd like to give you my number... In case you feel the ill effects from this fall and, well, you know. This way, you

316

can call me and complain about it," he finished with a charming smile. "I am a good listener."

"Oh, okay." Relief, which I tried hard not to show, spread through my chest. I reached for my purse, retrieved the phone, and handed it to him.

His fingers touched mine when he seized the device. I felt like I was about to melt under his stare.

He prolonged the touch for one beat too long.

I let go of my device.

His head bent down to enter the number. I watched him.

"Here you go. Now, you can get a hold of me if you want to," Chase announced with a warm look in his eyes.

"Okay. Thanks." *I can't believe I'm this stupid.* Unable to come up with anything else to say, I seemed incapable of finding my old self, not since that other night. I sighed — no sense in pretending. I was a dimwit.

His velvety voice broke into my thoughts. "Gen? Are you sure you're all right?"

I nodded. "Sure. Fine. Huh… Chase, would you like my number?" I finished asking the question and winced. *Can you be any more obvious?*

He handed me his phone. "I thought you'd never volunteer it."

As I punched in my number, I felt him studying me. I lifted my face and met his eyes, worried, profound. And calculating. I felt a chill run through me. My heart lurched in my throat. *What the hell are you doing, Gen, giving your number to a stranger?* It was bad enough that he would know now where to find me. I lowered my face back to the screen of his phone, and on impulse, I entered the last two digits with

317

false numbers. With a fake smile, I handed the phone back to him. I inhaled and whispered, "Thank you for the help."

I took a step back. This small gesture broke the mood. I needed to put some distance between us before I made a fool of myself. "Bye, Chase, and again, thank you for your help."

He watched me, hesitating a second too long before answering. It appeared as if a thought entered his mind, and he wanted to share it. Instead, he remained silent. Shrugging, he said, "Bye, Gen."

Did he regret that our encounter had ended too fast as it did?

He moved toward the door. He glanced back at me and waived before he pulled the door closed behind him.

Chase left, and I stood in the middle of my room struck hard over the head, with no thoughts other than those about this sweet guy I had sent away.

The tears came then, once I realized I was all alone. I shook so hard that I dropped to the ground and pulled myself into a ball, putting my palms against my mouth to avoid screaming.

After several deep gulps, I calmed down. My eyes landed on the door. The panel even closed, leaving me feeling unsafe. I got to my feet and rushed over to lock it.

I then grabbed my phone and called Jonas. "Hey Jonas, it's Gen… Someone stole my codes. I… almost got run over. Be careful. Watch your back. Call me as soon as you get this."

How did they do it? We hadn't left a trace… Or had we?

They sent someone to break into my room, subdued me, fondled me, almost raped me, and stole my stuff. My ignorance about who these people were and why they came here stared me in the face.

We had stepped on someone's toes. They knew where to find me. If so, they could also find Jonas.

The anger surged through me, dampening the fear. I breathed harder, ready to strike at anything in sight. How could I allow myself to fall prey to anyone in that way?

Double, triple hell.

I wanted to crawl in a hole and lay there, never coming out.

The truth of the matter surged through me. These men could be anyone, and I would not know it.

The reality hit me… And I got even more scared.

18
STRIFE
Chase

Harvard, Massachusetts - 2018

Chase sees the car speeding up. His protective instincts go on overdrive. Deep down, he knows that this incident, connected to the errand that brought him here tonight, is against everything he believes. He fights his anger, but guilt overwhelms him. In his mind, he has to settle the score. DAINN Annals – Summer 2018.

My arrival in Jonathan's apartment with a massive chip on my shoulders in the middle of the night did not go unnoticed. I barged into the small space without even asking and then turned on him, "Did you know?"

Emerging from a deep sleep, Jonathan took a moment to notice that I behaved like I was on the prowl, waiting for any reason to break something. He didn't answer, so I repeated my question, this time facing him.

"Did you know?"

"Know what? Do you mind telling me what you are talking about?"

"He ransacked the room, Jonathan. For goodness sake, why send goons?"

This incident was not what had held my attention. The girl standing in the middle of it did. She looked so lost but remained brave. My protective instincts awakened; I wanted to hold her in my arms as she cried and wished I could soothe her fears. My desire turned into one thing, taking the hurt away. None of this made sense, not out of the blue. Not like this. I passed my hands in my hair, disconcerted as I watched Jonathan. *What the hell?*

"I won't offer you coffee. You need to calm down," said Jonathan, un-phased by my outburst.

I faced him, my arms crossed over my chest. My experience in the cave remained unknown to him. I was glad for my silence. Even to this day, what had happened remained a complete mystery. The whole experience of my fall had been too weird. Still, after all this time, the drop slowed, keeping me alive, that I had heard a voice in my head, and that somehow, the tablet spoke to me appeared too surreal. Over time, I became convinced that all of it had happened. Although once outside the cave, I floundered just the same for an explanation. But deep down, I believed that somehow, I possessed some connection with the tablet. Tight-lipped, I said, "You owe me an explanation."

Jonathan shrugged. "Steven told me you would go off the rail. So he took other measures."

Whatever took place a while ago in the dorm sent my blood boiling, but I kept my cool. I refused to scare Gen more than she already was. But the more I thought about the entire evening, the more I got angry. "And you decided not to tell me?"

"A little robbery is nothing too hurtful, so what are you babbling about?"

"You bastard... A robbery? He attacked a girl, almost ran her over. If I hadn't been there, she would lay splattered on the ground in front of her building." Now, I wanted to flatten Jonathan against the wall of his living room. I took a deep breath to calm down.

Jonathan smiled, but it didn't reach his eyes. "You were there."

The punch I felt in my stomach resembled those times on the field when a play didn't go so well. Only this time, I stayed winded and had to sit down. They had played me. The whole of them had manipulated the entire situation.

"Come on, it's not the end of the world," said Jonathan as he left for the open kitchen.

Until that moment, I never considered the small living room of his apartment too small. It was practical, a little place kept for his trips into town. Those rarely happened these days, now that he spent most of his time near the site. Now, I couldn't fathom staying a moment longer. I couldn't bear to be this close to him. Nothing I did that night allowed me to escape the doubts creeping up in my head about the Center's role. Nothing I heard now reconciled me with any of it, to the contrary.

Jonathan poured me a drink and said, "We had to stop them from finding out what we are doing and going public with it."

I loathed my involvement with him. How could I ever trust him? I was a fool.

He came back with a glass in hand. "Drink."

I didn't take the drink. I couldn't move. My coming here tonight found Jonathan and me on opposite sides. *Damn him.*

Jonathan set it on the wooden surface and sat down in front of me. His face didn't show remorse, just a certain detachment as he explained, "The girl is fine. Her codes revealed in a matter of hours our cover-up and could have damaged the entire operation. There was no going around it."

I snickered. "So, you implicated me in something you knew I wouldn't go for."

"You may not like my… huh, our methods, but they produce results, and that means they safeguarded the project. Besides, no harm came to the girl."

"The guy driving the car almost hit Gen, Jonathan."

"It was never about harming her, just getting the codes and scaring her so she would stay away."

So it connected the guy to Jonathan. Steven and Sean had set this up. They both would deal with me in a big way. When I got hold of the guy behind the car wheel that almost ran her over, I would show him what I thought of thugs. I knew I would recognize him anywhere. I saw his face just long enough. "Only she fought back."

"So, it seemed she did. She's got spunk. I'll give you that."

I couldn't even look at my partner now. He disgusted me.

Gen Aubrey stood up to her assailant despite her size. She had been angry when she came down those steps inside her dorm. Gen Aubrey was an enigma I planned on figuring out. But I knew one thing from my time with her. I murmured, "She won't stop, Jonathan. She's not that type."

"That could be a problem. You must make Gen stop."

"You better understand that I won't play a part in this."

"But you already have. Besides, you were there when Gen needed someone, and that has to count for something when the time comes."

It caught me off-guard. "What the hell do you mean?

"We set you up as a contingency. You both are still in school. We figured Gen would trust you after this."

My ears picked up on his tone. He sounded quite satisfied with something.

"Trust me for what?" That Jonathan would set me up like this, for the sake of the Center, revolted me, but I wanted to hear him explain and justify what he had done.

"I think she'll be a good recruit. She is good, I told you."

"You can't be serious."

"We can use her coding, and she may help us get more out of the information we find," explained Jonathan. "She is a fighter. She'll be a good addition to our team."

Indeed she was. I remembered the fire emanating from her eyes as Gen stumbled on me. She radiated such a fury. Not that the girl could inflict much harm. I mean, I stood taller and bulkier than she would ever be. But no matter what, I wouldn't play her like that. She shouldn't have to fight for this venture. So, I got up. "I know your beliefs about this entire endeavor. Just remember how important this is to you, but know I won't take part in this, not on these terms."

"You'll come around. Our methods may not be perfect, but we are not hurting anyone. Besides, you're part of this. You brought it to me, remember."

I sputtered, dismayed, "Not hurting anyone? What about Harriet?"

A pained expression crossed Jonathan's features for the flash of a second. "We didn't have anything to do with that."

"But it did happen... And now, this." I walked away from him. "I won't be part of this."

"Why? She is a pretty girl."

"Are you kidding me?" I saw Gen again in that instant. Her green eyes filled with tears that streamed down her cheeks. She appeared so lost. She was captivating, even with the confused look crossing her features. Everything about her looked ideally put together. She was beautiful with soulful eyes, a small nose, and a gorgeous mouth. Her body, proportioned with a tiny waist, nice breast, and long legs, looked dreamy. Even her red hair was startling. Tossed around her head, she presented quite a presence even in that sad state. All her features fit together and delivered an image worthy of a portrait. "You think this is the only reason I find this revolting at the thought?"

"That explains your eagerness to protect her, but don't forget our goal. It's too important."

My temper spiked, but I held it. "Your methods are questionable. I didn't sign-up for this."

"Don't be so self-righteous. Do you think it will matter when the world goes up in flames?"

"I don't believe the end justifies the means. I have a code. You don't. What will happen when there is something more at stake?"

Jonathan looked like the cat that had just swallowed the canary. "What makes you believe there isn't already?"

The situation had called for face-to-face instead of a call. But now, I wanted nothing more than walk away from my partner. However, the certainty that he knew something I didn't rose within me once again. This plane trip confirmed it. I couldn't trust this man, not when it came down to his science. This friend of my father turned out to be a significant letdown. This night created a wedge I couldn't breach. I would have to find out what he knew on my own, especially now. I glared at him before I turned away and headed for the door.

"Think of Gen… The girl is part of this now."

I didn't trust myself to answer him and opened the door.

Gen's face floated in front of my eyes as I put my hand on the door handle. She kept the tears at bay while I was with her, but the moment I left, I thought I heard her sobs through the door. A small part of me wanted to be back with her, to watch over her. How in the hell was I going to keep her away from this? *Shit! It wasn't meant to happen.*

"Your choice. It's your discovery, as you told me so many times."

I wanted to punch him, but I knew I couldn't. He held too many cards for now.

"Just remember, you're not indispensable unless you remain helpful."

I turned around and challenged him then. "Really? Maybe there is something you don't know that I know; as you said, it is my discovery."

Jonathan hesitated. I saw the look in his eyes, and then he dismissed my warning. "You'll change your mind. Besides, we have reached the end of our preparations. Once we reach the Center, we can focus on the real work."

I then laughed… Hell, I could play his game. "You're not the only one to hold things back, Jonathan. Don't worry… I did the same eleven months ago. Trust is a rare commodity, isn't it?"

I passed the threshold, walking out on him, and never turned back.

19
GATHERER
Tesh

Deep Inside The Earth - 2018

The Origin training provides Tesh and her team with humanity's history in detailed strokes. It also bequests other resources like genetic engineering, imps skills, and technology, which arm them with powerful skills and tools to complete their mission. But the bonds they forge during their integration on the ground will impact their ability to influence events. And I warned them against this. DAINN Annals – Summer 2018.

The waterfall held me in its grasp until my EmVat boots kicked in. Water was not my natural element, but it was Leane's. Water did nothing for my abilities. It muddled my mind.

Taken by surprise when the wall broke, my reaction time, less than a beat, sent me tumbling through the hole in the bedrock. I went over the edge, shrouded in the cascading downpour, tumbling down faster with the weight of it. My vision, impaired by the gushing stream, detected a blurred wall of rock.

My EmVat engaged a split second too late. It responded to my mind, reacting beyond the surprise. It triggered my boots' engine, and when they fired, my body stabilized and stopped rolling. Once I regained an upward position, I glided away from the cascade.

Leane's alarmed voice broke through the overflow noise, and her face appeared on my visor. "Are you all right?"

Leane, always so gentle in her demeanor, became one of my closest friends over the years at the Institute. She possessed a calm and steadiness that I envied, but, at that moment, her poise was lacking.

Soon, Streak's voice resonated in my ears. His image, shrouded in darkness, opened on the other side of my screen. "What happened, Tesh?"

I swiveled my attention back to the pit beneath me. "I'm fine. The water breached the wall. Just got caught in it."

"Do you need help?" Leane said, sounding more troubled than I was.

I looked up. One high wall rising forever, it seemed. "No. Stay where you are and follow up with the chamber. I will check this out. The bottom looks deep because I cannot see the end. But I think we have our way out now, up above."

"NetRoger that," Streak said. He winks at me, right before his image disappeared from my visor when his screen closed.

I felt a warm tingle spread inside and smiled.

Leane's eyes registered it. "I see that things are better now."

I returned her look with a grin.

"Good. I don't think I could have handled the two of you at war. You are both scary when you're Netpissed."

"Huh, huh. You know it," I replied, feeling relaxed for the first time since we got here.

Leane's face looked serious. "Tesh... Can I ask you something personal?"

I paused. "Sure."

She hesitated and said, "What will you do now that we are here?"

I frowned, feeling uncomfortable. "What do you mean?"

"Well... You and Streak... What happens now? I mean, you two have a thing. You always had in Ang. We saw it. DAINN advised against it... D would... Not part of the plan, right? But we're in a new place. Our rules don't apply here if you don't want them to."

I tried to deflect, not wanting to talk about this. "Leane, you know we don't have time for this."

"I do... but my question still stands. Do you want to make time for this?"

I shook my head. "Why are we talking about this now? It is not a priority."

Leane was persistent. It was part of her make-up. "It is not, and I'm glad you see it that way because... I'm not sure it would be a good idea for you and Streak to become... Well, you know."

I sighed. Even here, the stupid judgment followed. Exasperated with the subject, I said, "I hear you. We need not concern ourselves with this. Not now. Never."

I saw Leane's face before the visor folded. She looked relieved.

I found myself alone inside the shaft again and tried to forget the conversation. It wasn't easy. We had carried with us all the perceptions, preconceptions, and limitations of our society into the past. The freedom that I hoped to find here looked once again unreachable.

By the look of it, my location was halfway down the sheer vertical wall from a small ledge below. The narrow overhang appeared wide enough to walk on. And past that point, darkness. My eyes drifted around the cave.

For the first time, I saw its vastness. The sheer wall in front of me glittered with tiny sparkling crystals in the bedrock. They resembled those my pulse made, golden hues shooting from the twisted sedimentary limestone. Only, they didn't spread in a ring formation. Instead, they shimmered like stars in the night sky of our dome, some bigger and brighter than others. It was joltingly beautiful in a raw and natural way, for the immensity of the cavern bespoke of eternity. The walls took unusual shapes in places, ready to unfold the mystery they held as I surveyed the depths below. I roamed through the cavern with silence wrapped around me.

The UniWrap pulse device on my wrist caused a small hole in the wall's surface. The Pulse pushed a powerful sonic wave ahead, creating rings molding the surface of the shaft. The opening in the bedrock of the tunnel grew ahead of me. This technology shaped smooth cylinders, merging rocks and creating safe underground passages. The golden fusion emanating from it could not have caused a weakness in the cavern's infrastructure. Measuring the rock's density with my PVZ, the number I got confirmed my suspicion. It had reinforced the structure, not weakened it.

The tunnels, which should have led us to the outside, tumbled in part. Only now, my knowledge that we had not caused it called for another revelation. What did?

Blast ran into this problem in the tunnel he followed. It created the torrential downpour from above. We neither foresaw nor expected this collapse. Our paths under the Earth should have led us outside easily after we cleared our way to the surface. Instead, we faced an unknown and had lost contact with Blast.

Something was going on in these parts.

I looked around the cave, puzzled. What caused the trembling of the Earth around us? The sonic noise heard earlier might have contributed to this weakening, but I saw nothing that could explain its provenance in this area of the cavern.

While Streak attempted to locate Blast, floundering his way underwater on the other side of one of these walls, I wanted to seek the cause. My eyes followed the path past the ledge below. I drifted toward it and landed on the small overhang. I leaned forward, seeing nothing but black emptiness. Not fond of heights, I picked up a rock nearby and threw it.

I counted the vertical length of the ridge. The weight of the stone, the velocity of the fall should give me an approximate height. I waited, my ears stretching for a sound.

Nothing. There was no noise resonating from the fissure inside the Earth. Indecisive, this left me apprehensive about exploring the abyss. I retreated. It would wait. We needed to secure the way out. I moved up the wall.

To my right lay the direction Streak and Blast found themselves.

Leane faced the incoming torrent at about the same time I did. Since the tunnel she was in did not crumble under the water's weight, she should have made it back to our chamber by now. I reluctantly reached out to her. "Leane, is everything stable with the chamber door?" My voice possessed an edge because of our last conversation.

"Almost there," she replied.

I surmised we had hit a snag, and a big one at that, because the waterfall didn't seem to decrease in power. Instead, it kept a steady stream, falling into the abyss below.

Every step since we separated had taken me further away from all of them. The EmVats communication system kept us linked, and despite the growing physical distance between us, it felt like my friends were in the next room.

Leane reassured me. "The door is fine." Her curt response showed that the turn of our last conversation had perturbed her. Too bad... At the moment, I didn't care what she thought.

Mage was fine. That was all that mattered to me. At first, I had wished Mage beside me in the tunnel. Now, instead, relief filled me because he remained safe inside the chamber.

I glanced up, gliding toward the rupture in the bedrock. How far did this shaft go past that point? My desire to see us out in the open fought an inner conflict. The bottom of the pit remained unattainable the higher I got, but the more I went up, the more I felt a strange pull coming from the abyss. This was odd. We would need to investigate this later.

The screen of my suit showed that only twenty-nine minutes had elapsed since we left the chamber. It seemed like hours. Blast's absence weighed on me. Saving my friend came first, no matter what lay in our path. I reached for him again. His silence, so unnatural, concerned me. *Blast... Can you hear me?*

I arrived near the opening. I should continue up the wall, but my instinct called me to stop. We were inside the mountain and separated by tons of rock. I needed to get to him; I focused harder. My mind stretched ahead in his direction. I touched the rugged surface, my palms spread against the wall, my thoughts crept forward, following the chain of long tunnels. I wished for Leane's gifts once again. Frustration rose, and I squashed it. There was no help for it. These were not my gifts. They were hers, and I couldn't acquire them no matter how much I wished for them. Her skills would help us in our search, and that had to be enough.

"Leane, can you scan the direction where Blast took off? Guide me through the pathways leading to him. I will merge with you."

"Hmm...." Her hesitation resonated loud and clear. "You want to do this now?"

I sighed. "Why not?"

"Maybe we should wait until we are... calmer? It could be more stressful otherwise."

She had a point. Our reservations regarding our last conversation couldn't interfere with the work. "Look, I'm not sore at you for asking the question before."

"Maybe not, but you did not like my position on it."

"Leane, we are friends... It's not about your concern. It's about stupid rules. I hate that we bring these with us here. That's all."

Leane frowned. "Some rules are not that stupid, Tesh."

"Maybe not, but then tell me... What about Blast?"

Her look gave her away... "What about Blast?"

I smiled... "You know..."

She shook her head. "There's nothing between Blast and me."

I laughed. "If you say so."

She shrugged, "Besides, if there was, we don't have any rules against it."

Here it was… The crust of the matter. A Giver of Life and a Molder of Things did not represent a threat. A Shaper of Thoughts and a Gatherer of Space did. "And who came up with that stupid rule? And what would you do if it existed?"

Her eyes reflected her thoughts. She felt terrible about the rules, but they didn't reach her.

"Look, I disagree with these rules the same way I disagree with some of the Council's decisions. I have for the longest time, and I will not hide it, but you have a right to your opinion."

Leane's smile broke through on my screen. "Okay. So, let's move on… Water is still high here, but I don't see any breach to the compartment. We'll need Blast to build a wall and contain it away from the door if it doesn't light up. I think it should, though. How much of the underground water reservoir could there be?"

"I'm not sure, but can you create another opening to drain the tunnel?"

"What do you want first?"

"Guide me. I'm worried that Blast has been unconscious too long."

"Give me a second, and let me walk toward his tunnel."

Leane reached the nearest wall bearing a greenish hue and put her palms on it. "I'm ready." She leaned toward the uneven surface and closed her eyes.

Scanning came quickly to Leane, with her skills performing in different ways according to defined wants. Her abilities had a surprising range, and many times I wanted to switch places with her. She had come to the Institute from the Faculty, and it was not by choice that she transitioned. On that point, we found common ground, for I came from the SRC as unwillingly as she did. Over the years, we had made peace with that. Our friendship flourished under the tests thrown our way by the Institute leadership.

I felt her breathing and heartbeat. Joining her mind to mine, I kept centered, opening a doorway to anchor her to me, giving her a thread to hold on to if she lost herself. "I'll monitor you. If it's too dense, let me know."

"I will."

Her voice disintegrated in my ears as I merged with her mind. And I was no longer inside the large cavern, but inside Leane, and abruptly, felt what she felt.

Rock... Heavy. Tons of it. Matter so dense it pressed against my body, crushing me like an invisible force on all sides. There was no escape from it. I began to fight for my breath and forced myself to calm down, centering my thoughts and relinking to her own. It was not real. It was me inside Leane, under tons of rock, deep inside a mountain.

She was not inside the rock, but it sure felt like it. Her ability for such a thing remained something I still grappled with every day.

Leane moved ahead of me, leading me through the rock formations. The heaviness didn't lift. Instead, it increased with every breath she took. I felt like I was suffocating. I held on to the link, disregarding the oppressiveness of it all.

She found a pathway. Fluidity replaced the immovable force of the mountain. We were now floating through it, carried by a current that pushed us forward, water. We followed the bedrock. The current pushed us away from our target. No, I wanted to say... In Leane's head, I whispered, *It's not the direction. We're moving away from them.*

I know. Let's follow the current. There is a way out, further ahead.

But I am in a cavern leading to the outside. We need not do this, Leane.

I want to see what lay beyond these walls, please.

Blast needs us.

Her frustration with me resonated deep in my head. *I know, but for once, follow my lead. Streak will take care of Blast. Let's do this.*

What did you mean for once? Do I ignore your recommendations?

Sometimes...

Fine... Go ahead.

We bobbed in the water, following the increasing stream along the massive walls on either side of us. *Wait... Wait it out. Tesh... We are in the sea. What we're feeling is the tide going out. Look... The water is clear, crystal clear.*

Turbulence caught us inside the undertow. We rolled, losing ourselves as we tumbled around and around. Leane kept her calm, but her breathing increased, coming out more raggedly.

Steady, Leane.

The undertow pulled harder, and we fought against it. Our release from the tide brought us to the surface.

I saw the glimmer of light — a blue sky through transparent waters.

We broke through the sea. We were outside... Swimming in the ocean and facing massive cliffs.

The tide moved around us. Our faces emerged into the sunlight from the darkness of the cave, like a cork.

Leane sounded quite satisfied in my head. *It is one way out.*

Yes, it is...

Our location, just beneath an expanse of cliffs overlooking a small beach, butted against the side of the mountain with the forest right beyond it. *Beautiful.*

Leane, satisfied, pulled back on the strings of her scan. Following a similar journey backward, she unwound the strands she had weaved moments ago and moved us toward the darkness of the mountain. This time, she ventured inside different passageways, still searching for Blast and Streak, and we found ourselves back in the cave at our original positions.

I withdrew from her mind. There were no traces of Streak or Blast.

"I missed something," said Leane, her brows furrowed in contemplation on the screen of my visor.

"Let's do it the old-fashioned way. Let's go meet them," I replied.

With assurance, I turned around and glided toward the tunnel's opening. "Streak... We're coming to find you and help."

Streak's face appeared distorted under the weight of the water. "No need, I'm following Blast's signal. Find us an exit instead."

"We already did... Leane found it." My voice sounded excited. I couldn't help myself, but I wore this massive grin on my face as I looked at Streak.

He smiled back. "That good, huh?"

I nodded. "Leane... Tell him."

"We found the ocean," exclaimed Leane with a laugh. "There's a beach, and the sky is so clear."

"So, let's get Blast out of the deep dark hole he put himself into and get the HellNet out of this place," I added with a newfound assurance. The sunlight made me feel powerful again.

Inside the chamber's infrastructure created to protect us, the lighting was soft and warm. The temperature remained constant, avoiding the dampness of the corridors underground.

I hovered back to the gap in the rock. Inside the tunnel, the water was at my waist. My boots propelled me ahead. I shot out from the water and glided above it within the tube. I arrived near Leane, who waited for me near the junction. Her hands plunged into the water, and she appeared in deep contemplation.

I slowed down when I reached her side. "Are you all right?"

"Hmm… Encharging," she whispered with a small smile. This process permitted her to retrieve the energy she had lost. Water was Leane's element and one she connected to strongly. She would derive a boost out of that connection, one she could store within her energy field.

I nodded. "Ready?" Scanning deployed an enormous amount of energy, and Leane often needed a few minutes to recharge.

"I am now."

We splashed through the water in the direction of Streak, who was now tracking Blast. Checking our visors, we followed the signals emanating from their locators.

Leane's voice whispered in the NetComm, "I hate to say it, but I hoped it didn't work… When we abandoned our Conclaves and lined up to take our places in the chambers, we expected not to return to what we knew. My mind, overrun by emotions, constructed what it wanted. I had hoped to arrive on the surface and find our world, even if it appeared broken."

"Now, we know otherwise, for we never saw our ocean like this," I whispered. We both wished it... She possessed the courage to say it out loud. We knew now; our wishes did not manifest. We were here at another time. I glanced in her direction and said, "I feel the same, Leane. I think all of us do."

Leane said, "Do you think the other programs made it? The SRC was so DarNet sure. They believed this would preserve us. Most of us, at least," exclaimed Leane. "You knew the odds, right?"

"I did." I sounded calm to my ears.

"Thirty-three percent, and you never said a word." Leane's voice wavered. "Apart from the fact that we should rejoice, we even woke up at all... We're the Institute's Conclave. We are the governors of our world, and we set the priorities. Our mission remains the same, lead all other Conclaves. Yet, we suspected nothing. We were in the complete dark. What does that tell us? I call this Netfucked."

"Yes, I know."

"I hate feeling guilty to be alive." Leane's voice was thick with sadness.

Streak's voice interrupted us. "Origin worked," confirmed Streak. "Since it did, we have work to do. We have three chambers to locate."

"...And our friends to rescue," Leane continued.

I shook off the misery this spun on me since the moment we entered Origin. It gave me pause. This blue ocean looked sparkling. The air appeared clear, and the sky remained pristine and devoid of clouds. It should bring my mood up. Regardless, I took a deep breath and focused on the goals ahead. "Talking about friends, how are you progressing to find ours, Streak?" As I inquired, I also projected my thoughts to Blast. *How are you doing?*

I received nothing back from him.

"Not like a fish in the water... Rather like a rock at the bottom," Streak grumbled. "These are great in the air, but in water, they are dead weight."

My mind heard Blast's thoughts. His response rang in my head. *Lousy, but what can I do about it?*

His voice resonated after that in the NetComm. He was furious... "I don't see why they didn't send Origin into space. The outcome would have been better than this. DarNet, I hate this place. HellNet, Streak, get me out of here." Confronted by his fears, Blast, pissed at finding himself inside the ground and submerged to boot, grew impatient.

"Well, if it's not sleeping beauty. Tweak your locator. Your signal goes in and out. Adjust it so I don't walk the entire bottom of this pool."

"Working on it, big boy. Why not space? That's what I want to know," continued Blast, grumbling to himself.

Only we all heard him.

"The risk they would notice us would have been too high, Blast," answered Streak.

"If you ask me, they did a lousy job. We have stealth, don't we? Why not use it?" Blast said.

"By the sound of it, you're fine," Leane said with a giggle. "What happened?"

"Blast this place... I got caught when the wall burst. I hit my head, and it knocked me right out. The current dragged me under a piece of rock I could not dislodge. Where in the HellNet are you, Streaky?"

"Coming... Hold your Netass... Leane and Tesh are also on the way. I'm letting the girls come to save you."

"Streak, you're a Netass."

The Chamber kept us safe, but time had moved past us and came back around to claim us, unfolding moment after moment. *How long has it been since we first went into the void?*

The only thing I controlled was me in that tiny second of awareness. Despite the amount of research done in decades to correct our planet's problems, we still live under domes for the most part. All the advances in science and technology could not combat the inhospitable climate changes on our planet's surface. Our innovations held in the palm of our hands did nothing to alter our potential destruction. *What awaits us behind the rock, a broken or an unknown world? We held the answer now. It was a strange world, in many ways novel to us.*

We found the entrance to the large pool below. It opened about three stories down.

Leane and I launched forward, dropping into the water. We broke the surface within seconds. Quickly, we sank downwards, touching the sandy bottom. Despite our lack of visibility due to the sediment that moved around us, we began our walk.

"Clave, we need your help. Blast got himself pinned down, and there is no way I can move this thing alone."

"Yeah, blame it all on me. I didn't choose the *DarNet* cave."

"We're almost there," I said, pushing forward faster, with Leane by my side.

Until now, the search of the caves remained centered on our chamber, near water. Soon, we would have to expand it if we found no traces of the other compartments. But first, we needed to retrieve Blast.

"Clave, I don't mean to rush you, but know that my EmVat is doing some weird things," groaned Blast.

"Is your energy field fluctuating?" demanded Streak, guessing the problem.

"Huh, huh... You could say that," murmured Blast, unsettled.

"Not surprising. This thing must weigh tons." Streak's voice sounded concerned.

Leane and I glanced at each other. It was a bad thing.

We were closing in on them. The light in the water ahead of us showed as much.

Until that moment, she had paced herself, but now in no time at all, she left me behind. She moved so fast across the water, gliding through liquid as if through the air, toward the massive wall standing just ahead of us. "We're here..." she said, sounding relieved.

I thought the barrier ahead was the mountainside. It quickly became apparent that it wasn't.

Streak stood beside a rounded structure, leaning toward something on the ground.

We were dealing with a large rock formation that dropped when the water poured from above.

Seeing the width and height of it caused me to pause. How in the HellNet are we going to lift this off of Blast? Our EmVats could move a lot of weight, but would the three of us be able to handle this enormous mass?

The Android inside the chamber would do a quick job of this, but we couldn't open the Chamber without risking the equipment, so long as the water remained high inside the tunnel. The continuous flow over the last hour showed that this might not abate soon unless we created additional shafts in the tunnel's flooring, which would allow the water to escape.

I scanned the bedrock, reluctant to consider opening more tunnels at the moment due to our ignorance of the topography of this mountain. We needed Blast and his molding abilities. Only our friend lay at the bottom of this pool, stuck. DarNet.

Leane kneeled near Blast on the ground. "Well, any suggestions?" she asked, with a light tone.

There was only one that I could see. "Molding," I whispered. "This is the way to move this thing."

"You transform it, Blast," said Leane, excited at seeing our friend free of the obstruction.

"Ouch…" groaned Blast. "Tesh, you're a genius. Why didn't I think of that?" His voice sounded half disgusted, half-embarrassed with himself.

I hid a smile, feeling relieved. The insurmountable setback would disappear in the course of the next few minutes. Until now, Blast had not thought of it because it rattled him from being underground.

Streak snickered at that one. "We can always count on you to make things interesting, Blast."

"Don't rub it in, Streaky. I must have hit my head much harder than I thought," said our very annoyed friend. "All right, take a step back for this. Make it two or three."

Leane pulled away from Blast after squeezing his hand and came to stand by my side.

Streak, closer to the end of the wall, moved back to the left of us.

"What will you mold, Blast?" Leane asked.

"Water... What else?" Blast responded, already focusing on the rock, pressing against his chest. His EmVat energy field fluctuated. For now, it remained the only thing preventing him from being crushed.

Blast pressed his hands against the stone. His palms glowed with a green hue, the mark of his energy signature.

In the next instant, the stone melted away, gaining a translucent quality before it disintegrated into water particles. Part of the wall disappeared, releasing part of its weight.

"Wait... Wait!" exclaimed Streak, suddenly.

Blast stopped, freezing the outpour of energy.

Streak pushed up against the ground with the thrusters of his boots toward the ceiling. He flew there, scanning the area supporting the roof of the cave.

Blast's chest, halfway out from under the rock, remained pinned down.

"The ceiling appears weak. It won't hold without this wall. Hurry, Blast. We need to haul ass from this place. Girls, get ready to shoot out."

"Wait... Hurry... I would like you all to decide," shot out Blast, but his hands reached out against the edge of the rock, and he began sending energy back into the wall.

The bedrock shifted, its matter transforming right under our eyes.

Blast's power as a Molder transmuted all forms of material into different elements, changing their composition and affecting atoms. The object lost its consistency.

A considerable rumbling resonated over our heads. The screams of metal against the bedrock of the mountain reverberated around us. Rocks detached from the ceiling, raining on us at once.

I said to Leane, "Get out of here; we will be right behind you."

"No, I'm not going anywhere without you guys."

Examining Blast's chest under the barrier, I reached for his arm, determined to pull him out. Filled with relief, he moved from the weight of his prison. I pulled him.

He slithered on the floor of the pool and rolled.

In the next instant, he stood up beside us. "Streak, I'm free. Let's NetScram."

The cave's ceiling gave way. The fissure opened under the weight of something big. An object, rounded and polished in a dark charcoal grey, shot down toward the pool floor. It appeared as a flat disc, whose even turned edge, we recognized. We had just found one of our chambers, and by the look of it, it was the EHAF's.

In the tumult that followed and among stones, twisted beams, broken rocks, and pebbles that came down with it, a sense of relief rose within me.

Our scientists came through, and two of our chambers had made it, one of them being the EHAF.

The EHAF was our ally, and my heart swelled with hope because we could count them on our side, according to President Langden.

The water, so bright before, became opaque and filled with silt, reducing our visibility. The wreckage surrounding us required that we retreat away from the area. Boulders came crashing down, and the vertical wall shifted toward us.

I pulled back, with Leane at my side. We both engaged the thruster of our boots and flew away, avoiding fallen debris without a word.

Blast appeared behind us within seconds.

The water dampened the cacophony of sounds, but we could still hear as rock tumbled downward, hitting the outer walls of the chamber and displacing the vast body of water, forming waves we fought against as we hovered away.

I screamed over the noise, "Streak, where are you?"

Our visibility, limited at this moment, hampered our movements. We advanced through the wreckage of the cave, avoiding traps in the uneven terrain. With each water displacement and the fallen rocks tumbling on the remaining surface, the pool became more unstable.

Blast pulled Leane behind him and pushed me ahead.

Concerned about Streak, who still didn't respond, I yelled again, "Streak... Where are you?"

Static. Silence.

We reached the entry point where the tunnels met, and I glanced back. The entire side of the cavern spread, covered in rocks, the rounded surface of our chamber ensconced amid them. The length of the whole cave was now blocked with parts of the twisted structure. Origin lay ahead in a pile of wreckage.

Leane lifted onto the tunnel with Blast in tow.

I hesitated, trying to see past the stilted water below. Everything appeared distorted and out of focus through my EmVat. Opening my visor, I searched for Streak's locator signal. My voice trembled when I called for him again. "Streak? You better answer me."

My heart tore inside. What if something happened to Streak? I breathed with difficulty as a sense of panic flooded through me.

Blast's hand reached for me and attempted to pull me up.

I resisted. "Wait… We have to look for Streak." My visor closed in the struggle.

"We will," answered Blast, in a tone edged with anxiety. "Just let the dust settle down there." His hand grabbed my arm and pulled me to safety, lifting me inside the tunnel.

"Let's look at the Vlogs," he said, with both of his hands resting on my shoulders.

I nodded, my visor unfolding again in front of our eyes. Searching for my monitor, I looked for Streak's locator signal. I rewound the actions of the last few minutes on the screen. Surveying the images recorded by our PVZ, I located where he had stood right before the cave-in. "He hovered right under the overhang there. It is where the ceiling appeared weak to him. Where did he go?"

Leane leaned over my right shoulder, pressing her hand on it as she checked the video stream with me.

We witnessed a larger piece of the ceiling dislodged, among other rocks. The column holding the cavern's roof fell right where Streak appeared to have been and dropped on our friend as he attempted to evade it.

Streak's signal moved underwater. It disappeared and reappeared a few seconds later. Our second in command swam fast, but his erratic trajectory suddenly changed, and a vast expanse of wall hid Streak from our view.

"He didn't use his Znet…" whispered Leane.

"Streak, are you okay? Streak?" My voice trembled. My agitation soon turned into full-on panic.

"What's that?" asked Leane, alarmed.

A small area on the screen showed his vital signs. In seconds, the signal disappeared. Streak was gone.

I reached out in my mind. Streak? Streak? No, I screamed, "No, no, no!" I didn't realize that I had spoken these words aloud until Blast enfolded me in his arms. I looked at their faces and saw my fears reflected in theirs.

Streak… Streak… Please answer me.

Frantically, I pulled away from Blast's arms, ready to dive down, but he held me back.

"I can't hear him… I can't read him anymore. Blast, look for him… Please, keep looking for him."

"I will, Tesh… But we have to get organized. It starts with the chamber."

I stood there, paralyzed. How could it be?

We had tech equipment. We had extreme powers. We were strong beyond measure. We were also fast. We were incredibly resourceful.

It was not possible, and my mind refused the obvious. Streak was there and then was gone in the course of a moment.

The event played back in my mind. Streak was there one instant, and in the next, he had vanished. A pattern of recognition formed in my head – he jumped.

Streak was a Gatherer... A Gatherer of Space. If he found himself stuck in a bad situation, it would be in his power to bail out and to move into a different place; even a totally different time. He could orb through locations, disappearing from here, only to reappear somewhere of his choosing. He could also bend time...

Tesh, Blast... Let's not panic yet... Chances are Streak bailed out.

Do you think so? He would only do that if he knew the place. Here, it's risky, said Blast.

Maybe so. But Streak still may have. Leane's words resonated as whispers in my head.

If he did... There's nothing we can do right now. We have to wait until he reappears.

I sure hope so, yes... That's it, said Leane.

Better be, muttered Blast.

Leane, Blast... I still don't feel him, and I should feel him. His vitals have vanished.

I screamed these words in their minds.

My feelings rocketed inside my chest. Raw pain twisted me. I felt as if I was drowning, as if I couldn't breathe anymore. The turbulence within me hit my body with the force of a tidal wave. It coursed through every fiber of my cells, paralyzing.

Suddenly, Leane and Blast winced with the force of my emotions.

"Stop, Tesh," screamed Blast.

I saw the hurt on their faces through the tears in my eyes.

Blast shook me. My friend said something else, but I didn't hear it.

I was trying to reach Streak.

A part of me knew I needed to focus on protecting them. Erecting a barrier between my mind and theirs was what they trained me to do. But my emotions spiraled out of control, bringing a brutal assault on my mind and rendering me erratic. Defending against it, protecting them and myself became impossible.

Over the noise of my blood rushing through my ears, Blast's voice reached me. "Tesh... Tesh... Stop it. You're hurting us."

OMG, said Leane in my head, and she shuddered against me.

I shut down the tumult of my mind, enclosing myself within a wall of my own. I turned myself off from everything and stood alone in darkness.

20 SHELTER
Gen

MIT, Massachusetts - 2018

Gen Aubrey shares the birth of an organization that will influence the shape of our future. I witness it in some parts, receiving the information in others. But for once, I do not helm the rendition of the design. DAINN Annals – Summer 2018.

Jonas was gone. He never called.

Fear never left me.

The night my data disappeared, it became my constant companion. Its presence during the day overshadowed everything, and at night it overwhelmed me. I felt alone, unable to turn toward anyone at the university because I had lived my college years aloof from most other students. Those few relationships I cultivated remained superficial. I didn't feel I had anyone to reach out to without Jonas. Besides, part of me permanently closed off in a time of trials. I didn't confide easily.

Sleep escaped me, even with the door of my dorm locked. The small lamp on my night table gave a glimmer of light in the room and kept the shadows at bay. Still, my eyes, heavy with sleep, remained open until the early hours.

I could only hope that Jonas was okay, although I worried about what had happened to him after my encounter. Panic set in over hours of waiting.

The following day, I got up early. I showered and put on some jeans and a shirt. I pulled my hair up into a ponytail, grabbed my keys and cell, and headed toward Jonas' dorm.

The grass looked wet from the early morning dew. I pushed over the double doors to Jonas' building and ran up the flight of stairs to his door.

Jonas never got up early. I expected to see his messy head and sleepy eyes when I knocked.

He didn't answer.

I texted him, puzzled by his absence. I made my way back to my building, but I didn't feel safe in it once inside. So, I headed toward the library.

I looked over my shoulders while walking the grounds of the university to get there. I ran through the campus, filled with anxiety. Even nestled in an oversized chair in the corner of the MIT library, I felt on edge. The hours turned the day into a grey landscape devoid of color. I left my makeshift hideout and headed out again.

Someone watching me burnt an imprint on the back of my neck. The feeling lasted. I turned.

A student wearing a hoody and jeans walked in my direction. His eyes looked ahead as if he didn't see me, and he passed right by me with the look that said, "What's with you? Freak."

I guessed I was a freak… An uneasy one at that. Searching the faces of those around me, I attempted to locate the individual behind the room invasion, but it remained an impossibility. No one looked like him.

An older man, looking out of place, turned the corner and entered a doorway. I thought he had glanced my way, but he disappeared inside. I was losing it…

The intrusion, left unreported, haunted me. My stolen codes and my lifted algorithms represented small losses compared to my ordeal at the hand of the pervert who assaulted me or even to Jonas' disappearance.

I searched for him on the grounds, at our usual spots during lunch, and my sense of paranoia increased over the hours, rendering me more anxious as time went by. Blast it.

Jonas never called or showed.

By early afternoon, the fear curled up in my abdomen catapulted me toward his dorm again. I unlocked his door. I pushed it open. His room, empty of any personal items, sent my mind into overdrive. No clothes, no books, and no posters reminded me of Jonas's existence. The room loomed in front of my eyes, devoid of personality. It looked like a blank canvas begging to be filled.

I knocked on the door next to him and waited.

"Just a minute," said a male's voice behind the panel.

A disheveled guy with a towel around his waist opened the door. "Yeah, what's up?"

"Hmm… Have you seen Jonas?"

"Do I look like I've been out and about?"

"It's afternoon."

"So?"

"His room is empty. We were supposed to meet."

The guy scratched his head and then his jaw. "Sorry, I can't help you. I haven't seen him."

"But his room is empty. You haven't seen or noticed anything?"

"Nah… I came back late last night. Cramming for an exam."

I looked around the hallway. Two students walked up the hall, laughing.

"Hey… Have you seen Jonas around?"

They looked at me for the beat of a minute and shook their heads.

"His room is empty… No one noticed anything?"

The tall one answered, "Exams…."

The podgy one said, "I haven't seen him in two days, sorry…." The door behind me closed as they entered their dorms.

Another door opened, and a guy holding a stack of books came out.

I moved in his direction. "Have you seen Jonas?"

He paused, "Nope, not since yesterday morning. Sorry, got to go." He walked away in a hurry.

I found myself alone in the corridor on Jonas' floor, unable to decide what to do.

The guy, next door to Jonas, came out of his dorm. This time he wore a pair of snug jeans and no shirt. He appeared comfortable in a state of undress. "Still here?"

He walked to Jonas' room. "I wouldn't worry about this if I were you. He bailed… early." Opening Jonas' dorm, he turned back to look at me. "He had plenty of credit to graduate. That's what he told me last week."

I watched him closely. He appeared unconcerned.

Another door opened a few steps away, and a young man looking every inch like a jock came out.

The guy in snug jeans turned and yelled. "Hey, Jonas is gone. Know anything about it?"

His voice looked every bit like his face, devoid of any thoughts, "Who's Jonas?"

The guy in snugged jeans laughed and shrugged. "Sorry,…" He went back into his room and closed the door.

In a few days, the semester ended. Some knew Jonas, and others didn't, but those who did, assumed he had left early.

Still, this didn't reassure me.

My popularity around my peers didn't score high either.

Unable to subscribe to this notion, I headed to the administration office.

They confirmed that Jonas had finished his classes early. Having accumulated more credits than he needed to graduate this last semester, he had left that morning.

Gone… Jonas is gone.

He didn't call. What kind of friend is that?

I meandered through the campus, my head reeling.

Jonas never mentioned graduating early. I didn't think he would hit the road without telling me. My friend didn't even say goodbye. He never returned my calls about my stolen codes. The Jonas I knew would not do that. Something terrible had happened to him, and it was my fault?

My feeling of responsibility lingered. I experienced it with my mother's disappearance. Guilt ate away at me; with every minute, the needle on my watch moved.

I left Jonas half a dozen messages and waited, keeping my panic from overwhelming me. When I reached out to hack land, and no one answered, I posted cryptic messages on the usual boards and waited. Later, I hit the gym, attacking the bag like an old enemy, working out my frustration. Then, I sent to Jonas more emails and text messages. And then I waited, waited, and waited some more. The emails got pinged back. Still, there was no word.

Chase's number drew my eyes several times during that day. Bringing a stranger into my life at this moment existed only as a wish list. I didn't even know if I could trust him.

I made a point of hanging around people and changed my routine. No matter how much I tried, I felt jittery and no longer safe in my room.

That evening, I poked around the internet, quivering at the slightest noise. It could not be happening to me. Millions of thoughts flipped through my head. *Bugger off.*

The next day, I walked around campus, avoiding the usual comfortable places, unable to focus on my last exam, and then I got lost when the little voice in my mind kept going off. *Don't take a chance. You don't know what you are dealing with, and the same can happen to you.*

The feeling of being watched persisted. Still, I couldn't spot anyone.

Worthless thoughts, but they prompted action.

I knew better than to believe Jonas vanished without a word. I didn't think he would go of his own volition without letting me know. Something had happened to him.

I got spooked even further, thinking about it. As improbable as it seemed, the fact remained that Jonas probably needed my help. The irony of our last conversation did not remain lost on me. These disappearances couldn't be a coincidence.

Run. To where?

I dialed my father's number. I needed to talk to him, to feel connected somehow. The phone rang. A message... My dad's voice resonated in my ear.

Par for the course. "Hey, Dad, how are you? It's me, Gen." *What to say?* "Everything is going well. I just wanted to hear from you. Call me."

Going to my dad occurred to me, but how would I explain everything to him without revealing that I was still hacking in search of my mother? Or that I had involved myself with the hacking of the computer system in the first place? I couldn't do this, and I couldn't risk him getting involved with something that could put him in danger. There remained too many things I didn't understand. Facing this alone appeared my only viable alternative.

I shivered and couldn't shake the feeling that I needed to run as I walked back toward my dorm.

The silhouette of a man walking behind me on the path across campus didn't reassure either.

After a few yards, I stopped and faced him. "What do you want?"

He looked puzzled and shook his head as he passed me, crossing the grass to another pathway to walk away from me, muttering to himself, "Crazy...."

That's it... I had lost it.

The image of Chase floated in my head. Should I call him? My instinct warned me to be cautious, and I intended to do just that. Only I had no one else to talk to since my superficial connections at school were only that, and they were not apt to deal with the stuff I found myself immersed in these days. So, feeling vulnerable, I ended up fantasizing about Chase. For a short instant, I felt safe in his arms. It was an attraction, feeling safe again. Besides, he was easy on the eyes. I groaned. I never behaved like these girls, never before. *What the hell is wrong with me?*

The whole situation rendered me restless. Too many people had vanished—first, my mother, the scientists, and now Jonas. The instances were too similar, and it felt as if I could never let go of the nightmare.

As often as I could, I went to our house, even when it didn't feel like home anymore. The difficulty of entering the household, knowing I would not see my mother again, became excruciating. I pretended she would spring up around the corner of a room. She never did... Every time a school holiday came around, I felt the hint of hope surface. What if?

My steps would falter as I approached the front door. A lump, lodged in my throat, almost gagged me when my hand touched the doorknob. My eyes searched in vain for my mother's silhouette when I pushed the panel. The experience repeated itself for a while, and then, I resigned myself to believing I would never hug her again. She would never welcome me back in her arms. This unalterable knowing devastated me. I came to accept it as penance – my way of paying for my selfishness that night.

Almost half a year went by. Eventually, seeing my father's face light up when he saw me arrive made the struggle worthwhile and eased the pain a little.

And now this…

I picked up the phone and called Chase. The phone rang… And rang… But I didn't wait for the line to pick up and hung up.

While I understood why my brothers acted that way, and I forgave them, it didn't mean that I forgot. We never spent another holiday together. A piece of my heart broke on that score too. My resentment at my brothers' selfish behavior didn't help, and ultimately, I let them go. There were no more calls, pleading for them to come for holidays or vacations. I made no more attempts to reach out to them, inquire about their lives, and give them news about us. It took one year, and I quit. I made peace with it and resumed my life. But sorrow ate away at the family we had become. Siblings split apart, turning into strangers. Family members detached from each other, indifferent.

Losing my mother caused us all to drift away when it should have brought us together. Some cases never close, they say. Determined that my mother's case wouldn't end up in that pile, I got a hell of a lot better at hacking. I wouldn't give up. And now… Jonas….

I took a deep breath to shake the loss. I wallowed in the emptiness too often. *Better get used to it.*

My phone rang.

I jumped at the sound. *Shit… I left it on after my last call.* Chase's name appeared on the screen.

I answered. "Hi."

Chase's voice said, "Who is this? Gen?"

I sighed… I gave Chase an incorrect number; no wonder he doesn't recognize me. "Hi, Chase. It's me, Gen."

Relief sounded in his voice. "Gen, I tried to call you. The number you gave me didn't work."

I grimaced. Better come clean… "I, huh… I gave you a fake one. I'm sorry."

He chuckled. "I figured. I'm glad you called. I was looking for you."

"You were?"

"Yeah." His voice sounded severe when he continued, "I need to see you. Where are you?"

"I have one last exam, and then I'm going back to my dorm."

"Where's your exam?"

"Simons building. It starts in twenty minutes."

"Fine. I'll meet you there afterward." Chase hung up.

I felt a warmth in my chest for the first time since my ordeal. I was not alone.

The moment I answered the final exam question, relief settled in my chest. I could get out of here, finally.

I sprinted out of the exam room, expecting to see Chase.

He wasn't there.

Maybe he waited outside the building. *I never gave him a room.*

I took the stairs with the other students. The crowd flowed inside the sweeping staircase. The sound of feet on the steps echoed, the voices rising in relief rose amid the laughter of my peers. We had done it. The year ended here at this moment. Surrounded by others so alike and so different, I relaxed, looking at all their happy faces.

A man approached from behind and reached for me, laying his hand on my shoulder. "Miss…"

My heart made a summersault in my chest. Sidestepping, I shrank from the contact. I didn't recognize the guy and didn't stop to talk. I evaded him, jumping several stairs, pushing past students. Voices rose all around me, upset, shouting. I kept going. I never turned to see if he followed me. With each footfall on the landing, I increased the distance between us. Frantic, panting, I only had one thing in mind: finding Chase.

The crowd moved as one.

Ogling would be appropriate to define my actions. What the hell… Everyone appeared as if they had it in for me. *Make sense, why don't you?*

Running the hall's length, I took one of the front exits with many people meandering outside. A glance at me passing through glass doors showed me looking like a zombie. Seriously.

The air on my heated face felt cold, but I knew it was not over. It was only a matter of time before the man came for me again. I screamed at the situation inside my skull.

Where was Chase?

The grounds were empty under the street lamps. Chase was nowhere.

The walk following the edge of the road leading to my building felt surreal. The small path reaching the wing of the Applied Science Building ended at the concrete walkway. It took a few minutes to scamper through the grass. This way lengthened my walk across campus. I wanted to get lost in the city. But I got lost in my thoughts instead.

Getting the hell out of MIT had become an obsession, but I didn't know where to go. My desire to see my family, hampered by the fear that whoever took Jonas and my codes could use my loved ones against me, kept me away from them.

My brain functioned on hyper-drive. Scrutinizing everyone and suspicious of any harmless actions, everything around me looked dark, bathed in shadows and heaviness.

Graduation didn't bring joy or excitement. The lack of news from Jonas killed that.

I needed sunshine, rays of it.

Suddenly, my hair rose on my neck. The feeling that someone walked a few steps behind me made me walk faster, crossing over to the upper floors of the next building.

The sensation lasted.

When I could no longer stand it, could no longer sustain the pressure, it happened.

"Gen…"

About to crack like a lunatic and scream, I turned. Bullseye.

Chase.

He stood about to talk… But I lunged toward him and threw myself in his arms. I didn't care that I made a fool of myself, and I didn't care what he thought of me at that moment. I didn't care because he showed kindness.

21
WARNING
Chase

MIT, Massachusetts - 2018

Chase Davenport struggles, knowing that Jonathan directed his team to act egregiously. Worried for Gen Aubrey, he not only warns her but takes action. DAINN Annals – Summer 2018.

She turned just ahead of me after I called her name. She threw herself in my arms before I could utter another word.

I held her close. Close enough to feel her against me. Close enough to smell the scent of her perfume drifting in the breeze. An essence of wildflowers rose and tickled my nostrils. There was a hint of spice there somewhere. I tried to place it, but couldn't, so I waited for her to calm herself and stop trembling.

My heart missed a beat. "It's all right… I'm here. Sorry, I'm late."

She looked frightened when she glanced up at me. "Where were you?"

"What happened? Did something happen?" My impatience got the better of me. "Gen, I've been looking for you everywhere. Where the hell have you been?" Gen was beautiful on the outside, but on the inside, she was a mess. Emotionally, things like an assault didn't just go away. Her state of mind was another thing altogether. One had to deal with it. She was a fiery little thing, though, but she appeared so unsettled at the moment.

She looked surprised and relieved to see me. "You have?"

"Yes. I told you that on the phone. I was worried about you."

Her face turned pink. "Look, I have a confession to make." She looked to the ground and faced me, straightened her shoulder, and said, "Oh, brother... I might as well tell you. I didn't know you called me. You see..."

I waved my hands in front of her in understanding. "You told me you gave me the wrong phone number. I figured that out on the third call."

She grinned at me. "You did?"

I was not thinking about what I was doing. "It doesn't take a genius," I said, caressing Gen's arms.

"You look terrific. How have you been?"

I laughed. Shifting on my feet... Unable to decide how to broach the subject. I found myself in the middle of a conundrum based on Jonathan's obsession to control a situation he had created. I wished I could bash Jonathan's head against the wall for his stupidity, or lay my hands on Steven and give him a piece of my mind, or corner Sean for lying after learning the truth of his orders play on my mind. They all had led me down a path I disliked. Regardless of these feelings and thoughts, I needed to tell Gen because she needed to know the truth.

At this moment, her pretty face was relaxed, and despite her smile from ear to ear, she looked damn exhausted. I couldn't help but say, "You look beat. Have you been sleeping?"

The smile disappeared under a flush of embarrassment. Gen's face closed off. The carefree moment went by. I wanted to kick myself.

"I'm fine. What about you?"

When Gen consented to show me the state of her room, I witnessed her vulnerability. This private moment only rendered her more attractive. My hand ran through my hair, "I've been worried about."

The grin reappeared on her features. "You've been worried about me?"

She somehow seemed happy about that. I grunted. "What happened that got you so scared just now?" I did not intend to give her the wrong impression. *Damn. I would have to be careful with that one.*

"I think... Someone is following me." She whispered.

"Why? Did someone try to approach you?" I wished I could take her away from all of this and provide some solace. The feeling she evoked was weird. Few people made me behave that way. I wanted to hold her in my arms and wished I could soothe her fears. The bottom line, I desired to take the hurt away. None of this made sense, not out of the blue, not like this. *What the hell.*

"Just minutes ago... as I was leaving the building. How would they know where to find me, Chase?"

Hell... I felt my stomach do a summersault. *It couldn't be that... now could it?* Could they have bugged my phone? I tried not to overreact.

"What's going on, Chase? You look like you have seen a ghost."

With calm, I said, "I needed to see you before leaving the campus. We need to talk." Although I wanted to know how she fared after the ordeal the other night, it was better to keep everything casual.

She frowned. She seemed to sense that this was not a social visit. Disappointment stared at me from her green eyes as she glanced in my direction. She whispered, "Okay."

I felt her anxiety, but with resolve, I walked with her toward her building. "When are you done?"

"This was my last exam."

"Good. When are you off?"

"Graduation is in two days."

I nodded again, somewhat relieved. If Gen put some distance between herself and the Center, she could walk away from all of this. I echoed my thoughts, "That's good."

"Where are you going? You said you were leaving?"

I tensed. "I have something to do... Look... What I am about to say will not be easy to hear, so please listen to the end."

She observed me in silence.

I waited.

She nodded and, with reservation, whispered again, "Okay."

I took her arm. "Let's go sit down."

We walked toward a bench near the path. I paced in front of Gen as she sat down.

The silence lengthened between us.

"Chase, you have me worried. What's going on?"

"The other night... I was coming to see you."

"You were?"

I nodded. "I began to tell you that, but with everything that happened… Well, I felt it was better to wait until later."

Although Gen's face looked calm, she folded her arms and said, "Why were you coming to see me?"

Diving in, I took a deep breath. "I need to talk to you about your codes."

Her voice shook when she said, "What do you know about my codes?"

"A lot and nothing at all." He sighed. "It's a long story."

"Did you have anything to do with what happened that night?"

He looked offended. "Hell, no… But I know who did it. I am not talking about the guy you chased, but the people behind it. Your codes were getting too close to their projects. I don't think they meant for any of it to happen the way it did. Not that it's any better, mind you. I disliked their methods."

"Who are they?"

He shook his head. "Look, it's irrelevant. These people are working on something that they want to remain contained. I'm here because I think they will try to contact you to recruit you into coming to work for them. Don't."

"How are you involved in this?"

"It's complicated. I didn't know any of it until the other night. Not about you or the codes. Just don't work for them."

She jumped up. "I can't believe you're involved."

I watched her green eyes in silence for a moment. Her face was smooth, her skin translucent. Even exhausted, she looked pretty, but now, she was angry.

"My involvement is not important. But the other night, I met your friend, Jonas."

At the name of Jonas, Gen jumped up. "You know about Jonas?"

Ignoring her interruption, I continued, "He is fine. You need not worry about him. I saw him that evening, right before I ran into you. He is somewhere in Europe. They paid him off to leave."

Gen's face reflected the horror she felt at that moment. "Jonas wouldn't do that."

I smiled, but it was more like a grimace. "Jonas didn't want to. He was sorry to leave you."

She moved away from me as if I had become a threat. "How the hell do you know all of this? Did you set me up? Is that why you were there?"

I got angry thinking about how they duped me too, but there was no sense telling her that. She already had enough to contend with, and I didn't want to make it worse. "I didn't know what was coming down that night. I already told you this. Just stay away from an outfit called the Center."

Agitated and angry, she confronted me. "Why? How do you know any of this? What are you not telling me? Are they behind the disappearances of the scientists? How do you fit into all this?" She let out the stream of questions in one breath.

I supposed that I should have expected that, considering how she reacted when she found the guy in her room. She would not back down from a fight.

My face must have given her the answer she sought concerning her last question.

"OMG. You're a part of all this."

She took a step back and another. "Stay away from me."

Contrary to what I expected from her, and before I knew it, she started to run.

"Gen... Wait!" I realized that I didn't want to remain a stranger, which had everything to do with the aim that brought me here.

She didn't look back or slow down. She just kept running.

I sat on the bench. It went well.

I grimaced, knowing full well it didn't.

22
REMORSE
Tesh

Deep Inside The Earth - 2018

The chamber keeps them safe, even in sleep, and rejuvenates them if needed. The DAINN Network, based on our technology of the future, accesses this world to integrate an obsolete system in this timeline, unaware that something else already exists here from another time. DAINN Annals – Summer 2018.

The machine, working with efficiency, brought me within range of the performance spectrum established by our scientists. As my body peaked, my mind's acuity received and processed the data despite me. Once accessible, my neurons responded, my brain activity connected the place, the context, the actions and meaning, and the moment of realization took me by storm. I emerged from my frozen cocoon with each passing instant.

I claimed myself again. My mind soared.

Pain seized me. It perforated my abdomen like a snake twisted around my insides, throbbing and cold. *Streak, where are you?*

My eyes opened on the glass of the MedPod in which Leane and Blast placed me after I lost consciousness. The enhanced platform monitored my functions and provided my body with the needed nutrients to overcome the surge of mental and emotional turmoil I faced in the tunnels. Through it, I saw our chamber's ceiling.

The overload had never happened to me before. It was a first.

I had lost it, really lost it. I had hurt my friends. For that instant, my training was but forgotten, and I shared with Leane and Blast the sense of overwhelming loss I experienced when Streak disappeared.

Now, I no longer stood in the tunnel, but I remembered what I had done. I breached our fundamental Universal Pledge. So, I recalled the minutes leading to the darkness that penetrated my mind when the pain became unbearable. Unable to contain it, I shared it with Leane and Blast. Then, I remembered The Pledge and closed off. *But I had broken the Pledge and hurt them.*

My training, meant to maintain disciplined control over my emotions, should have prepared me. I reacted to the pain and lost control. I always knew that it might happen but had never experienced it before. The eventuality that I could lose Streak never entered my mind, not even here, and not even now. I couldn't accept it.

My hope drove me. We could overcome everything together, including the dictates of the council. We could overcome anything if we fought for our freedom, even if we stuck to our known protocol. Streak must come back.

I recognized the surface of the MedPod under my fingertips. It opened upon my consciousness returning, having fulfilled its purpose.

Waiting outside, I heard the soft breathing of my dog beside me.

Mage watched over me as I slept.

Cian appeared at my side. "It is good to see you back, Phenom Tesh."

I glanced at Cian with tears in my eyes.

"How are you feeling now? You caused us great fear, Phenom Tesh. Phrenic Leane's hands trembled when she checked your vitals."

I nodded. "I... lost... control."

"You have never done this before, Phenom Tesh. They would not expect it of you."

My reluctance to move kept me still and my mind wandered back to Streak and his disappearance.

I sighed... Anguish twisting my gut. Where was he now?

Streak would have never broken the mandates, not any time, no matter how much he loved me. But I preferred him with me, by my side, even as a friend. Until now, perhaps because of now, there was hope for us. I held on to that. Only I had to find him first.

They altered our minds. They wiped our memories. The knowledge made me angry, and I shook inside. For years, I wanted to be close to Streak. I desired to spend my life with him. The bonds we shared remained strong, despite the voluntary restraints he erected between us. We had also boosted our defenses against one another because of that. The Council had eradicated and stolen our moments together. The false sense that our relationship existed based on friendship remained a betrayal that cut deep. But now that we were here and had awoken in this place, we discovered the truth. The lie had lasted for years, and now the road to our desires lay ahead. *How could they do this to us?*

Thinking back over the moments I remembered, I frowned. It was Streak, more so than me, that kept a distance. At first, I didn't understand what made him aloof. He had forced himself to stay away from me. He believed my role would be more significant than his within the Conclave. I understood all of it now. There was no way he could get through the blank spaces left once they removed his memories. The confusing signals he gave along the way opposed his desire to get close to me. He had no way to combat that. Not like I did. The interludes between us piled up, demanding more control when we stood alone in one room because there always was something between us - the fake wall they erected. Only we did not understand. The attraction, the need, the emotional tie was there. On every occasion, Streak always pulled back, leaving me empty and without a voice. They became a cycle of frustrating instants leading nowhere. These often existed in the last year, until a few months ago. Now, I wished he stood in front of me, knowing that we may never touch again.

I wished I could get my hands on the one responsible for this: that little rat, the Rodent. My hate for Sloan Roden Baker filled me, and the stench of it made me sick. If Ang still existed, I would go back there and unleash all my wrath on him.

Streak made a promise that he would take care of it, and I guessed that it would have to suffice until we returned.

I straightened inside the pod and swallowed the bitterness. I reached out to Mage and squeezed his fur between my fingers. It felt so soft... The memories were all there.

Mage… And the moments we shared, rolling down the hill of the city's nursery among the plants and trees or splashing in the water basin in the Plaza's park under the vigilant eye of our domestic bot. Those days growing up made Tesh in just the same way as the edicts and implants of the Institute.

The Spozor injection took root, speeding up and enhancing my organs like a stroke of lightning. It spread throughout my entire body in a rush of quicksilver, electrifying my mind, heightening my perception, and bulking up my muscles. I absorbed these sensations like a sponge and got up.

No sounds reached me in here. The air of the chamber didn't move. There was only stillness around me, unlike what happened inside me. My cells responded to the injection.

The process continued, unaltered, despite my instinct, with an aversion I could never quite understand.

I retrieved a mirror.

On the outside, my face was identical, a girl with regular features, dark, long hair, and hazel eyes that turned the color of deep beryl when upset. These were the same eyes as Mage, which dictated my father's choice when selecting him as my companion. I thought they were our best features. Only, I stood with something broken inside me, like my world, if it withstood the cataclysm at all.

None of these actions spoke of what I stood for or who I was. Not recognizing me, acting against every conviction I possessed, and despising myself for it, I still knew I would do it all again.

Where is your loyalty, your kindness, Tesh? How is your devotion to your Conclave?

I could hear DAINN's voice in the back of my mind… Only, I didn't need his words to echo in my head because I knew they were also my thoughts. I held back for the wrong reasons: to protect them from knowledge because it spelled danger in my world. I knew that too well from experience.

Seconds passed, moving ahead and dragging me in their wake. Hope for a different outcome than what lay ahead filled my heart. We were here to change the future. One we believed was not yet set.

I opened my visor. I called out. "Leane, Blast?"

Leane responded, "Oh, good. You're awake. I told Blast you would wake when you were ready."

Blast joined in. "How are you feeling?"

Ashamed for what I had put them through, I whispered, "I'm so sorry. Are you both all right?"

Leane grimaced. "We are… It wasn't pleasant, but we are both okay."

Blast grinned, "A little warning next time would be welcomed, although this gave us insight on what you go through daily. How in the HellNet do you keep all our thoughts at bay?"

I shook my head. "Practice. I promise… It will never happen again."

"Okay," replied Blast, relieved to hear that.

Silence fell between us. I looked at their faces on the screen. "Do you want my help?" My voice sounded unsure. *Why would they?*

Blast eyes looked serious. My friend glanced in Leane's direction.

She nodded.

He turned back to me and said, "I think you should get outside... find out what we are dealing with and what is out there. We need to know where we are, and you're the best person to do this, Tesh."

Leane added, "We've got this, Tesh."

A clump in my throat stopped me from talking. I nodded and closed the feed.

I had betrayed a friend to save another by electing to lie to Streak. While I manipulated his mind to save my dog, I also kept the truth from my friends. They didn't know what I had gathered. So, the hurt I inflicted on my Conclave needed to remain the last one. Losing my control and sharing my emotions with Leane and Blast was the last of my transgressions. No wonder they didn't want me near them. When would I act the way my parents taught me all those years?

I connected to my past. The shadows rested with Rodent and the Institute and what they called upon me to do. I wanted Rodent dead. Maybe he was already... The evacuation plans, months of planning, deadlines met, agendas weaved, and all well underway when I learned the truth. I could never change these because they never wanted them altered. And then time ran out. I knew now that the responsibility lay with five Council members, and within the missing Chambers, we would find additional answers.

I turned toward a wall drawer, one of many placed along with the main compartment's structure. I touched it, and it slid open without a sound. All the DAINN archives lay within, organized according to dates and subject. The MindTranscripts and Vlogs waited in front of me, urging me to watch them. I had never been privy to those in Ang. Could I retrieve my memories from them? I held the

Vlogs in my hand, knowing full well that now was not the time. Fighting with myself, I sighed and put them back. Streak was right. It would have to wait, at least until we got out of here.

These data files included the profiles of all the members of the other Conclaves, their skills, qualifications, gifts, affiliations, attitudes, characteristics, and even their implants. Based on what DAINN told me and what Langden confirmed, I would access their information and perhaps, get a clue about their agendas.

I shook my head to dislodge these thoughts. Their intrusion upon this moment slowed me down. Remembering the mission, I grasped the present instant. One that unfolded and one I intended to alter, shaping a better tomorrow.

We would succeed here and would go back. I vowed to make the Council pay. Minutes later, I closed the drawer, grabbed more Spozor, and dropped it inside my suit. Mage followed me. "You have to stay here with Cian until I return."

Mage stopped and sat down.

I reached for another drawer and retrieved some food. "Here is a treat for being such a good boy."

Looking at me, he barked once, waiting for his usual caress.

I dropped to my knees and hugged Mage.

My visor opened on Leane's face. "Tesh…"

I tensed, "Yes, Leane."

Her face looked sad. "I know you feel guilty. Please don't."

"You mean that I shouldn't feel like I failed you? I do. There is little to do about that."

"It's not your fault."

"Yes, it is. You warned me about this. You told me there were reasons, rules even…."

"I know, but one cannot always control one's heart. I want you to understand that Blast and I, well, we get it. We will find Streak."

I nodded, unable to speak.

The NetComm closed between us, and I felt relief.

My mind took me back to Ang and the rules we had faced in our time. Why did it matter how two people lived their lives so long as the greater good remained satisfied?

I held the answers. A conclave rule, broken and disregarded, no longer promoted the greater good. It belonged to another category in our world, one where anarchy ate away at a system meant to protect us. I hated remembering all of it. *DarNet, when will this control be over?*

"He is not your match, Tesh. You cannot cheat DNA." DAINN's voice echoed in my head. "The system provides you with plenty of choices. You know how it works… The selection criteria based on physical, mental, and emotional traits, qualified each candidate to their match."

I never cared about DNA. It was necessary up to a point. But for DAINN, it mattered. The Council also insisted that our society's demands came first before those of the individuals.

For DAINN and within our System, these amounted to rules promoting order. They enhanced the value of life according to our Universal Pledge.

The Inst trained us to behave a certain way. Imps influenced our behavior. The programming we all went through reinforced both, so we complied with mandates given to us during our time as a Transient, Aspirant, Proselyte, Phrenic, and Phenom. All candidates responded to the training in the same way. Only those of us destined for Conclave leadership existed to meet higher standards. The expectations from those at the top required a particular behavior, reinforced at their roots by DNA attributes designed at the time of our conception… And these called for us to be in service of our gifts. So, all this went deep, too deep for me to ever break it.

Where are you? I no longer feel you, Streak.

Streak denied himself what he wanted: me. He would do it because no matter where and when we lived, he remained the product of our world. He would never sway from our society's ingrained teachings and the course they gave to his life unless DAINN approved Streak's path. In our world, it could only happen if the Council released its hold on him. Only, this remained an impossibility unless we returned to an altered future. Understanding this all along, I still had hope. And now we were here.

Only now, I may have lost you for good.

My mind was my gift, and although probed and structured a certain way, it remained mine until they tricked me because now I suspected they erased my experiences with Streak. We both had felt something when we kissed. Memories… Capable of twisting past the shaped pathways, I overcame most of the programming my mind received, never thinking they had dared. But they had.

The others did not possess this gift. What would happen now once we found each other again?

The protection of every citizen remained the basis for everything set in motion throughout our time. The safeguard of everyone came first. While the quest for individual happiness during our lifetime came second, it remained an important priority demanding space for each of us to flourish. How could one ever believe the Council established rules meant to provide our lives with a better chance of fulfillment without including love in it?

I stomped toward the door of the chamber, irritated with the Council. It represented their way of influencing the stakes. Only, no one except them knew. *How can I help the Claves find you? Surely, there was something I could do.*

I was about to engage the door panel when I glanced at one of our Custodians. I suddenly got an idea. I reached out to Blast and Leane. "Insts... "Where are you?"

Their faces appeared, glowing slightly in the darkness of the cave. "We're back in the pool."

"What if we used our Custodians? I can program a few to find Streak?"

"We don't have a signal." Blast's face grim as he looked in my direction, reflected some of his fears.

"I get that... but we can program the Custodians to explore areas of the cave where we cannot go. They can provide us with an underground map of the area. Maybe this can help me find him as well...."

Leane's eagerness appeared in her smile, "It would not hurt. The important thing is to keep searching for Streak." The look of relief shone in her eyes.

"We got the Cygil1000 with us," replied Blast, "I thought by digging, we would find something, and we moved a lot of rubble, but so far, nothing."

His concerns became mine too.

The Cygil1000, one of our most advanced robots, didn't help in finding Streak. It was a setback. Panic rose in my solar plexus, but I said, with a hint of optimism, "He escaped the collapse. Now, we have to locate where he went."

"I guess the Custodians could save us time. I didn't think about that." Blast looked at me and nodded, "Do it. Send them right away. I love this Netbrain of yours…" said Blast, with a grin.

"NetRoger that."

The NetComm closed. I wish I could feel the same way.

I didn't care for my brains or my gifts, even if they were valuable. Using them to find independence of thought from the Inst, despite the teachings, had provided me with positive outcomes. Only, my dislike of my tributes from my ancestors was my truth. I considered them a burden. I would give up everything for Streak.

"Can I help you, Phenom Tesh?"

"Yes. Fetch the Custodians… Not the Hulkings, but the Malstroms."

"Right away, Phenom Tesh."

"This past allows us to change our future, Cian, and for that, we need all of us," I said out loud with an assurance I was far from possessing. "These will keep searching every nook and cranny out there." The price to pay, if I didn't keep myself together, would be Streak. "I'm sure he used his gift to get out of harm's way," I muttered.

"Well, he did," said Cian, her robotic arms carrying a tray of Custodians. Our leaders used these around Ang for security reasons and sometimes for scouting purposes.

Unlike the others, whose powers corresponded to something they loved, I always fought against mine. Indeed, knowing people's minds in the most intimate details, reading their thoughts, and shaping their actions represented for me a distasteful legacy, serving an ability, which was no more than an unwelcome intrusion on others. It meant a breach of everything I stood for under the Universal Pledge. I could choose not to exercise my gift with the SRC. Only, I never had a chance against the System once my parents died.

The Institute ferreted out people like me.

We were few. We served specific purposes. Primarily, they sought after us to establish and maintain control over others, working for the System. In that, I didn't say DAINN, although the Network was a huge part of it.

Streak, Leane, and Blast owned their gifts. These tributes were a part of who they were, and for them, as essential as breathing. Giving them up would change them irrevocably. If they had to choose to follow their hearts and let them go, it would surprise me they would decide to part with them. Abandoning these gifts would ultimately be too costly.

We never discussed this issue among us. My team didn't know that I would let go of my gifts without looking back.

I prepped ten Malstroms in a matter of minutes with Cian's help. They were now programmed to get back to us and the chamber.

Blast interrupted my train of thought with new communication. "Tesh, I want to check the other side and see if we are missing something. The Cygil1000 will help me get past the wreckage."

The considerable boom resonated in the distance, followed by the Earth once again shaking.

I stopped what I was doing to the last Custodian. "Do you feel this where you are?"

"You bet we do," responded Blast. "It's damn annoying if you ask me." After a pause, he added, "How long before you can send them our way?"

"I'm about done."

The ground shook again, and I held on. "Blast, measure the amplitude of this quake for me. What is your visor saying?"

Inside the chamber, the rumble reverberated all around, just as powerful as before. The walls of the compartment held sturdy. Our equipment didn't budge.

I pulled in one of our tablets on the nearest console with my UniWrap. On my visor, the images of Leane and Blast became fuzzy, disappearing even for a beat. Then they were back. My tablet focused on the area where I stood. It showed a 9.3 on the scale.

"I show a 9.1 according to my reading. Why?"

"When I was in the cave, there was a significant drop-off. I'm wondering if something down there is not causing this. My reading shows a 9.3, and I am closer to the cave than you guys are."

"It's an interesting theory, one we can explore later, Tesh."

"I'm thinking of sending one Custodian down that shaft when I head topside."

The trembling subsided just as before.

"Fine, do that... Things are unstable around here, and it's not getting any better. I erected a barrier outside the door. You have a straight shot sending the Custodians our way."

"Fine... I'm ready now."

"As soon as you clear topside, Leane will join you to transport our equipment out of the caves. This sonic wave is wrecking this environment. I want everything we need out, as fast as we can make that happen," insisted Blast.

I moved around while he was talking and said, "Agreed."

"Leane, give Tesh a hand," Blast added, hoping she would follow his lead.

Leane crossed her arms over her chest and shook her head. "I'm not going anywhere until you get back here first."

I smiled. There was no budging Leane for now. "I'll let you guys know when I'm out. If you can't find Streak in the next few minutes, get out. No sense in risking the two of you." I stopped before my voice cracked.

Blast nodded.

Leane winked at me as I closed the visor.

Looking at Mage, I said, "Okay. You stay here, and I will be back for you."

The compartment containment field lifted once Mage stepped inside my cubicle. On command, the mechanism of the door engaged.

My EmVat rose around me as I waited in front of the entrance. When the last of the layers peeled away, I looked in the eyes of a stranger.

23
CONSPIRACY
Gen

MIT, Massachusetts - 2018

Gen Aubrey runs away from Chase Davenport, feeling betrayed and knowing she cannot trust him, but she cannot escape her attraction toward Chase, even if she wants to. DAINN Annals – Summer 2018.

The grounds crawled with students as I ran. My steps followed the path on automatic pilot, and my mind didn't catch up to it, for I was still thinking about Chase. What a letdown he was. He manipulated his meeting with me, but I wasn't sure for what purpose. What did he hope to gain? I didn't know. Part of me felt crushed by his callousness; another part believed that his caring was genuine. Regardless, his involvement with these thugs didn't warrant my forgiveness for hiding it. I couldn't trust him. When I turned the corner, the park in front of my building lay ahead, filled with people, and I collided with a brick wall.

I ran smack into it… The chest of a brick wall.

The tall man didn't seem to suffer from it, but I felt the jolt, and it took me a moment to get my bearings. He was muscular, with broad shoulders and the height to give anyone pause.

He didn't look like a teacher. Too well-dressed for that. He didn't look like the guy on the stairs either. Too old for that. "Miss Gen Aubrey?"

I hesitated but took a step back all the same.

A few people passed… A confrontation in a place I knew well, right here, would provide answers. Could he be the one behind everything? I wasn't sure.

He appeared way too clean-cut for that, but then who knew what lurked inside people's heads?

I took another step back and got more distance from him. It was typical of the last few days — me avoiding contact with others.

"You have nothing to fear, I assure you."

Huh, huh. Say what you want. I don't believe you. With anger, I looked at the stranger, and my upset took over. I wasn't about to listen to him. Prepared to flee, I thought better of it. People surrounded us. Perhaps this was the best place to confront him, yet I was tired, so tired.

His eyes observed me as if he sensed my mood. "I mean, you no harm."

His voice, different from the guy in my room, sounded lower and raspy.

I stepped back again. Keeping a distance of about five feet between us seemed insufficient. My voice came out aggressive. "Stay where you are. What do you want?"

The man stopped approaching me. He looked relaxed, but his brows drew together as if trying to size me up. "I assure you, I'm only here to meet with you and our company's CEO."

"Knock yourself out. I'm not interested."

A smile played at the edge of his mouth. "My name is Steven Langley. You are Gen Aubrey?"

Cold sweat poured down my back.

My hand reached my chest. I shook my head. "Not interested."

A puzzled look settled on his face. "You're graduating, aren't you? And you are looking for a job. We've tried to reach you, but your phone is off. That's why I'm here."

"You're wasting your time."

"I wouldn't be here if we thought so. An interview with you and my CEO can't hurt, now can it?"

My gaze met his. His brows went up in a quiet challenge.

"You've been watching me." I seethed and held on to my bag pack. I just knew he was behind the feeling I experienced these last few days.

He nodded. "You're difficult to get to."

"What do you want with me?" I asked, my voice trembling. I straightened my shoulders, determined to fight the intimidation. *Way off.*

"We believe you will fit right in with The Center."

Here it was. Chase told me about The Center minutes ago. Now, I knew who was behind the whole thing. I possessed a name and a face to go along with it.

He continued… "Our director would like to talk to you."

"I don't trust you… or your motives."

His eyes ran over my face. "We're quite impressed by you."

"You can take your compliments and shove them where the sun doesn't shine."

In a calm and curious voice, he asked, "Are you always this pleasant? I get that your upset drives you."

"Damn right, I'm upset. How else would I be after the other day?"

"The other day?" A puzzled look appeared on Steven Langley's face.

"I have a good reason to be careful after what you pulled."

The guy looked lost. Either he was a darn good actor, or something else had occurred here. "What would you call what your guy did in my room? He assaulted me. He could have raped me." My voice dropped to a murmur in the last words.

Steven shook his head. "I'm sorry. It must be a mistake. We never would."

"Save it. I'm not interested."

He oversaw me for a beat. "I believe you might be if only to know why."

I didn't care what he thought of my behavior. "Why would I ever want to talk to him? You attacked me and stole my codes." I started to walk away.

At the accusation, "Attacked you? I don't understand." He began to follow me.

"As if you don't know. You've got my codes." I watched him from the corner of my eye and kept a safe distance between us as we walked. I was ready to bolt at the slightest move in my direction. But he seemed content to give me a wide berth as he walked by my side.

"We retrieved your codes, and that's one reason I'm contacting you. It was an impressive piece of work."

"Why do you think I would try impressing you? I don't know you or care to."

"Please, tell me what happened?"

Fat chance. I didn't want to go there. No way. "You know what happened... Why do you care? You hired a scumbag. He accomplished what you wanted. He did what you sent him to do. Now, leave me the hell alone."

He looked unimpressed, and he clipped, "I will sort this out. We will find a solution."

"Tell that to the guy who got into my room and pushed me around." I did an about-face then and said, exasperated by the entire thing. "Where the hell is Jonas? What have you done with him?"

His lips relaxed a little. "Jonas is fine."

Looking up at him, I shouted, "Where is he?"

Unaffected by my tone, he replied, "I presume somewhere in Europe. London, by now."

So Chase told me the truth. Surprise.

I didn't expect that. It took me a moment to assemble my thoughts. "What would Jonas be doing there?" I dragged out at a total loss.

Steven laughed at that. "Enjoying himself, I assume, with the money we gave him."

"So, you gave him a fat paycheck, and you assaulted me? That's what I call a double standard. I need to talk to him."

A concerned look passed over his face. "We ordered no one to assault you, and yes, we paid off Jonas under a confidentiality agreement, with quite a nice sum. As for you, we want to offer you a job with a nice salary to boot."

I heard the words coming out of his mouth, but they made no sense to me. Nothing that happened in the last few days did. "How do I know you're telling me the truth?"

Steven withdrew something from his pocket. "You can call him if you wish. Here's his British number." He handed me a card with a phone number written on the back.

He had prepared for this. A story planned to confuse me even more.

I didn't advance to take it, eager to maintain a distance between us. Getting any closer to the stranger than I was, was not an option, and so I said, "Give me the number. I'll remember it."

He shrugged. "One can never be too cautious."

I stared at this stranger, unsure what to think. Regardless, it changed nothing. "As if this makes a difference to me now."

He inclined his head at that, watching me with a curious look on his face. "Jonas' number is 44 76 39 45 67."

I repeated it in my head, memorizing it. It was easy to remember.

Steven tried to reach me again. "You gave us the runaround in the last few days."

I stared at him, only focused on understanding why the codes were so crucial that they had to take them. "It is about the scientists that disappeared?"

He nodded. "Some things must remain unnoticed... For a time, at least. We can explain."

I shook my head, and my hair, held in a ponytail, swung with the movement. "Why is it so important that you would want them in the first place?"

"Your codes are in good hands. You're talented, Miss Aubrey. Dr. Spallberg would like to meet with you." Steven continued, "My boss will be on campus in two days. Talk to him. He can explain everything."

I couldn't even respond to that. Why would I? There was no logic where I could even contemplate getting close to these people. Besides, Chase warned me not to.

He read my answer in my eyes. The silence expanded between us. *Genius.*

Steven shrugged. "I understand your misgivings… But… Never say never… He'll be in touch. His name is Dr. Jonathan Spallberg. In the meantime, please stay away from using a certain algorithm. We are interested in acquiring your codes legally. He'll explain everything. I suspect you'll have an interest in what he has to say."

Steven saluted me with a nod of his head and said, "Very sorry." He left after that.

I stood rooted in the same spot, unsure that I had not dreamed the whole thing. *Brilliant.*

Minutes later, I listened to the ring of my cell phone with anxiety. It didn't matter what time it was in Great Britain. I possessed a line to get a hold of Jonas, and I took it.

On the fourth ring, I heard his voice. "Hello."

"Jonas… Is that you, Jonas?"

"Gen? Hey, how is it going?"

Words spurted out of my mouth. "What the hell do you mean? Are you all right?"

"Hey, sorry about that. I'm fine. Living it up." Jonas talked fast, uncomfortable. He continued, his voice strained but brave, "Couldn't pass up the offer I received."

"Why didn't you call me?"

"It was part of the deal. I had to wait for the guys to contact you so you could call me."

I waited, expecting him to offer further explanation, but he didn't. "Why? What does it mean?"

"I'm out; Gen. Can't check out the stuff you and I were looking into because I have to hold my end of it."

"You don't say...." Sarcasm poured out of me. I couldn't believe what he announced so casually, but I was not about to let him know that his betrayal hurt a lot.

He sold out with little remorse.

There was nothing much I could say. I whispered, "So long as you're okay."

"Yeah... The Center gave me a great deal to walk away."

I shook my head, my eyes filled with tears. What else was there to say? I hung up the phone. The feeling that a cold hand punched me in the gut and crushed my inside remained.

He left without an explanation. He departed without a word of reassurance, letting me hang in ignorance and anguish. *So much for friendship.*

Not again. Never again.

24
BURST
Chase

Mountain Range, California - 2018

When Chase Davenport meets Tesh, he feels like he knows her. Undoubtedly, my intervention to save him through her caused it. Only, I did not expect the strength of the bond they forge. DAINN Annals— Summer 2018.

The silence brought haste to my movements as I rappelled down the wall. The cave appeared the same. No one had ventured here since the last time I escaped from it, a year ago. Still, I needed to be sure. Jonathan found something around these parts. It was my turn to discover what it was.

Perfect momentum.

Sleek gestures.

Smooth rhythm.

Easy mechanics. Easy decision.

The image of Harriet still haunted me. I didn't think of myself as soft, not about things like that. I mean, I've seen plenty of violence at the movies and on television, yet I still couldn't reconcile myself with her death. No matter what I did, my mind came back to Harriet lying lifeless on the street. How did she come to possess a gun? My thoughts jumbled; I recalled the moment she had fired it.

I shook my head. Damn it. I needed to get over it. Suddenly, I realized this thought alone amounted to the wrong conclusion. I didn't want to get over it. It demanded some remembrance and commanded attention. But it couldn't just be an incident; one quickly put behind. It required remembering what brought it on, always. Her body lay on the ground, pieces of her brain matter dripping on the asphalt. The Center had contributed to her loss, and now I doubted everything about what we stood for.

I shook my head. *Think of something else, anything.*

Gen entered my mind. To be exact, she never left my memories. Since the moment I met her, that girl had left her mark on me. Vulnerable, stubborn, fiery, beautiful. Her red hair and green eyes caused a stir in me. There was no point in denying it. Only, my determination not to get close so long as I remained with the Center drove me to keep my distance. I wouldn't risk her getting caught in this.

On the inside, I fumed about the way I got to meet her. When I entered the building that night, I did not understand what awaited Gen. And afterward, once I realized what Jonathan had done, I only thought of warning her. It was likely that it would compromise my chances with her.

I took a calculated risk. Hey, what other choice did I have? Thinking about what could happen to Gen if she joined the Center, I shuddered. She didn't need to deal with unscrupulous individuals. It was bad enough that I discovered that side of them. Disillusion stirred within me. I guess the unpleasantness of it all wore on me. I never expected that Jonathan would manipulate me into playing a part in this charade in the first place. But I understand now that he knew no limits.

I wanted another chance with her, but knowing that she had a tie to the Center now held me back. I hoped she would stay away from them, and I wasn't about to bring her back within range of them. *Move on. You have other issues to contend with now.*

The rope under my fingers felt rough. My legs moved down the wall. Soon, I would reach the mid-point if my memory served me right.

Rhythm and silence soothed me. But it didn't last.

A screeching noise reverberated inside the cave. The surface of the rock shook, propelling my weight on the cable sideways. I now hung over the abyss, holding on for dear life with the same feeling of despair I experienced in this place the first time around. A thought formed… *Not again.*

I never wanted to relive the moment of my fall. I couldn't conceive of it. Finding myself in the same position as before was unacceptable. But here I was again, putting my life to the test. All of it because of Jonathan and because I wanted to discover what he kept from me. *Shuffle the odds. Get the upper hand.*

Here on the ridge, I needed to come to terms with their behavior. Was tying myself to Jonathan something I wanted going forward? The choice presented itself. Despite what had happened, I couldn't let it go or walk away. I knew damn well what my course of action called me to do. I couldn't remain a part of it in all good conscience unless I controlled the Center's activities. Only, now, I was on the outside. Central's behavior and code of conduct called for the highest standard. It was the only way I would stay involved. That

Jonathan duped me showed his true colors. I needed leverage, so I came back here to find it. If I held something over his head, something he did not possess, like the tablet he kept under lock and key, well, maybe I could command different actions. I hoped this lurking around would provide the answers. *Once again, I called on lady luck.*

Hanging on the cable now that sand and pebbles drizzled over me seemed stupid. I knew the odds and could get myself killed here. But I didn't tell my family where to find me. Should I disappear inside this cave? Did I leave little to no bread crumbs? *Tell me something, Chase; how stupid are you?*

Although I wasn't about to hint at my whereabouts, should Jonathan come looking for me? I didn't plan on running to my father about the activities of his friends. It would be a farce of gigantic proportions to tell him that Jonathan ran a major elaborate plan to entice the foremost minds of our time in joining the Center. Chances were that he would get me admitted to a psychiatric institution for suggesting this in the first place, or he would derail any possibilities of reaching my aim.

The trembling subsided as it began. The sound disappeared, but the silence did not resume around me. Instead, a steady rumbling echoed. Pushing away from the wall, I got my bearings. I reached the half waypoint. I slid further down on the wire, trying to locate the sound, and saw the stream of water pouring down a hole blown in the bedrock.

It didn't exist a year ago and was something worth exploring.

I swung the rope over and landed near the opening, getting drenched. The water was cold. It would not be pleasant. Regardless, I grabbed the side of the gap and lifted myself inside.

Water rushed in, midway up my thighs, in a continuous flow. I was wet in seconds, but I didn't care. This outpouring came from way up on the mountain. I observed the tunnel. It looked uniform, smooth even, as a series of rings touching each other formed the shaft walls. Glittery golden particles embedded inside the rock formation gave the walls a unique look. They created millions of minuscule stars, dust-like, against the rugged background. I saw nothing quite like this before. I pulled out my camera and took pictures. The wall, compressed, golden, seemed in part harder as though a laser had fused the matter. Touching the surface left no residue on my fingertips. There were no molecules of dust particles breaking apart between my fingers, either. Instead, the scintillating fragments remained embedded in the rock, unbreakable. *What technology can make this?*

I moved ahead, following the tunnel. This path could lead me to answers. At least, I hoped so. Following this purpose gave me pause. Of all the things I could do, why this? I almost died in this place a year ago. *What the hell am I doing here again?*

It held a special meaning, for I had found the tablet here, which began the Center's endeavors. The facility, on the other side of the mountain, could now contain additional finds. Looking back at the last few months, I figured that my instinct had been spot-on. Seeing the breach inside the cavern and following this make-shift cylinder only confirmed this. Whatever lay in this cave had to be a whopper of a thing too. It was now my turn to dig up something else, some unearthed remnants of our future.

The shaft turned.

I never disclosed to Jonathan the exact location of my discovery, giving him a vague position leading to a different cave. There were so many of them in these parts. Vagueness appeared an excellent tool. Lack of memory seemed a good excuse. Okay, trust issues. I get that. It was my place where I found the tablet, and it may hold other secrets. I was counting on it.

Jonathan, in his way, had paid me back in spades. He kept control over everything. Besides, if he intended to claim the revelation himself, well, he better possessed reasons to claim it. Why would I make his quest easy?

These tunnels reinforced my conclusions. Only, I didn't know of any equipment that could dig with such a result. Was it part of a new device Jonathan had found? A twist of jealousy ran through me.

If Jonathan had discovered this part of the cave, I was in for a battle. The Center's expansion and its perimeter underground appeared to reach this side of the mountain. It surprised me. We had to do much to repair the old facility and bring it up to the newest standards. His resourcefulness in allocating the resources to dig this way gave me pause. Wondering what else he kept me out of the loop on, I followed the tunnel, slushing through the freezing water with my teeth chattering. Despite that uncomfortable numbness settling in my legs, I was glad that my determination had brought me here again.

The walls continued on either side of me with the same star-like texture. The tablet owners possessed advanced technology far beyond us, and this same technology carved these identical rings.

My mistake haunted me now. A year ago, I gave Jonathan the tablet so we could discover its secrets. Keeping it within reach of those working on it made sense, although our best team didn't get us very far. I never questioned that decision, even when it took the Center nine months to break its programming. Today, while we were still grappling with what else lay beyond some of the codes, I revised my opinion. My judgment had been flawed. Given what transpired with Jonathan and the fact that I could no longer lay my hands on it, I wished I had thought this through. My only consolation remained that the unbreakable, impenetrable alloys and their composition didn't give much away. I knew that much.

Venturing this far inside the cave gave me the information I didn't possess a while ago. Whatever the Center had found appeared substantial. Now, I needed to get my hands on it. *Let Jonathan keep his findings a secret. I will have my own soon enough.*

Give me some leverage, lady luck.

Without me, the Center wouldn't be here. Me not dying had to mean something. *Make the best of it… Hell, yeah. I'll make the best of it, starting by getting a hold of what lay around in here. Then I would get the NetFrig out of here.*

Climbing started as a dare between friends. It developed into a sport I loved. This sport led to this place. My life brought me here. I didn't believe in miracles. Still, something had kept me alive. There must be a reason for that. Something saved me. Based on this, I assumed who or whatever they were could only have good intentions. Was I stupid to believe that? Could they be awful, without morals, and barbaric? No. This notion held no validity in my mind.

I shivered, fighting the cold seeping through my skin.

A civilization so advanced that wisdom and generosity of heart dictated their action enticed me. Was such a conclusion plausible? I studied Anthropology, gearing my studies to figure out the human mind and its evolution. Neuroscience held answers to a path toward a future yet to be defined. It somehow had to be linked with my fall and my survival. Convinced that this shaft held the answers, I pressed forward.

The tunnel turned, and I went with it. Taking each step became more demanding with the frigid water splashing around me. The colder I got, the more I questioned my sanity.

The light on my head covered a large area, unlike the first time I had climbed these rocks.

According to the mountain range's topography, caves covering just beneath the summit connected deep below in some areas. My senses told me that their link opened a passage to the other side, near the Center. Only, I still had to locate the pathway.

The shaft on the outside of the tunnel went deep. The area where I walked now appeared to sit on a higher ledge. It continued toward the other side of the mountain, where the Center's facility spread underground. My compass told me as much. Venturing alone, in darkness and dampness, didn't do much to instill confidence.

I pulled a piece of paper and a pen from my backpack and made a map of the area so I could find my way back. I also designed an arrow made of chalk on the tunnel walls. It was crude but efficient if I needed to get the hell out in a hurry.

As I moved further ahead, the light changed. Above my head, an opening connecting to the path where I stood led to yet another rounded tunnel, one that was going up this time. The structure of the matter, different from the first, struck me. The particles glittered just the same but imbedded in the rock; they shone bright green instead of gold. Past the juncture, the shaft moved upward at a forty-five-degree angle. The precision of the cut through the rock formation was odd.

I shut down the camera. A picture of the intersection made its way into my bag. Suddenly, I stumbled into a hole on the ground. My advance into the passageway turned into an almost dead drop. The earth under my feet had ceased to exist.

Emptiness lay ahead. I stepped back, struggling to remain upright, but lost my balance. The few inches of water covering the incline cushioned my fall, although I hit my head on the wall as I reached the ground. *Damn... This cave doesn't like me.*

Stunned, I brushed the bump on my head with frozen fingers. They returned to my line of sight, sticky with blood. A headache, the sort one sports after a night of excess, reminded me of a bad hangover. Keeping my wits about me would preserve me alive. I didn't need a badass stupor to get me dead in here. *This cave wants to hold on to its secrets badly.*

Move or die. Supporting my weight on the wall, I got up, keeping away from the edge of the drop. What had kept me from falling? I could have. I snarled to myself, "Never mind. Get your priorities straight. Find what hides in here."

The little voice in the back of my mind kept saying. *But it's not possible...*

My pursuit of this quest and its unknowable ending raised tons of questions. I claimed no answers to any of them. *But that's why you came here. You want to know who is behind your survival. Best not to talk about it if you're not willing to acknowledge it. Just focus.*

My soul had no melody right about now. Yet, I ought to be grateful. Damned grateful.

I acted on crazy impulses, never thinking much about the consequences. Disregarding them caused me to be in a jam occasionally, even to face close calls, but it never altered my behavior. It never rendered me cautious. This experience here and now called for that. My instincts screamed at me to get out of the cave.

My mind, disoriented by the cold and the darkness surrounding me, created illusions. That was it. It had to be it because I began to act chaotically. My predicament affected my outlook. It took a lot to shake myself off this negative train of thought. I battled with myself, rejecting doubts about my sanity. *Not here. Not now.*

Questions without answers jumped into my mind. Doubt arose in my heart… *Do I have something to fear? Yeah, like losing my life in this place.*

The hole in the ground opened to a third tunnel and was about the same size as the other two. Someone had forged the tunnel that led me here, as well as the paths going above and below. On the other side of the drop, a fourth tube, this time with scintillating blue crystals embedded in the bedrock, lay ahead.

The equipment that made these perfect cylinders, almost too perfect in their shape, corresponded to technology with an exact calibration. Only, I did not understand how anyone achieved such power. The close quarters and this amount of consistency baffled me. Did Jonathan find the equipment and use it to his advantage to shape the underground of the facility and spread tunnels in this area? If so, where was it?

The turbulence earlier confirmed the presence of something unusual. The longer I walked in these passageways, the more convinced I became that I followed in someone else's footsteps. My doubts about my endeavor lifted. This underground passageway might connect to the one on the other side of the mountain. Or better yet, to a cave. Perhaps even the one where I would discover the thing I looked for so desperately. I survey my surroundings.

Find it. Dig deeper. There is something. I'm sure of it.

I grunted. A recess existed ahead, just on the opposite side from the intersection of the three corridors. I stepped towards it. The ground sunk under my feet, forcing me to test the terrain. Something wasn't right. I couldn't quite put my finger on it. I examined the ground, shifting my flashlight to one side and the other, then up and down.

The water level was uneven. Behind me, it rose at hip level. In front of me, nothing. It was as if I had walked through a dead zone - a water-free area. I stepped back. A transparent wall loomed now, inches away from me. Erected to the tunnel's height, it held the flood back and away from the area ahead.

My hand touched the invisible surface and passed right through it. Smooth. My fingers encountered no resistance. I extended my arm and passed through it, turning around to now face it. A force field held the water away from the area of the tunnel where I now stood. I moved back across the barrier to the other side. No resistance. No resonance. Only wet, cold water. I stepped through the transparent barrier again. Once on the other side, dry land greeted me. Looking across it, felt as if I inhabited a glass vase.

Four passageways formed a junction a few feet away from where I stood. The first one brought me here. The second went up, the third went down, pouring water out, and the fourth opened to the left just ahead of me. Tempted to follow it, for it went in the direction opposite to the one I came in, I glanced forth, several feel away from the transparent wall. I saw it then, ensconced inside the rock formation.

A rounded doorway meshed with the surface of the mountain.

Its size spread the height and width of the shaft. My hands reached for it. Cool to the touch. Smooth. Carvings edged in the metal above the door depicted unknown symbols. When I passed my fingers on these, they vibrated and emitted a sound. Whispers under my touch… Excitement filled me. My fingers ran around the doorway, looking for a mechanism that would open it. Nothing appeared on the surface.

I retrieved my camera; the lens focused on the details of the gate. The flash sprung to life under my fingers.

I shot the details of the carvings, seizing the image of each symbol. My skin tingled with anticipation at the thought of what lay behind this door.

Suddenly, a booming sound echoed across the tunnel. Its provenance came from the cave below. Its tonality seared my eardrums.

I cringed.

The noise reverberated across the bedrock for what seemed like long-frozen minutes. Then, the mountain, like before, stopped shaking as abruptly as it had started.

Within seconds, another noise shook the mountain. A crashing metallic sound resonated within the tunnel. Inside the cavern, in the bowels of the abyss, something substantial emitted a noise resembling dislodged beams and twisted blocks. It screamed as it slid against the surface of the bedrock. The screeching of twisted and crushed metal came to mind. It reminded me of fingernails trailing on a chalkboard, only amplified a thousand times.

I grimaced at the clamor echoing in waves around me.

The ground shook again. This time, harder. Chunks of rock fell, littering the tunnel, and blocking the way to the left entrance.

I flew back toward the barrier and into the water.

The Earth seemed to roar on all sides. Rocks dropped and tumbled near me.

My camera went underwater. *Shit...*

My hands searched for it. So much for my proof. I doubted I could salvage anything. My fingers closed on it and lifted it above the freezing water. Teeth chattering, I crawled toward the dry ground.

At the intersection of the four tunnels, more rocks went over the edge.

I reached the safeguard of the doorway. The structure, stronger around the door, appeared to resist the mountain's onslaught in that area.

When things settled, I saw the way to the other tunnel left of me blocked farther up ahead. There was no way for me to venture in the direction of the Center.

This time, the sharp noise built up into a strange melody like a broken cacophony of distorted alloys. *What now? You need to get out of here.*

A cold hand grabbed my gut. My hair rose on the back of my neck. I froze, attempting to determine its origin. Could it be our team reaching over from the other side? Unable to identify where it came from, I crept away from it, turning back in the direction where I had first entered the tunnel. In place of the gap in the bedrock, piles of rocks blocked my exit.

I now stood in freezing water again, only this time, cut off from the opening on either side of the tunnel. The impulse to leave propelled me to turn back around and look for a third exit point, but none existed within reach. Only the one tube moving straight up could provide a way out if I could get past the pile of rocks ahead of me. The size did nothing to entice me to try. When I examined it a while ago, the smoothness of the tunnel walls discouraged any attempts to climb it. Caught with no way out, I would either freeze to death or run out of air.

I shivered, getting colder by the minute. Contemplating my death again, I moved toward the only dry place in the forsaken mountain. *This cave has it in for me. Really... Every time you almost die.* My thoughts jumbled; I resisted my sense of panic. Dread threatened to engulf me.

The urge to go back to the broad gate and satisfy my curiosity won. It could very well be my best chance to survive this, and if nothing more, I would be on dry land. Nothing else came to mind.

I splashed through the frigid water. I stopped in front of the metallic door, watching it.

In the tunnel's silence, the locking mechanism engaged. Did it answer my prayers? A soft swoosh I almost missed whispered with the shifting of gears.

I watched it. The process was swift.

The rounded door unfolded in multiple layers, like the petals of a flower opening in the morning light. Many protective metallic leaves moved at once, revealing the entrance.

In the middle of the gateway, standing in a pool of light, an unmoving silhouette cast a shadow.

My stomach dropped. A knot lodged in my throat.

A red burst flew at me. In the next instant, I felt lifted from the ground. My eyes blinked. My muscles tightened.

Blood pumped like a flood through my heart. Life pulsed through my cells.

My body shook, tensing as I went down, legs and arms rigid. I sensed a feeling of weightlessness. I had no control over what was happening to me. But I was still here.

A net wrapped around me. On contact, I lost consciousness.

Everything faded at once.

25 RECRUITMENT
Gen

MIT, Massachusetts - 2018

Gen Aubrey, reluctant at first, meets the man behind her stolen codes. In so doing, she goes against her instinct. Her ability to assimilate and evaluate information remains overshadowed by her emotions. DAINN Annals – Summer 2018.

The appointments turned out to be most uninspiring. I needed fresh air, and I walked away from the hall and the interviews. Boring.

My steps led me to my favorite place. I took my shoes off and walked on the fresh grass, feeling the earth under my feet before settling myself on the ground.

I leaned back and looked at the cirrus clouds. Nature always anchored me. It provided a sense of belonging. The ground, this unique tie linking me to the world, felt sturdy under me. The sky, moving above in a pattern charted by the winds, brought me calm. Earth nurtured me.

A stone building, ivy engulfing its walls, rose in the middle of a lawn filled with old trees. Nearby, benches scattered around the trimmed grounds merged with the landscape. Trees, leaves, vines all contributed to the subtle palette of green colors, forming the myriad of shades that overran this grand old place.

Students walked around the park pressed for time. Those sitting on the grass flocked in small groups, their books in piles scattered around them.

Not too far away from me, two guys threw a football at each other. I witnessed their easy throws. They appeared relaxed, unconcerned, and in the present. *Lucky bastards.*

At the end of the park stood the Roth library. The windows shimmered in the sun of the late afternoon. These walls of knowledge connected the old and new.

Inside the building, aisles of shelves brought warmth to the halls. The rooms of the Rotch or Hayden libraries and the rotund of the virtual Barker Library, where one could almost taste wisdom altogether combined, fit the size of a football field. I enjoyed walking the rooms in the hushed whispers of voices permeating these grounds' otherwise silent atmosphere.

Bookshelves made of oak, and brimming with volumes of all sizes, opened a world to many subjects. They sometimes stood next to the computer stations lined up on individual cubicles. Wood tables shone under the lights with the scent of fresh lemon on opposite sides. This place mixed a picture of modern technology at work with the depth of ancient culture. *Somehow, I miss it already.*

The large windows framed the world outside, keeping at bay the echoes of life beyond the walls. In this island of silence, the ceilings, two stories high, encouraged the pursuit of lofty goals and shaped a new generation, opening minds to a landscape without limitation.

I wished my learning days would continue. But they had ended hours ago. I envied those who still possessed a reason to remain. These grounds would feel the imprint of my feet for another day. After that, I would begin my journey elsewhere. Bummer.

I had options… Few I would even consider.

Where would I go?

The football landed at my feet, startling me and distracting me from my thoughts.

One guy waved in my direction. "Hey… Can you give us a hand?"

I picked it up and threw it their way, like a girl. It bounced and rolled toward them. The same guy ran to it and grabbed the ball. "Thanks. Graduating?"

"Don't mention it. Yes…"

"Good luck!"

Damn. How did the guy know? Was it a guess? Or did I look older already, with graduating written on my forehead? *Honestly?*

Top of my computer science and electrical engineering classes and doing well with applied mathematics, the road ahead for me remained unknown.

What kind of person graduating from MIT stayed clueless about their future? Someone like me. Inadequate. Without a plan. The thought swirled in my mind, leaving its imprint.

Figures.

Will I ever select one thing, rave about it? Seeking challenges in fields I excelled at appeared impossible. I wanted more, a whole lot more. This desire seemed to be healthy. Why not? Why settle for less? Only maybe, just maybe, I thought more of myself than I ought to.

Undoubtedly, the experience of the last week began to make me reconsider everything.

My job search amounted to a routine, fulfilling others' expectations, but it bored me to death. Hard work never scared me. Boredom did. Complacency sent me running.

I had tackled several MIT degrees at once. Retention came easy for me. If I read something once, I remember it forever.

So, it didn't come as a surprise when, at graduation, I remained unchallenged — and depressed. The prospects before me dampened my spirits. *Blackhole.*

The clouds in the sky passed before my eyes. I named each shape to occupy my mind, postponing the moment I came to grips with the inevitable, settling on mediocracy. *Ugh...*

A shadow covered me.

I jumped, still too shaken by my recent experiences.

Ensconced in my thoughts, I never saw the man approach. Reacting fast, I got to my feet, ready to flee, purse in hand as a weapon. A puny one at that, but I had nothing else with me.

It wasn't my week. What the heck... Things were bound to turn around, right? The universe didn't see it that way. Bad things kept coming my way, and I began to resent them.

The guy stood inches away. "I'm sorry. I didn't mean to startle you. My name is Dr. Jonathan Spallberg. You've already met one of my associates, Steven Langley."

I studied him, taking a step back, not ready to trust anyone, much less any of these men who appeared so interested in me. He was tall, in his forties, about six-foot-four, and wore jeans with an old suede jacket over a polo. His face looked sun-kissed, framed by long and wavy hair touching his shoulders. His eyes looked thoughtful as he waited for me to say something. "I know who you are. I looked you up."

He pressed his lips together, annoyed at my reception. "Can we talk? I came here to meet you."

My face scrunched in anger. "So, it's supposed to make it all right?"

"I can't erase it or make it go away," he replied. "You need to deal with it, and by the look of it, you're not doing so well."

I knew what he said was true. I felt frustrated... Unable to forget the intrusion that still had me reeling. *Let it go.*

"What would you have me do? See a shrink? You guys should go to jail. What are you doing with my codes?"

Jonathan smiled. He seemed to think my outburst funny. "No... I don't think you need a shrink. I believe you need to claim back what you lost. Fear can fuel purposeful things if handled the right way."

"I'm not afraid of you." I told a lie, regretting it instantly. It didn't sound sincere, even to my ears. *Bugger.*

Jonathan overlooked it.

He acted gracefully. I gave him that. "I know someone who can help you. He can teach you how to fight."

Despite my initial reluctance, I became curious. "Fight?" I relaxed a little. "How would I do that?" The idea intrigued me. The anger within would find a way out.

"You can train with him once you join us," said Jonathan, taking off his suede jacket as he gestured at the ground around me. "Do you mind?"

I thought of training to fight after the attack. It seemed like a good idea. Only, I had never considered it, with me being neither violent nor the physical type. Inflicting harm corresponded to a new concept, and it didn't appeal to me. The notion of taking care of myself did. I tried to reconcile the two impulses. Looking around the area, I crossed my arms. "The place is big enough." I nodded… "Go ahead. You have the terrain," I said, referring to the large grass area around us, just as much as I was referring to the topic he had sought me out to discuss.

Jonathan sat down; his wiry frame twisted a little on the ground to find a better position. He now looked at me a few feet away and folded his long legs in the way a new colt stood on his, uncertain how to accomplish the act. "I'm here for you," he said, a stern look on his features.

Although I wanted to press him for more details, instead, I whispered, "Really? I rather think you're here for you. Besides, I'm not the violent type."

Jonathan snorted. "The right fighting is about avoiding violence altogether. I know the guy for that." He struggled to make himself comfortable on the grass.

I started feeling overwhelmed with conflicting thoughts. Jonathan had just provided me with something to reflect upon. Learning how to fight from someone who excelled at it without abusing it might be interesting. I would never again feel powerless. Still, why would I ever trust him or any of the men in his organization? I looked around. There were plenty of people on campus.

Jonathan seemed to read my thoughts because he patted the ground beside him. "I'm harmless, I promise."

I could believe him. He was a thinker, one that plotted the actions, one step at a time. But he didn't get his hands dirty. Instead, he had other people do it for him.

Curiosity killed the cat. Despite myself, I eased down onto the bed of grass. Recalling my brief conversation with Steven Langley, I heard the guy out.

Facing the campus lawns of the library, He continued, "I wish you had picked a more comfortable spot."

I laughed. This man ordered his people to maltreat me, steal my codes, send Jonas to Europe, and yet he couldn't sit on the grass. "You admit that you don't fit the part."

A shadow crossed his face, and he ignored my comment. "I'd like to offer you a job."

My heartbeat stumbled, and I snapped. "He told me you would."

"Who?"

"Chase... He also told me I shouldn't accept it."

He laughed at my jab. "So, how are your interviews for other jobs working out?" He continued. "I'm here to offer you a challenge - one that will change your life. I'm not kidding when I say this. You're brilliant in your fields, and I suspect you need more than a job to keep that analytical mind of yours active. I'll provide you with new boundaries. You'll break them. I expect no less."

"Not interested."

"I read your thesis in Applied Mathematics. Nice work... Don't bother to find out how it came to my attention. Why you? You fit our mold... A mold that doesn't conform. We don't have boxes. So, here." He handed me a USB key.

Pop quiz... What's in it? I looked at the key as if it was about to bite me. Trust issues. Definitely.

Since I didn't take the key, he dropped it on my lap. Jonathan went on... "You will find a contract with a sign-on bonus to work for the Center. It's confidential, so don't talk to anyone about this. Sign and return it to me. I will wire the money to your account. It is yours to do with what you wish. Keep it... Give it away... Where you are going, you won't need it. You will have everything provided for you."

My eyes grew wide. "Wait a minute... What kind of research are we talking about?"

His brows drew together, "A new beginning for all of us... In a brand new research facility, off the map. It will stay that way too. Just know that the best scientists in the world are working with us. You'll join them." His voice sounded fearsome now.

No way. I repeated, confused, "Join a facility that, as far as the entire world is concerned, doesn't exist and which kidnaps its employees to work there?" *Perfect.*

Jonathan shook his head. "We don't. Work with a team whose mandate is to change the world; only no one knows about it except those involved. You can say goodbye to the present, you know." Jonathan was excited now. I could tell from the shift in his tone. "If you don't, you'll regret this for the rest of your life."

"Yeah... Right. No, thanks." I choked on the words. Tears came to my eyes, and I shut up.

Jonathan frowned. "I'm sorry."

Feeling despondent, I shook my head. "Prove it. Give me back my codes, or nothing you say will convince me otherwise." I shuddered, playing with blades of grass. It still didn't make the anguish disappear. I had to live with it.

As if reading my mind, Jonathan continued, "Sean can help you. Be willing." His eyes appeared anxious, as if this mattered to him.

"Sean?"

"He is good at that."

"I pulled the grass without realizing what I did and found the blades between my fingers. I stopped and shook my hand, rubbing it against my jeans.

"Why would Chase be sore at you?"

"Hmm… Chase dislikes my methods." He shrugged. "He'll come around. The research matters."

I feigned surprise. "Really? Not in my book." I got up. "Research is just research. People matter, and if you don't see that, I can't help you." I pointed out.

He glanced up at me. "Not in this case. Certainly not when it's what dictates the methods. And not when the end changes everything."

I rolled my eyes, finding the implication hard to believe. I threw Jonathan a pointed look. "Bullshit. You think you're the only one who believes this and that the end justifies the means. And I know thousands of men like you."

I looked at Jonathan sideways, and he laughed, shaking his head. "No, I don't think you do. There is a legitimate reason for all this."

That blows. "That's what they all say."

He continued, unperturbed by my attitude. "We have great people working on humankind's greatest challenges. Brilliant scientists… I can show you a career, unlike anything else."

"So, I'm one of the lucky ones?" I snarled.

"We'll provide opportunities that will demand more from you than you can imagine."

I felt the challenge he issued in his stare. He dared me to look away, to ignore his call, to disregard the gauntlet. Transfixed, I hesitated. The allure of the position tickled the edge of my mind. I shook off the confusion. "What do you know about me that leads you to believe I need a challenge?"

"Please, let's not play games. I understand, you know, more than you think. I have watched you. I know more about you than you know yourself. You wouldn't be here if you found work that interested you," Jonathan mocked.

"You think you know everything you need to know about me?"

Part of what he said was correct. The somewhat sad state I hovered close to resulted from my lack of finding something that excited me. Still, I refused to agree with him. Stubbornly, I whispered. "You can't know what entices me."

He chuckled. "I know your motivation."

"Do you?" I said, looking down at him.

His piercing gaze taunted me.

I resisted what he offered. No way will I give in. I wanted more information from the people who had played us, Jonas and me. Thinking of Jonas, I grimaced.

Chase was right.

It was insane thinking that… Even to consider the possibility.

And so defiance rose its head.

My voice filled with irony, I said, "You can provide a path, so I don't end up on the couch of my parents' place, watching crappy television programs, and eating loads of milk chocolate-covered raisins and red licorice?"

Jonathan grinned. "Don't forget the coffee ice cream unless you go for one more degree."

The mention of the ice cream shocked me into silence. No way. He couldn't know what it meant. I caught myself holding my breath. Relax.

My silence and stillness caught his attention, and I felt his eyes on me, attentive and measuring.

Get on with it. Ask the man. "How the hell do you know about coffee ice cream?"

He shrugged. "In the fridge of your dorm."

Shaken, I looked at my hands and grasped them together. "You looked inside my fridge? You have some gall." My wavering voice got lower on purpose before I turned and walked away. Letting him know how much his statement had affected me was not my intent, so I created some distance between us without thought, breathing shallow.

Jonathan chuckled at that. "Where the hell do you think you're going? You need this."

Ice cream caused my mother to disappear that night. She went out to get a stupid gallon of it because we had complained that we didn't have any for dessert. Like spoiled brats, my brothers and I never suggested that we get some ourselves. Instead, we joked and prodded for some. Without that, my mother would still be among us today.

Since that night, I had kept the fridge filled with it. I didn't eat it; not anymore; I just stocked it. How can something as small as ice cream become such a significant factor in one's life? My mom would hate that I no longer ate ice cream.

My steps moved me toward the nearest MIT building. Now, I wanted to put some distance between Jonathan and me and required something familiar around me. I headed toward the tunnels I knew well by now.

It was not until a little while later that I realized Jonathan had followed me.

He now walked behind me. "Hmm... Gen, I need to understand people. Especially those I bring to my project. We research and watch them before we bring them on."

I inquired, "And why should I care?"

Jonathan thought for a moment, his head leaning to the side as if he listened to something only he could hear. "They are smart, all in different ways, and belong with the program, like you. But it brings heavy sacrifices. I make sure they can handle it." Behind the certainty of his tone, there was a sadness there.

"Sacrifices? What are you talking about?" Puzzled with his statement, I stared, watching his reaction.

The connection between us strengthened as we walked ahead. I wanted it to disappear. The ground turned into the concrete pathways leading to the steps of the building. Walking inside, I turned toward the lower levels towards the elaborated system of tunnels twisting below MIT. I wanted to escape his presence, but he kept walking at my side.

He didn't seem to care where we were going.

The location and the circumstances of our meeting contributed to my eagerness to put some distance between us. Jonathan's patience aggravated me. "How long are you going to keep this up?"

He ignored the question. His piercing eyes, the color of a deep, angry sky on winter days, stood out in a face dominated by a sharp nose and a mouth ready for a quick retort. "I do what I do because it's important," he added. A mop of unruly curly hair, touching his shoulders and turning salt and pepper at the temple, looked every bit at home on his head.

"Why?"

He had attempted to sell me on his organization. The way he conducted our conversation put me off-guard. I refused to let him in, but he was getting to me.

He tilted his chin toward me. "Would you like to know what I gathered about you? I have the personality profiles of all those who work for me."

I clipped, "Not particularly."

Too late.

His smirk widened, "I'll tell you anyway... You don't relate to certain people, girls especially, because all they talk about are boys. You don't go out with guys because you intimidate them, giving them a run for their money since you compute things faster than they can. You are an outcast and would be even worse except for your positive attitude, your sense of humor, and the fact that you play many games online. It keeps you social at a distance. You know how to adapt and handle unpredictability better than most. You have a strong survival instinct. Shall I go on?"

I got pissed off. It didn't sit right with me; someone who called out my personality characteristics as quickly as reading a menu in a restaurant. I challenged Jonathan. "So you think you got me pegged? What does it have to do with the work?"

The tunnel we jaunted in stretched ahead of us. I headed toward Harvard. Our steps resonated between the walls on the concrete and echoed all around us.

His calm behavior seemed weird, even for a renegade boss. "You will want to hear the rest," he continued, unperturbed by my remarks."

I increased my pace. My face scrunched as if I tasted something sour.

Jonathan insisted, "You belong with us."

I shrugged as if to shed the mantle he laid on me with that statement and countered, intent on getting to the real issue. "What is so important about the work that you need this screening?"

His gaze lingered on my face, watchful while he remained silent. "What did you think of Chase?"

Damn. I returned the gaze, blushing. I frowned. "Why do you ask?"

"He is very protective of you." His assurance kept my attention. But his eyes wore a kind of cynicism that spoke of dilemmas faced and conquered. His unusual approach intrigued me.

What did he mean by that? *Why does it feel like I face a man who knows the rules, how to break them, and make new ones?* He didn't subscribe to a norm, that's why. "Okay, you came to MIT to recruit me," I said. "You still haven't explained what for?"

Eager to join the ranks of a compelling organization, I demanded a little convincing. I hoped to find a company where I could play a role. But could I trust them? Chase told me I couldn't. My investigation into Jonathan landed me with his impressive curriculum and the paths in science he chose. He picked the fringes, every opportunity he got.

"I want you to join the Center," Jonathan said, without a hint of hesitation.

"The Center? It doesn't exist. I checked it after Chase warned me." *Persuasive? Not.*

Jonathan laughed. "You won't find anything about the Center, I assure you. We made sure of that. It is private."

"Any research facility worth its salt wants to be in the limelight. Publishing findings help with grants. So, why be any different?"

Jonathan, at ease under my gaze, answered calmly. "We don't need to because we are well-capitalized. But we need other resources. People like you to join the minds of those already on board."

I groaned… "The scientists that have disappeared." The notion brought about resentment. In the back of my mind, I thought of the codes that got me within their radar. "Why?"

I turned right, and he followed. His steadiness rendered me nervous. He didn't deny it. "We don't let people know. These are private and sensitive projects. The scientists all came willingly, you know," he added.

I swallowed, but the information intrigued me. I remembered Chase's warning. I wanted to find out more. Much more.

Jonathan handed me the USB key for a second time. He must have picked it up after I got up.

I lifted it from his hand.

He nodded and said, "You have 24 hours to call me and accept. If I don't hear from you, I'll assume you got a corporate desk job."

I couldn't hold my tongue. "Are you always this bossy?"

Jonathan scoffed at my question and waited for me to give him the direction ahead. I pointed to the right, and we resumed walking, this time in silence until we emerged outside.

The grounds here were familiar, for I walked them even in bad weather. The Harvard campus stretched in front of us, with Brattle Square just ahead. I headed toward the science building by the Tanner fountain.

Jonathan appeared so confident that I would join them. I asked with irritation, "What makes you think it would interest me after what happened?"

Jonathan's face turned cold. He looked at me straight in the eyes. "This experience will change you. It's the biggest challenge you'll ever face. There is no coming back from that."

"There never is...." I pointed out.

He talked as if he could teach me that as if I didn't know that already.

Jonathan began to walk again.

I advanced with him, falling into a slower rhythm. We now had a speed that matched each other's pace, and that made me uncomfortable. *What the hell?*

I heard the gurgle of the fountain before I saw it. The place that had become an architectural design icon sitting at the Old Yard crossroads between the Science Center and the Memorial Hall always gave me peace. It was a refuge among peers without requiring participation in conversations of any kind. I escaped here.

Jonathan looked at me and smiled. "You have nothing to worry about."

Excellent play, only I wasn't buying.

He shrugged. "Either you believe me, or you don't."

Dream on.

Jonathan leaned toward me, no longer relaxed but intense. "What would you do if… Hypothetically…. You understood without a doubt that there would be no future. For anyone, not for ourselves, nor our children, unless we make it so?"

Ludicrous.

Get out of here. Reluctant to consider this, hesitant to reject it altogether, disbelief played a dance in my mind. In my heart, I recognized the truth. Although I wanted to ask questions, Jonathan wouldn't answer any of them. *I'm out of my depth here.*

But I looked at Jonathan's face. I searched his eyes and saw that he believed this, without any doubt.

Is he crazy? He had not stepped into the off-limit yard of those geniuses too brilliant for their own good.

I took a deep breath. "You believe that we have no future? Do you know about an extinction event?" I processed the information I possessed and contemplated the odds. Possible, but unlikely. Unless I didn't have all the factors, maybe it was possible because I did not have the data.

He did.

Only a significant event would cause scientists to join a cause that demanded they disappear; if they had done so willingly. I watched the man in front of me. Intrigued beyond words, desiring to know more, I still held back. Everything sounded like a conspiracy. It also seemed so real.

He just stared at me. "We have work to do."

My gaze darted around the grounds that positioned landscape architects as artists before I glanced back at him. No future? How could it be possible? All this, eradicated somehow? I tried to hang on to reality. "You know this is unreal, right? I mean, crazy stuff."

"Understand… We begin right away. You get a few days. Time to settle your affairs. The sooner, the better."

Hold on to the story. Sure. Have at it. I whispered, "How do I verify anything you tell me?"

As if we were holding the most benign of conversations, he explained, "You will talk to one of the foremost scientists in your fields within twenty-four hours. After that… You decide. I'll be expecting this signed the day after your conversation with him."

"You're good at the cloak and dagger stuff."

He chuckled, "He will be in touch with you… It is the phone he'll call you on. Keep it with you. We can't trace it. It's encrypted."

Anything less wouldn't fit under the circumstances. I looked at the USB key in the palm of my hand. And I was tempted, more than tempted, but with everything that happened and Chase's warning, I couldn't accept. But I handed it back to him. "I'm sorry… But it's not for me." Then, I breathed a sigh of relief. I had done it… I had refused.

He smiled, confident, and added with certainty, "You'll change your mind because… I will help you find out what happened to your mother."

What? I took a step back. Then two. Here it was… The incentive I could never pass up. *How did he know?*

Stunned, I retreated again from him on weak legs. "How do you know about my mother?"

He stared, "I know how much this means to you."

I narrowed my eyes on him. "Why would you think you can help me find out what happened?"

He shrugged, "We have unmatched resources."

My hopes flared, but I fought them off. I had been there before. Without thinking, I took another step back. I could barely contain my excitement at the prospect of shedding light on something that haunted me every second of every day. Was he real?

Jonathan tried to warn me. His hand reached for me, but it was too late.

I moved back another step. My heel caught the side of a stone bordering the fountain, and I landed in the water as it splashed around me.

The coldness of it caught me by surprise, but it was nothing compared to what Jonathan had just sprung on me.

All this was a tall order, and yet, could I pass it up?

26
CONCURRENCE
Tesh

Inside the Mountain, California - 2018

Our broken compartments hold the key to changing the future. The success of the mission hinges on all chambers fulfilling their roles. Our five Conclaves must take their place in the past, and all members must move into the light so that the technology of the future, unbeknown to most everyone, spreads the DAINN shadow system. DAINN Annals – Summer 2018.

His face looked every bit as surprised as I felt at seeing him there.

My reflexes took over. In the next second, I threw the Znet and trapped him within it.

His eyes widened, and his mouth opened to say something, but he dropped unconscious before a sound came out.

The thought flashed like quicksilver through my head resonated in my skull. *DarNet… We have some company.*

I approached the man on the ground and retracted the ZNet from him. The sleep state would last hours unless I gave him an injection. I grimaced. I had overreacted… Again. Pondering what to do, I weighed the pros of letting him sleep while I glided my way up the wall versus waking him up and getting the answers we needed. Trying to decide on my next move, I observed him.

A sense of knowing came over me. The man's energy registered somewhere in the back of my brain, swirling within me with an awareness of the man. I puzzled over it… Thinking of DAINN and the message he had left me.

The Custodians waited in the chamber for my order. I launched them, and they floated toward me, past the Chamber's threshold, gliding inside the tunnel. Made of our most durable alloys, they provided advanced functions for our population with our latest technology. They executed security, scouting, or infiltration missions on command. They hovered away from me, following different directions.

My mind reached out to Leane and Blast. *I launched the Custodians.*

Some took to the left, others to the right, while a few followed the tunnel up and the path downward. There was no telling what the elliptical shapes with their electronic eyes would uncover inside our prison.

I watched them disappear and returned my attention to the guy unconscious at my feet. Deciding that waiting around for him to wake up didn't suit our situation, I went back inside the chamber and picked up the Hypo Transmitter, which I loaded with a capsule. This opportunity to talk to him, even question him, would prove helpful, and I was better off doing that without Leane and Blast.

I received their signals within seconds of the launch.

My visor opened on screens coming from the Custodians. They showed blocked passageways on either side of us.

DarNet... A Cave in.

Stopped in front of the rocks, they waited for their orders. I gave it. *Insertion mode...* The command prompted the mechanism to respond — the authorization to slip through the rock fissures without drilling.

I came back into the tunnel and kneeled beside him. Injecting the NetCap, I waited at his side, knowing that I could control him if he gave me signs of aggression.

My thoughts went back to the moment inside the chamber where I had connected to this guy, curious to discover who he was. I remembered the flood of charged emotions that reached me. Ignoring the pull between this stranger and me turned into an inconceivable notion. How did he come to be here? The area seemed isolated enough that there shouldn't be anyone around.

My ears, attuned to the silence, reached out beyond the rocks to determine if anyone else was moving within the subterranean terrain. I got nothing.

A huge sigh escaped my lips, hitting the glass surface of my EmVat and bringing me back to how we came to be here. Could it be that we had created issues with the Pulse inside the caves despite our advanced technology?

I waited for the unconscious guy to wake up. Passing the time until he did, I examined his outfit. It looked different from our own. He wore a light blue Thermoball vest that looked insulated but was now wet. A shirt glued to his chest was underneath it, revealing broad shoulders, tight abs, and a soaked pair of khaki pants.

431

What would this encounter mean for us?

I scanned him. His breathing was regular. Within minutes, he would awaken. Would he play a role in our future here? I did not know.

There was plenty to worry about, knowing our planet's history. Humanity did not demonstrate much acceptance for the unknown. Most people got freaked out.

Our presence in this timeline, if it became known, would undermine our mission. The defense mechanism caused by an undisciplined mind created scenarios and brought significant tension to situations otherwise controllable. It affected potential relationships. Integrating within society might prove impossible. Establishing connections and making friends would become more complex, if not impossible. Allowing this series of events might well represent the failure of our project.

Keeping people in ignorance of our presence was paramount to the success of our mission. This man provided a test. His reaction would dictate ours. Regardless of the outcome, I possessed a recourse. Unsure what to expect from him, I waited.

We entered Origin, a unique program devised by the Institute. Four chambers, similar to our own and within it, four people belonging to each of the four Conclaves: Institute and Academy, almost one and the same, SRC, Faculty, Company, and EHAF.

Origin… We remained underground until the portal took us to another time. A time before ours that led us to this mission. If it succeeded, no one would reach out to us because our people no longer could. The past engulfed us.

We knew when we left our world behind that we faced two distinct possibilities. Two different scenarios. The first... The operation to save our people failed. Nothing and no one survived. Otherwise, they would have found us. Everyone who entered Provenance, Alpha, and Aurora knew of our mandate. Our people in the stations around the Earth, those in the fleet in space, possessed our destination and location. Even the population in the underground facilities had the maps and the beacons pointing to our Chambers.

They would search for us. Like we would look for them. Unless everything and everyone dear to us disappeared in the cataclysm. Then, Origin would stand alone if we were alive at all.

The second... If successful, we broke our timeline. Our lives, as we knew it, to this very instant in this place, no longer existed for our world, had officially ended. We were here now, beginning anew.

Our standing in the chamber, behind the Earth's dense barriers, meant that we already were no more, for otherwise, we would not have seen the ocean such as it was or the sky during Leane's scan. And my people would have rescued us. The Origin experiment would have then failed.

In which case, our race would disappear. Our species would be nullified. But this outcome was yet to unfold.

We had traveled through time. Origin, outfitted to respond to Streak's mind, took us away from our time, and we ceased existing from the old life. We transported through the Accelerator into this new place where this stranger lived here and now. We had succeeded...

If we carried on and reached our goals, we could save everyone. Unless, once again, the Council had lied.

His eyelids fluttered. Disoriented at first, he took a deep breath and opened his eyes. His gaze never left mine as he saw me looking over at him.

"Easy now. You'll be fine. Just breathe."

His eyes locked on me, accused. "You knocked me down." The tone of his voice, laced with an accusation, amused me.

The murmur of his voice reminded me to go on privacy mode. There was no need for my friends to know yet. I grinned. "I did. A bit of an overreaction at seeing you here."

He stared at me through the headset of the EmVat, and he appeared confused.

I stood up, giving us both some distance. When I peeked down at the man, his eyes showed recognition.

"It's you... Again. I saw your face before."

I tilted my head, trying to understand what he meant. "You saw my face when the door opened?"

He shook his head and grimaced at the sudden move, and convinced he said, "No. Last year..."

Struck by curiosity, I gazed down at him and said, "You've seen my face before?" I frowned, wondering what this statement meant under the circumstances.

He was confused. The NetCap should not have muddled his mind.

"I did. Last year... After you slowed my fall."

I mused, thinking of DAINN and the connection he had created between us. "I need to know what you remember. Please tell me." My voice shook despite my attempt to remain calm.

The stranger shrugged. "If it's that important to you... I don't like to relive that moment. I was on the ridge and fell. I went down to the cave where you found me. The only thing that saved me was what you did. You slowed my descent enough that I soft-landed on the ledge."

My breath caught. The only way I could have interfered while in Cryo existed through DAINN. Our A.I. would have known of the fall, and it most likely reached out with our nanotechnology to save him through me. My Nanos embedded in my DNA provided the path to use my abilities. Tapping into my skills, DAINN would possess the ability to influence specific outcomes. It was a first for our A.I. to intervene through any of us. Usually, we were awake and aware, so DAINN never needed to attempt it.

The chamber we awoke in remained intact, with no breach from the outside. How did DAINN reach out to stop this stranger's fall? The only way it could have happened was if one of our other chambers had experienced some breach. Various scenarios entered my mind, some worse than others. I needed to find out more. I inquired, "What happened after that?"

"I thought I had gone crazy... You got into my head, talking me up the wall."

"I did?" My voice, carrying a tinge of surprise, caught him off-guard. I registered his gaze.

I confused him. "You don't remember it?"

I swallowed and repeated with more assurance, "I did."

DAINN acted according to its protocol, even here.

I sighed.

This action made things much more complicated. I didn't want to use my powers on Chase. I refused to start my new life in this way. Still, the more time I spent with him, the more likely I would need to use them.

Netshit. No one expected that the underground Chamber would be discovered, not this soon. The plan to leave the Chambers underground for our protection had failed. No one foresaw the eventuality of our detection while we were asleep.

He continued, "I was pretty beat up, but in good shape considering… So, I climbed out and found the tablet in a fissure in the bedrock." He paused, assessing me, lost in his thoughts.

"You did?" My voice sounded strange.

The stranger ran one of his hands through his silky hair again. It must be a gesture familiar in times of confusion or stress. We all developed these unknowingly.

I possessed my own as well now; my hand moved to my throat and betrayed my personal feeling of alarm when he mentioned the tablet.

He was not to know this.

I dropped my arm.

"Who are you? You speak our language… Where are you from?"

He had the tablet… My mind reeled with this new knowledge. My demeanor didn't change, but I felt my heart rate increase. I didn't want him to know about my dismay. *One of our chambers got damaged. One of our tablets found its way into the cave. DAINN got out.* As advanced as it existed, our technology in the hands of people of his time would give us away, create questions, and entail investigations, perhaps even some digging around these parts. *Stay calm, Tesh.*

"Are you alone?"

He nodded and smiled. "Not very smart of me to admit this… but you saved me, so you can't. You know." He shrugged.

He was nervous… He needed to relax and tell me more. "Why wouldn't I speak English?" We have possessed the knowledge of all the languages spoken and unspoken since the beginning of time. Our database saw to it. What explanation should I give him? None. Instead, I asked, "A tablet, you said? Where is it now?"

His hand went to his forehead as if trying to clear it. "What are you doing here?"

He didn't look right. I ignored his question, "How do you feel?"

"I have a pounding headache, but I'll live."

I nodded. "You're bound to have one. It's the side effects." Even DAINN possessed limitations. Still, it had saved Chase.

He tried to get up and lost his footing. He shook his head as if to get his thoughts in order. "How long have I been out?"

"A little while." It was my turn to be puzzled.

His hand shook, making its way to his hair again. "We're running out of air."

I smiled. "You're right. There was a cave-in."

He shook his head. "It's hard for me to breath."

I frowned. I didn't feel it because my EmVat provided me with all the air I needed. I scanned him. My visor showed that his vitals were dropping. They became worse with each passing minute, and it began to concern me.

I waved at the panel of our chamber. It closed behind us. I appraised the stranger and asked, "Can you walk?"

He nodded.

"Follow me…" I advanced in the tunnel toward the large cave. The connection I possessed with him grew stronger the longer I remained in his presence. *DarNet, the Nanos… It was DAINN's doing.*

The water, now at thighs level, made our progress slow. Using the pulse might further compromise the stability of the environment. I opened my link to Leane and Blast once again. "Claves… I have to use the NetPulse."

Leane's face appeared, followed by Blast. "Tesh, what's going on?"

"There are two cave-ins… One on both sides of the tunnel. We have to open them."

Leane's eyes filled with concern. "The vibrations could weaken the passage to the pool. Blast is still searching the other side."

"Anything?" My voice sounded eager to my ears.

"Not yet."

A hole opened inside my chest. "NetRoger that. I'm using a low modulation to breach the wall."

Blast's face appeared on the other side of my visor. "Hey… Do whatever it is you're doing fast unless you want to bury me."

Leane's voice cut him off. "Blast… Cut it out."

He growled, "Well, what in the HellNet do you want me to say? The whole side is about to drop."

"Get the HellNet out of the pool then. Just come back. I'm digging us out on the right side." I said these words, and all the while, my mind rebelled against abandoning our search for Streak.

"I'm not leaving until I've explored every inch of the pool on the side where Streak disappeared," insisted Blast, with a stubborn look on his face.

A sigh escaped from my lips, but I said nothing. The glimmer of hope in my heart got rekindled. "Fine… One large burst, and it's over, so stay out of harm's way," I replied, just as stubbornly. "Otherwise, I promise you, you'll regret it."

Blast chuckled. "NetRoger that." His screen folded.

Leane's face remained a moment longer. "Tesh… As soon as you are out, let us know."

I smiled. "Promise." She was running out of patience down there.

Leane disappeared from view, and our communications turned off.

I glanced back toward Chase. I should have let them know about him. His skin shade told me that time was running out for him.

He looked about to pass out, leaning against the wall of the tunnel. His teeth chattered. He took a huge breath… And several others, leaning forward with his hands on both knees. In between, in a reasonably weak voice, he murmured, "How many are you?"

Say as little as possible, the voice inside my head told me. "There's four of us."

Splashing through the distance between the stranger and me, I grabbed him under one arm and supported him toward the opening.

In between gulps of breaths, he muttered, "What's your name? I'm Chase, Chase Davenport."

I answered without looking at him. "My name is Tesh."

The closeness we shared in that instant brought a new dilemma to the surface. The MindLink created by DAINN strengthened between this man and me. How could that be? A visceral reaction followed. What about Streak?

Limits eventually occurred with everything we touched. Some were more visible than others. Still, most remained hidden by uncontrollable powers. My mind allowed me the possibility to influence others.

DAINN had thrown a wrench into the equation when it exercised its judgment and activated a channel between us. Did it even realize that by linking my DNA to the stranger, I would experience this reaction?

Our society thrived on a structure meant to serve the individual. Selecting positions within a Conclave also helped to tie us down. A natural ability brought a precise selection process. These characteristics became untouchable for once into the System; a person belonged to a Conclave forever. I could not change this, nor anyone else for that matter. But by providing choices under the guise of attributes identified as belonging to one person boxed us in. For most of our population, these evolutionary steps remained unattainable factors that distinguished the classes within our world. All this existed as the foundation of our entire system.

I walked and took on more of Chase's weight against me.

His steps faltered several times.

The searing noise of a sonic wave brought me to a stop. I adjusted my PVZ to see the tunnel in resonance mode. The ripples appeared, moving toward us. This time they were more powerful and closer. What was going on? The movement would not affect me, but it would my companion, whose state disintegrated with every minute.

I placed myself in front of him, extending my EmVat shield to protect him. Looking into his eyes, I whispered, "Hold on." We were close, too close.

According to our System, and based on DAINN's recommendations, there was no path between Streak and me. Yet, I responded to a perfect stranger from a different world than our own time and time again. Talk about confusing… My reaction complicated everything and brought the entire issue to new heights.

The power of the surge came at us fast. My boots kept me steady on the ground. The impact the field released caused the ground to shake. The pattern set by the crest hit us hard.

I held on to the stranger. It collided with my EmVat. The force of it affected my balance. The EmVat compensated, keeping me standing. My shield, extended around Chase, acted as a buffer. The wave passed us. Its strength was powerful enough to shatter bones.

Whereas I would have broken the imposed guidelines of the Institute before, out of individuality and freedom, I would cross over the lines after the knowledge of the Council betrayal fell on my lap. Maybe it was too late when it came down to Streak even now, but I refused to let my emotions abduct my life. It was true, given they were engineered.

Those damn Nanos affected me in ways I didn't care for and couldn't explain. I wanted to drop the stranger right there and then and let him figure out how to make it the rest of the way, but I couldn't do it. Impeded by our code of conduct, demanding that we help the weak,

I had to see this through since, in this circumstance, he was the most vulnerable of us.

The tunnel floor shifted within the zone affected by the transonic barrier, and I balanced on my legs. It was like riding air sliders in Ang. The old muscle memory kicked in, and I went with it, taking the total weight of Chase in my arms.

"What in the hell is that?" Muttered Chase as he straightened in my arms after the surge passed us.

He no longer stood on his own volition, relying on my strength, and so he held on to me with the energy he had left.

Parts of the tunnel formation gave way: a massive rock wall dropped nearby amidst smaller rocks. The water moved around us, rendering our situation even more precarious.

I looked at my companion, almost unconscious in my arms.

He had little time left. I needed to keep him alive, so I moved to drag him with me. My thoughts got interrupted by Chase's voice, coming in between labored breaths. "Where do you come from?"

"Sure? You want to know now?"

"I'd like to know before I die...."

"You're not going to die."

Suddenly, the loudness of the shock wave abated. The silence reclaimed its place within the cavern.

"Tell me,..." he murmured.

Stubborn, this one... Netshit. How do I answer this? I came from the future, in an underground chamber you got a glimpse at a few minutes ago, and that remained buried a few feet away under this mountain for some time. I came through a time portal while in Cryonics. And there were others still in their chambers. They should have awakened at the same time we did, but we didn't know where they were or if they were even all right at the moment. No way could I tell him that, not a chance. I responded, "It's complicated."

"It doesn't... seem... complicated to me."

"It is. Trust me."

Think fast, Tesh. The one thing you don't want is to encourage his curiosity. Turning the tables on him preempted his questioning me further. "What do you remember happened?"

His breath brushed against my ear. "Tesh... I'm... I will not make it. But thank you," murmured Chase.

His weight shifted in my arms, and he wavered on his feet. Had I not been holding him, he would have made a face plant in the water. I lifted him over my shoulder and moved faster toward the cave-in blocking the exit.

"You will make it. I'll see to it." I switched on my UniWrap.

The low hum echoed in the tunnel. It amplified as I regulated the vibration rate for one powerful burst, one loud explosion. I opened my NetComm. "Sending the NetPulse now."

I splashed through the passage, aiming for the barrier.

The sonic pulse resonated inside the tunnel. Keeping my eyes on the wall, I pushed the pulse forward, hoping this wouldn't weaken the environment inside the pool. The modulator containment parameters, more restrained than we had experienced a few minutes ago, hit the bedrock.

The ground shook. Rocks flew back, sending debris across the gap now opened into the cave. The water poured out, lessening the level around my legs.

"Are you all right?"

Leane's voice sounded over the vibration. "Yeah. Still breathing."

"I'm good too," muttered Blast.

"NetRoger that. I'll let you know when I'm out." The NetComm dropped on my command.

I turned toward my companion and leaned him against the rocks, plastering one side of the inner tunnel. I switched the UniWrap to LifeLine and began the reanimation process. My hand in shock treatment mode infused an electrical charge on his heart. A small jolt surged between my fingers. I pulled back and waited, watching the minutes on the lower side of my PVZ. A few beats… Nothing. I placed my hand over his chest again, sending a more substantial charge. "Come on, Chase," I murmured and waited. I was about to do it again when his vital showed a heartbeat and another. I leaned back, relieved.

Chase took several breaths and looked at me again. "You're making a habit of saving me."

I laughed. "It seems someone has to."

My emotional response triggered memories of Streak and me. It was only an echo of moments where we were together in such proximity: hope, excitement, and nothing. I frowned at the feeling of emptiness.

Chase looked at me with interest.

In my thoughts, there was never any follow-through. Instead, I recognized frustration. The sensation rose in my gut. The recognition showed that we had tested the terrain, and it folded under our very feet, for I held no recollection of us as a unit. No instants that put us together as a girl and a boy. No history to build upon. Everything about us as a couple remained a blank slate. Bitterness shook me. I shrugged, "It's nothing."

"It didn't look like nothing."

I acted under the belief that Streak showed an inflexibility in breaking even the slightest of decrees all these years. I tried to retreat emotionally. Now, I wasn't sure about anything.

I shook my head to clear my thoughts and looked at his face, strong, handsome, and tanned. His brows, darker than his sandy blond hair, stood drawn above gorgeous blue eyes that, at the moment, were focused on me. A slight stubble of beard ran across his square jaw, forming a shadow around his mouth. A beautiful one at that... His sandy blond hair shifted on his forehead as he leaned forward. One of his hands pushed the longer strands away. He was warm, friendly, and... Unafraid.

I felt trapped again. Only this time, it was different. My hormones acted up despite me. I took a step back. Perhaps, it was me... I was defective, attracted to Streak, and not seeing the wrong in our attraction and now, feeling some ties to Chase. What in the HellNet was going on with me?

With a louder voice, Chase pursued his inquiry. "Are you, huh... causing this?"

Well, there it was... Accusations were hovering in Chase's mind already.

I didn't relish explaining anything to this guy, but I couldn't let him believe we had anything to do with what was going on in here. I didn't want to tell him I didn't know what caused this, either... for I knew. Only a contained sonic wave would produce these results. Lies never worked. They just demanded more lies. I whispered the truth.

"I'm sorry. Only some advanced technology can cause this, but we have nothing to do with it."

Chase nodded. "How advanced?"

"Why do you ask?"

"Just wondering if my people had something to do with it."

"Do you think they could experiment around here?"

"It's possible." Chase looked thoughtful for a moment and then said, "You didn't have to save me the first time around. Why did you?"

Did he always act with this curious streak?

I cleared my throat. "I did it because I could."

"How?"

I remained motionless, thinking back to the experience inside the chamber. Something happened while I slept — a vague recollection of a fall and fear.

DAINN had caused the rescue to take place while I remained in the void. Reluctant to explain anything, I said, "How do you remember it?"

The stranger released a chuckle. "Trust me; this is not an experience one forgets. Hell, I thought for sure I was a goner. Didn't you see the height of the cavern? Huge. But here I am... How is that possible?"

How was it possible that a fall would not result in death, such as what he described? In his time, it would never be possible. In ours... Well, we had technology that allowed much.

I searched for his face. "Humor me, please."

He tilted his head to the side, watching me in the same way I had observed him earlier. "Who are you? What was it... That you used?"

I shrugged, unprepared to answer him, and so I asked a question of my own. "What are you doing here?"

"I should ask you… that question." Pointing at the chamber's entrance, he said, "The door back there… That's not from here." He leaned back against the wall feeling better.

Exasperation surged through me. *HellNet…* The guy had been willing to croak in this place to get answers. I turned back toward the rocks. "Do you have any idea what is going on?"

"Nope." Chase's face looked worried. "That's why I'm here… To find that out."

"So, there are others around here? You're not alone?"

"I am… But there are others on the other side of the mountain. People I know."

"DarNet…" The expression, released without thinking, made Chase chuckle.

I laughed with him. But I needed to stop this. I was better off keeping some distance. Thinking about Streak and focusing on him, not Chase, was a better alternative. *No. You need to focus on yourself and the mission.*

I confronted an emptiness within myself. Strength, logic, and self-preservation had demanded that I wised up, and I did. Now, I found myself in another place where fighting a product of that system became imperative: freeing myself from the effect DAINN had caused when he saved Chase's life through me. The connection influenced my reactions. I rejected it. "Let's look at this cave of yours."

We had wondered what we faced. Looking at the guy standing by my side, I knew. The experiment had worked. I had to come to terms with it. Waking up in a different time than the one we had left

447

behind, we now possessed one mandate. We belonged to the future still, witnesses to our potential demise, unless we corrected the present's trajectory. It rendered the possibility of our extinction even more real if we failed in this new timeline.

Either way... For us, only one outcome. We lost our world while we slept.

The realization hit me, and the pain almost knocked me off my feet. I turned away so Chase could not see it in my eyes.

The moments since we were in Cryo vanished before we could comprehend their meanings, before we understood the consequences of our actions, even before we took our next breath. One after the other, they pulled away from us. Our core as perfect humans no longer existed. The very thing that made us who we were; had vanished with the universe we left behind. Now, everything that created us, the things we understood and knew, was lost.

The knowledge rang in my head. I am in an unknown world.

Maybe, just maybe, they had been right to send us here. If we could achieve our goal, our people would survive, and that's what mattered.

"Are you sure you're all right? Because you don't look all right." Chase persisted, as usual, in his quest for answers.

Quickly, I played back the events of the last few hours in my head, analyzing what I knew of him. I needed to convince him to help us, and for that, I needed time alone with him. I needed to understand what he knew. Could I trust a stranger?

There was only one way to find out. "I'm fine." I was about to continue when a shrill sound interrupted the silence of the cave.

The screeching noise of metal burst in a painful yelp and resonated again inside the mountain.

Immediately following, a sonic wave echoed just as loudly. The ground moved under my feet, and the walls of the tunnel trembled once more. Rock fragments fell around us from the breach made by the force of the water. I looked past the opening. This time I identified its provenance.

A light glammed brightly in the pit's darkness, shooting straight up. The beam created a white hue coming up the cavern beyond the small promontory, jutting out several feet down the wall.

Something was down there.

Chase, at my side, leaned forward to see over my shoulder. "What in the hell...."

I shook my head. "This is not natural... Something... Someone is causing it."

"I take it; it's not yours?"

"No. I told you. We have nothing to do with this."

"Shit. Tesh, I don't think we possess this technology."

"Of course, you wouldn't..."

He looked offended. "You don't have to be so smug."

I shrugged, "We've studied your scientific advancements..." trying to amend for my lack of sensitivity.

"So, if it's not yours, who does it belong to?" He showed genuine concern, looking at it.

I understood why. I shared Chase's anxiety.

My tension rose a nudge when I saw a fluctuation in the field. Who and what was it?

I didn't know what we faced, so I used my PVZ to identify the energy. Its components didn't give much in terms of raw data. I registered the power at its core, much higher than around the edges. Its levels pulsated at different rates. That much I could tell. For the rest, though, our technology left me in the dark.

The beam of light thinned and stretched.

"Back up, Chase," I murmured, assuming the worst.

Our movement or the shifting of the rocks caused a reaction because the burst stretched further. Bam... Like a bullet released from the barrel of a gun, the oscillation throbbed. And a scintillating pulse shot out toward us.

I tensed.

Chase's face looked stricken when he saw it coming at us. "Shit."

The vibration increased as the center sphere moved around against the black hole and disappeared below. Its glow vanished in the abyss. The sound that until now pierced our ears evaporated into thin air. Only, the small strobe, which was like a dot when it shot out toward us, grew as it continued its course in our direction.

I froze. My EmVat, reacting to me and sensing a threat, erected its protective energy field around me. Rules of war... Don't engage until you know what you're fighting.

Chase took a step back and another.

The intense pulse grew to the size of a ball, emitting a constant whistle. It amplified to a higher pitch.

It came at us fast.

I grabbed Chase by the waist, yelling, "Hold on." My boots propelled us back into the tunnel and away from it.

Not fast enough.

It manifested behind us three feet away and gained ground.

I flew toward our Chamber.

Retreat and regroup… Our mentors at the Academy said.

I attempted to do as much, not waiting to determine what we faced.

Although I could fight, and stand my ground, what would happen to Chase?

He could not face this thing.

The only thing I could do to protect him was to open and close the chamber on him. The energy of the EmVat enfolded Chase inside the protective envelope of the suit. I could extend it a bit, but I would have to stand in the beam's way to shield him. So be it… It was what being Conclave meant—the duty to lead and protect. I had trained for this all my life and no matter where the same rules applied.

"Run…" I said, releasing him. "Get ahead. When you get to the door of the chamber, I'll open it. You'll be safer inside."

"What about you?"

"I've got this… Go."

I turned around to face the light.

27
TIMELESSNESS
Tesh

Inside the Mountain, California - 2018

The abyss holds a secret. Something awaits… Unleashing an energy so strong on my people that it overpowers them, destroying the rock formation inside the mountain. Its presence breaches our defenses and endangers our purpose. DAINN Annals – Summer 2018.

Did I say I got this? Foolish.

I didn't have this… I didn't even know what this was. I stood inside my EmVat, extending my shield as far as I could. My boots anchored to the ground; I increased my suit's power to maximum and faced it.

The bean kept on coming. The burst flashed.

It wasn't enough.

The mechanism of the suit's NetJet boots identified the strength of the attack. The EmVat's visor said, "Unable to withstand. Brace for impact."

The release grounding me in place gave way. Choosing between two evils, my EmVat protected my legs first.

The force of the blow sent me flying.

Before I knew it, I got slammed against the side of the tunnel. Winded, but otherwise unhurt. The suit had protected me.

Before I could get up, I heard a crushing sickening noise against the wall.

I looked in Chase's direction. He had flown several spaces away and landed on the ground, with one of his arms in a weird configuration. No doubt, Chase had tried to cushion his fall with his arms instead of rolling. Classic novice moves.

Sprawled in the mud, he looked in pain with the water turned into sticky silt around him.

So much for protecting him.

I shifted position on the ground and got up.

Another burst of light came crashing in my direction.

This time, I put up a shield ahead of me and leaned against the tunnel wall.

The light pulsated and moved in front of Chase. We now stood in the area it lit up.

DarNet. It outplayed me. "Chase, don't move."

Chase rolled his eyes. "I have no intention of moving."

I followed the wall of the tunnel toward Chase.

The pulse vibration increased.

I got closer to Chase... One location provided a better defensive position.

It watched me, adjusting its position with mine.

The glimmer at its center turned bright white. It was a light that burned the retinas, snow-white, so much so that snowflakes would appear grey and dull compared to it.

I compensated with the help of my visor.

Chase lifted his unaffected arm, shielding himself from its overwhelming glow with the palm of his hand.

The burst came at me again.

The EmVat mechanism spoke again, "Reflecting."

My shield turned to a metallic surface that shone the light right back at its source. My eyes burn, looking at it through the darkened visor.

The change didn't do much.

The EmVat spoke again, "Suit recharging. Incoming. Power at 80 percent."

DarNet. It won't be enough.

The burst passed right through the shield. The salvo blasted. My shield slowed it down and folded, losing its energy. I received the blast right in the middle of my chest.

I closed my eyes under the power of the light, and tears began to stream down my eyes.

It felt like the ray got right inside the suit, removing the protective barrier of the EmVat. When it withdrew, I choked as if the air moved out of my lungs with it.

Pain spread in my chest. Searing... I fought against it, refusing to give in. But I needed reinforcements. I called for it. *Custodians... I need you.*

My legs gave in... I dropped to the ground about two feet away from Chase's position, fighting for breath.

The light released its hold on me.

I reached out to Chase with my mind. *Chase, get ready to run when I tell you. Don't speak, think.*

A surprised look flashed on Chase's face.

I heard his thoughts, *Tesh, is that you?*

Who else knows your name in this place?

He blinked. *Are you telepathic?*

Now is not the time, Chase. Just get ready to run... You're halfway there. When I open the door, you get in. For now, don't move.

If you don't mind me asking, what do you have in mind? Because, no offense, but you don't look in any position to fight this thing.

I shifted, planting my feet on the ground, fighting to catch my breath.

Maybe, you could try talking to it?

Chase's suggestion came too late.

I didn't even have time to respond.

The Custodians were here. They flew inside the corridor from both sides. Then a few more arrived from the passage up and the one going down. All positioned themselves around the sphere, covering all angles. They surrounded the light, and their laser went into action next. They attacked mercilessly.

The light moved, attempting to avoid their fire. But there was nowhere to go inside the tunnel. The eyes of the Custodians hit the beam over and over.

It grew, protecting its center.

The lasers focused on their target, the intensity of their beams penetrating its outer layer.

I didn't stop watching. Instead, I got back to my feet. My thoughts went to Blast and Leane. *We're under attack...*

I didn't wait for the next flare. Activating the door mechanism to get a more powerful weapon, I prepared to run. *Now, Chase.*

The door opened slowly.

My limbs tensed, filled with adrenalin.

Springing into action, I reached for the chamber's entrance. It was a stretch. The distance and the speed played against me.

But I tried it anyway.

The giant burst that followed blew me off my feet.

Chase went flying too.

I never made it to the door.

I rescinded my order as I floated in the air.

The doorway responded. The mechanism began to close.

Tossed against the wall near the doorway, I saw Chase land nearby, this time unconscious.

It had been the wrong move. When the pulse blew, the Custodians got blasted away. Tossed to all corners of the tunnel, they lay inert on the ground with their mechanisms dismantled.

DarNet... What now?

The luminescent ball hovered, turning on itself. It shot out again, closing in on the doorway.

It couldn't get through.

I lunged at it.

The next burst blew me toward the door of our compartment and almost crushed me, despite the EmVat. My back hit the panel so hard that my teeth rattled in my mouth.

But the door closed behind me. In between boots of pain, I breathed a sigh of relief.

I saw a fluctuation in the light. It lifted me off the ground, holding me, suspended in mid-air. *Netshit...* What now?

My PVZ protected my eyes and body, its power at sixty-five percent.

The energy field of the EmVat vanished. The air withered inside me, sucked out.

My lungs burned. My chest cavity became hollow.

I saw stars from the lack of oxygen. *How in the HellNet can it penetrate the defenses of the EmVat in such an effective way?*

A perfect weapon. One cannot fight if one cannot breathe.

We ought to have thought of that. I panted, trying hard not to lose consciousness.

Battles, fights, even here, we faced attacks. We had trained for that. HellNet, at the Institute, we prepared for that every day. Our skills, fine-tuned over the years, enhanced by implants, and some of our genetically engineered DNA, proved lethal. We had learned to move without sound and be deadly in close combat. My mind remained my most reliable power. Most of us could handle three opponents and sometimes faced one twice our size. Yet, I didn't possess a weapon in all my arsenal to take this thing down in this confrontation. I didn't even have an idea of what this thing was.

It was always the same burden. I sighed and coughed. Why could we not all get along? The hostility remained no matter the time or the place. Maybe our species attracted it. Maybe our actions called for it. Perhaps we were just doomed with the inhumanity of our aggression against others.

How long would I last without air? My head pounded. Blackness beckoned…

The pulse behaved as if it sensed my discomfort.

Air…

This creature was intelligent… No doubt. So, what does it want?

I inhaled, grateful. I coughed again, breathing hard and taking because my lungs allowed. Rendered defenseless by the most basic of needs, I fought to regain my equilibrium.

I glanced toward Chase, leaning against the wall without a sound. I wondered if he was conscious.

He grunted. "Talk… don't fight."

The object remained still, as unmovable as an immovable object.

Only I knew better. *Are you all right?*

His whisper answered me. "Huh… not in the least. Stop moving. You're making things worse. It hasn't attacked me since I hit the wall. I don't think it likes movement."

I waited, unwilling to raise its ire.

It did the same. Death itself couldn't be that still, as we faced one another. Looking into the ball of energy, I was unable to grasp how it behaved or even identify its weaknesses.

The white light created a pattern as it hit the tunnel wall, rendering the area misty. It spread over the rock as if it penetrated the matter itself.

This weapon was unlike anything I had ever seen before. It functioned by launching a powerful blast at a target. The area covered by the wave rendered one vulnerable. Its range spread, hitting wide. Its elasticity and scope grew on impact, adjusting to the size and opponent strength and handling multiple adversaries without effort.

A conscious weapon. Made of energy had penetrated my EmVat field, like butter. Did we provoke it?

Chase's advice made sense.

The longer I remained still, the longer it did too.

I watched it. Maybe Chase was right. I could talk to it.

Chase was giving me advice. A first. He was unknown to us but behaved as an ally, although his hide counted in the balance too.

Another pulse cleared the first, pushing away from it, and hovered in front of me. Was it reading my thoughts? "What do you want?" I said, my voice weak.

It glided closer to our chamber. Too close to it now... Opening the panel attracted its attention. It appeared once again that I took too much of a risk.

I sighed. Talking was my gift. Why not use the power of my mind? I had seen stranger things in my world. I turned to the second flash of light and said, "What do you want? Why did you attack us?"

The orb shifted position as if examining the door. It understood me.

My hand slid over the surface of the door. *Don't even think about opening it.*

The thought registered somewhere within the energy sphere. It shifted again in my direction, coming toward me.

I refrained from moving.

It floated in front of me.

I shook my head. No.

The small move provoked a glide closer. It sought to intimidate.

I erected a shield around my mind. I hoped the thing would listen, although part of me doubted it. *Blast, Leane... Stay hidden...*

The core of the light increased in intensity. The energy field surrounding it grew. It spun faster, although I couldn't be sure it was turning on its axes, spinning fast.

My eyes watered under the light.

It brought itself closer to me.

"I'm not opening it," I said, between clenched teeth, determined to protect our secret. It was the wrong thing to say. Besides, Mage was inside. I wouldn't risk him.

It positioned itself a few inches from my eyes. I saw double, my vision impaired.

The pulse, sensing my dilemma, pulled back.

My PVZ got nothing on the globe's composition.

It was intelligent. So why did it feel threatened? We did nothing.

Open it—the thought formed in my head.

I held the answer. The pulse appeared to be an independent, thinking organism.

Who are you? Who is Mage?

The energy read my mind.

Not good. I struggled to keep protection around my thoughts. My emotions flared up...

It was a first.

No other encounters had prepared me for this. Usually, I had the upper hand, reading people's thoughts without giving mine away. It was not what I expected.

Why did you attack us? My question jumped at it. I attempted to regain my composure, calming myself down the way we had learned at the Institute.

You do not belong here.

Did you attack because you felt threatened?

You do not threaten us. You do not belong here. Why did you come?

Chase belongs here. You attacked him.

He brought others here. They are not welcome.

I glanced in Chase's direction. "You brought people here... It doesn't want them here."

Chase nodded. "So, it talks."

Another dot emerged from the second light, gliding in Chase's direction. It stopped a few spaces away from him.

Chase, cautious, observed it.

I didn't blame him. The field of energy acted as if it had a claim on this place.

I returned my attention to it. *What are you doing here?*

You also brought people here. You need to leave.

Is this why you made the ground shake? So we would go away?

The glow shifted, flickering with the next question. *Tell me about Mage.*

My brows creased. This thing wanted to know about my dog. Why?

Is Mage a dog?

The entity could read my thoughts. I attempted to close myself off from it.

The light pulsated even more as if it didn't like my mind's defenses.

It burned brightly, turning its intense shine on me. I felt the heat emanating from its center. The glare around its core blazed, dazzling, growing more diffused as it spread out. Pale filaments formed a slight pattern around it.

Mesmerized… It took every inch of willpower I possessed to think, fighting its influence.

It was getting ready to fire again. I sensed it. Don't.

I want to know about Mage.

My energy dwindled. Keeping the shield around my mind made me feel weak. *Why do you want to know about Mage?*

You thought of protecting Mage. Why is a dog vital to you? Is it a weapon?

DarNet… *Mage is dear to me. It is my friend, my companion.*

Chase's voice got my attention. "What is going on?"

The third pulse moved closer to Chase.

He stopped talking.

You hurt Chase. Let me help him.

I want to see Mage, continued the pulse in front of me. Filaments moved with the thoughts.

Chase groaned. "You broke my arm. Did my people hurt you?"

The burst's velocity slowed in front of Chase as if it knew he posed no threats but remained in place, not engaging.

Do you have a name? I murmured. My friend needs help.

Do you have a name? Your friend Mage?

No. My friend Chase. I pointed at Chase. My name is Tesh.

Tesh, I want to see Mage.

Why?

I have seen dogs here but have never seen a Mage. He is different.

How… How do you know this?

You told me.

DarNet... The energy glow read my mind way too well. The occurrence was not going the way I had hoped. So far, I didn't see weaknesses in the sphere. I sighed.

Will you let me help Chase?

Why?

It is the right thing to do. Let me help, my friend.

His vitals are fine. He is in no danger.

He is hurting.

It is a condition of his race. They know hurt; they are used to it.

How do you know this? How long have you been here?

I dislike your questions. Show me Mage. I want to know why he is important to you.

He is... I will not open the door, no matter what you do to me.

I dislike your answers.

The air inside the tunnel shifted.

The burst of light in front of me hovered faster. It grew.

I saw the movement toward the junction in the tunnel. As I tried to think about something else, I also strengthened my grasp on my mind.

The struggle increased as if the energy field read me. *What are you hiding?*

I shifted my thoughts to a song my father had taught me — anything to divert its attention.

The field grew in front of me, cutting me off from the action behind it.

I didn't dare transmit information to them for fear of revealing their presence. Giving away Leane and Blast's location endangered them. My thought focused on the words. *Gentle into the night you go.*

What are you doing?

We arrived here and fought for our lives when all we wanted to do was get out of this mountain, the very same that buried us. You go, you go... My friends were lost somewhere inside it, and we had not located them yet. *Tomorrow, you will see the sun again.* We couldn't leave until we had. This much was clear. *Somewhere, in another world, in another place.* Not only were we discovered when we shouldn't have been from people in this time frame. *You will feel the wind on your face again.* But we also faced a threat, the likes of which we had never seen and that we didn't understand.

Blast and Leane emerged from one of the connecting tunnels, weapons in hands.

I closed my eyes, averting from giving them away.

It didn't work.

The sphere moved away from me.

They aimed in perfect unison. Their ZNet deployed, spreading like a red sheet over the distance between the first pulse and them. It trapped it in place.

A few Custodians moved in, those not disabled. They aimed, their electronic eyes sending their lasers against the target, attempting to disable it once and for all.

The first sphere near the door grew and turned red.

The other two joined it, growing its center on purpose.

Together, they engulfed the entire width of the tunnel. The blast moved like a tidal wave across the distance that separated it from Blast and Leane.

No... Wait.

Too late.

Already, the laser guns from Blast and Leane aimed at the pulse.

The pulse blazed hotter, redder.

And the energy of the lasers changed color. It made contact with the field and disappeared in it, swallowed by the sphere. Somehow, they gave it more strength.

The translucent sphere grew more prominent, its light turning a darker red. The energy around the core of the globe sent a flare against the members of my Conclave.

I screamed a warning... *Duck.*

The wave of light absorbed the energy from the lasers as if it was nothing. The surge shot out toward Blast and Leane, catapulting them backward.

Their bodies flew against the tunnel's wall and landed several feet away.

My friends didn't wait to respond with another salvo. Only this time, Blast changed tactics. He blasted the tunnel with our NetPulse.

Leane followed his lead, this time pulverizing the walls around us.

The sphere moved, avoiding the blast.

The debris from the rock fell all around. One of them hit my shoulder.

The EmVat field protected me from the weight.

I crawled away from the area, reaching for Chase.

Blast continued, pulverizing more of the tunnel.

Stop... Stop firing. We now stood in the middle of a collapsing structure.

The sphere moved around, spinning faster to avoid most of the blast.

Crimson red emanated from its growing core.

One of the NetPulses hit the tunnel again. This time, it created a deep hole in the ceiling, and more rocks fell around us.

I touched Chase's leg just as everything came crashing down.

The EmVat protected us.

Stop! My thoughts hit against my skull. *Stop... all of you. We can talk this out.*

The sphere grew. It spun even faster now. The filaments of white extended wider, turning red, and forming multiple rings around the core. Dark, angry, and increasing.

The burst that emanated from it shook everything around us. Its salvo unleashed a small storm within the confined area.

Netshit. White, okay, red, not okay.

The fiery display formed a sonic wave, displacing everything in its wake. But the swirling motion became nauseating to observe. A violent noise cracked against the startled air in the tunnel, spreading its burnt tinge of acrid scent, depositing on everything it touched dark frost. Rocks tumbled in the corridor, collapsing the ceiling on my friends.

My nostrils flared.

My friends disappeared under another cave.

The weapon bore a hole so big that it claimed everything in its path. The air mixed with ashes, right before the particles froze, suspended in a cocoon without motion. This enduring vision of horror imprinted on my brain.

No, no, no… We didn't do everything we did to come here for things to end this way for us. We didn't go through all the trials, made all the sacrifices to save our people, and our world so that we would be in this predicament.

We were the last of our race. We would not perish here. We didn't go into the void of Cryo to emerge here and die without ever seeing the light of day in this world. I wanted to feel the air in my face. I demanded that for all of us. *Stop! Please stop this nonsense. We are not your enemies.*

I don't know if it heard me. I thought it did…

Regardless, it stopped.

I crawled away from Chase.

The worst of the assault ended as rapidly as it began. The sphere remained intact. It didn't move as I slithered on the ground to reach my conclave.

It watched me.

I called out to Leane and Blast.

They never answered.

I pushed past the rocks, dragging myself over mounds of dirt and ashes. *Be alive; please be alive.*

I resorted to the only thing I knew, my scanner, to locate them. Getting past the zone of this broken world took everything I had. *Leane, Blast… Answer me, please.*

The EmVats blocked the onslaught. It had to…

Desperate, I searched... Past more rocks, piles of debris, and past the tunnel's burnt surface, through the sections destroyed by the wave blast.

They had to be all right. Leane and Blast had to... *Where are you?*

Their signals were faint.

I had found them...

As I moved, inch by inch, dragging myself onto frozen Earth, I cried their names. *Leane... Blast... Be all right...*

They didn't answer.

My EmVat Emergency signal told me not to go there. The suit wouldn't last.

I disregarded it. I kept ongoing...

The energy of my suit fluctuated, sending shivers on my skin.

I didn't care. I didn't want to survive this without my friends.

It had to be all of us or nothing at all.

The atmosphere was cold... Too cold for the suit to sustain me.

I got a few spaces before my breath began to freeze. I could no longer move. I tried to advance regardless of my arms and legs, useless from the cold.

Their vital signs showed on the base of my screen. It was the only signal still emanating from our technology.

The pulse watched me. It didn't make a move to subdue me.

Why are you doing this? I made my way toward my friends until I could no longer.

You care about your friends. You don't care in the same way about this one. Why?

I hesitated. My answer could get Chase hurt. *Of course, I care. It's different.*

He is not as strong as you.

Why are you hurting us?

They attacked.

No… My friends defended me. You attacked us with the earthquake you created.

Because you should not be here, you bring danger.

Trust me; we want to leave this place.

And you shall, for you cannot win this.

Lying on the frozen ground, I took another breath. It came in a ragged, shallow gasp. My chest froze, my insides felt as they were liquefying. I froze, entombed in an icy numbness.

Silence reigned in the tunnel, and it was deafening after the noise of the fight.

My brain stopped functioning; the lack of oxygen sent everything into a downward spiral. My world splintered all around me.

The pulse of light grew to reach a large size.

I felt feathered light.

The sphere, white again, grew big enough to envelop me. It increased further in size to contain all of us. But it drew me in first.

My body lifted from the cold ground, pulled toward it. Hovering above the wreckage, I lost control over my limbs, my will, my entire being. Trying to fight against it, I was too weak. And I knew I was dying… Now, I glided toward it until I reached it. My movement was not of my volition. My body passed the transparent perimeter of the sphere. Released inside at its center, I dropped and landed gently at the bottom.

The temperature shifted.

I no longer felt cold.

My eyes opened... My lids were so heavy that I fought to keep them open. Black danced at the edge of my vision.

Leane flew into the sphere and dropped inside.

Blast came next.

They were both unconscious.

My friends, lying beside me inside, were in oblivion while I still maintained a sense of something, observation, no doubt.

Chase dumped on top of us, protested with a groan of pain.

The sphere didn't like Chase.

How odd? My thoughts floated...

Enfolded in a cocoon, we lay there, unmoving. The sounds resembled white noise, diffused yet leaving no room for anything else, as it amplified around us.

We moved above the ground of the tunnel in a bubble of light.

I saw the ceiling change.

The perimeter of the immense cave spread in front of me.

I didn't hear Chase's voice when he talked. I couldn't even hear my heartbeat. Every cell in my body resonated with the hissing. My presence within the sphere reminded me of the day after Imps' surgery when my head filled with a cotton-like stupor.

A torpor made my limbs heavy.

My lids slid closed. I lost track of time and found myself undone inside the sphere, falling into an unconscious state where time no longer had meaning.

Time no longer counted—neither joy, sadness, nor hunger. There were no needs, no desires, not anything—just this suspended state of nothingness.

Then... Much later, it seemed, my body lifted as if I was weightless, and I heard in my head.

You wanted to talk; let's talk.

The talk came and went.

I don't recall any of it. It happened, of that I am sure. I saw the light in front of me, and then nothing.

I awoke later on the ground just in front of the doorway of our chamber.

Lying beside me were my friends, Leane and Blast, and further Chase. All of them intact, as if the battle we had fought never happened.

Blast woke up after me, shaking himself off as Mage would do after a bath in the fountain.

It made me smile.

He moved as if he had a dream he couldn't quite get out of and shook his head. "What in the HellNet happened? I thought I bought it out there. He looked at the chaos of the tunnel and glanced toward me. "Will you tell me what in the HellNet, was that thing?"

"I would if I could... but I have no idea."

Leane's sleepy voice resonated as she moved. "We're alive; that's all that matters for now." Her face looked calm. "I know we don't have answers, but we have a purpose. Tesh convinced them to give us time, and we have little of it, so let's get to it. Shall we?"

I nodded, unable to find my voice. So, I tried to get my memories in order, unable to remember the talk. But I had talked, giving us a chance.

There was no confusion about that part.

We knew the event had taken place. Only now, we understood every bit of time in this place counted.

Chase muttered something, "Well, if that doesn't beat it all… How are you all doing?"

Blast turned toward him. "Who in the HellNet are you?"

I chuckled…

Blast hated remaining in the dark. "This is Chase, a new friend."

He barked… "Tesh… I need to know everything, every DarNet thing since we left you in the chamber. Because I really, really, really don't like not knowing anything!" With that said, Blast got up, checking Chase out.

Oh, boy… It would be interesting.

Getting out of the mountain became paramount. The urgency of it drove us even more.

We knew something would happen. Something big… Something bad…

Before that took place, we needed to find the exit, locate Streak and the rest of our people. Our survival and theirs demanded it.

Other than that, we remained in the dark.

DAINN Ang City – 2040

The second Bane triggers a need to centralize our world. Now, the Network assimilates data on all our citizens. Soon, we rely on the information to structure our society. Among the changes in our infrastructure, the DAINN System expands to monitor the health of our people. Prevention enters a new age in healthcare measures, including infectious outbreaks. DAINN Annals – 2040.

Inside the Control Center, the dead overwhelmed the screens. Dead eyes looked up at us, their spark extinguished. Dead faces, frozen in permanence, stared at the living, no longer carrying the fire of life. Dead bodies piled up in the air transport bound to their final destination, waiting for their turn in the city's incinerator.

Dr. Rene Paladock, the creator of the DAINN Network, viewed the latest images from our feeds. They came from all around

Ang, reaching from the Golden Ghetto to Water's Edge, ArchwayPass, BridgeView, CliffTops, and Emerald Field. It didn't matter that we had closed off the various sections of the city.

"How many today?" said Paladock in a broken voice.

"Seven hundred and sixty-eight," said the EHAF guard standing beside him. He was still a young man with a sweetly proportioned face, but the last several weeks brought a different look to him. His eyes bore shadows, and his shoulders seemed to carry an unbearable weight.

The guards were switched often because of the work that brought them face to face with death every minute of every day. And while the System could keep the count on its own, Paladock visited every day, and no one wanted to see him alone inside the Control Room to face the awful reality. No one knew how to stop it.

By the time we realized the threat, it had turned into reality overnight. The outbreak spread in all our cities, and as we attempted to identify the source, the infectious disease continued its course. Our health officials declared it a world emergency, demanding a quarantine for everyone. The warning to the Federation soon followed, and the EHAF went into overdrive, alerting our people to remain indoors and take precautions. Our Conclave leaders issued orders and mandatory stay at home for non-essential personnel. The head of each five Conclaves implemented measures to ensure our operations' safe continuity, providing for our citizens, and meeting their needs within the various blocks.

It was sixteen months ago.

"You don't have to stay here, young man," said Paladock, looking grimly at the images.

"Sorry, Sir, I am not at liberty to leave until you do," said the young guard. "They don't want us to be here for very long and certainly not alone. Bad for morale and all."

"Huh, yes. I understand," said a conflicted Paladock.

Today, death was everywhere, permeating every task we undertook.

There was no way to imagine the death toll. There was no amount of preparedness to face this horrendous pandemic.

Now, worldwide, death reached nine million people. We dealt with one hundred and ninety-nine million people infected.

As Dr. Paladock watched the System monitoring our people, I could see the stress on his face.

The automation of the Network took over for people. He had achieved much in the last year.

Within our online education system, things remained pretty much the same, with courses delivered individually. But some programs expanded to include in-home robotics training to maintain the curriculum of recruits and candidates aiming for official government service. Old training grounds were extended, making room for more classes. Isolating our youth into smaller groups for physical requirements preparation led to more intense training. More Apps produced by the Company and covering various fields were developed to carry on the workload from remote locations.

"Someone needs to know, notice you know… Pay attention to them on their last journey. It's probably stupid," said Paladock after a few minutes of silence.

"No, Sir. It's good of you, Sir." The guard looked at the screens again and got a stunned look on his face. "There's just so many."

Paladock just nodded.

The research facilities around the world developed new prototypes to take over some essential functions. Robotics took more significant roles within domestic households. They even provided care for sick individuals remaining at home. These included better Domestic bots' capabilities to handle simple tasks within residents' quarters, including fetching and delivering things on the grounds within various locations. It also covered additional drones, now replacing delivery systems overseen by men. The DAINN System took over these new undertakings.

Many companies competing for sales leverage and market shares built these with no respite. Our manufacturing facilities assembled more drones and robots to cover increased demands, and the lines moved non-stop, day and night, to fill the requests. These new robotics advancements served multiple purposes, with some programmed to provide backup care to our medical units. Others oversaw security in our streets to eliminate the risks to our people and support individual police forces. Now they crowded our buildings and our passageways, serving as a go in between.

But there was nothing worse than what the Healthcare field faced as the illness spread like wildfire within our walls. Our world medical board responded to cover immediate needs, dispatching personnel in the most infected zones. But they were overwhelmed.

"We don't seem to get a handle on this virus," said Paladock. The man seemed beaten.

Our scientists were doing all they could to create a vaccine, but we had found nothing to obliterate the virus so far.

Everything stopped at once in our cities as everyone retreated inside their doors. Fear rose, touching all our kind, as the outbreak did not discriminate. Personalities, celebrities, and unknown people were all affected. Rich and poor fought for their lives. Young and old were brought down. Across all walks of life, death touched us all.

Earth became silent overnight. Our world froze under threat, blanketing our entire way of life. The Planet obtained a respite from the long and agonizing demise we imposed on it.

"I suppose we should go then. I can't keep you here; you have better things to do," said Paladock as he made his way toward the door.

As we fought this world catastrophe, buried deep inside within the SRC Conclave, under the aegis of Dr. Paladock, the core of the DAINN System spread its influence.

Slowly, the Network took over our infrastructure.

**2
SURFACE
Tesh**

On The Mountain, California - 2018

Tesh looks at the sky for the first time. It is clear, so clear… Unlike the air of Ang City. As she stands under it, warmth radiates through her body, and a grin spreads across her face. I feel her joy. DAINN Annals – Summer 2018.

I couldn't wait to get topside, so I engaged my glider with the propulsion engine in my boots, adjusting the velocity for the weight of two. Then, I grabbed Chase by the waist and launched us over the tunnel's threshold and into the large cave. He rotated his frame to face me. His body glued to mine, we now hovered upwards in the shaft, following the column of rock.

Chase's reaction did little to calm my misgivings about our proximity.

A smile reached his lips as he held on to me, looking down into the abyss as if nothing was abnormal with the experience we had just escaped from together.

I glanced at him with his head bleeding. He looked pale. Until I reached the surface, there was little I could do for him besides until Leane arrived. His wounds would have to wait. She was the healer among us, the one who possessed the power I envied. She knew how to bring back life from the brink of death into every living cells. I wished that I could have her gift so many times. My early years growing up in Ang brought unfulfilled wishes. Until I no longer cared to wish for anything.

Talking through my NetComm, I said, "We're going up. There is an opening above. Blast, can you take care of bringing Mage up?"

"What?" Blast's question carried over the NetComm induced a smile I quickly repressed. Although Blast was fond of Mage, they, surprisingly, didn't get along. It wasn't Blast's fault as much as it was Mage, who appeared way too affectionate with Blast every chance he got. It made Blast on edge and rendered the situation fluid between these two.

"Get the equipment ready and secure the chamber. Then, you can join me with Mage. Leane, I will need you here. Chase needs your help as soon as you get the equipment fixed. Chase needs your help."

"NetRoger that," Leane said. "How is your arm?"

"Better. Stronger. Don't worry about me." No doubt, she was concerned about the effect of the Nanos on my left limb, but the feeling had returned. My strength had doubled, although it was nothing compared to what we had faced a while ago. I was still adjusting to the feeling.

"We won't be long, Tesh." The sound of the Pulse reverberated far below us. Blast had things in hand with Leane. Soon, they would join me.

"Do me a favor, Blast. Make sure you harness Mage before you let him out of the chamber. He hates close quarters as much as you do."

"Having something in common with a dog doesn't quite do it for me, Tesh." Blast emitted the comment through a voice filled with frustration.

My companion laughed out loud at that comment.

"What was that?" Blast said. "It's no joke, Chase..."

"Can we discuss Mage and our exit strategy later?" I said. "I'll see you on the surface."

The propulsion engine in my boots increased velocity over the abyss as I held onto Chase. I sped up, hovering upward faster inside the shaft and following the massive column of rock in front of me. I needed some space between us.

Looking up at the shaft, I kept moving upward until we reached an opening in the rocks.

We rose toward the light,

The opening in the rock formation broadened slowly, revealing a patch of sky.

I contained my excitement, fearful of what I may find. What if it is terrible outside like in our time?

An awkward beat passed between us before I asked, "How long before we reach the surface?"

He chuckled with a hint of humor. "Hum... I've never experienced this mode of transportation before. So it's hard to tell. I daresay a few more minutes." He smiled. "I owed you thanks for not having to go up the old fashion way. I owe you for more than that. Now, I must make it up to you."

I could see the light outside. Soon, we would reach it.

The sunlight got closer with every breath we took. I inhaled again, trying to calm the excitement I felt seeing a little piece of the sky. Just ahead, the mountain formed two vertical walls close together but separated by a large fissure.

He held on to me and grinned, apparently unfazed by the upward movement.

I glanced at his face.

He winked. Until I reached the surface, there was little I could do but maintain the contact. "You must have an idea. How much further?" I inquired with a slight growl.

He laughed. "Did you just growl at me?" he said, with a charm that was difficult to ignore.

Near the opening, the light shimmered, and Chase closed his lids, adjusting to the brightness and giving me time to compose myself.

I ignored his comment. I didn't want to get any closer, nor did I desire to know what he thought at this moment. Instead, I asked, "How do you feel?"

"I have a pounding headache, but I'll live."

This climb gave me time to consider our predicament. Could I trust a stranger? There was only one way to find out. Only I didn't want to think about that.

I could feel his gaze on me, steady, unwavering as he observed my reaction.

Besides the glass barrier of my EmVat around my head, our mouths were inches apart from one another. *Good for that.*

I turned away from his lips. His breath formed a fog on the precise contour of my headset, right at the level of my jaw. I needed to break the silence between us. The contact had turned intimate, almost embarrassingly so. Still, it was also comforting.

Chase was still too close.

I wanted to get even closer. *Not smart, Tesh. What in the HellNet is wrong with you?*

My visor suddenly unfolded between my face and that of the stranger. I pulled back to give us more room.

Blast's face appeared beside Leane's, way too close to my eyesight for comfort. "We're done here. Making our way back. No signs of Streak, so he bailed out."

"Oh…" I mused, looking toward the guy in my arms.

Leane joined Blast with a big smile on her face. "It's great news. He must be too far out for us to read him. He'll find his way back to us."

"I hope so," I murmured, but I could feel a blush on my cheeks.

I saw an eyebrow raised in my direction, and I heard a sigh of inquiry from my passenger. My brows furrowed together. He was about to speak, and I silenced him by pressing two of my fingers against his lips.

"Tesh, what's wrong? What do you see?" asked Blast.

"Huh… Nothing. Why?" Distracted by the heat of his lips against my fingers, I felt the tips tingling.

Chase appeared content now, and he seemed amenable to remaining silent.

"You look upset. Is everything all right?" demanded Leane.

I forced a lopsided grin and looked at them both, avoiding the distraction of the blue eyes in front of me. "I'm almost out."

Leane's voice resonated over the NetComm, and I could sense her unease. "What do we do once we're outside?"

"I'm not sure," Blast responded while I remained silent as I figured out what Leane had referred to minutes ago.

All of us wondered what we faced, only now, looking at the guy in my arms, we knew. The hope that still existed inside us died with the stranger inside the cavern.

Chase moved against me, tightening his hold as if he wanted to help me with his weight. It only contributed to us getting closer, and now we barely had any air between us.

I gasped.

He smiled, lifting both eyebrows at me in a questioning way.

I changed my focus.

He wouldn't have it… He kissed the tips of my fingers.

I removed my hand.

His expression fell, with his features turning severe. He spoke again.

My fingers settled on his lips again.

Chase seemed satisfied for now, but I still scolded him with my eyes, forgetting that both Blast and Leane watched me through the screen.

Leane's voice inquired, "Tesh, you're acting strange. What's going on?"

"I concur," added Blast.

With a sigh, I looked at my two friends. I had never believed in the experiment. Yet, here I was…

As Perfect Human, we had left behind our very core. The thing that made us who we were, the universe in which we evolved with

DAINN in our heads, a system that created us, and everything we understood and knew.

We were in a time we didn't belong to and in an unknown world.

Blast groaned over the NetComm, "Is our new friend giving you trouble?"

I glanced at Chase. "Don't worry. I can handle him." I smiled when I saw the look in his eyes, now filled with a challenging glare. *Um… what have I done?*

I needed to convince him to help us. I needed time alone with Chase.

When I peeked down on him again, he observed me with a satisfied grin on his face. Regular and tanned, his features were handsome in a rough way. His sandy blond hair shifted under the breeze as we emerged from the darkness.

We had reached the outside, and I glided over a small promontory. We stood at the summit and dominated the other mountain tops surrounding us.

Settling us on the rock, I released my hold on Chase. Some distance between us felt safer. For the first time in a very long while, I turned toward the sun and felt the fresh air on my face.

More coming soon with NEWDAWN CENTRAL
Order Your Copy NOW!

Glossary

Alpha - A program launching the fleet into space, along with an entire armada to safeguard the population of Ang due to an impending extinction-level event.

Ang - Angel City is one of the largest Megapolis on Earth in 2098 and known as such for the sake of efficiency and brevity. After their initial destruction, most of our major cities, rebuilt to sustain the great floods and impending massive storms, now bore new names.

Aurora – A program that created underground safety chambers for the main population to prepare for the impending cataclysm.

BeautyForm – The latest product with technological advancement for the reformatting and remodeling of body parts developed by the Company's research and development under the initial product enhancements created by the SRC (Science Research Center).

City Vigil – Robots built to oversee the population's security and safety with advanced protocols allowing them to face many situations and replace the police force in the city.

Custodians – Robots implement security measures and enforcement policies citywide and within government buildings. They replace today's security personnel. They look like spheres of different diameters. Based on their capabilities, Custodians carry one or multiple ZNets, which are zapping mechanisms designed to put people into a sleep state. Using nets deployed around their targets, they bring their passengers to detention centers.

Council – The Council of Nations or Great Council represents multiple countries and runs the Planet and its infrastructure under a public mandate.

Cryogenic Chamber – Located inside the Institute, with a unique team of technicians dedicated to welcoming those who emerge from the Cryo modules, many such rooms contain one hundred to a thousand pods. The total number of modules is unknown. We also refer to the Cryogenic Chamber as NDCryo.

DAINN – The Distributed Artificial Intelligence Neuro Network and A.I. is a planetary mind whose tentacles reach all over the globe to monitor our entire infrastructure.

DarNet – An expression that has evolved from the word "darn" or the phrase "darn it." It became "DarNet" because of the influence of the Network over people in our future.

DarNetWash – An expression suggesting "never mind," or more used to mean "nullify" this or that.

Domestic Bot – Robot or Bot designed and located inside each population quarters, apartment, or house to serve as domestic, doing chores in society's upper echelon. The Bot is programmed for basic tasks, deals with cleaning, cooking, and running errands but can do much more. Linked to the DAINN System and Network, they monitor all our needs.

EmVats – A defensive unit or suit linked to the DNA of a user. EmVats provide protecting ambient suits with combat readiness based on specific programming.

Encharge – An exchange of energy between conclave members to unify, recharge, and strengthen a link between people.

Flycar – A motorized vehicle with lower flight capability, designated for personal use to higher level conclave members. Flycars configured on-demand can carry one or two people.

Gatherer – A Gatherer, also called a Gatherer of Space, can move through time and space based on DNA, implants, and technology.

HydroSheath – Metallic tube or cylinder containing Nanos pushed through a perfusion head.

Institute – The Institute is the government's arm that implements the DAINN System according to the government's mandates. It keeps up with A.I. and population demands.

IOGel – A gel-like substance composed of water and nutrients. An energy drink for Conclave leaders and members.

HellNet – An expression replacing "hell."

MindTranscript – DAINN reads a subject's mind to understand where a person is emotionally at a certain point in time. Monitoring thought patterns in different situations and used to learn everything a person thinks and feels.

NetComm – The planetary telecommunication network linking everyone on the planet.

Netdumb – An expression replacing "dumb" or "dummy."

NetRoger – An expression replacing "Roger that" based on the influence of the DAINN Network.

NetWash – An expression signifying "Shit" or "F... It..." Depending on the inflection of the subject.

Nuzar – Purple drink with energizing nutrients.

Origin – A safety chamber designed to safeguard a few of the Conclave members chosen to travel back in time to prevent Ang's future destruction.

OxyPure – A breather or breathing mask, delivering oxygen to survive.

Phenom – A title gained by accumulating accomplishments and implants to master skills and knowledge in various disciplines. Phenom is one of the highest levels attained by individuals within the DAINN System.

PodBot – Robots designed to implement and oversee the Cryo process inside the Origin chamber.

Provenance - A program designed to safeguard the population and some conclave members in space facilities surrounding the planet. Using multiple space elevators and ships, Provenance began a mass exile to deliver people from Earth who expected an impending extinction-level event.

Pulse Device – A sonic wave pulse creating such energy on the subatomic level displaces matter and reshapes it according to pre-programmed designs.

PulseTube – The level of a Pulse Device creating tunnels into the Earth based on sonic waves.

PVZ – Personal Visor Z, linked to the ZNet or Communication Network on the planet, is a system that replaces the cell phones of today. Implanted in a human being at an early age, the PVZ serves multiple purposes, including health monitoring, location tracking, and the facilitation of communication between members of the population and the DAINN Network.

Roamers – Members of the Conclave selected to become Time Travelers as part of the Origin program.

Rovers – A particular group formed to survey the timeline under assignments from the Council of Nations, enforcing specific dictates.

Spozor – A liquid gel with exceptional qualities and nutrients and developed by the Institute.

Shaper – A person capable of reading thoughts, shaping minds, influencing perceptions, and altering decision processes.

SkyFarms – Vertical agricultural complexes spread over the city and designed to grow food.

SoulLife – A greeting form used by residents of Ang City to express mutual appreciation, and based upon an Allegiance to the Universal Pledge, recognized Life Energy as a unique source of power.

The Institute developed Spozor to facilitate immediate recovery in those waking up from Cryo.

SRC (Science Research Center) – The Science Research Center is the governing arm that develops all new technology and science on behalf of the government. The SRC works under the Council and the officials dictating policy.

UniWear – Underclothing worn beneath a uniform.

UniWrap - A bracelet that wraps itself around a user's wrist, the **UniWrap** carries the energy and can adapt to a user's needs. It is an advanced weapons system comprising Nanobots and used as an offensive or defensive tool in combat.

VLogs/VideoLogs – A process qualifying as a work report facilitating a person's information dump into DAINN. During a Vlog, the A.I. asks specific questions relating to one's work. A recording of the subject is launched during the interview. Each VLog ends up in the DAINN archive.

WatGel – Water-like gel used for baths or showers.

ZNet – An apparatus incorporated into the Custodians in the form of indestructible netting. Also available for EHAF ships (Earth Homeland Alliance Force).

Note from the Author

To all my readers, please visit the retailer's product page and leave a review.

Also, Tesh and her team have great merchandising for you. So, please check our store: www.newdawnshop.com.

Reviews help me with sales, as you know, and allow me to keep creating. It also provides me with knowledge about what resonated with you in the story, the many plot lines, and what characters you enjoyed best so I can create future environments that you will love even better.

You are the reason I write these stories, and I wish to continue taking you on this journey.

I feel blessed that I can share with you what I love. I hope to take you with me on the adventure you seek every time you open the NEWDAWN Saga book series!

From science fiction to science facts… The bridge between today and tomorrow must provide us with a better way of life. Whether through stories in books, television series, films, or games, scenarios give us a path, one to follow or one to discard. As a content developer, I wish to establish a global brand to support and safeguard the planet. Strategic world-building gives us insights. New technologies allow us to reach a greater audience that can resonate with multiple outcomes, providing choices for tomorrow's world. The advances in science and technology unfold more rapidly and lead us down a road where keeping control over human values for fear of losing ourselves is essential. Building a network looking at tomorrow and what it can be to impact massive shifts, influencing the choices we make along the way, requires context vs. content. Therefore, I write. It is the why behind my books and what I endeavor to do beyond them.

As an author and futurist, I seek to influence results with passion and purpose to create outcomes and develop a sphere of influence, building awareness about the possibilities ahead. A platform providing resources and ideas to shape a better future is a huge undertaking. Yet, it provides exchange, enhances collaboration and community, and can reach a new generation of people. Designing these experiential environments in a global digital landscape makes possible outcomes more real. We will soon face the challenges of climate change, food distribution, technological advancements, and scientific achievements that will temper who we are, challenging us in new ways. Our need to survive will dictate decisions, yet ensuring that humankind remains relevant in the future must be our ultimate purpose. While empowering disruption and divergent thinking in search of knowledge, our humanity must remain rooted in the betterment of our species. The NEWDAWN Saga is one of the unique pathfinding exercises for consciousness in the future world besides being an entertaining read!

Thank you for your support.

Please share this book with your best friends!

If you wish to learn more about the world of NEWDAWN, please visit our sites:

www.windommedia.com

www.newdawnworld.com

www.dominiqueluchart.com

www.newdawnblog.com

www.newdawnshop.com

Follow me to see more books from DominiqueLuchart

Follow me on Facebook, Twitter, Instagram, and Pinterest
Also available in the NEWDAWN Saga Series:
The next novel – Volume 2
NEWDAWN CENTRAL
Coming to you in 2020.

My name is Tesh. I am with my team… Out of twenty of us, only four are now awake. The others are still buried somewhere inside the mountain. The warning we received from the entity was clear. Time is running out to find all of them spread across five different Chambers. When it unleashes its power, it will destroy everything, but I don't have a choice and have to risk it. So, despite the odds, we have infiltrated the space below the Center and found something else. A structure with an energy signature we have never encountered before. *Can we decipher what it is in time? Could this be where Streak is?*

I am asking you to support me and help in any way you can.
I am looking for readers, partners, sponsors,
ambassadors, and members.
Sign-up and receive our latest updates:
www.windommedia.com/newdawn-readers.

Contribute by buying merchandising: www.newdawnshop.com.

Give your support at: www.windommedia.com/newdawnimpact.

Biography

Transmute the now and transcend tomorrow. Dominique Luchart is the forward-thinking author of the NEWDAWN Saga, a YA science-fiction, fantasy, romance adventure series about the state of our world from 2018 to 2098 and beyond. NEWDAWN ROAMERS is the first volume of the series, followed by NEWDAWN CENTRAL and NEWDAWN RISING, in a chronological timeline. But NEWDAWN REBOOT was written first, culminating with the chain of events that unleashes everything in the NEWDAWN Saga. Soon after comes NEWDAWN RETRIBUTION; while in between, the adventure continues in a suspenseful epic story spanning time and space.

Dominique Luchart, the founder of WindHorse Entertainment and Windom Media, is a multi-faceted creative. As an Author and Futurist, a Media Platform Architect, Director and Producer, and Speaker, she is a masterful innovator, changing how people interact with content. As a universal storyteller, she delivers the next generation of information and entertainment networks based on science and technology using new media technology. One of her goals is to create trailblazing experiential environments delivering enhanced user experiences in storytelling. Mixing content distribution within a social network, she is working on a platform for the world of NEWDAWN, inside which the readers of NEWDAWN and SciFi lovers can take part in the stories and contribute.

"These experiences can serve as a roadmap for the future, determining what is on the horizon for all of us in the hope of building a socially conscious world where generations can thrive." Knowing what is to

come is the first step to manifesting awareness and maintaining our choices in a world where technology will run our plane*t. "Only we can decide if this is the world we want."*

Credits

Dominique Luchart